The Secret Language of Stones

Center Point
Large Print

Also by M. J. Rose and available from
Center Point Large Print:

The Collector of Dying Breaths
Seduction
The Book of Lost Fragrances
The Witch of Painted Sorrows

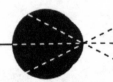

The Secret Language of Stones

M. J. ROSE

CENTER POINT LARGE PRINT
THORNDIKE, MAINE

This Center Point Large Print edition
is published in the year 2016 by arrangement with
Atria Books, a division of Simon & Schuster, Inc.

The text of this Large Print edition is unabridged.
In other aspects, this book may vary
from the original edition.
Printed in the United States of America
on permanent paper.
Set in 16-point Times New Roman type.

ISBN: 978-1-68324-091-4

Library of Congress Cataloging-in-Publication Data

Names: Rose, M. J., 1953– author.
Title: The secret language of stones / M. J. Rose.
Description: Center point large print edition. | Thorndike, Maine : Center
Point Large Print, 2016.
Identifiers: LCCN 2016022743 | ISBN 9781683240914
    (hardcover : alk. paper)
Subjects: LCSH: Large type books. | GSAFD: Occult fiction. | Gothic
fiction.
Classification: LCC PS3568.O76386 S425 2016b | DDC 813/.54—dc23
LC record available at https://lccn.loc.gov/2016022743

To my dear friend Alyson Gordon,
who heard a one line idea and
helped me find its story.
And to Paris—my inspiration.

I love you as certain dark things are to be loved, in secret, between the shadow and the soul.

—PABLO NERUDA

Prologue

Every morning the pavement in front of our shop in the Palais Royal is washed clean by the tears of the mothers of dead soldiers, widowed wives, and heartsick lovers.

Look to the right and left. There is grit and grime in front of Giselle's Glove Emporium and the family Thibaut's umbrella store, but at La Fantaisie Russe, the walkway is sparkling like newly polished stones.

Here inside the mythic Palais Royal arcade, the stores are not as busy as they were before the war, except for ours. In fact, it's the war that's responsible for our steady stream of clients.

There is nothing to identify what we offer in advertisements.

Visitez le Palais Royal, invites the dark-haired seductress in the prewar poster painted by a friend of my mother's, who signs his work simply *PAL*. The posters, first printed more than a dozen years ago, have been reprinted often, and you can see them, a bit worn and faded, plastered onto kiosks on rue de Rivoli.

Unlike the women who come to see me, the lady in the poster is untouched by war. Swathed in pearls around her neck and wrists and crowned with an elaborate bejeweled headdress, she smiles at potential shoppers. Her low-cut, jewel-studded teal gown shows off her creamy skin and ample breasts. Her delicate fingers, decorated with the loveliest diamond rings, beckon and point to the arcade, showing clients the way.

Walk in through the main entrance, a stone archway stained with centuries of soot, down the pathway, past the fountain, through the Palais's gardens, halfway to the end . . . but wait . . . Before you turn right toward the shops, stop and admire the magic of the garden first planted over two hundred years ago.

Some of the most glorious roses in all of Paris grow here, and even now, in the midst of all our strife and sadness, the air is fragrant with their perfume. The flowers don't care that their blood-red petals and razor-sharp thorns remind mothers and wives of loved ones' lives cut short, stolen by the war. The bees don't either. On some afternoons, their buzzing is the loudest noise you hear. On others, just an accompaniment to the drone of the air-raid sirens that frighten us all and send us running for shelter.

In *PAL*'s advertisement, in the bottom left corner, is a list of the shops in this oasis hidden away from the bustle of Paris.

Under *Maisons Notables & Recommandées*, jewelers are the first category. Our store is listed at the top. After all, Pavel Orloff trained with the famous Fabergé, who is a legend even here in the land of Cartier, Fouquet, Boucheron, and Van Cleef and Arpels.

La Fantaisie Russe is tucked in at number 130. There are a total of six jewelry stores in the arcades beneath what were once royal apartments built in the mid-1600s by Cardinal Richelieu so he could be close to the king. In the late 1700s, Philippe Égalité's theater was built and elite stores moved into the arcades facing the glorious inner courtyard.

Royalty no longer resides here. Rather, the bourgeoisie inhabit the apartments, including the well-to-do shopkeepers who live above their stores, famous writers and poets, established actors, dancers, directors, and choreographers. The theater in the east wing of the complex draws the creative here despite the darkness inhabiting this ancient square. For the Palais is not without its tragedy. Égalité himself was beheaded here, and some say his ghost still roams his apartments late at night.

Monsieur Orloff's wife, Anna, whose amethyst eyes see more than most, has warned me about the spirits haunting this great and complicated warren of stores, residences, basements, and deep underground tunnels. But it's not just the dead who contribute to the mist of foreboding that sometimes falls on the Palais. The miasma of dread that seems to issue forth from the ancient stones themselves is perpetuated by the living as well.

Behind the closed doors and lowered window shades, in the shadowy stairwells and dusty attic rooms, scandals are enacted and secrets told. Some of the elegant quarters are sullied by brothels and others by gambling dens.

Rumors keep us up at night with worry that German spies crisscross under the Palais as they move around the tunnels and catacombs beneath the city's wide boulevards and grand architecture.

But for all its shadows, with so much tragedy in Paris, in France, in Europe, in all the world, our strange oasis is all the more precious. Physically untouched by the war, the Palais's fountain and gardens offer a respite from the day, from the year. Her stores are a distraction. All of them, including number 130. The doorway to marvelous displays of precious gems and gleaming objects of adornment but also the unknown, the occult, and the mystical. Number 130, the portal to the necromancer, to me.

Chapter 1

JULY 19, 1918

"Are you Opaline?" the woman asked before she even stepped all the way into the workshop. From the anxious and distraught tone of her voice, I guessed she hadn't come to talk about commissioning a bracelet for her aunt or having her daughter's pearls restrung.

Though not a soldier, this woman was one of the Great War's wounded, here to engage in the dark arts in the hopes of finding solace. Was it her son or her brother, husband, or lover's fate that drove her to seek me out?

France had lost more than one million men, and there were battles yet to be fought. We'd suffered the second largest loss of any country in any war in history. No one in Paris remained untouched by tragedy.

What a terrible four years we'd endured. The Germans had placed La Grosse Bertha, a huge cannon, on the border between Picardy and Champagne. More powerful than any weapon ever built, she proved able to send shells 120 kilometers and reach us in Paris.

Since the war began, Bertha had shot more than 325 shells into our city. By the summer of 1918, two hundred civilians had died, and almost a thousand more were hurt. We lived in a state of anticipation and readiness. We were on the front too, as much at risk as our soldiers.

The last four months had been devastating. On March 11, the Vincennes Cemetery in the eastern inner suburbs was hit and hundreds of families lost their dead all over again when marble tombs and granite gravestones shattered. Bombs continued falling into the night. Buildings all over the city were demolished; craters appeared in the streets.

Three weeks later, more devastation. The worst Paris had suffered yet. On Good Friday, during a mass at the Saint-Gervais and Saint-Protais Church, a shell hit and the whole roof collapsed on the congregation. Eighty-eight people were killed; another sixty-eight were wounded. And all over Paris many, many more suffered psychological damage. We became more worried, ever more afraid. What was next? When would it happen? We couldn't know. All we could do was wait.

In April there were more shellings. And again in May. One hit a hotel in the 13th arrondissement, and because Bertha's visits were silent, without warning, sleeping guests were killed in their beds.

By the middle of July, there was still no end in sight.

That warm afternoon, while the rain drizzled down, I steeled myself for the expression of grief to match what I'd heard in the customer's voice. I shut off my soldering machine and put my work aside before I looked up.

Turning soldiers' wristwatches into trench watches is how I have been contributing to the war effort since arriving in Paris three years ago. History repeats itself, they say, and in my case it's true. In 1894, my mother ran away from her first husband in New York City and came to Paris. And twenty-one years later, I ran away from my mother in Cannes and came to Paris.

In trying to protect me from the encroaching war and to distract me from the malaise I'd been suffering since my closest friend had been killed, my parents decided to send me to America. No amount of protest, tantrums, bargaining, or begging would change their minds. They were shipping me off to live with family in Boston and to study at Radcliffe, where my uncle taught history.

At ten AM on Wednesday, February 11, 1915 my parents and I arrived at the dock in Cherbourg. French ocean liners had all been acquisitioned for the war, so I was booked on the USMS *New York* to travel across the sea. A frenetic scene greeted me. Most of the travelers were leaving France out of fear, and the atmosphere was thick with sadness and worry. Faces were drawn, eyes red with crying, as we prepared to board the big hulking ship waiting to transport us away from the terrible war that claimed more and more lives every day.

While my father arranged for a porter to carry my trunk, my mother handed me a last-minute gift, a book from the feel of it, then took me in her arms to kiss me good-bye. I breathed in her familiar scent, knowing it might be a long time until I smelled that particular mixture of L'Etoile's *Rouge* perfume and the Roger et Gallet *poudre de riz* she always used to dust her face and décolletage. As she held me and pressed her crimson-stained lips to my cheek, I reached up behind her and carefully unhooked one of the half dozen ropes of cabochon ruby beads slung around her neck.

I let the necklace slip inside my glove, the stones warm as they slid down and settled into my cupped palm.

My mother often told me the story about how, in Paris in 1894, soon after she'd arrived and they'd met, my father helped her secretly pawn some of her grandmother's treasures to buy art supplies so she could attend École des Beaux-Arts.

Knowing I too might need extra money, I decided to avail myself of some insurance. My mother owned so many strands of those blood-red beads, certainly my transgression would go unnoticed for a long time.

Disentangling herself, my mother dabbed at her eyes with a black handkerchief trimmed in red lace. Like the rubies she always wore, her handkerchiefs were one of her trademarks. Her many eccentricities exacerbated the legends swirling around "La Belle Lune," as the press called her.

"*Mon chou*, I will miss you. Write often and don't get into trouble. It's one thing to break *my* rules, but listen to your aunt Laura. All right?"

When my father's turn came, he took me in his arms and exacted another kind of promise. "You will stay safe, yes?" He let go, but only for a moment before pulling me back to plant another kiss on the top of my head and add a coda to his good-bye. "Stay safe," he repeated, "and please, forgive yourself for what happened with Timur. You couldn't know what the future would bring. Enjoy your adventure, *chérie*."

I nodded as tears tickled my eyes. Always sensitive to me, my father knew how much my guilt weighed on me. My charming and handsome papa always found just the right words to say to me to make me feel special. I didn't care that I was about to deceive my mother, but I hated that I was going to disappoint my father.

During the winters of 1913 and 1914, my parents' friends' son Timur Orloff lived with us in Cannes. He ran a small boutique inside the Carlton Hotel, where, in high season, the hotel rented out space to a select few high-end retailers in order to cater to the celebrities, royalty, and nobility who flocked to the Riviera.

Our families first met when Anna Orloff bought one of my mother's paintings, and Monsieur Orloff hired my father to design his jewelry store in Paris. A friendship developed that eventually led to my parents offering to house Timur. We quickly became the best of friends, sharing a passion for art and a love of design.

Creating jewelry had been my obsession ever since I'd found my first piece of emerald sea glass at the beach and tried to use string and glue to fashion it into a ring. My father declared jewelry design the perfect profession for the child of a painter and an architect—an ideal way to marry the sense of color and light I'd inherited from my mother and the ability to visualize and design in three dimensions that I'd inherited from him.

My mother was disappointed I wasn't following in her footsteps and studying painting but agreed jewelry design offered a fine alternative. I knew my choice appealed to the rebel in her. The field hadn't yet welcomed women, and my mother, who had broken down quite a few barriers as a female artist and eschewed convention as much as plain white handkerchiefs, was pleased that, like her, I would be challenging the status quo.

When I'd graduated *lycée*, I convinced my parents to let me apprentice with a local jeweler, and Timur often stopped by Roucher's shop at the end of the day to collect me and walk me home.

Given our ages, his twenty to my seventeen, it wasn't surprising our closeness turned physical, and we spent many hours hiding in the shadows of the rocks on the beach as twilight deepened, kissing and exploring each other's body. The heady intimacy was exciting. The passion, trans-forming. My sense of taste became exaggerated. My sense of smell became more attenuated. The stones I worked with in the shop began to shimmer with a deeper intensity, and my ability to hear their music became fine-tuned.

The changes were as frightening as they were exhilarating. As the passions increased my powers, I worried I was becoming like my mother. And et my fear didn't make me turn from Timur. The pleasure was too great. My attraction was fueled by curiosity rather than love. Not so for him. And even though I knew Timur was a romantic, I never guessed at the depths of what he felt.

War broke out during the summer of 1914, and in October, Timur wrote he was leaving for the front to fight for France. Just two weeks after he'd left, I received a poetic letter filled with longing.

Dearest Opaline,
We never talked about what we mean to each other before I left and I find myself in this miserable place, with so little comfort and so much uncertainty. Not

the least of which is how you feel about me. I close my eyes and you are there. I think of the past two years and all my important memories include you. I imagine tomorrow's memories and want to share those with you as well. Here where it's bleak and barren, thoughts of you keep my heart warm. Do you love me the way I love you? No, I don't think so, not yet . . . but might you? All I ask is please, don't fall in love with anyone else while I am gone. Tell me you will wait for me, at least just to give me a chance?

I'd been made uncomfortable by his admission. Handsome and talented, he'd treated me as if I were one of the fine gems he sold. I'd enjoyed his attention and affection, but I didn't think I was in love. Not the way I imagined love.

And so I wrote a flippant response. Teasing him the way I always did, I accused him of allowing the war to turn him into even more of a romantic. I shouldn't have. Instead, I should have given him the promise he asked for. Once he came back, I could have set him straight. Then at least, while he remained away, he would have had hope.

Instead, he'd died with only my mockery ringing in his head.

My father was right: I couldn't have known the

future. But I still couldn't excuse myself for my thoughtless past.

The USMS *New York*'s sonorous horn blasted three times, and all around us people said their last good-byes. Reluctantly, my father let go of me.

"I'd like you to leave once I'm on board," I told my parents. "Otherwise, I'll stand there watching you and I'll start to cry."

"Agreed," my father said. "It would be too hard for us as well."

Once I'd walked up the gangplank and joined the other passengers at the railing, I searched the crowd, found my parents, and waved.

My mother fluttered her handkerchief. My father blew me a kiss. Then, as promised, they turned and began to walk away. The moment their backs were to me, I ran from the railing, found a porter, pressed some francs into his hand, and asked him to take my luggage from the hold and see me to a taxi.

I would not be sailing to America. I was traveling on a train to Paris. Once ensconced in the cab, I told the driver to transport me to the station. After maneuvering out of the parking space, he joined the crush of cars leaving the port. Moving at a snail's pace, we drove right past my parents, who were strolling back to the hotel where we'd stayed the night before.

Sliding down in my seat, I hoped they wouldn't

see me, but I'd underestimated my mother's keen eye.

"Opaline? Opaline?"

Hearing her shout, I rose and peeked out the window. For a moment, they just stood frozen, shocked expressions on their faces. Then my father broke into a run.

"Hurry!" I called out to the driver. "Please."

At first I thought my father might catch up to the car, but the traffic cleared and my driver accelerated. As we sped away, I saw my father come to a stop and just stand in the road, cars zigzagging all around him as he tried to catch his breath and make sense of what he'd just seen.

Just as we turned the corner, my mother reached his side. He took her arm. I saw an expression of resignation settle on his face. Anger animated hers. I think she knew exactly where I was going. Not because she was clairvoyant, which she was, of course, but because we were alike in so many ways, and if history was about to repeat itself, she wanted me to learn about my powers from her.

I'd been ambivalent about exploring my ability to receive messages that were inaudible and invisible to others—messages that came to me through stones—but I knew if the day came that I was ready, I'd need someone other than her to guide me.

Years ago, when she was closer to my age, my

mother's journey to Paris had begun with her meeting La Lune, a spirit who'd kept herself alive for almost three centuries while waiting for a descendant strong enough to host her. My mother embraced La Lune's spirit and allowed the witch to take over. But because Sandrine was *my* mother, I hadn't been given an option. I'd been born with the witch's powers running through my veins.

Once my mother made her choice to let La Lune in, she never questioned how she used her abilities. She justified her actions as long as they were for good. Or what she believed was good. But I'd seen her make decisions I thought were morally wrong. So when I was ready to learn about my own talents, I knew it had to be without my mother's influence. My journey needed to be my own.

"I'm sorry, but I plan to stay in Paris and work for the war effort," I told my mother when I telephoned home the following day to tell my parents I'd arrived at my great-grandmother's house.

When my mother first moved to Paris, my great-grandmother tried but failed to hide the La Lune heritage from her. Once my mother discovered it, Grand-mère tried to convince my mother that learning the dark arts would be her undoing. My mother rejected her advice. When Grand-mère's horror at Sandrine's possession by

La Lune was mistaken for madness, she was put in a sanatorium. Eventually my mother used magick to help restore Grand-mère to health. Part of her healing spell slowed down my great-grandmother's aging process so in 1918, more than two decades later, she looked and acted like a woman in her sixties, not one approaching ninety.

Grand-mère was one of Paris's great courtesans. A leftover from the Belle Époque, she remained ensconced in her splendid mansion, still entertaining, still running her salon. Only now she employed women younger than herself to provide the services she once had performed.

"But I don't want you in Paris," my mother argued. "Of all places, Opaline, Paris is the most dangerous for you to be on your own and . . ."

The rest of her sentence was swallowed by a burst of crackling. In 1905, we'd been one of the first families to have a telephone. A decade later almost all businesses and half the households in France had one, but transmission could still be spotty.

"What did you say?" I asked.

"It's too dangerous for you in Paris."

I didn't ask what she meant, assuming she referred to how often the Germans were bombarding Paris. But now I know she wasn't thinking of the war at all but rather of my untrained talents and the temptations and dangers awaiting me in the city where she'd faced her own demons.

I didn't listen to her entreaties. No, out of a combination of guilt over Timur's death and patriotism, my mind was set. I was committed to living in Paris and working for the war effort. Only cowards went to America.

I'd known I couldn't drive ambulances like other girls; I was disastrous behind the wheel. And from having three younger siblings, I knew nursing wasn't a possibility—I couldn't abide the sight of blood whenever Delphine, Sebastian, or Jadine got a cut.

Two months after Timur died, his mother, Anna Orloff, who had been like an aunt to me since I'd turned thirteen, wrote to say that, like so many French businesses, her husband's jewelry shop had lost most of its jewelers to the army. With her stepson, Grigori, and her youngest son, Leo, fighting for France, she and Monsieur needed help in the shop.

Later, Anna told me she'd sensed I needed to be with her in Paris. She had always known things about me no one else had. Like my mother, Anna was involved in the occult, one reason she had been attracted to my mother's artwork in the first place. For that alone, I should have eschewed her interest in me. After all, my mother's use of magick to cure or cause ills, attract or repel people, as well as read minds and sometimes change them, still disturbed me. Too often I'd seen her blur the line between dark and light, pure and corrupt, with ease and without regret. That her choices disturbed me angered her.

Between her paintings, which took her away from my brother and sisters and me, and her involvement with the dark arts, I'd developed two minds about living in the occult world my mother inhabited with such ease.

Yet I was drawn to Anna for her warmth and sensitive nature—so different from my mother's elaborate and eccentric one. Because I'd seen Anna be so patient with her sons' and my siblings' fears, I thought she'd be just as patient with mine. I imagined she could be the lamp to shine a light on the darkness I'd inherited and teach me control so I wouldn't accidentally traverse the lines my mother crossed so boldly.

Undaunted, I'd fled from the dock in Cherbourg to Paris, and for more than three years I'd been ensconced in Orloff's gem of a store, learning from a master jeweler.

To teach me his craft, Monsieur had me work on a variety of pieces, but my main job involved soldering thin bars of gold or silver to create cages that would guard the glass on soldiers' watch faces.

To some, what I did might have seemed a paltry effort, but in the field, at the front, men didn't have the luxury of stopping to pull out a pocket watch, open it, and study the hour or the minute. They needed immediate information and had to wear watches on their wrists. And war isn't kind to wristwatches. A sliver of shrapnel can crack the crystal. A whack on a rock as you crawl through a dugout can shatter the face. Soldiers required timepieces they could count on to be efficient and sturdy enough to withstand the rigors of combat.

Monsieur Orloff taught me how to execute the open crosshatched grates that fit over the watch crystal through which the soldiers could read the hour and the minute. While I worked, I liked to think I projected time for them. But the thought did little to lift my spirits. It was *their lives* that needed protecting. France had lost so many, and still the war dragged on. So as I fused the cages, I attempted to imbue the metal with an armor of protective magick. Something helpful to do with my inheritance. Something I should have known how to do. After all, I am one of the Daughters of La Lune.

But as I discovered, the magick seemed to only make its way into the lockets I designed for the wives and mothers, sisters and lovers of soldiers already killed in battle. The very word "locket" contains everything one needs to know about my pieces. It stems from old French "*loquet*," which means "miniature lock." Since the 1670s, "locket" has been used to describe a keepsake charm

27

or brooch with a personal memento, such as a portrait or a curl of hair, sealed inside, sometimes concealed by a false front.

My lockets always contained secrets. They were made of crystal, engraved with phrases and numbers, and filled with objects that had once belonged to the deceased soldiers. Encased in gold, these talismans hung on chains or leather. Of all the work I did, I found that it wasn't the watches but the solace my lockets gave that proved to be my greatest gift to the war effort.

Chapter 2

"Yes, I'm Opaline Duplessi," I said to the woman who'd stepped into the workshop. "Can I help you?"

"I hope so. I was told you are able to—" She broke off. "It's about my son—" She couldn't finish.

The desperation in her voice told me everything. This tall woman with dark curls framing her pale face, with almost night-sky navy eyes, with her lovely lips trembling just a fraction, was shopping for solace.

My stomach clenched. No matter how often women called upon me to help, no matter how many lockets—or "speaking talismans," as I called them—I made, each time I took on a new assignment I felt as if I were being cut and bleeding afresh. The pain never lessened, and I never became inured to it.

"My name is Denise Alouette and I have a son—" She shook her head. The curls fell, hiding her high cheekbones. "I had a son . . . who . . ." Her voice reduced to only a whisper, she couldn't finish.

"I'm sorry."

She quickly lowered her head, but not before I saw the single diamond tear.

"My only son."

There was nothing I could say.

She took a moment to compose herself. "I've heard about you," Madame Alouette continued, finally raising her face. "About what you do. At first I thought surely you must be a fake and make it all up. There are so many charlatans in Paris now, the police are finally cracking down."

I knew all about the ancient French laws that were once again being enforced forbidding talking to the dead and reading fortunes. Monsieur Orloff warned me and his wife almost daily. With his strong Russian accent, the caution carried gravitas.

Madame Alouette fussed with her reticule. Taking out a lavender-colored tin, she opened it and offered me one of the deep purple sugar-coated violets and then took one for herself. In a moment, the candy's sweet scent suffused the air.

"A friend of mine told me about the message you passed on to her from her son. She seemed better afterward . . . almost at peace. So I've decided it might be worth a try."

I'd heard a version of this same speech many times before. Women who visited me at the shop were usually both skeptical and desperate.

"Let's go into the showroom, it's more comfortable," I said as I got up. "It's this way." The workshop was no place for clients. In the middle of the well-lit room were four U-shaped wooden tables, all facing one another like a four-leaf clover. Now only two of the stations were occupied, Monsieur Orloff's and mine. I was the sole full-time jeweler employed by the firm. Not only were precious metals and gems on our tables, but dangerous apparatuses also lay about: soldering guns and metal files.

"A piece of jewelry should be a marvel," Monsieur Orloff once had told me. "A little miracle the buyer looks at with awe and amazement, not understanding how it came together." He wore a perpetually serious expression and had deep frown lines etched upon his brow, but when he spoke about his jewels, a child's delight shone in his eyes and echoed in his voice.

He loved invisible settings and was famous for them, as well as the otherworldly gems he searched out and used in his pieces. His artist's eye found rubies that resembled wine turned to stone, emeralds as clear as a pool of water, sapphires that captured the essence of night, diamonds like stars pulled out of the sky, pearls glowing with the luminescence of the moon.

"How do you do it? How do you speak to those who have passed?" Madame Alouette whispered as I escorted her toward the private viewing room.

"I don't think I do speak to them directly," I said as I opened the door. "It feels more like I am able to access messages soldiers left behind as they passed over." *Or,* I considered, *it could be that I read your mind and hear what you wish he were saying.* But I'd never admit that to a client.

"As if the messages are in the sky and you pull them out?"

"Yes." I shrugged. "But I can't be sure." I held out a chair for her. "Here, have a seat," I said.

She sank down with the relief of someone who'd been on her feet for days.

"Can I get you coffee or some tea?"

"Coffee, yes, please."

Returning to the workroom, I turned on the kettle, prepared the press with grinds, then stocked a silver tray with Monsieur Orloff's Limoges china service: cups and saucers with a green, gold, and purple Russian imperial pattern.

Milk and sugar were often scarce because of the war, but we tried to always have some for clients, even if it meant going without ourselves.

Arranging the silver pitcher, sugar bowl, and coffee, I returned to the showroom to find Madame Alouette no longer at the table but standing, studying *The Tree of Life.*

Monsieur had wanted La Fantaisie Russe to be as much a work of art as the jewels inside its walls. An Art Nouveau masterpiece, the shop was one of the architectural commissions my father was most proud of. He'd chosen the themes of the wisteria vine and peacocks, the wisteria for welcome and the birds for their jewel-toned feathers. Walnut-veneered panels inlaid with purplish amaranth wood, to represent the cascading blossoms, covered the walls. The dual motifs were carried out in the carved showcases, as well as in the furniture, doorknobs, drawer pulls, lamp bases, and cabinet handles. Climbing vines carved into the wood led up from the floor to give way to blossoms hanging from the moldings, and vines framed the cabinets, doors, and windows. When it came to the lighting fixtures, standing lamp bases echoed the vines' twisting trunks and the glass shades evoked the clusters of blossoms. The peacock color palette—amethyst, turquoise, sapphire, emerald—carried throughout the upholstery, rugs, and tiles laid around the shell-shaped fireplace and on the mosaic floor.

No artwork decorated the walls; rather, tall mirrors, their carved frames suggesting peacock feathers, reflected back the jewels. In each corner, overlaid on the mirror, were peacocks, their jewel-toned feathers fashioned from stained glass.

Only a limited amount of Monsieur's wares were ever on view in the shop: two or three pieces showcased in each of the two display cases in the main gallery, another in the front window, and one in the private showroom.

It was the latter that I found Madame Alouette

inspecting. It held but one magnificent piece, *The Tree of Life*. Sculpted from silver, the oak tree stood almost three feet tall and sat in a glass case set flush with the wall. Instead of leaves, over 150 small gleaming guilloche enamel eggs, in a myriad of rich shades of green, from lime to forest pine, hung from its many branches. Each luminous egg designed and executed by Monsieur Orloff.

Like the more elaborate fantasies he had created with Fabergé for the royal family and upper crust of Russian elite, these simpler charms, set with fewer stones, were created with the same engine-turned process. Monsieur Orloff used a machine that engraved the metal with a perfect pattern of wavy or straight lines so when the enamel was poured it created an optical illusion and iridescence no other jeweler had yet been able to replicate.

"These are lovely," Madame Alouette said. "Are they for sale?"

"They're samples, but you can order them in any color you prefer. I have a color chart if you'd like to see it."

We'd sold hundreds of eggs throughout the war. While some clients still bought and wore extravagant jewels, others considered it bad taste to show off during wartime and were more comfortable buying modest pieces like the eggs. Fashion in general had changed rapidly since

1914. Almost all women worked now, fulfilling jobs men at the front had once held, and our clothes needed to be more efficient. Long light-colored dresses that soiled easily and dusted the floor gave way to darker, shorter, and more streamlined skirts and blouses. Since you could see our ankles, boots gave way to shoes. Bobbed hair became not only acceptable but chic and very much in style. Even our underwear became less constricting since the steel once used to construct corsets was needed for weapons. Brassieres and undergarments made of jersey had become the norm.

"Are these eggs your work?" Madame Alouette asked.

"No, Monsieur Orloff's. Enameling is not my forte."

"But you make the lockets?"

I nodded. "Yes, lockets of all kinds."

A month earlier, Monsieur Orloff had displayed a suite of mine in the window—a necklace and a pair of earrings featuring diamond crescent moons strung together with the thinnest platinum chain, interspersed with pale blue diamond stars. Each star, a locket that opened. Inside, a single teardrop ruby.

Unlike with those creations, the demand for my talismans wasn't determined by style or gem quality. Women like Madame Alouette sought me out because of the talismans' unseen beauty. It was the spirit and memory of their loved ones that made them exquisite, if not to a fashion connoisseur's eye, then to the heart.

Many of the descendants of La Lune had unusual talents, each different. One of my great-great-aunts was able to move objects by visualizing them. Another could manipulate the weather. There were stories that the original La Lune had been able to camouflage herself to her surroundings and seemingly disappear.

Since childhood, I'd experienced a special relationship with stones. Lights radiating from their opaque density that my brother and sisters couldn't see. Far-off music emanating from their masses that no one else could hear. Sometimes, I could hold a stone and sense danger, or calm, or good fortune or bad. I could also perceive the emotions of whoever had been holding it before me.

I had been afraid to tell anyone. Did these abilities prove I was a witch like my mother? The idea both excited and worried me. Like most little girls I wanted to be like her. She was beautiful and talented. Special. But at the same time I didn't want people to think I was different and strange. I wanted to be normal like the other children at school. Not someone to be singled out and whispered about.

When I was old enough, I searched my mother's library of occult titles, researching various phenomena, searching for a description that fit what I did. A combination of psychometry and lithomancy came closest to matching my abilities. Psychometry is the ability to touch an object and learn about its past and the person who owned it. Lithomancy is the ability to tell the future by throwing thirteen stones, each assigned to an action, and reading the prophecy based on how they land. While similar, neither really fit me.

But everything changed when I came to Paris and began to make talismans. Once I began combining stones with locks of hair and mementos from the dead, the noise I'd heard before became voices delivering messages.

Anna was the one to explain what was happening to me.

"Your talent *is* a variation on the art of lithomancy with a soupçon of psychometry. You can receive knowledge from stones. When you work on the watches, the materials you use are benign. They don't belong to any particular soldier. It's when you create the lockets, when you combine the soldier's personal object with the crystal and add his loved one's presence, that you ignite the magick."

Over the centuries, starting in ancient Egypt, mystics, priests, shamans, astrologers, doctors, and witches assigned properties to each earthly material. They knew all stones, including gems and crystals, are living things. Made up of water, earth, air, minerals, they are all related. Certain stones function better as conduits. Crystal, jet, white and blue and black diamonds, which are all coal based, and moonstones are the best conductors.

Once dug up, stones need to be uncovered or split open, cut, polished, or sometimes heated for them to reveal their beauty and offer up their powers.

Symbolically, they are reminders of the beauty within, of time, of life and death, of the permanence of the earth and the impermanence of those of us who inhabit it. These rocks will exist long after all the people who trod over them, who dug them up, who touched them, are gone.

Their beauty is not just in their colors and shine, their luminosity and glitter. The energy the gems possess can be read like a book if you understand its language. *The secret language of the stones.* A language that I spoke—though often wished I did not.

I poured the coffee and handed Madame Alouette a cup. "Would you like milk? Sugar?"

She looked down into the steaming dark liquid as if the answer lay there.

"No, black is fine." She took a sip and then sat quietly for a moment.

I didn't like to rush clients into talking. It often took a few minutes for women to begin the conversation they wished they didn't need to have. But when the silence lasted too long, I gently prodded.

"You said a friend of yours came here to see me?"

"Yes, Colette Maboussine, do you remember?"

"I do." I remembered every one of the fifty-nine grieving women I'd worked with, but especially the first one. Of Madame Maboussine's sons, one had been badly hurt in the war but survived; the other had been killed. The locket I made held his hair.

"Colette Maboussine told me how you helped her," Madame Alouette repeated. "She said you made her a piece of jewelry. An amulet or a talisman? I'm not sure what the difference is."

"An amulet possesses properties that can protect you against illnesses and accidents. Even evil spells. And anything can be an amulet, from a shark tooth to a scarab. A talisman is an amulet, but it can also help you create or orchestrate events or actions. Books I've read explain that talismans are enhanced with magick symbols that reinforce the attributes of that stone, gem, or metal."

"So there's more magick attached to a talisman?" she asked.

Madame Alouette didn't seem disturbed by the idea. Few of my customers did. After all, since the middle of the last century, séances and psychics have been very much in vogue, often discussed and dissected, despite whatever laws were in effect to tamp them down. Famous figures from Victor Hugo, more than seventy years ago, to the present-day author Arthur Conan Doyle were convinced there was more to our world than what we could see and hear and rationally know.

"Yes. Magical powers can be produced by tapping and then trapping astral influences."

"Which do you make?"

"Talismans."

"How?"

"I enclose an object belonging to the soldier inside a piece of rock crystal that I've carved with the soldier's name, astrological symbol, his birth and his death dates. I fill in the crevices with powder from his birthstone. Then, using gold wire, I enclose the crystal and lock it in."

"You know, I'm a sculptor," she said. "I never realized it until I heard you talk just now, but jewelry is miniature sculpture, isn't it?"

"I've never thought of it that way before either, but of course you are right. What kind of sculpture do you do?"

"Before the war I did portraits, mostly busts. But three years ago, Anna Coleman Ladd commandeered me. She's the American who opened a studio here to make metallic masks for soldiers who return from war with facial disfigurements. To give them back some dignity. She believes each of us has a divine right to look human. That is how Madame Maboussine and I met. She brought her older son to our studio. He had extensive cheekbone and ear damage."

I knew about Anna Coleman Ladd. The newspapers had printed a series of reports about her "Studio of Miracles," as they called it. Shrapnel made a horrible mess of many soldiers' faces that couldn't be repaired with surgery. Some men lost sections of their noses, chins, chunks of their cheeks, an ear. Ladd's studio provided a noble service to those boys. In London, another sculptor, Francis Derwent Wood, did the same work.

"It's really a pleasure to meet you then. I've read about the amazing work you are all doing. This war is . . ." I shrugged.

What more could be said about the never-ending war?

"I prayed my son would never need me to help him . . . but now I wish he did. At least then he would be alive . . . Well, it doesn't matter what I wish, does it? . . . Now I am here."

"Tell me about your son," I said, steeling myself for a fresh onslaught of heartache.

With measured motions, she unclasped her purse, reached inside, and pulled out a piece of paper that fluttered to the floor. I bent to retrieve it and found myself holding a black-bordered obituary notice, carefully cut out of a newspaper.

"No . . . no . . . that's not what I wanted to give you." She held out her hand.

As I returned it to her, I tried to read it, but it was upside down and I wasn't able to make out the details.

Returning the notice to her purse, she pulled out an envelope and gently emptied its contents on the desk, as if handling something as fragile as a spider's web.

I examined the lock of hair, the same dark chestnut as her own, tied with a faded blue satin ribbon.

"He had his first haircut at three years old. How he hated it," Madame Alouette said, reaching out and touching her son's hair with her forefinger.

I remained quiet while she lived out the memory. Her sorrow overwhelmed me and sent chills down my back. Any time a client began to recall her loved one and share her story, each word spun an invisible thread that connected us. Her emotions traveled via those byways, and I experienced them as if they were my own. I found no escape, no option but to suffer through each woman's mourning.

"But he needed that haircut. My husband said he looked like a little girl with all those curls. And he did."

She stroked the strands, and I pictured the child in the barbershop chair.

"The barber did everything he could to distract him, but my son fought back, covering his head with his arms so ferociously none of us could pry them apart. Such a determined little boy." She looked up, her eyes bright with tears. "Who became such a determined man."

"What did he do? Before the war, I mean."

"He was a journalist. Maybe you read some of his pieces? Since the war began, he's been writing a column of weekly letters from a soldier at the front to his fiancée."

"She must be devastated."

"Oh, he didn't have a fiancée. I'm not even sure if he left a special woman behind." She smiled sadly. "He told me there wasn't one—except for me." She smiled again. "But his editor wasn't interested in a soldier's letters to his mama. So my son writes to an unnamed, imaginary lover every week and in the process shares what the war is like, what he's feeling."

The suffering in Madame Alouette's voice as she spoke of her son in the present tense was difficult to listen to. It always was. The mourners' pain reached out and ensnared me. Encircled and paralyzed me. It infected the air I breathed, got into my lungs. I felt their anguish in my own heart.

"What is the name of the column?"

"*Ma chère.*"

"But isn't *Ma chère* written by Jean Luc Forêt?"

"Ah yes, Alouette is my second husband's name. His father died in a fire when Jean Luc was only four."

"How terrible."

She bowed her head a bit and nodded.

"So Jean Luc Forêt is your son. My father and I read him all the time . . ."

Now it was my turn to be lost in thought. Before the war, my father and I had always read Forêt's column on the avant-garde art scene. Like us, Forêt believed art was the highest form of individualism. He believed in beauty. In rage. In the pure form of expression through the arts. A fearless crusader for those artists who forged ahead, he never seemed to care how much criticism he got for it.

My father and I both admired him and worried for him whenever he went so far as to make a new enemy from what he published in the pages of *Le Figaro*. I remembered one column in particular he'd penned about a young artist being ridiculed for his work—for it being too ugly. Jean Luc argued that art frees us from our prejudices and gives us the chance to become our best selves, individuals who dare to dream. And even if those dreams aren't always as pretty as we'd like, or don't conform, or frighten us, it is our duty to encourage art to flourish. All art. Every kind.

I'd torn it out of the paper and glued it in my sketchbook. Without knowing him, I'd felt as if the writer in *Le Figaro* had spoken directly to me, offering a credo I'd taken to heart.

But once Jean Luc started reporting from the front, I'd stopped reading him. The war was too much of a presence in my life. Timur's death still too fresh in my mind. And now Jean Luc was dead as well? My heart seized up, sharing Madame Alouette's grief in a way new to me. I'd never before known of any of the soldiers I'd messaged.

"I got the telegram last week," Madame Alouette said. "Jean Luc's entire outfit was killed. All his men . . ." She shook her head desolately. "And for each is a mother and father, perhaps a wife or a sister or daughter or son." She stopped speaking, closed her eyes, collected herself, and then continued. "I am trying to accept his death, but I find I'm in limbo. I have a sense Jean Luc left something undone he wants me to know about. My husband thinks . . . Well, it doesn't matter what he thinks. Do I sound crazy to you?"

If she did, I shared her craziness. Of course, if you think you can commune with the dead, then you must be a little crazy. We all knew it was impossible. Except was it? Did I imagine it, or did I actually hear their voices? Did the souls of the dead soldiers whose lives had been stolen by the vagaries of the war really speak to me? Did they hover somewhere in the dark sparkling ether that we call eternity and communicate their last thoughts through the talismans I made from their

belongings? Did those little bits of their lives—
a lock of hair, a photograph, a baby tooth, a
handkerchief with a shadow of scent clinging to
it—function as tunnels through time and space,
enabling one last message to reach their loved
ones? Did they operate as doorways through
which I gained access to another plane, where
I received messages? Or was I, as Madame
Alouette implicitly suggested, crazy?

After making a talisman, I would decorate it
with jet and gold, lock it, and hang it from a cord.
A small gold key, attached to the knot on the
chord, dangled at the back of the wearer's neck.

Once completed, I would present the charm to
my client. After putting it on, I would instruct
her to clasp the talisman, and then I would cover
her hands with my own. Shutting my eyes, I
focused. Typically, I would hear a cacophony of
all manner of noise at first. Human voices, wind,
rain, the ocean's waves, train whistles, auto-
mobile horns, ambulance sirens. Withstanding the
onslaught, fighting the discomfort, I would
concentrate, and in a matter of minutes, as clearly
as if he were in the room with us, one soldier's
voice would rise above the rest. Inside my
head.

Sons to mothers, husbands to wives, fathers to
daughters, brothers to sisters, lovers to lovers,
the communiqués were deeply personal, and
often I blushed with embarrassment at having

to speak their words aloud. But my discomfort only lasted a few minutes; it was clear to me that the solace I gave would probably last forever. From what I could gather from their messages, the soldiers seemed trapped in a kind of purgatory like the one Dante wrote about in his great poem. They were souls awaiting entry to heaven, unable to completely leave this realm until they found some kind of release I didn't yet understand.

In all the time I'd been doing this, none of the soldiers had ever spoken to *me*. Their spirits seemed unaware of a conduit.

"What you said to Madame Maboussine, you weren't making it up, were you?"

"What kind of monster would I be to lie? We don't make profit on the charms. I have nothing to gain," I said.

"You might be looking for fame."

"As you yourself said, what I do is now illegal. Fame is the last thing I'd want." This interview wasn't getting off to a good start. I didn't blame Madame for being suspicious, but her questions bordered on rudeness. There was more I could have said. I could have told her how frightening it was to dwell in the land of the dead and that I would never willingly journey there. I could have told her it was like entering what one might imagine hell to be like. If I could, I would have boarded up the gateway that connected me to these souls.

"I'm sorry," she said. "It's just that I've never believed that what you do is possible."

"Neither do I, actually." I smiled at her.

Madame Alouette returned her son's hair to the envelope, which she handed to me with a reluctance that tore at my heart. As I reached for it, the scent of apples materialized, and a combination of nausea and dizziness descended over me.

Pulling out one of the boxes we use to encase our jewels, I quickly slipped the envelope inside, trying to outpace the headache coming on. I'd learned that if I could tuck the soldier's item away fast enough, I could prevent myself from becoming ill in front of my client.

Taking an ivory label from the desk, I picked up my pen, dipped it in the Baccarat inkwell on the table, and wrote out Madame Alouette's name. After placing the label on the box's lid, I slipped the package inside a drawer.

"Are you all right?" Madame asked.

Usually, so caught up in their own turmoil, my clients failed to notice mine.

"Just the beginning of a headache. How did you know?"

"I'm a sculptor, I study people's faces, I recognized the changes on yours. Are you all right?"

"Yes, I'll be fine."

"It began the moment you touched the envelope, didn't it?"

48

I nodded.

She placed her hand on top of mine. "This ability you have, is it painful?"

"Not compared to your pain."

"Can you describe it?"

I hesitated.

"I'd like to try and understand."

"The objects often cause me distress when I first come in contact with them. As if my body is rebelling and doesn't want me to take on a new assignment."

"You have to steel yourself?"

I nodded.

"Yes," she said. "It's like that when a new soldier comes in to see me. I pretend I can deal with his deformity. That my stomach isn't churning. That I didn't wish I could look away. What happens to you exactly?"

"I smell apples, even if there are none to be seen. And my head fills with noise, starting an avalanche of pain."

Madame Alouette nodded, but I stopped. She didn't need to hear more, and it wouldn't do to share any more details with a stranger, especially one suffering her own crisis. There was no reason for her to know that once I finished fashioning a locket I was so exhausted and depleted that often Monsieur Orloff sent me to bed. Anna would serve me hot tea sweetened with jam and laced with brandy and sit with me.

Neither did Madame Alouette need to hear about the despair that would follow the next day, that fell like a thick heavy curtain around me and made me feel as if I inhabited some other world . . . not quite here on earth . . . but not quite in the land of the dead either.

"And yet you do it? You willingly put yourself in this state of distress." Madame Alouette wasn't asking me a question. She was telling me something she knew about me because she shared that willingness with me. "You are very brave, Mademoiselle, and very kind."

Tears came to my eyes. I shook my head. "Neither brave nor kind," I said. "If I can help, I must."

Yes, it all started with helping. That was what I had come to Paris to do. Or so I thought. I now know it was more selfish than that. Offering comfort to strangers, I tried to assuage the guilt I lived with. Timur had died without any hope. That was the real reason I forced myself to help these mothers and wives, sisters and lovers. As physically ill as it made me, as frightening as it seemed, it was my penance for what I'd done to one boy who'd gone off to the war and died without the comfort I could have given but withheld.

Chapter 3

"The tsar has been shot," Monsieur Orloff said, looking up from the newspaper trembling in his hands like leaves buffeted by the wind. "The reports we've received since June twenty-fourth are all true."

"What exactly does the article say, Pavel?" Anna asked.

Twice he tried to read it out loud, but his voice shook worse than his fingers. Anna put her hand on his shoulder.

"Let Alexi read it," she said, taking it from her husband and giving it to their friend and fellow expatriate Alexi Vanya.

Often during the week I joined the Orloffs for dinner, as did an assortment of Russian émigrés. In Paris, there were thousands of tsarists, Russian refugees who despised the Bolsheviks and their actions against Mother Russia. Most White Émigrés, as they were known, had arrived in 1917. But others who were more insightful and less stubborn started to see what the future held as early as 1905. Every day still more escaped. And many of them found their way to a secret political opposition group called the Two-Headed Eagles, founded by Monsieur.

Named after the Romanov dynasty's symbol,

the group aimed to overthrow the Bolsheviks and restore the imperial family to the throne so they might all be able to return home. Fearful that Bolshevik spies would somehow infiltrate the group, the Two-Headed Eagles met clandestinely in one of the labyrinthine underground chambers here beneath the Palais Royal.

Vanya began to read. "'At the first session of the Central Executive Committee' . . ." His voice cracked. He fished in his jacket for a handkerchief, wiped at his eyes, tried to read again, and then gave up. He handed the newspaper to Grigori, Monsieur Orloff's eldest son from a previous marriage. After three years of fighting, an injury had ended Grigori's career as a soldier and he'd moved back home, taking an apartment on the other side of the complex and opening an antiques shop next door to La Fantaisie Russe.

"'At the first session of the Central Executive Committee elected by the fifth Congress of the Councils, a message was made public. Received by direct wire from the Ural Regional Council, it concerned the shooting of the ex-tsar, Nicholas Romanov' . . ." Grigori's husky voice did not break, but he did hesitate.

"Go on," Monsieur Orloff ordered.

Making an effort to control his emotions, Grigori continued. The story detailed how Yekaterinburg, the capital of the Red Urals, had been seriously threatened by the approach of

Czechoslovak bands and a counterrevolutionary conspiracy was found. When its objective—to wrest the ex-tsar from the hands of the council's authority—was discovered, the president of the Ural Regional Council decided to shoot the former tsar. The assassination had been carried out on July 16.

" 'The wife and the son of Nicholas Romanov have been sent to a place of security.' " Grigori's voice came to a halt. I saw the shadow of his eyelashes on his cheek. He took a breath and then continued.

" 'The Central Executive Committee has now at its disposal extremely important documents concerning the affairs of Nicholas Romanov— his diaries, which he kept almost up to his last days; the diaries of his wife and his children; and his correspondence, among which are the letters of Rasputin to the Romanov family. These materials will be examined and published in the near future.' "

Monsieur Orloff took the newspaper from his son and looked down at it as if searching for other words. Then he put his head in his hands. The sound of his anguished sobs broke our silence. Anna went to her husband's side. Vanya began to pace.

Grigori walked to the window and stared out into the black night.

I watched him, thinking I should go to him but

not quite sure I knew how to ease his suffering or that my ministrations were wanted. We had a complicated relationship.

We'd only met a little over six months before, in January, when he had been sent home from the front after shrapnel had shattered his left leg, leaving him severely lame. He'd gone to war a strong, able-bodied man and come back a cripple. He didn't understand that despite his injury he was handsome. Especially when his thick brown hair fell over his broad forehead. When his smile, when I could get him to smile, dimpled his cheeks. When his sleepy eyes, the uncommon color of brown diamonds, sparkled as he forgot about the war and talked to me about his passions.

Like his father and his half brother Timur, Grigori had a keen appreciation for beautiful things. It was what I enjoyed about him the most. On a walk, he was quick to point out a fine architectural detail or a particularly beautiful shade of blue in the sky. In a gallery of mediocre paintings, he could always spot the one hidden masterpiece, and in the workshop he always gravitated to the finest stones among those I was considering.

And yet he was full of bitterness about his handicap. He was angry he wasn't at the front with the rest of his company; jealous that Leo, his younger brother, remained, proving himself a hero. Grigori could also be irascible and prone to long fits of depression. Never having met him before the war, I couldn't know how drastically the war had changed him. But occasionally, I heard Anna or Monsieur remark on a cynicism creeping into his conversation that hadn't been there before he'd gone away, and a new darkness that had seemed to alter his soul.

To some, that would make him unlikable, but his moodiness and tendency to isolate himself endeared him to me almost as much as his exquisite taste. His faults and the secrets beyond his shine made him unique and roused my sympathies, just as my secrets and scars roused his. Knowing that sometimes, even after a wound heals, it can still cause pain, Grigori was surprisingly sensitive about how my relationship with Timur continued to haunt and trouble me, and it strengthened the bond between us.

Sometimes I believed we might have a future. Other times I sensed we were like inmates who turned to each other in desperation rather than desire.

Watching him at the window, his shoulders rounded, his head down, my pity got the better of me and I went to him.

"I'm sorry," I whispered as I took one of his hands.

His long fingers intertwined with mine.

"It's very difficult to believe our tsar is truly dead," Grigori said without turning to me, but his fingers gripped mine with a force that surprised me. He was usually more gentle.

Behind us, I heard Monsieur Orloff's voice, weaker than its usual growl. "We need to call a meeting. We do not have the luxury of mourning." His tone strengthened, his resolve already over-taking his pain. "Our goal has not changed. We still must restore Russia to its rightful rulers, even if that means its next generation of rulers. We need to do this so we can return to our homeland. This news of the tsar's death only makes our imperative that much more urgent."

Pushing himself up from his chair, Monsieur went to the telephone, which held a place of honor on a small table at the end of the couch. He didn't sit but remained standing, almost at attention, as he picked up the receiver and waited for the operator.

Because of his fear of Bolshevik spies, organizing a meeting had become a clandestine operation. Monsieur's former countrymen were now as much the enemy as the Germans.

Suddenly, static split the silence and then we all heard the operator's voice booming out of the earpiece. Monsieur gave her the exchange for Tatania Tichtelew. I knew her as a woman in her seventies who frequently came to the shop in the late afternoon to gossip with Anna over a cup of tea from the silver samovar. They both drank it the way so many Russians do, in a glass cup with a cube of sugar between their teeth. Often, Tatania would order a new string of pearls. I never counted, but in the time I'd been working for Monsieur Orloff, I must have strung at least thirty strands for her, in subtly diverse colors, from dark green-black to pure star-shine white.

"Madame, forgive me for calling you at this hour," Monsieur Orloff spoke loudly into the telephone. "But I know you are anxious to get your pearls and the stringer has finished."

The cryptic message sent and received, we sat down at the table, beautifully set with a cream tablecloth, sparkling crystal, and fine china. The heavy and ornate silverware, decorated like the plates with the tsar's imperial insignia, took on a greater poignancy.

Our conversation continued to revolve around the tragedy, and no one had much of an appetite, even for the cook's tempting food. Only the wine was consumed with any relish.

"This is the kind of night when I could drown in a bottle, but will stop at two glasses," Vanya said when Monsieur Orloff attempted to refill his wine goblet for a third time. "We have work to do and plans to make."

After the plates were cleared, Monsieur Orloff and Vanya went to the library to prepare for the meeting. Anna went to the kitchen to speak to the cook.

"Can I see you to your rooms?" Grigori asked.

"I'd appreciate some brandy if you don't mind. This has been a trying night."

I'd come to Paris expecting to live at my great-grandmother's fine mansion on rue des Saints-Pères. But with the city under siege and without the light from street lamps, the half-hour walk was far too dangerous for me to undertake alone at night. And so, Monday through Saturday, I lived beneath Monsieur's shop. The Orloffs had created a warren of rooms in their large basement, including a stock room, with enough tools and workbenches to serve as a second workshop, as well as three bedrooms. Two of them were often used by new émigrés during their first few nights in Paris. The third room, actually a suite with a bedchamber and sitting room, belonged to me. The walls had been covered in pale aquamarine blue with dark sapphire trim and matching upholstery. This tiny enclave was my sanctuary in a way my room at my great-grandmother's house wasn't. Her mansion offered no solitude. Open to soldiers on leave from the war who craved excitement, titillation, and escape, her salons and "fantasy bedrooms," as she called them, had never been busier. In the old days, only rich men had been able to afford the many pleasures found in them. But now, this was Grandmère's gift to the soldiers fighting. Whatever the desire, there was a room to match. One recalled the mirrored palace of Marie

Antoinette; another resembled a monk's chamber with a narrow bed, straw rug, and religious frescoes on the wall. There was an Egyptian room, as well as a Chinese pagoda and a Persian garden room with fanciful walls painted with trees and flowering bushes against a midnight blue sky complete with stars, a perfect crescent moon, and the onion-shaped minarets of Persepolis in the distance.

When I visited, I made a habit of hiding from the forced gaiety as soldiers overindulged in food, wine, and sex in order to forget. My great-grandmother provided a great service, but for me, being at Maison de la Lune, as her house is called, was like attending theater and suffering through a desperate, debauched, and sometimes depressing play.

As Grigori and I descended the staircase leading to my room, both of us were all too aware of the uneven cadence of his steps as he struggled with his damaged leg. I hated the sound for his sake.

At my door, I invited him in, as was our ritual. Whenever he dined with Anna and Monsieur, or whenever he surfaced from his melancholy and asked me to the theater or dinner, an art show or opera, at the end of the evening I would always invite him in and he would always accept my invitation.

He made himself comfortable on the couch

while I poured us both brandies and sat down next to him. Usually we talked for a while, but that night he seemed unable to wait and reached out—almost as if it was causing him pain—and pulled me to him.

His hands and his lips were, as usual, insistent, hungry. As if he were capable of devouring me. He slid his hand up my skirt. The feel of his fingers on my stocking leg sent shivers farther up. He moved from calf to knee to thigh. I heard my breath catch. Grigori's lips moved against mine, and I returned his kiss. His hand moved farther, finding my cleft, tickling me, making me buck. He unbuttoned my blouse, exposing my skin to the cool air. The oblivion his passion promised excited me. I thrust my breasts up toward him, and he pulled down my brassiere to kiss my nipples, holding first one then the other between his teeth. I ran my fingers through his soft hair. He moaned, and I felt him, hard against my thigh, ready for more, ready for me.

But we didn't reach a pleasured place because that night, as Grigori always did, he suddenly stopped, turned from me, and stood, leaving me on the couch, gasping and waiting, ready.

I felt sympathy, despite my frustration. As long as he eschewed that ultimate intimacy, as long as he continued to be ashamed to be with a woman because of his mangled body, we would never move past the awkward stage of undressing. But I didn't know what to do or what to say. I wasn't an experienced enough lover to know how to coax a man into relaxing. I'd lost my virginity to Timur, but we'd only been together a few times. I remained naïve in bed. One of my great-grandmother's courtesans would have been of more use to him.

I longed for the connection women whispered about, the desire to be one with your lover, the willingness to give up your body, especially in a time of war, when romance had been swept away and replaced with fear, when most eligible men my age were off fighting. But my shyness and his embarrassment kept us apart.

"I'm sorry," I said.

He spun around, his brown-diamond eyes flashing. "For what? I stopped because I cannot take advantage of you. Not in my father's house, not under his roof. And not when I have a meeting to attend." He pulled out an elaborate ruby-studded gold pocket watch. "And not when my meeting starts in fifteen minutes."

Grigori left my suite abruptly to collect his father and Vanya for the meeting. For a few moments, I contemplated getting into bed with a book. Far too restless, I straightened out my clothes and returned to the shop.

Chapter 4

I sat at my workbench, prepared my tools, and listened to Monsieur, his son, and his friend Vanya descend the steps leading deep beneath the store's basement.

Under the marvelous Palais courtyard and fountains and gardens lay a mysterious world where no light penetrated and the only sounds were made by rats, falling rocks, or men stealing through secret spaces.

At least that was all most people heard. Other sounds, terrible sounds, haunted me.

All of Paris sits atop limestone and gypsum mines, known as the *carrières*, some of which date back as far as the thirteenth century, when the stones that built the city were first excavated. No longer worked, the mines run for miles, a long network of empty tunnels and caves. Some were appropriated for the metro, others as havens for criminal, religious, and occult groups. During the war, the underground had turned into a secret highway for spies as they maneuvered around the city undetected.

Soldiers policed the caves, trying to protect us from enemies who might attack us from underneath, but the labyrinth was too complex for them to safeguard all of it at any one time.

Ironically, while spies hid in some caverns, Parisians used others as shelters during bombings. There were several beneath the Palais. The small one we used could hold approximately twenty people comfortably. Monsieur Orloff also held his Two-Headed Eagles meetings there.

Close by the shelter, through a door and down an incline, was another cavern that Monsieur had transformed into a vault for his materials and assets. Access to both was gained through the store. Continuing on past the shelter and the vault, one came to a locked door. Through it, a series of secret tunnels eventually led to the other side of the river.

There are no signs, no landmarks aboveground, to advertise the entrances to Paris's subterranean world. I'd heard stories of people who wandered for days, never finding a way out, who were buried alive in an avalanche, or who died taking a wrong turn and falling down a shaft.

It's easy to get lost. Once, after an air raid, I decided to explore, thinking maybe I could discover the source of my unease about going underground. I unlocked the door and ventured into the mine.

Missing a turn, I spent over an hour trying to retrace my steps, my panic building. Suddenly I heard a loud and terrible noise. I took another step and looked into a cavern converted to a tomb. The deafening sound seemed like a nightmare come to life. The catacombs were clearly the source of my torture.

Starting in 1777, in reaction to health problems caused by overcrowding in aboveground cemeteries, the city started to exhume bodies and rebury the dead in some of the empty caves. Over six million were buried in the ossuaries, and I'd stumbled upon one of the chambers.

Standing on the threshold, I stared at the skeletal remains, bones arranged in a macabre design, the source of the thunderous noise, the cacophony of terror and tears. Here resided the last thoughts of so many who had died in pain. Their suffering trapped in their bones.

Similarly to how I was able to hear the dying thoughts of the soldiers via the crystals in the talismans, I heard these poor souls' final moments through the stone-studded earth. En masse, magnified, the storm of cries, curses, and calls terrified me.

And yet, when the sirens rang out or Monsieur sent me down to the vault, my only choice was to steel myself and endure. The same way I endured the voices of the individual soldiers whose loved ones came to me, like my most recent visitor, Madame Alouette.

I placed the box holding the envelope with her son's lock of hair on my worktable, but I didn't open it. Not yet. First I needed to prepare the object that would hopefully allow me to help her find peace.

Sorting through two dozen chunks of rock crystal, I chose an egg-shaped orb about the size of my thumb. Once a month I brought the lapidary a dozen or so crystals, which he cut into eighths, like segments of an orange, and then polished. I did all the engraving myself. And although the work was painstaking, it absorbed me. While I sat at my table, all thoughts disappeared. I connected with my tools, and they became extensions of my hands.

Sometimes, while scratching out the words and numbers and runes, I would crack a crystal, but the night of the tsar's news, the operation went smoothly.

On one segment, I carved Jean Luc's name and the numbers of his birth date: *18/8/1890*. And the date of the battle in which he died: *8/7/1918*.

Knowing his birthstone was a peridot, I looked through the assortment of stones I kept for the talismans. None of these were of the best quality. Because of what I do to them, occlusions don't matter. I found a lovely rounded light lime-colored stone with a crack running through it, which made it ideal for my purposes.

Hawaiians believed peridots were the tears of the goddess Pele, quite apropos for a mourning jewel. Placing the stone in a metal bowl, I pounded it with a small iron hammer, shattering it into fragments and then into powder.

Next, I chased a chasm in the crystal, like a

small stream, and filled it with the glittering green residue.

Placing that section aside, I picked up another slice of the crystal and began to carve the Egyptian hieroglyphs for immortality, youth, and victory.

I'd worked for two hours and was tired. Beneath my feet, Monsieur Orloff, Grigori, and Vanya were still meeting with their fellow Russians, trying to absorb and make sense of the fact that their beloved Nicholas had been shot dead. Did they find solace knowing he'd died honorably for his country? Did women like Madame Alouette find any solace knowing their sons had died for theirs?

I finished all the engravings. I knew I should stop, but something propelled me to keep going. I was eager to see how this talisman would turn out. I knew of this soldier. I had read his work. I felt a kinship to him, and I'd never experienced that before.

The next step was to add the personal memento. One by one, I placed four segments of the rock crystal egg into a vise to hold them steady. Removing Jean Luc's dark brown lock of hair, I smoothed it out, separated the strands, then laid them down in the core. Then I added the rest of the segments one by one until I'd rebuilt the whole egg again.

Those last steps often took more than one

attempt. I wanted the hair or other personal items to become part of the design—in this case, to lie symmetrically, forming a core, not just looking like hair encased in crystal. If the strands separated in the building process, I'd need to start all over. But that night everything turned out perfectly on the first try.

Taking a length of gold thread, I began to wrap the egg. Sometimes I left more crystal showing, other times less. With Jean Luc's egg, I left more because the look of his hair against the rivers of peridot was so pleasing I wanted it to be visible.

Once all the threads encircled the orb like curving, twisting vines, tight and determined, sealing the treasure within, I picked up my soldering gun and went to work attaching the gold at several junctures, creating a tight meld. I loved how the hot metal fused the disparate threads, like lovers separated for too long finally coming together and not wanting to let go.

Finished, I cupped the orb and inspected it. As I'd expected, quiet prevailed. Although I could hear cries in the catacombs, without a living conduit, I'd never received specific communications from my charms. In order for me to hear the actual words the talisman carried, a mother, wife, lover, or daughter needed to put the locket around her neck. It was simply a piece of jewelry to me. An artifact until its owner's love made it come alive and I heard the message it was meant to pass on.

But something quite different occurred that night. As I sat cradling Jean Luc's crystal egg in my palm, I experienced a fluttering in my chest. A tremor of exertion. As if I were a cage and some creature with wings were making a herculean effort to break free.

My body began to shake, and one of my terrible headaches blossomed. I smelled apples, which didn't surprise me, and something else that did . . . graphite and wood . . . I smelled the scent of paper.

Then, as if it were blowing in on a great wind from a distant place, I heard a grumbling noise. Dozens of distant voices? Birds screaming? I couldn't be sure. Listening harder, I tried but failed to pull any one sound out of the mélange. Yet I sensed a force trying to impart information.

Impossible. I needed some headache powder and water. Or wine. The soldiers' talismans had never before spoken to me alone. I had to be imagining these sounds in anticipation of the terrible words I would hear when I gave Madame Alouette the talisman and she put her own hands around it. Often the soldier's last thoughts frightened or shocked me and left me disturbed for days. I told myself I must have been dreading that.

I mixed the headache powder in a tall glass

of water and drank it. My equilibrium restored, I returned to my worktable and stared down at the crystal. All was quiet in the workshop and in my mind. But as soon as I picked up the talisman, the noises started again. I heard that same howling wind. Distant shouts. Or maybe a rush of water against rocks. None of it made any sense. All of it was deeply disturbing.

My fingers began to shake so badly I had to put the talisman down and clasp my hands together. Cold washed over me. And the wind that I'd only been hearing before seemed to actually be blowing past me.

What was happening? Had I been working too many nights? Hearing too many stories about dead soldiers? Or was I spending too many hours studying stones? My great-grandmother had warned me of this. Madness had descended upon some of the descendants of La Lune when they welcomed and embraced the talents she passed down.

The remedy I'd taken wasn't helping. With my head pounding I wasn't thinking clearly. The echoes and hums and crashes kept building. I'd never been in a hurricane, but I'd read about them. This must be what a storm of that magnitude sounded like. Wind that tore through trees and flowers. Upending objects, sending them flying. Destroying property, doing terrible damage.

Where . . .

One word flew out of the cacophony. I'd heard a word. But I was alone. Unless Monsieur had returned and was just outside?

"Hello?" I shouted out into the dark workshop.

No answer.

The storm continued to rage on inside my head. There must be an explanation for the word. Could it have been one of the Russians from Orloff's meeting, lost on his way out? That had happened before. Was some anomaly making a word spoken in the outer hallway reverberate strangely?

"Is someone there?" I called out.

No answer. I needed to clean up and leave. Sleep would help. I would just put away my tools and then I could—

Where am I?

I heard it more clearly. A deep and dark raspy voice asking me for help.

"Hello?" I shouted. "Is anyone there?"

Where am I?

I heard pain accenting the distant words. Was he standing outside the store? Or was his voice traveling up from the underground chambers? Could he be hurt? Or was it a ploy? It might be one of the Russians, but just as likely a German spy pretending to be a lost Frenchman. Or it might be a thief, making sure the shop was empty before he stole from us.

From the table, I grabbed one of the long metal

files with a point sharp enough to be a weapon. Creeping out of the workshop into the darkened hallway, ready to pounce or help depending on what I saw, I peered into the shadows, searching for a figure. But the hallway was empty. I checked the door to the staircase down to the basement below, but it was shut tight. The showroom was empty too.

Skulking down the hall and over to the entrance, I kept my back to the wall so no one hiding could attack me from behind.

The locked front door exhibited no evidence of an attempt to pry it open. Neither of the large windows on either side was broken.

Where am I?

Like the sound inside of a shell, the voice reverberated. I turned. My eyes, now totally adjusted to the dark, searched every corner. This had to be some strange echo coming up from a shaft in the mines I'd never been aware of before.

Where am I?

"I don't know, I don't see you," I whispered into the darkness.

Where am I?

Listening harder, I realized the shadowy blue-green voice echoed inside of me. The sad and desperate words weren't coming from outside. I was manufacturing them. Overtired, my imagination was playing tricks on me. I needed to leave, to go to bed, to sleep.

Please, tell me.

I put my hands up to my ears and pressed as firmly as I could to block out the voice, the wind, the words.

"No," I heard my voice groan. "No."

Please.

"Go away."

Please, tell me where I am.

This time I screamed: "Go away. Go away. Go away." I needed to shut down the voice. To prove to myself I wasn't losing my mind the way so many women in my family who had succumbed to the darkness and been its victim had lost theirs.

I knew all their names and the dates they were born and died—all tragically. Some accidentally, some by their own hand. Only one living past thirty-three.

EUGENIE 1664–1694
MARGUERITE 1705–1728
SIMONE 1734–1777
CAMILLE 1782–1814
CLOTHILDE 1800–1832

My great-grandmother had escaped by not believing in the legend. My mother by embracing it and willingly inviting a fate that the others had thought was worse than death. But I wasn't my mother.

I'd succeeded in quieting the voice. The wind slowed and softened to a breeze. The workshop was silent once again, save for the sound of my own heart beating, still a bit too fast. My back dripped with sweat. My hands continued to tremble. But the worst of it was over. I knew if I just rested for a few more minutes, I'd be all right again. And then I'd go downstairs and go to bed and in the morning this would all be a—

Where am I?

I shook my head. "No, no . . . go away."

I tried to stand, but my legs wouldn't move. My feet seemed cemented to the floor.

Please . . . Just tell me. Where am I?

I gave up. What else could I do? Maybe if I answered, he'd leave.

"I don't know where you are. On the battlefield where you died? In our shop? What can you see of where you are?" I whispered.

What would be worse? For him to answer or not to? I didn't know anymore.

When I received no response, I deluded myself that the episode was over. The breeze was even softer than before, wasn't it? In fact, I wasn't sure I could even feel it anymore. Yes, the episode was over. I willed my hands to stop trembling. I didn't need to put away my tools. I just needed to leave and go to bed.

You. I can see you.

Alarmed anew, I spun around. The workshop

was empty. There was no doubt of it. There was no living being here with me. My head ached worse now. The powder hadn't helped. Yes, yes. That must be it. At last I'd figured it out. The entire episode was a manifestation of my headache. An exaggeration of my ability to hear the stones and an overactive imagination.

Yes, I seemed to receive messages for mourners. I tried to convince myself the communiqués were the product of my mind reading the mind of the woman who sat across the table from me, desperately wanting to hear the words I shared with her. I had almost talked myself into believing I was a mentalist, not a necromancer. That I spoke the words I sensed the woman needed to hear. Not that I really was picking up messages the dead soldiers left in the atmosphere for their families so they could move on.

And it was possible, wasn't it? Accounts of mentalists who were able to receive others' thoughts went back to the Old Testament and ancient Greeks. In 1882, Frederic W. H. Myers, a founder of the Society for Psychical Research, invented the word "telepathy." But I preferred "mental radio" to explain the phenomena I experienced—the theory being that, in the same way the newly invented radios in the news transmitted sound, our brains transmitted thoughts to one another.

Over and over, I told myself that's what I heard, what the noises were. Transmissions from people around me, in the same room, the next room, the street. That what I saw and experienced was no different from my father's ability to imagine a building, from Edith Wharton's ability to imagine a story, from Picasso's ability to imagine a painting.

But that night, speaking to a voice in the ether, I couldn't fool myself. I was the daughter of a woman who called herself a witch and who could spin spells to prevent aging, cure illness, or alter the thoughts in someone's mind.

What *was* my curse? Or my gift, as Anna insisted I refer to it. Yes, I spoke the language of gems and minerals. But I didn't just hear their energy and sense who had touched them last or what they'd been feeling. I received audible messages through the stones as well. Or, more accurately, I was able to sense the energy between stones and humans and sometimes receive messages from the dead. Yes, I'd heard the dead's cries in cemeteries, in the catacombs. And through the lockets I'd heard messages meant for their loved ones. But *I'd* never *spoken* to the dead before. I'd never known I was capable of doing that.

I remained sitting at my workbench, staring down at Madame Alouette's charm. A simple rock crystal egg in eight sections with a soldier's hair—her son's hair—sandwiched at its center.

I still felt ill, but I knew I couldn't stay in the workshop all night. Forcing myself to clean up, I swept the gold dust and scraps into the leather apron strung under my table. Nothing is wasted in a jeweler's workshop. A year's worth of scraps of the precious metal is worth a small fortune.

After putting away my tools, I picked up the crystal egg once more, this time intending to put it too away.

Surprised by its warmth, I closed my palm around it. An exotic and pungent scent tickled my senses. Lime and verbena with a hint of myrrh. I heard the wind again but warmer and calmer this time. And with it came a tangle of voices. I listened harder and heard, inside of them, a single voice. His voice whispering softly. I leaned forward, thinking the voice emanated from the egg. But I was wrong. He was all around me.

I'm not on the field.

"No?"

I was on the field. The last place I remember. I made a call. The wrong call. What happened next was all my fault.

"What happened?"

My unit . . . all my men . . . all gone.

Did the voice belong to Madame Alouette's son? It had to. I'd been working on his talisman all night. And she'd told me he'd been in charge of his unit. Was it really him? And why was I scared to address him? Because he wasn't alive anymore? Because I was talking to—what? A spirit? A ghost? A fragment of a trapped soul needing to communicate before he moved on?

I'd heard other soldiers' voices before. But they were final thoughts left behind. A last sentence or two, preserved. Like an insect frozen in amber forever. Those soldiers weren't speaking to me. Not to Opaline Duplessi. But this one was.

It was never my mother's magick but rather my father's love that kept me feeling safe when I was a child. When she opened the door, her darkness and her secretive powers would overwhelm me, while my father's words and his touch would soothe me.

But that night I was alone in Paris. My father wasn't with me. He couldn't comfort me and convince me I had nothing to fear. And I was afraid. Somehow I'd opened a door of my own, and now I would have to live with what was on the other side.

Chapter 5

The next evening, once the shop closed, I followed my typical Saturday routine. I changed from my work clothes—a simple black midlength skirt and white blouse—into an mandarin orange sleeveless chemise, matching satin-heeled shoes, and opal earrings and necklace I'd designed. Ten minutes later I crossed the Pont du Carrousel to my great-grandmother's house. I would sleep there overnight, and we'd spend Sunday together before I went back to the store Monday morning. The normalcy of our time together would make me feel better, I was sure of it. Grand-mère discouraged exploration into the spiritual realm. My inner turmoil would calm, as it always did around her.

The sun hadn't yet set and an almost festive feeling blew in the breeze. Bertha hadn't dropped any bombs in two weeks, and a false sense of security was making all of Paris nearly giddy. As I strolled, I thought about how alone I was. I could have brought Grigori with me; he was always willing to accompany me to my great-grandmother's. But I'd endured enough of his melancholy the night before.

My destination was located on a lane blocked off from rue des Saints-Pères by wide wooden double doors. One of a half dozen four-story mid-eighteenth-century stone houses, it shared a courtyard that backed up to rue du Dragon. Hidden clusters like this were a common configuration in Paris, affording privacy within the bustling city. Usually the porte cochère was locked and one rang for the concierge, but on busy nights the heavy doors remained ajar and I didn't need to wait for service.

I stood on the stoop and lifted the hand-shaped bronze door knocker and then let it drop. All the noise emanating from inside muffled the sound. Dismayed but not surprised, I found Maison de la Lune more crowded than usual. In the salon, my great-grandmother entertained her visiting crop of soldiers with food and drink, music and conversation.

"I don't know how to turn any of them away," she confided as she offered her cheek for me to kiss. "I hope you won't be too cross with me, Opaline, but I put two of them up in your bedroom and made up the daybed in my suite for you."

Of course I was, even if I didn't show it. But I was never completely comfortable in this house anyway. It hardly mattered where I slept. The ancient maison was too old and there were too many secrets and too much history here. I always felt as if I'd just missed learning something about myself and my family that I needed to know. And the overflow of strangers—most of whom drank too much and enjoyed sex too loudly and took what I thought was advantage of my great-grandmother's largesse—made it feel even less like a home.

"You are cross with me. I see it in your face. Just like your mother, your anger pinches your eyes and, like me, flashes there."

We were in the grand salon. The most opulent room, where my great-grandmother held court. The colors of the fabric wall coverings and carpets chosen to complement her coloring—dark red hair, peach skin, topaz eyes with fire opal high-lights. The museum-quality furniture was ornate. The walls were crowded with paintings and the tabletops laden with treasures—all holding special significance for her.

I worried the visiting soldiers might be tempted to lift some of the objets d'art. It would be so easy. In between the windows stood an almost full-size marble sculpture of Diana wearing her crescent-moon headpiece. The double string of gray pearls that hung around her neck was worth a fortune. My great-grandmother's favorite lover had put them there more than forty years before, and Grand-mère said she left them because they reminded her of him.

With just one gesture they could be off her neck and in someone's pocket. And the pearls weren't the only valuables to make off with.

Enticing, curious oddities and fanciful amusements gleamed and shone from every corner.

A priceless collection of Japanese netsukes of men and women in erotic poses graced one table. Silver repoussé vases studded with onyx, turquoise, and amethyst and decorated with iridescent peacock feathers were tucked in corners. On the mantel were a half dozen birds' nests made from spun silver, each holding eggs carved out of precious stones. On the top of the grand Bösendorfer piano sat a collection of tiny enamel- and jewel-framed miniatures of women's eyes and breasts painted on ivory.

But my great-grandmother was too happy taking care of her *boys* to worry about losing a jade frog with ruby eyes or a salamander made of gold. She wasn't alone in her war efforts; she just offered more delights than most of the other godmothers, or *marraines de guerre*, as they were known, women who wrote to soldiers at the front who had no family. Too many people had lost their homes because of the bombings and in the wake of the destruction had scattered and lost touch with their sons and brothers, fathers and husbands, at the front. The godmothers sent long letters and care packages and did wonders at keeping up the armed forces' morale.

Generously, my great-grandmother's letters to the boys always included an invitation to the Maison de la Lune when the soldiers came to

Paris on leave. She opened the doors of her elaborate house, put them up, fed them, soothed them, and made sure there were lovely girls to offer them the kinds of entertainment they most craved.

The men fighting for France deserve nothing less than to be treated like the most wealthy industrialists and bankers who we have always catered to and lived off of, Grand-mère often told me. She thrived on what she did for the troops, and while I admired her for it, I hated being in the house with all the soldiers, all strangers, all trying to forget where they'd been and what they were required to go back to. Even if they bantered and joked, ate and drank and laughed and danced, I could see the suffering and fear in their eyes, the residue of the nightmares they'd lived. Their suffering overwhelmed me. I soaked it up like a sponge and became subdued, depressed, and haunted by it.

"They need your good cheer and smiles," my great-grandmother would chide me. "Not your pity and tears."

But I had nothing else to offer, so often, instead of dining with them in the overcrowded dining room, I asked for a tray to be brought to me in my grandmother's suite and went upstairs, past the haunting portraits of all the female descendants of the original sixteenth-century La Lune.

My great-grandmother's boudoir nestled in the

far corner of the second floor. I opened the door and, for a moment, stood enthralled anew by its loveliness. Here too the fabrics and carpet were chosen to set off Grand-mère's red hair. But the murals captivated me the most. My father's friend, the celebrated artist Alphonse Mucha, had painted a pastiche of the four seasons covering the walls. In high Art Nouveau style, winter scenes segued into spring, then summer, and finally fall. Through each season, a woman wandered, a younger, stylized version of Grand-mère who could have been me with her long russet hair, almond fire opal eyes, and pale skin.

In the corner of the room, an ornate wrought iron staircase led up to my great-grandmother's private library. Beside the expected classics and volumes of exotic and provocative erotica, I'd been surprised to find shelves devoted to the occult as well as gothic and horror fiction. Ever trying to understand and come to terms with the storied history of the house and our ancestors, she read everything, looking for clues and answers. Sharing her morbid fascination and equally curious, I'd made my way through Bram Stoker, Henry James, Edgar Allan Poe and Maurice Level and Villiers de l'Isle-Adam. I'd even stumbled on a book with my grandfather's ex libris plate pasted in the inside cover, *The Picture of Dorian Gray*. Seeing me reading it, my great-grandmother told me my mother had brought it with her when she'd first come to Paris.

While I ate my dinner, I read from a book of ghost stories by Edith Wharton. There was, for many of us, a great escape in reading about the fantastic and supernatural during wartime. Terrors more terrible than those we were living through gave us an outlet for our anxiety. Some found it strangely hopeful to read fiction suggesting there was more to our existence than what established religions suggested.

I fell asleep reading Wharton's *Tales of Men and Ghosts*. Some hours later, I woke up from a terrible dream. But it wasn't a dream. The sound of weeping was real. Lonely and anguished, these were the kind of tears that could only be shed in the darkest hour of the night. Could it be my great-grandmother? I looked over at her bed. No, she was quiet and calm. I should have known better. I'd never even seen her eyes fill. She'd told me once she'd used up her quota of tears when her son, my grandfather, died the year before I was born.

Tying my robe around my waist, I went out into the hall and followed the sound. When I reached the end of the corridor, it grew fainter. I retraced my steps. The hallway was dark and the house otherwise silent. Only the forlorn crying echoed. Concentrating, I tried to locate its direction. Was it coming from above? I climbed the steps to the third floor.

Yes, the sound was more pronounced. I walked down another long hallway, past rooms used by servants. At its end, in front of another staircase, I stopped to listen again. It seemed the weeping was still coming from above. Was that possible? Were soldiers sleeping even in the attic?

I followed the crying through a warren of storage rooms and a last ancient stone staircase leading to the bell tower, the one remaining structure from the sixteenth-century church that had once stood on this plot of land. This was where, in the late 1500s and early 1600s, my ancestor, the famous courtesan La Lune, entertained her paramours, including the king of France and the famous painter Cherubino Cellini, the man for whom she learned the dark arts in order to regain his love. After he died, she became a celebrated artist herself and lived, according to the family legend, into the 1700s while retaining the appearance of a forty-year-old woman.

As a little girl visiting, I'd been drawn to this very staircase. I would ask if I could go up and see the bell tower, but my great-grandmother insisted it wasn't safe. Too old and too fragile to hold the weight of a person.

"The steps are broken, and you could trip. Inside the tower is only scaffolding now," she'd warned. "If you even tried to walk there, you would fall right through!"

My mother, overhearing this, would laugh.

"But what is funny, Maman?" I asked. "It sounds dangerous, no?"

"Your great-grandmother told me the same thing once upon a time. And I believed her too. But it's not true. You should see what is up there, it's part of your heritage."

Over my great-grandmother's protestations, my mother took me up the last flight of steps. Yes, they were narrow and steep, but also sturdy and strong. My mother told me three hundred years of bell ringers had tramped up and down them and the tower they led to was constructed just as well.

At the top of the steps was a door carved with tiny bas-reliefs, each detailing an alchemical event and other amalgams of magick and religious symbols sprinkled through the rest of the house.

I tried the door, but it was locked. But when my mother put her hand on the knob, it opened for her. Inside was an artist's studio with marvelous murals of Cupid and Psyche on the wall. To an impressionable child their suggestiveness was titillating, but it was the book of spells, hidden in a concealed cabinet, that made the biggest impression on me.

"Why is it here if it's so valuable?" I asked my mother as she turned its old vellum pages.

"It's safer here than anywhere else. No one can enter this room except for a Daughter of La

Lune," she explained, telling me about the legend for the first time. But the way she told it frightened me, and I ran crying from the bell tower, down the steps, into the arms of my great-grandmother, who held me safe. Glaring at my mother, Grand-mère insisted the story wasn't true and that my mother was just indulging in make-believe.

That Saturday night, when I tried the door, it didn't open. I stood still, frustrated, listening to the sound of weeping coming from within. The soldier's plaintive cries sent chills through my body. I pulled my robe closer around me and leaned against the door.

"Can I help?" I called out softly, not wanting to disturb him, and at the same time feeling certain it was important I let him know someone was offering aid if he needed it.

There was no response.

Focusing, directing my energy the way I did when I read the talismans for my clients, I tried the knob. This time it turned, and with a single creak, I opened the door.

"Can I help?" I called out into the moonlit chamber.

No response.

I stepped over the threshold. Everything looked just as I remembered from when my mother had brought me here. The amazing murals, even when illuminated only by the lunar light, were still mesmerizing. The daybed, where I'd expected to find the soldier, was vacant, the silk coverlet and overstuffed pillows undisturbed.

The weeping ceased. The tower now was as quiet as it was empty. Confused, I stood in the middle of the chamber and waited. But why? I should go. There was nothing to discover here. Yet something kept me glued to the spot.

I'm not sure how many minutes I stood in the darkened tower, but it was long enough to become accustomed to the musty scent of a room untouched for years, to notice warps and bleached patches in the floorboards and crevices in each stone in the wall. As the moon progressed westward, lunar beams illuminated parts of the tower and I noticed a pattern on the southern wall that hadn't been visible before. By utilizing slightly darker and lighter rocks, some long-ago mason had designed a pentagram. At least as tall as me, the motif was totally invisible before the moonlight hit it at exactly the right angle. The path must have been calculated precisely.

Tracing the outline of the circle-enclosed star, I wondered what purpose it served. As I ran my hand over stones in the center of the star, I noticed they felt more uneven than those around them, with the rock dead center rougher still, prickly with points and clefts and crannies. My fingers found holds where they fit, almost as if the rock was sculpted to seem rough and natural but was anything but arbitrary. My curiosity aroused, I followed my intuition and pulled open what turned out to be a drawer.

A screech sent shivers down my spine. The sound of the stone scraping against itself was harsh. Ugly and rough, it disturbed the quiet and made me afraid. How long since someone had opened this drawer? Was I brave enough to peer inside and see what it contained? My imagination ran wild. What if it was proof of some awful deed committed here? I knew this had been La Lune's studio in the sixteenth century and my mother's just twenty-four years ago. I knew they were witches and that this star shape was a powerful occult symbol.

The moonlight fell into the drawer, a pool of it collecting, shining on silver, reflecting in my eyes. I reached in and pulled out a pile of metal sheets, stacked to create an object roughly the same size and heft of a substantial book. Examining it, I could see each sheet was engraved front and back with signs, symbols, equations, and words. Some in Arabic or Greek, others with medieval French spellings.

I studied the inscriptions, marked only here and there with fingerprints. I recognized them as formulas, some I'd even seen before in a book Anna Orloff had lent me when I'd first started making mourning jewelry.

These paper-thin sheets of sacred silver held secret rituals for creating talismans. I turned to the last page.

Make of the blood, heat.
Make of the heat, a fire.
Make of the fire, life everlasting.

I'd read a similar inscription on a painting hanging above the fireplace in my mother's studio. A self-portrait of her and my father, done in this very bell tower. They stood in front of a marvelous stained glass window, its ruby light bathing them and casting a shadow on the stone floor. The words painted on the window's border said something about stones too.

I closed the drawer but took the sheets and carried them carefully downstairs. I didn't return to my great-grandmother's bedroom but continued past the second floor to the ground floor and the kitchen. I needed a glass of water . . . or maybe wine. I was too shaken to go back to sleep.

It was past three AM, so I was surprised to see my great-grandmother at the stove. From the smells in the kitchen, I knew she was making hot chocolate. Nothing like the powdery cocoa my relatives in Boston drank, this was pure melted chocolate with just enough milk added to make it drinkable.

"You heard him too?" I asked my great-grandmother.

"Who?"

I told her about the weeping. She shook her head sadly. "No, I didn't hear your soldier tonight, but I've heard other soldiers other nights."

"Then why are you up?"

"I don't sleep more than two or three hours anymore. It is the curse or the blessing of old age or a fear that I have so little time left I don't want to lose any."

She smiled at me, and her fire eyes sparkled. Her astonishing youthful appearance was an inheritance of sorts. Like my mother, she seemed never to age.

"So many of the soldiers endure battle fatigue and terrible dreams," she said.

"Are there two ways to exit the bell tower?" I asked.

"No. Why?" She looked suddenly agitated.

"The soldier I heard was up there."

She shook her head. "No, *mon ange*, he couldn't have been. The door is always locked."

"Mightn't he have found the key?"

"It's in the safe in my closet so I don't think so. I doubt anyone was up there."

"But I was up there—"

"You were? I thought we agreed you would stay away from the attic. It's not safe."

"It's perfectly safe. Solid stone that's been standing for over three hundred years."

"That's not what I mean and you know it. How did you open the door?" Before I could answer, she put up her hand. "No, don't bother. I know. It simply opened for you. The way it did for your mother."

"Well, however it opened, I heard him." I needed the cries to be real, to be coming from one of her guests.

"Couldn't it be your voices?"

She knew about them. I had told her about them when they first started.

"I only hear them that clearly when I'm with a client," I said, forgetting until the words were out of my mouth about hearing what I'd thought was Jean Luc's voice the day before.

Changing the subject, I laid the silver sheets out on the table. "Look at what I found." I explained about the moon and the pentagram. "Who do you think put these instructions there? They are directions for exactly the kind of work I've been doing, making talismans. Almost as if they'd been waiting for me."

My great-grandmother sighed. "They have been."

"What do you mean?"

"Nothing happens by accident, Opaline, you know that. And I'm too old to fight this house again." She shook her head. "I blame your mother. It's all Sandrine's fault and will just continue now, generation after generation." My great-grandmother's voice always grew resigned when she talked about my mother. As if she was a lost cause. "I don't like that magick and never did. I kept our family curse locked up in that bell tower for over forty years until it seduced your mother. Sandrine should have exorcised the spirit of La Lune. What business did she have embracing a long-dead ancestor and allowing her to transmigrate into her body? Going so far as signing her paintings with La Lune's name?"

"My mother couldn't help who she became."

"Of course she could have. Don't defend her, Opaline. You don't know all the things that went on in this house between your mother and me. And you don't need to. Let me put those inscriptions back where they belong." She reached for them with her bony, hard veined hands. The perfectly manicured oval nails making a screeching sound on the metal.

I put my hand on top of the silver sheets I'd taken from the drawer to keep them where they were.

"Listen to me," she said. "Concentrate on the jewels you are making. Become the artist I see emerging in you." She put her hand on top of mine and stroked my skin. "My darling Opaline, don't throw yourself any deeper into this shadow land of voices and spirits. Has it given you anything but grief so far?"

I shook my head.

"I know people who can help you rid yourself of all connections to that world. Will you let me take you to them?"

I wanted to say yes, that I'd heard enough dead soldiers and seen too many of their wives and mothers weep. But was I really ready to give up what I was doing? Especially now after I'd been stirred by Jean Luc's deep velvet voice?

"No." I gestured to Grand-mère's kitchen, to her house. "Just like what you are doing here, entertaining these soldiers, what I'm doing helps those who the soldiers leave behind."

"At what price? Here you are, up in the middle of the night, nervous and exhausted, hearing things, your imagination spinning out of control."

The diamonds in my great-grandmother's many rings glittered as she poured out the chocolate into two fine china cups, white with a border of violets and green leaves. "Drink this, it will restore you."

Grand-mère liked diamonds she could scratch on the mirror to prove they were real and pearls whose veracity she could check with her teeth. She liked paintings and sculpture and listening to the raucous laughter of the men she entertained. She dwelled in the world of flesh and passion. Of men's needs and women's struggles to survive. Magick, second sight, speaking to the dead . . . she was suspicious of all the dark arts. She'd never attended a séance and didn't believe in anything she couldn't touch or see, except love. And she'd argue she could see even that. When I first came to Paris, I yearned to be more like her than my mother, and in many ways I did still. But I was beginning to question if that was at all possible.

Chapter 6

"You're not eating," Anna said as she watched me refill my wineglass. "What's wrong?"

We'd closed the shop for *l'heure déjeuner* as usual at twelve thirty and, since it was the first sunny day in two weeks, brought our lunch out into the garden. The velvety ruby and pink pastel roses were open, perfuming the afternoon, and birds sang as if there were no war, as if men were not dying and mothers were not mourning, and as if I weren't hearing voices.

In addition to the wine was cold roast chicken leftover from the night before, mustard, cornichons, and a coveted baguette from the bakery. With so many supplies acquisitioned for the front and rations in effect, white flour was a luxury, but Anna had secured a rare loaf.

"Nothing serious," I said in answer to her question, and picked at the chicken.

"From the look in your eyes, I doubt that. What's wrong, little one?"

I'd been hesitant to tell her. Like my great-grandmother, she'd want me to take action. But whereas Grand-mère wanted me to divorce myself from my potential abilities, Anna wanted me to do the opposite: embrace my heritage and explore the gift my mother had given me.

"You know it might make you feel better to talk about whatever is troubling you. I believe you need to delve deeper into what you might be capable of, but I won't push you, Opaline. You have to make up your own mind that you're ready . . ."

Maybe she was right. I was exhausted trying to understand on my own. I told Anna about the voice I'd heard on Friday in the workshop, the weeping that woke me up on Saturday night, and the sheaf of ancient silver leaves I'd found in the bell tower.

"I read in my book of gems that Arabs during the time of Mohammed believed opals came to earth on bolts of lightning. Another legend claims that in ancient times, of all gems, the opal was considered the most magical and the multi-colored stone bestowed the power of prophecy. What does that say about me?" I asked her. "The opal is not just my birthstone. It's part of my name. Is that why these things are happening?"

"You are double cursed and double blessed," Anna said as she gathered up our plates and put them in her wicker basket. "Let's go upstairs to my reading room and we'll see what we can see."

We walked through Anna's sitting room, all done up in a mauve silk, and into her closet. Here, behind a rack of the lavender- and deep-amethyst-colored clothes she favored, all scented with her powdery iris perfume, was the secret door

leading to her reading room, her *monde enchanté*.
Anna's hidden enclosure had been built by the
apartment's previous owner. We often wondered
who might have required such a hideaway. What
nefarious, clandestine business had been trans-
acted here? Had it been an opium dealer's den?
A lover's trysting place? A torture chamber
dating back to Richelieu's reign?

Using the ambient light from the closet, Anna
lit an ornate silver candelabra. One by one, the
five candles burst to life, revealing a wondrous
cave.

The room was half the size of a bedroom and
windowless. Antique mercury-spotted mirrors
covered the ceiling; midnight blue wallpaper
covered the walls. Sitting on the floor, on shelves,
and on tabletops, Anna's vast collection of crystal
balls sparkled and shone and reflected in the
mirrors, like hundreds of dazzling stars in an
infinite universe.

Anna, descended from gypsies, had inherited
the ability to use these orbs to see someone's past
and into his or her future. Combined with the
fortune-telling, she used astrological readings in
order to fully divine the complex paths a human
psyche traveled and where that person was
headed.

"Choose one," Anna said to me, gesturing to
her collection, her bracelets jangling and sending
more rainbow flecks onto the walls. Being

married to a jeweler, Anna could have worn different jewels every day, but she always wore the same pieces: three bracelets on her right wrist with ancient cultural, mystical, religious, and astrological symbols dangling from the gold chains; an Egyptian amethyst scarab ring surrounded by diamonds; and amethyst teardrop earrings hanging from diamond studs.

Scanning the shelves, I spotted a sphere on the third shelf with slightly bluish occlusions that looked like starbursts. I placed it in the depression in the leather-topped table, a hollow made from all the readings Anna had conducted over the years.

Pulling out a chair, I joined her at the table and watched as she leaned in and began to study the orb.

After a few moments, Anna looked up. "When was the last time we did this?"

"About four or five months ago."

"Something has changed." She smiled. "You've met the man you are going to love."

"The only man I've met is your stepson, and that was seven months ago."

She looked into my eyes, back into the ball, then shook her head. "Yes, you are on a path with Grigori, but . . ." She hesitated. "But I'm not sure he's who I see here. I'm trying . . ." She hesitated as she focused. "Your aura has definitely altered. I believe it has to do with the voices, Opaline."

"What do you mean?"

"I'm not certain. What you described, it's the first time a voice has interacted with you, yes?"

"Yes."

She studied the ball again. The quiet was profound in the small room. If there was an air raid, would we hear it so deep inside the apartment? The thought of bombs was never out of my mind for long.

"Have I ever asked you when you began hearing things others couldn't?"

"I'm not sure when it started. I remember being a little girl sick in bed. My mother would bring me her large jewelry case, covered in silver sharkskin, and let me rearrange her treasures. Mostly she had rubies, blood-red earrings, rings, bracelets, and brooches. They shone with purple and deep blue highlights. And if I held them up to the light, I could find a rainbow of colors inside them. She owned a shell-shaped pendant set with opals. I used to put it up to my ear and listen to it."

"Did you hear anything?"

"I heard the sea. My mother came in one afternoon and found me lying in her bed, the pendant up to my ear, and asked me what I was doing. When I told her, she seemed pleased. She explained that opals were layers of water trapped in a stone and maybe that's what I could hear. I asked if she could hear it and offered it to her.

She listened for a minute and then shook her head. 'No,' she said, 'but I'm proud of you that you can.' And then she smiled and gave me the pendant to keep."

"Did you know why things were different in your house?"

"Not really. I thought it was because my mother was beautiful, the same way our house was exquisite, hanging off a cliff, high up in the hills, overlooking the sparkling bay.

"Only when I turned thirteen and my menses started did I begin to understand all that beauty contained. My awareness came with the extreme cramps that made me double over. Suddenly a layer covering my world lifted. All that had been invisible and inaudible before was revealed.

"To help ease the pain, my mother fed me tea and lavender honey that helped me sleep. When I woke, I would feel better until she came to check on me and the cramps would return. When she asked how I was, her words would turn into pearls rolling around on the floor. When she left, her footprints glowed red.

"One night, when my father had returned home, she brought him to my bedroom. Half asleep, I heard my mother tell him she was worried because she herself had never suffered so badly.

"'The difference,' my father said, 'is that Opaline is your daughter.'"

"I opened my eyes then and saw a glance pass between them I didn't understand. 'What does that mean?' I asked.

"She shook her head and said I shouldn't worry about anything. Then she gave me more honey-laced tea. After I drank it, the pain went away. I tried making the same tea on my own when I got cramps and she wasn't there, but it never helped. Only when she made it. The tea was bewitched, I know that now."

"Or dosed with laudanum," Anna suggested, smiling.

"Do you think so?"

She nodded. "Much more likely than a spell. What about the stones? Were they more audible after that?"

"Yes, the day after I first became unwell, I went into my mother's room for something and noticed a topaz bracelet on her vanity rattling like a snake. I went to find her. As soon as I entered her studio, a bowl of smooth round black stones started humming. When I explained, she told me not to worry. But the expression in her eyes informed me she was holding something back, keeping a secret from me.

"I became a spy in my parents' house after that. Listening at doors, peering through windows, stealing into my mother's room and rifling through her things. I didn't know what I was looking for, but I was determined to find something that would explain it all. My trespassing yielded nothing until one night the summer I turned fourteen.

"Well after midnight, I woke up hearing a high-pitched hissing. I pulled on my robe and went out onto the balcony. A full moon splashed diamonds across a calm bay. The noise couldn't have been coming from the sea. I crept around to my parents' balcony and peered into their bedroom through the open window. With the moonlight's help, I saw my father asleep on his side of the bed. My mother's side was empty.

"Creeping downstairs, I went outside. A glow emanated from her studio. I padded across the dewy grass toward the separate structure far enough from the house to afford her privacy. Not easy to spy on, the studio didn't have any ground-floor windows, expressly because she didn't ike people looking in while she painted. But since a painter needed light, there were skylights. And so the only way for me to see what was going on was to climb up one of the oak trees hanging over the structure.

"I'd been climbing trees all my life. Secure in my ability, I shimmied to one of the topmost branches, then inched my way out to the end of the limb and peered down.

"My mother sat cross-legged on the floor, her eyes closed, surrounded by what appeared to be burning embers. In her hands, two of the orange glowing stones. It was those stones making the terrible fizzing, hissing, whistling sound that had awakened me.

"Petrified, I watched as she just sat, unflinching, unblinking, encircled by the fire, holding the fire. One of the orange flames licked at her sleeve. Why wasn't she moving? Was she unconscious? Did I need to wake my father? Did I have time to get him before her clothes burst into flames? The hissing sound intensified, hurting my ears.

"So rapt by the scene, I didn't realize I'd climbed out too far and was stressing the end of the tree limb until it broke off. I fell, crashing through the tree, branches scratching me. I crashed onto the studio roof, my body missing a pane of glass by millimeters.

"I'd landed on my arm, which was screaming with pain. My left shoulder hurt too. Certain I'd broken a bone, I looked around, trying to figure how to get off the roof. Then I saw my mother staring up at me from below, from inside, a horrified expression on her face. Despite my pain, I noticed there were no burning embers anywhere beside her. Only large egg-shaped agate stones in a circle on the floor.

"Hours later, I woke up in my own bed. Nothing hurt. I flexed my hands. Rotated my shoulders. There was not a thing wrong with me. At the end of the bed, I found my robe, which I was sure I'd ripped in the tree, but it was neither stained nor torn.

"Dazed, I made my way down to the glass-enclosed breakfast room. In the distance, the sea sparkled like blue-green sapphires.

"'Good morning, *mon ange*,' my mother said.

"My father looked up from his newspaper and smiled, angling his cheek so I could kiss him.

"Remnants of my brother and two sisters' breakfasts were at their places. The twins were seven, Jadine was five. All of them had too much energy to sit at the table for long and were probably already down at the beach.

"'Did you sleep well?' my father asked. I glanced over at my mother, but she didn't look up from her newspaper.

"'Maman?'

"She picked up her head. 'Yes?'

"'What happened last night? What were you doing?'

"I still remember her little insouciant shrug when she said she'd been painting until two in the morning.

"'I saw you. You weren't painting, you were sitting on the floor with burning stones in your hands. I was in the tree and then I fell, but nothing hurts.'

"'What a terrible dream that sounds like, Opaline,' my father said.

"'You need to start drinking chamomile infusions before bed,' my mother added. 'There's no reason to suffer so in sleep. Dreaming should take you to places of wonder and delight—not terror.'

" 'It wasn't a dream. You *were* holding burning stones in your hands. I saw you.'

"My mother held her hands open to me. Her palms were pale, unscarred, the pink color of the inside of a shell.

" 'Dreams can be like that,' she said. 'More real than the life we live awake. And nightmares can be confusing. Sometimes when you wake up, you can think it's real for hours and hours.'

"By the time I finished my café au lait and croissant, I'd almost been convinced everything I'd seen had been a dream.

" 'After all,' my mother pointed out, 'if you'd fallen, you would have scratches, you would be in pain. And you're not, are you?'

"It wasn't until I went back to my room to dress and fix my hair that I found a tiny twig caught in my brush. Only when I confronted my mother with it, telling her I knew what I witnessed was neither a dream nor a nightmare, did she finally admit the truth to me, that we were descendants of a sixteenth-century courtesan accused of being a witch. And the same bloodline ran in me and I too had abilities. But mine were unlike hers, she said. I could hear stones.

" 'And when you are old enough,' she said, 'I will teach you their magick.' "

Anna took my hand and held it. "But she never

did, because I wrote you and told you we needed jewelers and you ran away to come here," she said. "I interrupted an important step in your development."

"No." I shook my head. "They were sending me to college in America, remember? You didn't interrupt my training. My mother never taught me because I wouldn't let her. Because I wasn't sure I wanted to be different like her. And I convinced myself I wasn't. Not even during that last summer I lived at home, working at the jewelry shop, spending time with Timur, when my abilities took on a whole new level of intensity. I wasn't prepared to deal with what was happening to me. And didn't know what to do, other than eventually backing away from his affections."

Suddenly I worried I'd said too much. But Anna's eyes held mine as she gave me a small, sad smile and then nodded, encouraging me to continue.

"That's when I began to wonder if there was someone who might help me understand what was wrong with me. And when your letter came those months later, I knew you were the one who could."

"And now that you can't escape the magick, you want to learn how to stop it?" she asked.

"No, that's what my great-grandmother wants me to do. I'm not ready to stop it. Can I learn to control it? I need to. Can you help me do that?"

She took my hand. "Opaline, every practitioner has a choice to make: enter into the darkness or stay on the side of light. Some of your ancestors made the choice to be swallowed by the dark. Your mother has always kept the light as her goal, but her methods sometimes take her over the line. You need to realize you're different from all of them. You don't just have your mother in you. You have your father in you too. And he's clear and clean and pure. You were born into the light. You'd have to choose to go dark. I promise."

Chapter 7

Like a screaming child caught in a nightmare, the sirens rent the late afternoon and startled me. I dropped the rag I'd been using to buff the gold bindings on Madame Alouette's talisman. I should have been accustomed to the interruptions. They happened at least every other week. Sometimes for days in a row. But I wasn't used to it. The sirens were a nasty personification of the war itself: ugly, disruptive, brutish, and impossible to ignore. We all despised the danger signals, especially when they came after days of calm. False calm. For we were never able to keep thoughts of impending doom far from our minds. One day there was no heat. Another no milk. Hardly ever white flour. Every morning the papers brought news of shortages. And new troop activity. And the ever-growing casualty numbers. The endless warnings of German spies infiltrating our city accompanied every story about another enemy soldier caught in or around Paris. We were never safe, and we never could forget that for long.

As the alarm continued, I carefully followed Monsieur Orloff's routine. The door to the shop was always kept locked, but I was supposed to double-check it nonetheless. Next, with now-shaking hands, I pulled down the shades in the front window so our wares weren't visible. When all was secure, I took the first flight of steps to the basement. Then down one more flight to the chalky and chilly subterranean level of the shop to the two rooms carved out of rock: Monsieur Orloff's vault and the makeshift shelter. There, under the Palais, in the dark, with only candles and matches to shed any light, I settled in.

Hoping to make the shelter less depressing and more comfortable since no one could ever be sure how long an air raid would last, Anna had decorated the room with two old couches covered in forest green velvet and a dozen pillows in shades of purple and blue. She'd added worn-out, ruined Persian rugs. Their reds and blues didn't match the couches but did hide the rough dirt patches. A low table in front of the couch offered magazines, books, and hard candy in a cracked crystal bowl. Chairs were stacked against the walls in case we brought clients with us and needed more seats. There was even a small kerosene burner for boiling water to make tea and a tray of chipped Limoges china cups. These flawed items, no longer fit for a home, gave the shelter the illusion of grandeur.

I hated being down there alone, too deep in the earth. I worried about the building on top of us. If a bomb hit, would the Palais collapse and trap us here—or, worse, cave in?

To keep myself busy, I started to make tea but abandoned the effort halfway through. I didn't really want the strong Russian tea the Orloffs favored. I didn't want to be down in that room. I wanted the war to be over. I wanted to stop making mourning jewelry and create jewels celebrating birthdays and anniversaries, accessories that would give delight and joy, that would dazzle rather than depress.

I hated the eerie silence in the bunker. Not a calm quiet, but a nerve-racking one. Had the raid ended? Sometimes they were over in less than an hour, but often, if the bombs hit, not for several hours. I'd stashed a stack of books under the tea things and riffled through it. The last time I'd been in the shelter, I'd started reading Gaston Leroux's popular gothic *The Phantom of the Opera*. I picked it up again and found I didn't remember anything from when I'd read it the last time.

I'd only managed a few pages when I sensed someone outside. I waited in vain for the door to open and, when it didn't, wondered why anyone would linger in the hallway. Should I check to see who it was? Only Monsieur Orloff's paranoia about German spies using the underground, a fear fueled by the press, stopped me.

As I sat waiting, listening, trying to ascertain if anyone was there or not, I grew more nervous. No one came in, but I still thought someone was there. And then, I became aware of warmth against my thigh, directly beneath the pocket of my jeweler's apron, which in my haste I'd forgotten to remove. When my skin started to burn, I reached into the pocket and found Madame Alouette's crystal orb. Had I slipped it into my pocket when the siren started?

And why was it so hot? Yes, I'd been polishing it and that heated up the metal, but only while the process continued. The warmth could not have lasted this long.

I turned the piece over in my hand. The crystal was almost all clear, with a single star-shaped inclusion in the center of the lower right segment, like a piece of the night sky captured in glass. Like the orb that I'd chosen in Anna's reading room.

I had hoped I'd never hear it again, but there was that howling, sad wind. And the mixture of voices and screams, water rushing, stones breaking. I tried to block it all out. To shut it down before it began. But I didn't know how and the voice broke through.

I think I'm lost.

I wasn't sure I heard the words as much as sensed them. I didn't know what to do. Where to go.

Can you help me?

I recognized the dark voice. The voice I'd prayed was my imagination.

"Are you . . ." I hesitated. I still couldn't bring myself to name him. If it were true . . . If I'd conjured him, then it meant that like my mother, I was . . . Except I had to know. I took a deep breath and whispered my question.

"Are you Jean Luc Forêt?"

Yes.

Even though I'd assumed he was, I was stunned.

How do you know my name?

"From your mother."

Can you help me? I don't know where I am.

"I'm not sure."

Was his soul trapped between this world and the next? I'd read about the Bardo in Anna's books. A Buddhist concept describing the place a soul waits between the end of life and being reborn. She'd thought some of my soldiers might be speaking from that astral plane, but I didn't know what I believed.

Before, it seemed as if the dying soldiers had somehow left behind messages for their loved ones as they moved on, and all I'd done was sift through the detritus of everyone's thoughts to find the right ones.

With Jean Luc I still had to sift through the clamor and racket of the universe, but his voice pulsed with urgency and desperation as he communicated directly with me.

Am I with you? Where you are?

"I'm not sure. I'm in a shelter underneath a shop."

A shop?

"In Paris."

This was bizarre. Impossible. Beyond reason. Irrational.

I'm not actually there, though. Am I?

"I don't know." I looked around the shelter in its shadows. I waved my hands in front of me and to the side. I felt nothing.

"I don't see you. What can you see? Can you see me?"

I'm staring into darkness, but up ahead I can see light where your voice comes from.

"Light?"

Lovely light. It's the light that you're made of, I think. It's almost the shape of a woman.

"But you can't see anything else? Nothing around you?"

Nothing around me. Just your form made of light. Golden light streaming from your outline.

"Golden light?"

Yes. It's beautiful. As if you were made of gold.

"I'm a jeweler."

He sighed. As if the color of the gold made sense to him now.

How did you find me?

"I think you found me. Through the jewelry I was working on. I make mourning jewelry. Sometimes I get messages from dead soldiers to give to their families. I was making a talisman for your mother."

There are a dozen soldiers dead because of me and . . .

His next words faded out, and I leaned forward into the gloomy shelter as if that might help me hear him more clearly. Jean Luc's voice sounded anguished.

It was all my fault.

"You couldn't have known a bomb was going to hit. You can't blame yourself."

All my men.

"How can I help you?"

Can't. No one can. It's too late.

"You must need something."

Why do you think so?

"Because I can hear you. Why else would I be able to hear you if it wasn't so I could help you?"

I'd never had a conversation with one of the soldiers before, and even as I was having this one, I knew the impossibility of it. My imagination finally had taken over. The war and the endless reports of more soldiers dying and the sadness that multiplied with every passing day and the ever-present threat from the bombs that kept coming . . . it was all too much. I'd snapped like the soldiers who came back, I thought. My fate was mirroring theirs. Surely I was a victim of the same war fatigue as so many others in Paris, in

France, all over the world. Too much death, too much grief, too much fear. And now I'd manufactured my own soldier so I could help someone and feel I was pulling my weight.

No, not your imagination.

I heard his frustration. He wanted to prove to me that he was real. Or as real as a dead man might be.

Suddenly I felt a bit of warm wind in the shelter, almost as if someone had opened the door, but it remained shut. Then a lock of hair blew off my forehead. I quickly reached my hand out, as hopeful as I was terrified I might feel his fingers.

You felt that, didn't you?

My shoulders started to shake. Inside of my chest I felt the wings of the trapped bird fluttering to be let out. My fear. I didn't want to feel it. I closed my eyes. The wind brushed against my cheek.

I'm here. At least right now, I'm here. You believe me, don't you?

The very last thing I wanted to say was that I did. For surely it would be proof of only one thing: my madness.

Do you believe me? Haven't I proved I'm here?

"Are you here all the time?" My voice sounded like a child's.

No.

"And you don't know where you are the rest of the time?"

No. I don't know.

I shivered; his voice was heartbreaking. The wind slowed to a breeze and then the breeze was gone. All was still. I shivered again. The room temperature had dropped, and I knew Jean Luc was gone.

If he really had been there at all.

The door opened, and Grigori stepped inside the shelter.

"I heard you talking . . ." He looked around. "But it appears you are alone."

I gestured to the room and tried to act as if nothing out of the ordinary had occurred. "You can see for yourself. No one's here."

"Yes, but I thought I heard you talking."

"Only to myself." I smiled, trying to make light of his question. I didn't want to start a conversation with Grigori about my talents. Just like his stepmother's gypsy readings, my ability to relay messages from the departed disturbed him. Russia, he'd told me, possessed a long history of mystics who attempted to control people with their powers. Like Rasputin, he said with disdain, as he blamed the self-proclaimed holy man for much of Russia's misfortune.

"You're too young to be talking to yourself."

"It's an occupational hazard of working so many hours alone," I said.

"Spending too much time by yourself is unwise. It can lead to troubling, even frightening thoughts, especially in a place like this dungeon." He shook his head as if trying to dislodge a thought. Or memory. "I saw what the trenches could do to a soldier. Confinement is a harsh punisher."

Noticing my abandoned effort at making tea, he took up where I'd left off. "And why *are* you down here alone? Where are my father and Anna?"

"Both out. I thought you'd be down sooner, though. What kept you?"

"Seeing a customer."

I smelled kerosene.

"I insisted we take shelter, but he was adamant to get back home. I went with him as far as the gate where his car waited. Stupid of me, but he couldn't carry his purchases himself."

"Couldn't he return for them?"

"It was his wife's birthday and he wanted to take them home."

"What did he buy?" I asked, happy to move the conversation away from myself. I didn't want to think about the voice, but the charm was still warm in my hand.

"Two small end tables inlaid with porcelain."

I nodded, picturing the delicate tables in Grigori's store. His eye for antiques was as fine as his father's for jewels.

"I'm sorry to see them go, but he didn't even haggle on the price," he said, as he poured the water. While he waited for the tea to steep, he looked over at me. His dark brown eyes were unreadable but penetrating. Although he seemed to be able to see through me, I couldn't even guess what he was thinking.

After Grigori had been wounded and was on his way back home from the front, Anna warned me her stepson was prone to moodiness and quite enigmatic, and she feared his injury would exacerbate both traits. I found his mysteriousness attractive and his sulkiness poetic, but lately his inscrutability had been frustrating.

"This is such a godforsaken hole, isn't it?" he said. "Let's imagine we're in Ladurée, enjoying afternoon tea with delightful pastries." Unlike his eyes, his smile was uncomplicated, his dimples appealing.

"Yes, let's."

He took a handkerchief from his pocket and put it over his forearm, impersonating a waiter. "Would you like some tea, Mademoiselle?" he asked in an exaggerated accent.

"I'd love some." I laughed with relief that his mood had lightened. And that I could, at least for a while, pretend that mine had too.

He poured the tea with a flourish, placed it on the tray, and then came toward me with a pronounced limp. He'd almost reached me when his knee gave out and he went sprawling and teacups fell and the liquid soaked the rugs.

Too stunned to talk, I immediately went to his aid, but he brushed me off and struggled to get up and then clean up the mess. I knew better than to try and make light of the situation. His infirmity embarrassed him enough. I believed if there were not an air raid going on, he would have bolted.

I let him pick up the cups and the tray and remained silent. I'd let him choose when to talk and what to say. Instead of making more tea, he pulled out a silver flask engraved with ornate initials and poured vodka into one of the cups. He downed it in one gulp, turned to me, and offered me the flask.

I nodded, and he splashed some in one of the cups and handed it to me. After he poured more for himself, he sat beside me as if nothing unusual had happened.

The crystal egg still in my hand grew warmer. I looked down, surprised.

"What are you holding?" he asked.

I didn't want to show it to Grigori. Didn't want to share it. I realized I didn't even want to give it to Madame Alouette. I wanted to keep this one for myself.

Yes, please, hide it.

Even with Grigori there, I'd heard the voice. Or thought I had. Quickly I looked at him. Had he heard it? Or had I imagined it?

"Are you all right? I asked what you're holding."

I'd forgotten to answer his previous question.

"Opaline?" He looked at me strangely. Because he'd heard the voice too? I needed to find out and at the same time distract him from wanting to see the talisman.

"Did you just hear something?" I asked.

"Only the silence following my question. Why won't you tell me what you are holding?"

So he couldn't hear Jean Luc. I was glad for the confirmation. Now for an explanation of why I wouldn't show him what I hid in my hand.

"It's just one of the talismans I've been working on, but I've messed up the soldering and I'm embarrassed." I closed my hand even tighter over the crystal. No, I wouldn't give it to Madame Alouette. It might be wrong of me, but I didn't want to give it up. I'd make another for her and keep this one for myself. But what about Jean Luc's hair? Could I get a lock from someone with the same coloring? She'd never know. But what of my transgression? Would I somehow be punished? I almost laughed. By who? I'd never kept one of the talismans before, but I needed to keep this one.

"Let me see," Grigori insisted, half teasing and half annoyed. "My father says you are one of the finest young jewelers he's worked with and I haven't seen one of your famous talismans."

Grigori didn't spend much time in the jewelry shop—he was too busy with his furniture and art—and I never displayed the charms. They seemed sacrosanct. A private icon meant only for the one in mourning.

"All the more reason then not to show you this one." I slipped it into my pocket.

"I promise not to criticize you. Besides, I doubt it is anything but perfect." He put his hand on my forearm.

He was so close I was afraid he'd feel the heat emanating off the charm and I inched back. Grigori looked askance. Our physical relationship should have allowed for such a simple touch.

"Don't pressure me," I said. "I'll show it to you when I'm finished with it and happy with the workmanship. I don't want the first one you see to be damaged."

Yes, damaged is fitting. I don't deserve to be called any less.

Jean Luc's sad voice brought tears to my eyes. What had broken him? Why was he still suffering when death was supposed to be a relief for those hurt and destroyed by war?

Grigori was still close enough to me that I could smell his peppery patchouli cologne. Other days, other nights, I'd found its spicy darkness seductive. I tried to remember that and focus on him and his scent and not on the voice in my head. Here was an actual man, not a— What was the other? Surely just a manifestation of my imagination. I was reading too many of my great-grandmother's books and believing the fiction.

My ability was curious to be sure, but I was no different than a telephone or telegraph operator receiving messages over wires. Mine were just invisible. Either I was mind reading the mourners' wishes, or reaching out into the ether and picking up the last lingering thoughts of dying soldiers. The one thing I wasn't doing was actually speaking with the dead.

"Thank you for the drink," I said, and took another sip.

"So you are refusing to show me your jewel?"

"Yes."

"I'm quite bereft," he teased, his dark mood lifting, thanks to the vodka.

"Oh yes, I can see that." I forced a smile. "Tell me about your client's purchase. How much did you discount the tables?"

"Not a franc," Grigori said, and began to regale me with the nuances of his transaction.

Anna once told me Grigori left his best self on the battlefield and the man who'd come back was an exaggeration of all of his worst traits. She tried to help him, offering all manner of talismans and brews, some to make his physical pain lessen, others to help heal his broken soul. Jealous and angry because one of *her* sons with his father became a hero and died on the battlefield and the other was on his way to becoming a hero, he dismissed her and her efforts.

"But how did you convince him to buy both tables?" I asked.

"I showed him how the lovers' tale that begins on the first continues on the second. They were clearly created to be a pair, one on either side of a settee, together for almost two hundred years. To separate an artist's work like that would be a travesty . . ."

This was the time I enjoyed him the most, when he forgot about his mangled leg, when he could smile and talk about beauty and art.

"And that convinced him?"

"Not quite. It wasn't until I threw in the pièce de résistance, telling him about a centuries-old legend that it was bad luck to break them up. Russians are so susceptible to superstition."

"Is that true?"

"Would I lie?" he asked slyly.

"You might. Was it true?"

"I made a lovely profit on them and feel like celebrating something going right in this forsaken mess of a world. Would you join me if we can find a café that isn't closed because of the raid? Champagne might help us forget we've spent the afternoon in a bomb shelter. We can pretend . . ." He left the thought unfinished as he reached out and touched my cheek with one finger, moving a curl behind my ear. I tried not to notice that the talisman remained warm against my skin.

"What? What would you like to pretend?" I asked.

"That the lamps all over Paris are blazing and we're carefree lovers living in the city of lights."

His voice sounded as melancholy as I felt. Such a small wish, yet such an impossible one.

Sometimes at my great-grandmother's, her "friends," as she referred to the men who frequented her salon, would flirt with me, the way Grigori flirted and I would try to enjoy it. Wasn't a girl supposed to? But I never did. I sensed the sadness beneath the outward show of gaiety. I had real affection for Grigori. Yes, his moods and aborted efforts at seduction took their toll. But he was my penance for Timur. I'd hurt one soldier; I couldn't hurt another. And so yes, I would go out with him and drink champagne and bring him back to my room once more and give him what encouragement I could. I owed that to him, just like I felt I owed it to the men at Grand-mère's to endure their flirting. They'd fought for us. Been damaged for us. Lost brothers and friends for us. Would be scarred for life for us. The least I could do was smile and drink or laugh with them. Let Grigori kiss me and smooth my hair and whisper promises he couldn't keep. That was the hardest part, to witness his failure over and over. At least with Grand-mère's friends, it couldn't go further because, as her granddaughter, I was ultimately off-limits. Yes, they thought I was her granddaughter. Since she looked to be only about sixty—and young for that age—we kept it a secret that she was my great-grandmother.

No one would accept she was closer to ninety. Just as Grigori couldn't accept he'd ever be healed, which is why he rejected Anna's potions and brews. In our war-torn world, no one believed in enchantments. They thought witches and spells and conjurers were the stuff of fairy tales. The only mystery anyone believed in was ghosts. And only because memories of the war's endless dead haunted the living.

Chapter 8

Grigori and I never drank any champagne because we'd only gone a few blocks in the dark, moonless city when the heavens opened and a heavy rain poured down on us. We ran back to the Palais.

Our puddle splashing wasn't gleeful. It depressed me and reminded me of the futility of trying to get out from under the clouds of war, even for a few drinks at a café.

At my door, Grigori leaned forward and kissed me. I'd enjoyed his attentions before, but that evening, his lips pressed too hard on mine, his beard scratched my face, and the scent of his cologne, mixed with a lingering cigar, made me queasy. When he didn't suggest coming to my room for a drink, I didn't press him. Not until I'd dried off and pulled my nightgown on, and then just before I got into bed and slipped Madame Alouette's crystal over my head, did I realize why.

I preferred even the frightening possibility of hearing Jean Luc to engaging with Grigori. Rather than Grigori's touch, I chose to feel the crystal against my skin. Instead of listening to a man who was my friend and who I might be able to help, I wanted to listen to the dead soldier far beyond help.

Lying in bed, my head cushioned by a thick feather pillow, I tried to draw a picture of what the amulet's soldier looked like, but could cull no clues from his voice. I closed my eyes and waited to see if an image would reveal itself, but none did. I lay there alone, in the quiet of my body under the covers, and experienced a curious anxiety. Would he come if I called him? Could I entice him? And most of all, why did I want to?

I tried, but after what seemed like a long time, gave up and was falling asleep when I finally felt a warm breeze. Impossibly, because there were no windows in my basement apartment.

"Jean Luc?"

Yes. I'm here.

"I'm glad."

I was lonely.

"I was too. Till you got here." Despite myself, I smiled.

But now neither of us is. How is this possible? We don't even know each other. I would have remembered if we'd met.

"No, we don't know each other. But I used to read your columns about art. I was a young girl playing with stones and metal . . . I wanted to change the way women wore jewelry and have my pieces viewed as art. The way you spoke about artistic endeavor . . ." I shrugged. "It's hard to explain what your writing meant to me.

127

You said the things I thought. I feel as if I've known you for a long time."

Then me being with you is all right?

"Yes," I whispered into the darkness.

I felt the warmth between my breasts, where the talisman lay. Had I been more awake I might have been nervous, but instead, I allowed the sensation to lull and comfort me, relaxing in its embrace. After the warmth encircled me, it seemed to enter me, heating not just my skin but my blood. Heating not just my blood but my bones. These were the sensations I'd always hoped Grigori might rouse in me, but he hadn't.

Was this what lovers were supposed to experience?

Yes.

Only a whisper, I heard his voice all throughout my body. As if the word were being said inside of me, in my blood, against my skin.

Yes. This is what we would have been together.

Almost as if he were the puppeteer and I the marionette, Jean Luc's voice moved my hand to rest in between my legs and my thighs clamped, trapping it there. I rocked against the pressure.

Yes.

The pressure became a rhythm. The rhythm a dance. The dance a slow build of sensations, growing, growing in intensity until my whole body reduced to a few inches of flesh, until my whole body began to vibrate and shudder and pulsate with pleasure. Jean Luc moved my hand faster and faster until sparks leapt into a fire burning inside of me. Flames, bright orange flames, the colors of fire opals, burst, exploded, shaking me at my core.

My breathing slowing, drifting off to sleep on waves of pleasure, I heard him say *yes,* again and again, and I fell asleep with his warm hand on mine. Sure of it.

I woke up in the morning convinced I'd dreamed it all. And wouldn't have doubted myself except the talisman I'd put on before I went to sleep was no longer around my neck, lying between my breasts when I rose.

The unhooked chain, shaped into a crescent, with the talisman nested inside the curve like a single star hanging on the moon, sat on my bedside table.

I had no memory of having removed it, much less taking the time to configure it into a design. Anxiously, I looked over at the key in the lock in the door. Had Grigori come into my room? Somehow been the one to induce my nighttime abandon? I raced to the door and tried it.

No, still locked. What's more, the bolt Monsieur Orloff had installed so I could rest easy was thrown. It could not have been opened from the outside even with a key.

Since no one had come into my room, there

existed only two possible explanations: either I'd removed the talisman and configured it in that curious design, or Jean Luc had.

But he wasn't real. The soldier was a manifestation of my mind. A mind overwhelmed by war and sadness and grief and guilt. Even if I were to entertain the idea that his spectral form existed and was capable of such a thing, how would he know the symbol of La Lune? For the necklace was arranged in the exact crescent motif she'd adopted and all of her descendants throughout time were born with, imprinted on our skin. I bore two such marks: the one I'd been born with that hid in a dimple at the small of my back, a faint blemish, a simple birthmark unless you understood its significance, and another on the fleshy part of my thumb, the result of an accident with a sharp engraving tool.

When I arrived at the shop that morning, Monsieur Orloff was waiting impatiently. He needed to visit the stonecutter, but wanted to speak to me before he left. After issuing some instructions, he donned his hat and departed. Locking the door after him, I went into the workshop.

The studio at La Fantaisie Russe was Monsieur's realm, and while I felt privileged to put on my jeweler's glasses, sit at my station, and work alongside him, I was always a little bit relieved when there alone.

Monsieur Orloff was indeed a magician when it came to jeweled creations. His reputation was impeccable, as might be expected for someone taught by the master Fabergé. Monsieur created the same kind of exquisite enamel pieces his mentor's studio was known for; from gem-encrusted picture frames to desk sets and decorative boxes of all sizes. He also excelled at objets d'art made from onyx and jade, amethyst and quartz. My favorites were the bouquets. Until you touched them, you believed you were looking at a crystal vase filled with water and cut flowers. You even began to smell the sweet scent flowers give off. But it was all illusion created with gemstones and enamel.

In Paris, Monsieur Orloff took his art to new heights using trompe l'oeil techniques to manufacture creatures of the seas and skies. A most delicate bumblebee made of gold, yellow and white diamonds, and slices of onyx sat on one of the creamy pearls in a necklace. A small fish, pavéd with tsavorite, rubies, and emeralds, swam between the aquamarines in a diadem.

For all the delightful whimsy in his work, Monsieur Orloff was a suspicious man who smiled only at his wife and regarded everyone who entered the store as a potential bother. It was no wonder Anna handled sales while her husband remained behind the scenes.

At his workstation that morning, he'd left an

unfinished miniature easel only eight inches high. The gold frame was complete, and he was in the process of creating the design he'd soon pack with enamel.

By eleven, I'd completed my daily requirement of four trench watches and pulled out Jean Luc's talisman, glad Monsieur was still out so I could make the finishing touches while I was alone.

After a final polishing, I filled in some of the spaces between the gold wrapping with ancient jet. Once driftwood, jet fossilizes and becomes coal in a process that, according to scientists, takes over a million years. Unlike diamonds, which form in the same manner, jet is a soft stone. My book of gems says jet can be used to protect against evil and psychic attacks as well as enhance spiritual quests. Until that morning, I had incorporated it into my designs solely because of its ability to help those grieving by bringing deep-rooted sadness to the surface where it can be calmed and healed with comfort. But suddenly, I was more interested in its properties that enhanced spiritual quests. Would adding the jet help me reach Jean Luc?

No, I chided myself. He wasn't real. There was no spirit to reach. No magick to help me connect to this ghost. I was overindulging in some romantic notion brought on by all the books I was reading. Between Wharton's stories, *The Phantom of the Opera*, *The Picture of Dorian*

Gray, and Poe's tales, I was becoming too morbid and susceptible.

Turning my attention back to the jet, I inserted another piece in a triangular space. Although it's dull when harvested, polishing jet turns it into a dark mirror. I always thought that also made it ideal for mourning jewelry. While the black stone honors the dead, looking into its reflective surface, you see yourself, the one left behind. Both a memorial and a reminder that we must go on living.

One of jet's oddest properties, which I thought could explain why my talismans became conduits, was that, when rubbed on fabric, the stone becomes electrically charged. That spark, I believed, brought the piece to life.

Done with the talisman I would be keeping, I slipped it around my neck. Then I chose another rock crystal orb and went to work creating a new amulet, the one I would give to Madame Alouette.

Since I'd promised it for that evening, I didn't stop to lunch with Anna but instead went out on a hunt.

The Palais was like a small village where we all knew one another. During lunchtime there were always children playing in the gardens. Without any trouble, I spotted one whose hair was the same shade of dark brown as Jean Luc's. For a few sous and a piece of chocolate,

Ricard was happy to let me cut a small lock.

Back in the studio, ashamed of myself for the deception I was planning and exhilarated at the same time, I set to crafting a piece similar to the one hiding under my dress.

I inserted the crystal segments into the vise, etched Jean Luc's name and birth and death dates and the symbols into the crystal, positioned the lock of hair, and sprinkled peridot dust. Then, to save time, I used a gold binding made of chain so it wouldn't need polishing. Guilt tempered my elation that I was going to be able to keep the talisman that connected me to Jean Luc while not disappointing his mother.

I worked without stopping all afternoon. Finally, after soldering a gold ring to the top of the crystal, I hung the egg on a length of silk cord and looked at the clock. I'd finished a half hour before Madame Alouette was expected. Taking up another trench watch, I awaited her arrival. The phone ringing interrupted my work.

"It's Madame Alouette," she said. "I'm going to be late. I ran into some complications with some last touches on a mask. And now I'm afraid I won't make it there and back in time for the soldier who is coming to pick it up. Can I come at six thirty?"

"Oh, I'm sorry, but we close at six and Monsieur Orloff won't allow me to keep the store open past that."

"Not even for a half hour?"

She sounded so tired and unhappy, I asked her if she'd like me to bring her the talisman after I closed up.

I didn't mind going out of my way. I'd be glad to get the appointment over with.

I left the Palais and headed toward the river. Under a peach-colored sky turning twilight blue, I passed over the bridge and continued through Saint-Germain and cut across the Luxembourg Gardens. Paris wore a veil that summer. Like any woman in mourning, she never took it off in public, but her beauty was still visible behind the fine black mesh. Especially by her river and in her parks. For a moment here or there you didn't see her misery but her irrepressible joie de vivre.

That evening, the plane and chestnut trees were in heavy leaf and the flowers in full bloom. Children too young to be preoccupied by war played in the grass with one another, running around pedestrians, chasing balls, crying out with laughter.

The stroll gave me time to think about what message I would give Madame Alouette from her son, for surely the talisman wouldn't work and I'd need to fake the results.

Passing the fountain, I stopped to watch a group of four little boys sailing toy boats, focusing on their progress, serious about the race. Had Madame Alouette brought Jean Luc here? Did he remember days he'd spent innocently playing? In that netherworld where he hovered, how far could his mind travel? Would he know I'd tricked his mother? Would he be upset? And the most important question of all: What was I doing? Why was I holding on to his talisman?

Once I exited the park, it was only a few blocks more to 70 bis rue Notre-Dame-des-Champs, the Tin Nose shop, as it was known. Outside the building, a small sign identified Anna Coleman Ladd's studio by its formal name, the Red Cross Studio for Portrait Masks—a division of the French Bureau for Reeducation of the Mutilated.

I was about to ring the bell when the concierge appeared, helping a soldier out to the street. Moving haltingly, the young uniformed officer made his way across the cobblestones. When he saw me, he started and pulled back and then, as if remembering something, smiled and continued forward.

"*Bonsoir*," I said.

"*Bonsoir, bonsoir*," he sang back enthusiastically, and doffed his cap to me with a grand gesture.

I smiled, not sure why his greeting was so ebullient. I must have looked surprised because he answered my unasked question.

"Mademoiselle, you are the first stranger in four months to look at me without grimacing and looking away."

"Ah," I said, now realizing. "So you've come from the studio?"

"Yes." He tapped his cheek, and I heard the hollow sound of his knuckles on metal.

"I didn't notice you were wearing a mask," I said sincerely.

"I know. I could tell. Isn't it wonderful!"

Tears welled up in my eyes.

"Don't," he said. "I'm one of the lucky ones."

I nodded, not trusting myself to speak. No one was lucky. They called it the Great War, but that implied worthiness and grandeur, not violence and helplessness and the utter waste and devastation our country, our city, our people endured.

Like so many buildings in Paris, the gates at number 70 opened into a courtyard. Since the war, many of them had returned to seed with no one to take care of them. Most of the men were off at the front, and women were forced to take on more of the jobs they left unfilled. Ministering to trees, bushes, and flowers was now a luxury few could afford.

But number 70 was well tended. Ivy and wisteria twisted up the sides of the building and grew around the bases of the many classical Greek and Roman sculptures. Brightly colored geraniums filled window boxes on almost every sill, and dozens of old olive trees grew in mossy terra-cotta pots.

I was nervous about what I was about to do,

and so for a moment, before making my way upstairs, I paused in the courtyard, breathing in the calming, cool green scent.

After climbing five stories, I opened the door into a large studio full of activity, tall windows, and a bank of skylights, but it was the wall of faces, ghostly and immovable, that stopped me from taking another step. Each haunted stare represented a man who'd lost part of himself in battle.

The numbers of men who'd died and were wounded were abstractions. We read them in the paper, little black marks separated by commas, or we learned a name, one at a time, from a client or neighbor. Sometimes we saw a grainy photograph. But here were dozens of specific, sightless faces staring out at me, reminding me of the disfigurement and loss, the waste and the travesty of the war.

"Mademoiselle? Can I help you?"

I turned to find a young woman wearing a white smock.

"I'm here to see Madame Alouette."

She offered me a seat on the bench under the masks and went to fetch her. While I waited, I took in the studio, which was surprisingly cheery, with vases of flowers and brightly colored posters of American and French flags.

Two soldiers hunched over a table played dominoes, glasses of wine and a plate of chocolates nearby. Another soldier, his back to me, sat in an armchair by a window, sipping something hot and reading one of the many newspapers spread out on a coffee table.

Much like at the workshop at La Fantaisie Russe, there were stations for the sculptors. I counted six. At a seventh, an artist, paintbrush and palette in hand, sat in front of a soldier, touching up the mask on his face.

"It's the best way to match the skin tone," Madame Alouette said.

I'd been so engrossed I hadn't heard her approach. I turned to greet her. "This is amazing."

She looked around, as if seeing it through fresh eyes. "Even so, it's not enough. These soldiers suffer so much before they get here. From the terrible battles where they were wounded, to overcrowded field hospitals, then traveling in ambulances on stretchers or with crutches, all to come home to doctors who operate on them, often several times, often to no avail. Finally, when there's nothing the doctors can do to restore their shot-off jaws or empty eye sockets, they come here. We're their last resort. With copper and foil and paint we create an illusion so each of them has a way to face the future. They won't ever be handsome. Most of them won't even be ordinary looking again. But at least they can go out into the world and back to their families and not suffer stares and grimaces."

She was quiet for a moment. "I hope you don't find it too disturbing—some people do. I appreciate you coming to meet me here."

Remembering what I was there to do, I became nervous again. I'd never deceived a client and was beginning to regret my decision.

"Would you like some tea or coffee?" she asked. "Or a glass of wine? We try to make it as pleasant as possible for them."

"If it's not too much trouble, I'd like a cup of coffee."

"Good, so would I. As you can see, we work long hours, and I have a long night ahead of me. So many boys need masks, but each takes weeks to make. There's never enough time. Eloise," she called to another young girl wearing a white smock. "Can you bring two coffees, please?" She turned back to me. "Let me show you around."

The studio's slanted ceiling was fitted with skylights separated by wooden beams functioning as a design element to section off the big space into stations. As we went from one to the next, the artists stopped what they were doing to explain their process.

"After we meet with the soldiers, we bring them here." Madame Alouette indicated a small room off the main space with a comfortable chair, several cameras on tripods, and a table with various pencils, paper, and calibration instruments. "In addition to photographing the subjects, we need measurements of their features."

She opened one of the folders on the table. Inside were four photographs of the same man. The front view showed a missing chunk of his right cheek, a scarred crater where there should have been bone. Then a right profile shot, a left profile shot, and a photo of the back of his head.

Pointing to the red notations I'd noticed on the photos, Madame Alouette said: "In addition to making a plaster mask of the soldier's face, we also measure everything by hand—the length of his nose, if it's all there, the distance from ear to ear, the space between the eyes."

"What a difficult job."

"Yes. Our measurer is Madame Sisley. She is very gentle and knows how to put the soldiers at ease."

Next Madame showed me the stations where the models were made. There were twelve in progress. Looking at the heads, each deformed in a terrible way, I shrunk back. The right side of one boy's face was blown off, and only part of his right ear remained intact. Another was missing his chin. Each immobile white head was mangled in a unique way.

I thought of Timur and couldn't help wondering if the bomb that killed him had damaged his face too. And what of Madame Alouette's son? Jean Luc had become such a vivid presence in my mind, and yet I had never even seen a picture of him. If he looked anything like his voice sounded, he must have been handsome. When the end came for him, had he been disfigured, his beauty destroyed?

Following Madame Alouette, we arrived at the station where the masks were painted. Next, she showed me the wall of spectacles, where dozens and dozens of pairs of glasses stared out at me.

"Why are there so many?" I asked. "Does something happen to the soldiers' eyesight?"

"No, we attach the masks to glasses as an anchor. Sometimes we need to paint an eye onto one of the lenses, other times we just use unmagnified glass. If the soldier has lost his ear, it's more complicated. There is an elastic that attaches—"

The young woman arrived carrying the tray of coffee. Madame Alouette took it from her and thanked her.

"We can visit in the consultation room, Mademoiselle Duplessi, it's this way."

We sat down in a small, comfortable room set up much like a sitting room in someone's home. There were two couches, a card table with four chairs, a vase of roses on the fireplace mantel, landscape paintings on the walls, and decorative carpets on the floor. Suddenly, it occurred to me there were no mirrors anywhere.

Everything about the studio had been designed

with the soldiers in mind. The first part of their journey back to life started here, and clearly great pains had been taken to lessen their anxiety about being stared at and prodded and measured.

"It's quite a lot to take in the first time you see it, isn't it?" Madame Alouette asked, as she poured the coffee.

"Yes. It is . . ." I searched for the word. "It is heartbreaking."

"Do you take milk?" she asked.

I asked for a little, and she poured it in.

"Sugar?"

We all knew how hard it was during the war to get sugar, and I'd learned to drink my coffee unsweetened. "No, thank you."

"It is heartbreaking," she said as she handed me the cup, "but at the same time positive and hopeful. You need to see it that way too or you won't be able to bear it." She sounded desperate for me to understand. And I did.

"You give them back dignity."

"Yes." She nodded vigorously. "The masks aren't the same as faces. People still sometimes stare, but with curiosity, not disgust, not horror. The boys can meet women, court them, or go home to their wives and make love to them. They can hold their children, they can get jobs."

But in the dark, I thought, in the dark they are still wounded.

"Did you bring the charm?" she asked.

I pulled the leather pouch out of my pocket-book and slid it across the table. She reached for it, opened it, and took out the talisman. Letting the silk cord hang from her fingers, she studied the jewel. The crystal egg swung in the soft light, glowing a little with energy.

"How does this work?" she asked.

"You put it on . . ."

She slipped it over her head.

"And hold it between your hands." I showed her how to clasp the talisman between her hands as if she were in prayer—not because of religious significance, I explained, but because, enclosed, the talisman contained its energy. "Now, I put my hands over yours," which I did. "And in a moment or two . . ." I stopped talking, closed my eyes, and waited.

Normally the scent of apples would overpower me right away. Nausea would follow seconds later along with a terrible pounding in my head. And then, in the midst of the discomfort, the messaging would begin. The dead soldier's voice would flood into my awareness.

I didn't expect any of those effects. The hair in the locket wasn't Jean Luc's, but rather from the little boy who lived in the Palais upstairs from our shop.

Except, within seconds of putting my hands over Madame Alou-ette's, the distress began. The scent, the headache, the nausea all descended on me, and the voice was the same one I'd heard at the workshop, in the shelter, and in my bedroom.

But of course, I thought. I'd performed so many sessions, my body anticipated the reactions and delivered them. And I'd manufactured the voice before—why not again?

Often the messages I pulled from the ether contained information too personal for me to understand, but sometimes they were generic enough to be clear even to me. I'd planned on giving Madame Alouette one of the more comprehensible communiqués I'd heard over the years. I knew them all, those sorrowful farewells were lodged in my heart.

But I didn't require some other soldier's thoughts; I heard Jean Luc's.

No pain. Tell her there is no more pain.

"He's not in pain anymore," I whispered.

"Jean Luc? Is he here?"

I nodded.

She is worried about the pain because of the accident I had when I was little.

"He knows how much you always worried about him being in pain, since the accident when he was a little boy, and he wants you to know he's not in pain anymore and you can stop worrying."

I could see it in Madame Alouette's eyes, in the set of her mouth. She would never stop mourning her son, she would never miss him less, but with just that one sentence, she gave up her fear. Silent tears fell in silvery tracks down her smooth cheeks as she smiled. Even though I'd witnessed similar transformations before, they always stunned me. How little and at the same time how much it takes to give succor.

"He grew so fast, he was always too thin and so always cold. He gravitated to warmth, playing too close to the fireplace, despite my warnings. One day an ember sparked and flew out. Jean Luc didn't understand—he was only about four— he just felt its warmth and thought it was a toy—and so picked it up and put it on his palm. He only suffered minor damage to his fingertips, but his palm was severely burned and he was in pain, terrible pain, for days . . ." She paused. "Do you have children?" she asked.

"I don't, no," I answered, astonished at the coincidence. I already associated Jean Luc with warmth and fire, and fire and warmth were the nucleus of the story his mother had recounted.

"Watching my child in pain and not being able to take it away was excruciating. Worrying he died in pain has been agonizing. I can bear my own suffering. But his? Knowing I could not make it better, could not take it away? Torture."

I let go of her hands, and she let go of the talisman. It fell against her white smock.

"Thank you," she said. "I didn't believe you

would really be able to channel him . . . but I was wrong. I'm sorry."

I shook my head. "Don't apologize. I'm just glad if it helps, even a little."

"It will."

Eager to leave, I stood. My heart raced. I was perspiring. I didn't understand what had happened and didn't wish to think about it while there.

Madame Alouette escorted me to the door. I extended my hand to shake hers, but she grabbed me by the shoulders and held me to her. At first I recoiled, in fear she'd feel the talisman hanging around my neck, hidden under my dress. Then I realized that, even if she did, she wouldn't question it. There was nothing suspicious about me wearing one of my own pieces. As she held me, I experienced a sudden longing to talk to her about Jean Luc. About the sound of his voice. How special he seemed. About how he was the only soldier who had ever spoken directly to me, not just through me. I wanted to know what he looked like and how he dressed and what pleased him and what didn't.

But I couldn't, of course. She had what she wanted. Even though I hadn't used Jean Luc's hair in the talisman I made for his mother, he'd sent her the message she needed to hear. And as I crossed the courtyard, peopled with cold marble statues, I wondered how any of it was possible. How indeed?

Chapter 9

The next day, I put down my tools as soon as the shop's ornate silver clock struck noon and the lyrical bells rang out the hour. "I'm going out," I announced to Monsieur Orloff, who looked up from his enamel work.

"I have an errand on rue Drouot. Is there anything you need me to pick up on the way back?"

"The newspaper office?" he asked.

I nodded.

"Why are you going there, Opaline?"

It sounded like a simple question, but he would never take a simple answer. Monsieur examined, thought, angled, delved. He reminded me of my friend Lucille's father. When I was younger, I was jealous at how he inquired about her every move, thinking he must love her more than my father or mother loved me for they gave me so much freedom and questioned me so little.

"I want to see some back copies of *Le Figaro*."

Of course the answer didn't satisfy him.

"Which back copies?"

I took my hat off the rack and put it on, adjusting it in the mirror.

"One of our clients told me her son was a columnist who used to write for the paper, and to please her I thought I should read some of his work."

He liked my answer—anything to ensure a sale.

"You might keep your ears open in case anyone is talking about the royals."

In the Orloff home, as in every Russian émigré's home, endless hours were spent pondering the fate of Tsarina Alexandra and her five children. No news at all had emerged from Russia since the announcement of the tsar's assassination, and everyone was tense and anxious.

"I will."

"And don't talk to anyone about anything we discuss here. Remember, there are spies everywhere."

At least several times a week, Monsieur Orloff had warned me and Grigori and Anna there could be Bolsheviks lurking around any corner.

"Why would they be watching you, Monsieur? You're a jeweler who has been in Paris for over ten years. What would Bolsheviks want with you?" I'd asked the same questions before, but was never given a satisfying answer.

That day was no different.

"Anyone close to the royal family is suspect, Opaline. All sympathizers are threats, I've told you that. Don't forget, don't say anything about the shop, about our inventory, about the vaults. Not a word about our business to anyone."

The same warning. As annoying as it was, it

also made me sympathize with the stern man who was teaching me to become an artist. How frightening to watch your country thrown into a revolt and your way of life despised by your fellow country-men. Even though the Orloffs had already been in Paris during the revolution, the émigrés who'd arrived in the last year, the community they all formed, were a constant reminder of what was now and what was no more.

I opened my umbrella as soon as I stepped out of the shop. The morning's light drizzle was becoming a heavy rain. The dreary weather exacerbated the malaise hanging over the city. Every day was bad, but that day was worse. Morning news reported the threat of more bombs, and the air hummed with anxiety. Parisians tried to remember before the war, and the wonders of that past grew in our minds. We yearned to take off the mantle of mourning. We wanted our beautiful women to dress up again, to wear too much perfume, throw parties that were too lavish, that went on too late. We wanted the food restrictions lifted and to gorge on gastronomical delights. Our city no longer shone, never glittered. It was drowning. In so much rain. In so much sadness.

I reached the newspaper's office in fifteen minutes. A receptionist asked how she could help me and, after I explained, directed me to a second-floor office. The nameplate on the door identified the occupant as Marie Lund.

I stepped inside, introduced myself, and asked if I could buy some *Le Figaro* back copies.

"Can you tell me the dates?"

"I'm not sure actually."

She was young, probably about my age. Another woman in a job that had belonged to a man four years prior. There were so few men of a certain age left in Paris, and many were either too infirm to begin with or were soldiers who'd come home. Men like Madame Alouette's clients or Grigori, somehow damaged.

"We've published a paper every day for over ninety-two years." She smiled. "You'll need some dates."

"I wanted to read Jean Luc Forêt's columns."

Mademoiselle Lund gave me a knowing smile, which I didn't understand. And then, her face fell as she remembered what she'd forgotten for a moment. "It's so sad, isn't it?" she said, assuming I knew his fate. And since I did, I nodded.

"Women have been writing us condolences since we announced his death. Hundreds of letters arrived. It's as if they knew him."

"Does every columnist for the paper engender such admiration?"

"Admiration? It's not admiration. Half the women in Paris were in love with him."

When I didn't say anything, she cocked her head and gave me an appraising once-over.

"Have you ever read any of the columns?"

"Not the *Ma chère* columns, no. I met his mother recently and she told me about him . . . She made me curious."

"Ah, I see. Well, he's been writing this column since he went off to war. It's called *Ma chère* because each column is written like a letter home to his lover, you see. He never uses her name, and so we can all imagine we're her. And we all want to be her because we all want him to be in love with us. Oh dear, I can't get used to the idea he's gone. We published his last column just three weeks ago, with a note from the editor at the end."

"Did you know him?"

"I met him twice," Mademoiselle Lund said. "When he came home on leave, he would come to the offices."

"What did he—" I stopped myself. I didn't want to hear this woman's description of him. I wanted to keep my own impression of him intact without anyone sullying it. Jean Luc was a glimmer in the darkness, a deep voice with a musical undertone like a cello playing a solo on an otherwise empty stage.

"Can I buy some of the papers with his columns?"

"We keep copies of the paper for our records, of course, but we only sell copies going back a month."

"So then I can buy the last four weeks?"

"Yes, but just the first week has a column in it."
She sold it to me.

I stood in the street outside the building and opened the paper, but as soon as the first fat raindrops fell on the newsprint, I tucked it under my arm and looked around for a café.

Minutes later, I was ensconced in a corner table, and while the rain beat on the windows and I waited for my coffee, I opened the paper again, searching for the column.

The waiter brought my café crème. While it cooled, I started to read.

Ma chère,
Missing you has become a scar I keep opening. Just as it begins to close, I think of some moment we were together, and afresh it tears like a new wound. Is it this way for you? Do you miss me as much as I you?

The trench is wet tonight. It has been raining for days, and I think of you and your pretty blue-and-green umbrella with the silver handle and the blue agate gems set in the top of the curve. I picture you walking down the Champs-Élysées and stopping to glance in a shop window. If I were by your side, I'd take you inside and buy you whatever you liked, just to see the delight in your eyes.

Pining for you, I think of other lovers like us, separated unfairly and through some injustice of society. You and I never went to the tomb of Héloïse and Abelard, did we?

I want you to go there today or tomorrow, and if you can find some anemones, leave them there for me. Do you know the story? Bring this with you and read it while you are standing with them. Put the flowers at their feet, where the dog lies, a symbol of faithfulness . . .

My eyes took in one word and then the next and then I wasn't reading anymore. I was hearing Jean Luc speaking to me. Whispering the words printed on paper.

I closed my eyes.

His voice continued.

"And then turn to your left and walk. There is another tomb . . ."

I looked down—yes, those were the next words.

I shut my eyes once more. The voice continued.

". . . there. I don't want to tell you too much, but it is a message for you. From me because . . ."

I checked these words against the words on the paper. The same. No, it was not possible.

My heart raced. My hand trembled.

I lifted the coffee, some of it splashing in the

saucer. My hand none too steady, I sipped the hot liquid, sorry it wasn't hot enough to burn my mouth because I wanted a distraction from thinking about what had just occurred.

There must be an explanation, I thought. I wasn't a scientist, not well educated in how the mind works, how the eyes work, but surely I'd read ahead without realizing it.

I closed the newspaper, folded it, and put it in my pocketbook. I didn't want to read any more of the column there at the café. Jean Luc planned for it to be read at Père-Lachaise Cemetery. I'd never been. I looked at my watch. There was no time to go that afternoon. It was at least a fifteen-minute ride on the metro, and once there, I wasn't sure it would be easy to find the tomb that Jean Luc wrote about. I would need to go on Sunday.

There were soldiers buried there as well. I'd seen photos of funerals in the paper. Some services held without caskets, tombs without bodies.

I hadn't asked Madame Alouette for any of the details of Jean Luc's death, but suddenly it felt imperative to find out if his body was in Père-Lachaise. Maybe if I could face the reality of his death, I could quiet his voice.

Perhaps the paper had reported his funeral service. I left some coins on the table and went back to Marie Lund's office at *Le Figaro*.

"I'm sorry to bother you, but did the paper print

Jean Luc Forêt's obituary and information about his burial services?"

She said she thought so and asked me to wait. While she went to get it, I watched the large room fill up as the lunch break ended and reporters took their desks. Most of them were women; the only men were either over fifty or wounded. Nothing good came of war, but at least this one was showing the world how capable women were of doing jobs previously held by men. Like my own.

I heard a commotion to the right and inched toward it, straining to listen. I suddenly remembered Monsieur Orloff's request and wandered farther into the offices to listen for talk of Russia, the royals, or the revolution.

"They found them under the Montparnasse catacombs," said a gray-haired woman with a telephone receiver up to her ear. Covering the mouthpiece with her hand, she relayed information as she received it to the group of reporters who'd surrounded her desk.

"How many were there?" one of the reporters asked.

"Two of them," she said.

"How long have they been underground?" another asked.

She asked the question of the person on the other end of the phone. Everyone waited.

"At least a week," she said.

"What are they going to do with them?" another reporter shouted.

"They are spies, you fool, they are going to throw them in prison," someone in the crowd answered.

"Based on information the police were able to collect, they think there are dozens more Germans who've infiltrated the city."

"Spies under our feet," one of the reporters said. "In the tunnels and the mines."

"Mademoiselle?"

I turned. Marie Lund held a copy of *Le Figaro*.

"He died on July eighth," she said. "Here is his obituary."

The black border was the same as the one on the clipping I'd retrieved after it had fallen out of Madame Alouette's purse.

"There was no formal burial," she read. "No bodies were recovered from that explosion. There was too much damage and all the soldiers—" She broke off.

With the war all around, with its never-ending reports of casualties, there were only so many barriers one could erect. Some stories still broke through and shook you to your core. You'd find you could endure hearing about the unnamed troops—the hundreds, the thousands, yes, the millions of soldiers—who died, but not any one of those lives that touched yours, and it wasn't so easy to just buck up and go on as we were supposed to. Sometimes you needed to stop and bow your head and give in to the loss and grieve for the one who always said hello, or once waited for you at the door to help you carry your packages, or kissed you good night, or gave you your children. We could not be like the amazing automatons we'd seen on display. We were not just flesh and blood; we were also tears.

Marie Lund wiped hers away and handed me the paper.

"He was just such a lovely man," she said with a last little sigh.

Chapter 10

I returned to the shop in an even worse rain than when I'd left. Inside, Monsieur Orloff raised his eyebrows at the time of my arrival. I didn't apologize as I put away my umbrella and hat. I stayed in most of the time. Ten minutes of tardiness should have been overlooked.

"Did you hear anything about the Bolsheviks or the Romanovs?"

"No, but there was news about some German spies," and I told him what I'd overheard.

"Above us and below us." He shook his head. "There are Bolsheviks underground too. I'm sure of it. Where else would you hide in Paris?"

I didn't answer. He'd asked a rhetorical question I heard at least once a day.

"You remember the last piece we made for the actress Paulette Gillard, yes?"

"Of course."

I knew her lover Pierre Zakine well. A longtime friend of my great-grandmother's, he owned an art gallery and met my mother when she'd lived at Maison de la Lune. He'd become her dealer over twenty years ago and visited us in Cannes often. Once I moved to Paris, he'd started coming to the store just to check up on me and always picked up a little trinket, as he called the ready-made pieces in our cases, sometimes as a gift for his wife or his daughter. After many such visits, he commissioned a piece of high jewelry for his mistress and, liking it so much, began to order more of Monsieur Orloff's creations. Like many men of the upper classes, he'd not allowed the war to interfere in his life any more than absolutely necessary. After all, the nightclubs were still open and Maxim's still served. As long as you could pay, there were still oysters to feast on and champagne to buy and lovely ladies to bed.

"Well, we're making another gift for her," Monsieur said. "So let's go over it."

This was how Monsieur Orloff mentored me, by involving me in his own pieces. First, he'd show me his design, always a gouache on fine paper from Sennelier's store. After discussing the piece's intricacies, he'd explain about his choice of gems and color values. Then I'd estimate the number of stones, and together we'd visit the vault to choose and collect them. Monsieur Orloff often allowed me to make the first selection; then he inspected and either approved or replaced my choices, always explaining why.

When I first came to work for him, he rejected at least three-quarters of what I'd selected, but we'd reached a stage where he rarely found fault with any of my picks. If I couldn't find stones that were the right shade or size, Monsieur would send me to the gemologist, Monsieur St. Croix, to purchase what we required.

"This is a daunting design," Monsieur said that morning. "It's a necklace, yes, but the flowers can be removed from the stem here and here and worn as a clip. And then, I want the petals to be *en tremblant*."

I stood by his shoulder and gazed at the gouache study. The new piece comprised two roses on stems, with leaves. The bud and the bloom met in the center, their stems wrapping about the neck. Because Monsieur wanted the petals to tremble, they would be mounted on hidden springs.

"We'll use rose-colored diamonds, Opaline. As well as pink sapphires. Dark rubies for the shadows and folds of the petals. We want to complement her complexion, so you know the shades to pick. Tsavorites and emeralds for the leaves and brown diamonds for the stems. I'm expecting a client, so why don't you go down today on your own, find what you think will work, and I'll join you later and see how you've done."

I nodded, too excited to trust myself to speak. Monsieur had taken me into the vault hundreds of times but had never sent me down alone. Going on my own constituted a large step. In addition to jewelry and gems, the vault contained objets d'art Monsieur was safekeeping for émigrés. He also kept some of the smaller antiques Grigori had bought but hadn't put on display yet. And I knew from overhearing an argument between Grigori and his father that Monsieur did not allow even his son to visit the vault alone.

"If you'd become a jeweler, you would be going into the vault," Monsieur said whenever Grigori complained.

"Is that the only thing you can ever say to me? 'If you were a jeweler' this . . . 'if you were a jeweler' that . . . ," he'd spit back, and storm out of the room.

I ached for Grigori. As much as I admired and revered Monsieur, he was too angry at his eldest son for being the only one of his children to not follow in his footsteps. Making jewelry is not just a profession; one needs passion to sustain oneself through the long hours of sitting at a bench, sometimes wearing cumbersome glasses, using minute tools and always being careful and meticulous.

While Grigori possessed a great love of beautiful things and an excellent eye, he was best on the floor, describing with just the right phrases the artistry of a piece. Why it was a worthwhile investment. The joy it would bring.

With great ceremony, Monsieur Orloff handed me his keys to the vault.

After lighting a kerosene lamp to take with me,

I unlocked the first door just outside the workshop. Downstairs, at the landing, instead of going right toward my suite, I went left, walked past the bomb shelter down an incline and reached a second locked door.

I unlocked that door and opened it, immediately getting a nose full of the musty scent rising from the quarries. Walking the long twisting hallway to the vault, I held my breath at every turn. As always, I feared what I might hear. Some days the hum of the burial chambers, even though they were far away, was more audible than others. I'd gone down a few times without being assaulted, but most days I heard the dead's whispers and they frightened me.

That afternoon was one of the worst days. Twice I thought about turning around and running from the din, but the image of Monsieur's disappointed face kept me moving.

Using Monsieur Orloff's keys, I opened the next door, which led to a narrow hallway only wide enough for one. The rough-hewn stone walls and floors and thick wooden crossbeams hadn't been rebuilt since the seventeenth century. In the dark, the lamp's beam and my form cast more shadows. Twice I tripped on rocks, only barely finding my balance before falling. Heart pounding, I kept going till I reached the very last door.

Made of steel, it was the only modernity in the

ancient passageway. Using the last of the keys, I opened the heavy portal and shone my lantern in, setting alight an Ali Baba's cave of riches.

I never could enter the vault without sucking in my breath. I'd been to the famous gilt Palais Garnier opera house, seen the ornate riches of Versailles, visited the Louvre and examined the cases of ancient jewels and objets d'art, frequented the finest jewelry stores in Cannes and in Paris. None of them was preparation for the Orloff vault.

The long narrow room consisted of a series of archways carved out of stone walls. Each fitted with wooden shelves covered with forest green felt. Altogether, there were five archways on the right wall, three on the back wall, and five on the left. Ninety-one shelves crammed to overflowing with gold and silver jewelry and objets d'art. Platters, goblets, plates, picture frames, pitchers, creamers, teapots, coffeepots, candlesticks, and candelabras. Head mannequins with necklaces of pearls and diamonds and rubies and emeralds and sapphires encircling the painted flesh-colored wood. Velvet cases, some holding rings, others with earrings. Almost nothing was enclosed; everything was on view. I once asked Monsieur why. He said stones need to breathe like we do. They need to be seen and show off their colors; gold needs to shine.

Monsieur was a man of few words. Often curt.

Difficult to read. But when he talked about his gems, I saw the lover he must have been to Anna, the poet's soul living inside his craggy exterior.

Since so few Russian émigrés trusted the banks after living through an overthrown regime, they used La Fantaisie Russe to store their most prized possessions. Inside the vault, a large leather ledger sat on a podium. Every piece was recorded with a drawing, the name of whom it belonged to, and its particulars—weight, height, dimensions. Many of these items were heirlooms, and if I focused on them and touched them with my bare skin, I could sometimes be connected to the spirits of their owners and hear messages. An experience I had come to dread. Since we were supposed to wear white cotton gloves when we handled everything in the vault to avoid scratches, I made sure to keep mine on during the entirety of my visits.

At the far end of the room, I knelt beside the small safe. The enormity of the trust Monsieur placed in me worried me. I turned the tumbler to the right and then the left in the sequence he'd taught me. What if someone was to break in while I was there? I knew a pistol sat on the shelf to the right of the safe. Identical to the one upstairs in the showroom in the top drawer of the desk. Even with my small hands, I could hold it.

When I first went to work for him, Monsieur Orloff took me to the Bois de Boulogne and taught me how to use the gun. After several weeks of practice sessions, he declared me fit to defend the shop if I ever needed to. I was surprised at how brave I became with that small cold metal weapon in hand. In the midst of an angry war, with Paris going dark every night and rumors of spies infiltrating the city, knowing how to protect myself provided at least a kernel of comfort.

For a half hour, I sat on a small stool beside the safe and searched through pink diamonds, rubies, sapphires, brown diamonds, emeralds, and tsavorites, picking out my choices for the jeweled flower.

Finally, I heard the distant footsteps of Monsieur coming downstairs. Nervousness fluttered inside my chest. I wanted him to approve of my selection and perhaps even offer a word or two of praise.

Looking up from the glittering gems, I listened. Something was wrong. The sound wasn't coming from the right direction. The footsteps weren't descending from the stairs, but approaching from behind the vault's wall. From the tunnels running behind the section of the subbasement owned by Monsieur Orloff.

The noise increased in volume, sounding more like voices than footsteps but still muffled and hard to decipher. Was I picking up the hum from the dead and mistaking it for sounds being made by the living? Concentrating, I thought I could hear levels and tones of several people speaking.

It seemed that in a room or a cavern abutting Monsieur Orloff's vault, people were gathering.

I put my ear against the back wall and listened, almost able to make out the chatter, but there was too much noise, too many people talking all at once, as if there was one set of voices on the other side of the wall itself and another beyond it.

I have a bad ear for languages. I know how to speak English since my mother was born in America and talked to us often in her native tongue. While I certainly heard the Orloffs speaking Russian often, I'd never picked it up. To me, Russian, Polish, German, Czech, and Yiddish were almost indistinguishable and equally indecipherable.

Choosing yet another section of the wall, I put my ear against the cold stone and tried again. No clearer. For a few minutes, I moved around, repeating the same action, searching for a spot where the sound would be more distinct, but the walls were too thick.

Was I hearing German? Could these be spies? Or was my sense of direction off and it was Monsieur Orloff hosting a Two-Headed Eagles meeting? I just couldn't tell. Too many voices, too much noise.

As I worked my way around the room, I noticed one of the alcoves was set back farther, deeper into the wall. Maybe the sound would be more audible from there. As I quietly moved items off the shelf, I continued listening. Was it a mélange of unconnected voices from the heavens? Had I turned on some kind of psychic switch? Even though I wore gloves, was I hearing the people who'd once owned the antique objects in the vault before they were handed down or bought by their present owners? Had talking to Jean Luc opened a portal? Was I now a receptor even when I wasn't trying to be one? I needed Anna's help more than ever. I had to learn how to control my abilities so I could step out of the nightmare when it overwhelmed me.

Succeeding in emptying the shelves and removing them, I stepped into the alcove, put my ear up to the wall, and listened.

The only thing I became more sure of was that whoever was beyond this wall was speaking neither French nor English. If they were, I would have been able to pick up a hint of a word or accent. Pressing closer, I knocked over a candelabra, which clattered as it fell from a table onto the floor. The crash surprisingly loud.

The noise on the other side of the walls ceased for a moment. Then, just as it picked up again, I noticed a flicker of light above and to my left. Investigating, I found a slim crack in the rocks with half an inch of loose mortar. Using a fingernail, I picked at it, dislodging another half inch more, creating a peephole.

I moved the lantern away to the other end of the

vault. If there was someone beyond the wall, I didn't want them to see its glow and find me out.

Finally, afraid I would spot German uniforms—or, worse, not see anyone and discover the sounds were not of this time or place—I leaned forward and peered into the room beyond the vault.

Men's legs. Hands. A long cream-colored cylinder I couldn't identify.

The dimness of the chamber, the angle and size of the hole, didn't allow for much visibility. As far as I could tell, my peephole was only a few feet above the floor. I was almost eye level with chalky, muddy shoes. Five—no, six—sets of feet. Maybe seven. Too much movement, too many shadows. The noise was no more distinct. I realized I had, in fact, been listening to what these men were saying as well as hearing voices from the antiques around me. I couldn't separate the sources.

This was some kind of new hell.

Closing my eyes, I tried to remember Anna's advice on how to control the messaging. But we'd only worked on my psychometry, on what to do when I was touching something, not how to deal with untethered responses.

Stop, I said to myself. *Stop listening.* And miraculously, after a few moments, some of the noise dissipated. Maybe now, if I looked through the peephole and focused, I could pick out their words, identify their language.

I took a step forward, but before I got close enough to peer through, I saw a man examining the crevice from his side. A flash of hair the color of burnished bronze, heavy eyebrows, topaz eyes shining with suspicion. Could he see me, or was I deep enough in shadow? What did the vault look like from where he stood? I'd moved the lantern, but was its light reflecting off the gold and silver objects?

I dropped to the floor. Waited. Listened. Still unable to make out the words or the language. Inching backward as quietly as I could, I reached the lantern and pushed it farther into a niche. I picked up a large onyx box and moved it in front of the opening. Now, if the men on the other side looked in, there was nothing to see but their own reflections. I studied my watch. I'd been down in the vault for almost an hour. How much longer before Monsieur came looking for me?

For the next fifteen minutes, I sat still with my back up to the wall, my head pressed against its stony unevenness, listening, trying to pull apart the noises and recognize a single word so I could discern what might be going on. An innocent meeting of people who worked somewhere in the Palais? French soldiers searching the underground? Germans planning an attack?

Finally, I heard shuffling and a door closing. The only sound remaining was the din I usually encountered in these dungeons. Slowly and carefully, I moved the box and then looked through the peephole. On the other side was nothing but darkness. All lights extinguished. All men gone.

What had I seen? Monsieur Orloff's émigrés meeting in a new place? A gambling den? Rumor suggested there were at least a half dozen such dens in the Palais. Or was it German spies? Were the cylinders rolled-up maps?

Quickly, I replaced the shelves in the arch and arranged the objects sitting on them. I'd just begun sifting through the stones again when, for the second time that afternoon, I thought I heard Monsieur Orloff coming downstairs.

"Let's see how you fared," he said after closing the door behind him.

While he examined the stones, I tried to figure out what I should do. Ask him? What exactly? Or just tell him I saw men in a room beyond this one? What if it made me sound paranoid? Would he become hesitant about me doing my job?

Maybe I was letting my imagination get the better of me. After all, there were stores on both sides of us and each of them retained access to basement chambers. I couldn't be sure of the vault's orientation. If we were beneath Grigori's antiques shop, then on the other side was a coin collector's shop. And if we were beneath the jewelry showroom, on the other side was a perfume shop. There was also the possibility that the vault backed up against tunnels that were not part of anyone's shop and that the men were city workers. Maybe a sewer needed maintenance and the cylinders were maps of the sewer system. Or could there be a series of tunnels stemming off the metro line needing attendance?

"Opaline?"

"Yes?"

"What are you daydreaming about?"

"Nothing." I hadn't figured out how to explain.

"Is it your voices again?"

"No, no voices."

The less we talked about the voices and my talismans, the better. As much as he tolerated it, Monsieur Orloff was not in favor of my messaging. Married to Anna, of course he was sympathetic about my abilities, but also nervous about the police discovering what we were doing since talking to the dead and reading people's fortunes was against the law and there were stories in all the newspapers of the prefecture cracking down. Monsieur wanted nothing to do with the police. In Russia the proliferation of secret police, spy organizations, and corruption had left him suspicious. He trusted no one. Almost obsessed, he went out of his way to avoid bringing the authorities in on any matter—even when we'd discovered a client shoplifting. I wasn't sure why and hadn't found a polite way to ask, but assumed it was related to him harboring refugees from Russia below the shop.

As well, Monsieur wasn't a spiritualist of any kind. Neither was he religious. To him, precious metals and gems were paints on a palette. A necklace or bracelet, ring or brooch, a canvas. He used gems to create art to adorn its wearer, not to stare into the faceted depths of the crystals and see the past or the future, as his wife was prone to do. He never closed his eyes when he held a stone and felt for its vibration, as I did. Monsieur Orloff bowed to its beauty; he didn't commune with its mystery. So he tolerated Anna and her crystal balls and me and my voices. He watched us disappearing into her lair after dinner with a rueful smile.

"This is good work, Opaline. Thinking to include the darker brown diamonds was an excellent idea."

I smiled. Compliments from someone who does not offer them often are all the more precious.

"There's not much left to teach you. Now I just need to push you to spend more time refining your designs and not be quite so impatient."

I wanted to laugh. He'd done nothing but push me since I'd first arrived almost four years ago.

"Take the stones upstairs," he said. "I'll lock up—there are some things I need to get from the safe. Monsieur and Madame Bouchard are coming tomorrow to pick out a stone for a pendant."

Dismissed, I took the tray of stones upstairs to the workshop. As I climbed the steps, I worried that I hadn't found a way to tell Monsieur Orloff what I'd witnessed. But what if it had been him and his group of Russians? He might be insulted I'd been spying. Besides, what had I seen? Really nothing suspect. Men in a chamber on the other side of the vault. Why was that suspicious? There were over fifty shops in the Palais and hundreds of residences.

I'd spent too long listening to the voices of the soldiers, collecting messages for their mothers. My imagination was overworked.

Later that afternoon, while I was still sorting the stones into gradations within their color groups, Grigori came into the workroom. Fresh from purchasing a collection of antique jewel-encrusted goblets, he wanted to show them to his father for an estimate.

"I'm going to make some coffee," I told them. "Would you like any?"

They both declined. As I stood up, I knocked a pair of tweezers off my worktable.

I bent to retrieve them. They'd fallen close to Grigori's feet, and I couldn't help but notice pale gray mud on his shoes. Like the shoes of the men in the room next to the vault.

This was more proof I was being melodramatic. We were having the rainiest summer on record. Mud covered all the streets in Paris. It was on all our shoes. And so, once and for all, I put the incident out of my mind and made my coffee.

Chapter 11

That night, after a light supper with Anna—
Monsieur Orloff and Grigori were picking up
someone at the train station—I retired early and
nestled into the sanctuary of my basement suite.

Strangely, I didn't mind it being windowless.
My great-grandmother had contributed a few
objets d'art to make it special. An old carpet, too
worn in spots for her grand mansion but perfect
for me. Dark green with lavender wisteria flowers,
it set the tone for the colors of my room. She also
had contributed a magnificent stained glass screen
with a scene of Leda and the Swan on the shore
of a pond in a forest. Cleverly, she'd told me to
place a lamp behind it, and the screen lit up and
offered a spectacular rainbow of magical blue,
green, and lavender hues. My bureau was a fine
piece of rosewood carved in an Art Nouveau style
along with a matching headboard my father had
brought from his factory. And I had a comfortable
armchair upholstered in pine-green velvet, which
my great-grandmother had donated. Retiring to
my room was like escaping into the deepest part
of the woods, where ancient pagans enacted
rituals by the shore of a bubbling brook.

A pale green glass globe Anna had given me sat
on the bureau. Beside it a bowl of stones, for

practice. I'd picked out and polished each precious piece. There were chunks of jade, amethyst, lapis lazuli, jet, and three opals. Usually at night, before I went to bed, I worked with one of them, trying to control and fine-tune my ability. Anna believed I must embrace lithomancy completely in order to learn to control it. She'd taught me how to meditate using one of the stones. How to relax and concentrate fully, feeling the stone's energy and connecting to it. To become one with the precious object. To lose myself in its depths and search its secrets without fear. To just be and see what came to me. Anna cautioned me she'd been practicing her art for over thirty years and still found much to learn. I'd only been studying mine for three. But as Monsieur observed in the studio, I was impatient.

Instead of practicing, I unbuttoned my chemise and withdrew the talisman I'd originally made for Madame Alouette. All day I'd been feeling its pull. As if it was calling to me, begging me to wrap my fingers around it and enclose it in my palm. Because the rock crystal lay between my breasts, it was warm. But it warmed even more as I examined its star-shaped inclusion. Wrapped in its gold cage of stem-like wires that wound around and then met at the top of the loop to create a link, it hung from its silk cord, shining in the room's soft light. Removing the cord, I took a heavy gold link chain from my jewel box, strung it through the loop, and then lowered it over my head again. As the egg nestled once more between my breasts, I thought I heard a sigh.

Preferring low light, I shut off all but a small reading light and the lamp behind the glass screen. Bathed in a peacock blue glow, the room really might have been in the middle of the woods. The night stretched ahead before me. After work, after supper, without obligations, I could do whatever pleased me. Most evenings, I read of other times and places to dull the sharp edge of reality we lived during the day. I was still making my way through my great-grandmother's book of ghost stories by Edith Wharton and opened it to my silver bookmark—a gift from the Orloffs on my twenty-second birthday.

Other women read love stories to forget the war; I preferred to go deeper into darkness, into manifestations of evil, to help understand the nightmare around us.

I read a few pages but was distracted. A presence imbued the room. Not a shadow, not a scent. Almost a blur.

Against my chest, the talisman seemed warmer than a few moments ago.

"Hello?" I whispered to the darkness, feeling a little foolish talking out loud to myself. I waited. If I'd imagined my previous conversations with Jean Luc, then surely I could manifest another now.

"We always need to weigh what we think we see and hear with our wish life," Anna once explained to me. "Those of us with access to the future or the past, or who can speak to people no longer here, are prone to creative thinking. The line between reality and fantasy is so thin for us. Imagine a psychic says you'll meet a tall stranger at the opera and marry him. The next time you go to the opera you find a tall stranger in the box next to yours. Believing in the reading, you might go out of your way to meet him, flirt with him, and entice him. If he then begins to court you, did you create that scenario, or was the psychic right? It's important to learn to be strict with yourself and not manifest what isn't there, what isn't meant to be there."

I vacillated between believing I was going mad and concluding I just had conjured him the way children create imaginary friends. Maybe the conversations were proof of insanity. Or maybe just a manifestation of my loneliness.

While Grigori provided some companionship, it was fleeting and there was no true passion. Without both, I felt alone. But since Timur had died, I felt it wise to deny that part of myself. Not only out of guilt but because passion had stirred my powers and I feared anything that would magnify them even more. Despite myself . . . was I yearning for it now? Yearning for love, despite the danger? Even knowing I had little hope of finding it? History had invaded my personal life. The war had stolen all our dreams. Women who were supposed to have had houses full of children would probably remain childless now; men who otherwise might have made their fortunes were now dead in the trenches. Even if I was brave enough to go searching for love, my chances of finding it were slim.

If I was going to invent a companion, why not the author of the wonderful columns about art and individualism that had influenced me so long ago?

"I went to the offices of *Le Figaro*," I said out loud. "I met a receptionist who has quite a crush on you." A moment passed in silence. Just about to be convinced yet again that, yes, I'd imagined it all, I felt an almost breeze blow through my room. There should be nothing suspect about a breeze. Except it was impossible. There were no windows here. Yet it brushed my face, ruffled my hair. The very air moved. I smelled limes mixed with . . . I sniffed again . . . mixed with verbena and a hint of myrrh.

Why did you go there?

"I used to read your columns about art, but then when you started writing about the war . . . I couldn't anymore. I lived with too much news and reality from the front. But now that we've . . ." I hesitated, searching for the word. "Now that we've met, I want to read them. I planned on buying back copies, but only one was available. Who did you write them to? Who was *Ma chère?*"

At the time I didn't know. Now I think maybe I wrote them for you.

"Me?"

I think we were supposed to meet but I messed that up.

"What do you mean?"

It's all my fault, I misread the signs, I delayed issuing orders . . .

The words ceased. Silence. And then I heard what sounded like a sob.

"Jean Luc, what do you mean about us meeting? About messing that up?"

I think if I hadn't made those mistakes in the field, I would have come back to Paris and visited your store and looked at the jewelry and seen something to buy for my mother and would have met you.

I put my hand up to the talisman to touch it. To touch him?

"But now you won't."

No.

"I'm sorry."

Yes. Me too. For you. For so many, many things.

I didn't say anything.

Don't cry.

He could see me?

"How did you know I was crying? So you really can see me? Where are you?" I was so frustrated and confused.

Until you started to make the talisman I was asleep, floating . . . and then the closer you came to completing it, the more aware I became. When you touch it, you come into focus. Through fog. As if there is a certain distance between us. Yet more clearly than makes any sense, considering I am a world away from you.

"I don't understand," I whispered. "And I am a little afraid."

And then I felt, or I thought I felt . . . no . . . I *did* feel his hand brushing my hair off my forehead.

I don't want to make you afraid.

His touch made me shiver and begin to tremble.

I can't bear for you to be afraid of me. You, here, it's the only time since . . . since it happened I don't feel as lost.

I tried desperately to quell the shaking. Pressure increased against the spot he'd cleared. Not lips, no. But a force suggesting lips. Perhaps from the shock, my shaking stopped.

When I kissed you just now, you felt it, didn't you?

I nodded.

And now, do you feel this?

Somehow he'd taken my hand. I looked down and saw nothing but my own hand in my lap. I didn't feel flesh. Instead, it was as if I were holding smoke. And where our hands met, my skin warmed to his touch.

We sat like that, or I did, for several moments. I should have become more afraid, but instead my fear calmed. Jean Luc being there comforted me. Excited me.

My mother has a book of all of my Ma chère *columns. Including some never published because they were too risqué. I'd like you to read them. Then you'll understand. More than I can tell you here in the time left to me. I can't stay. Will you read them?*

"What do you mean you can't stay?"

It takes an effort to be here. So much effort. Have to . . . learn how to . . .

He continued speaking, but from an ever greater distance. His voice fading.

"Jean Luc?"

Silence.

And then, my tears came. As if I'd known him for years and just found out he'd died. I glanced down at my hand again. It looked no different from before and yet was cold. I touched my right hand with my left. Trying to find where his amorphous fingers had lain, trying to pick up a sense of him. But there was nothing there. He'd gone. And I was alone. Again.

Chapter 12

I practiced what I planned to say to Madame Alouette on my walk back to the mask studio. I came up with various reasons I might want to examine her book of Jean Luc's columns. All of them logical, but were any of them believable?

Upon arrival, an assistant informed me Madame was working with a soldier and asked if I could wait, or would I prefer to come back? Afraid if I left I'd lose my nerve and never return, I agreed to wait.

When Madame Alouette came out, her hands and smock smeared with gray clay, she seemed excited to greet me.

"Have you received another message?" she asked right away.

Taken by surprise that she knew, I started to answer without thinking. "I have been—" And then I stopped myself. In my nervousness, I almost admitted something that I could not share with her, certainly not yet. "No, not that. I came because I have been thinking"—I tried covering my error—"about your son's columns. I went to the newspaper's office to buy old issues, but they only sell a month back. The woman there told me," I lied, "sometimes family members keep scrapbooks of newspaper stories a loved one has written and I thought—" I needed to stop rambling. Her expression suggested I'd made a very odd request.

"Yes, I do have a book just like that. All the ones that were printed as well as some that weren't. You're interested in reading them? Because of something else he told you?"

"No, there's nothing . . ." I tried to make light of it, but what could I say that would make any sense? What had I been thinking in going to see her? I'd upset her and now I owed her something more.

"I'm sorry," I said. "Sometimes the voices of the soldiers, of the soldiers I talk to, get inside my head. Almost as if once I've heard them they get stuck there. It's happened now with your son. I'm not sure why, but I thought if I could read the columns, get to know him better . . . perhaps I might be able to . . ." I searched for the word. "Dislodge him."

Behind me, one of the other mask makers or soldiers must have opened a window because a strong gust of wind blew at my back. I turned. All the windows but one were shut against the rain. No one stood beside the opened one.

"Eloise?" Madame Alouette called out. "You need to get the concierge and tell him one of the windows needs to be fixed. It just flew open." She circled back to me. "The lock must be loose. Things are always going wrong here. It's such an old building."

I nodded, even though I was certain the concierge wouldn't find anything wrong with the lock.

"The book is at our apartment. Would you like to come by this evening? I'd be happy to lend it to you." She smiled. "It's comforting to be able to talk about him, you know. So many people just tiptoe around his death and that doesn't help either."

At seven o'clock, I rang the doorbell at no. 5 avenue Van Dyck. A dog barked somewhere inside. After a few moments, Madame Alouette opened the door and a little Maltese rushed out to greet me.

"Meet Maxime," she said as she ushered me into the vestibule.

I bent to pet the fluffy white fur creature who was pawing at my legs.

"Enough now," Madame Alouette scolded the dog as she scooped her up. "We are on the first floor," she said as she led me to a sweeping staircase with an ornate wrought iron banister.

Jean Luc walked on these stairs every day coming home from school, I thought, as I stepped on the well-worn marble.

On the landing, Madame Alouette ushered me through large lacquered doors into their apartment. Into *his* apartment, I thought.

I followed her through a beautifully appointed foyer, decorated simply with a black-and-white marble floor and a round table with a tall art glass vase in its center. Instead of flowers, it held creamy white peacock feathers the same shade as the walls. The high ceilings were capped with baguette moldings of repeating floral wreaths.

After seeing the simple entryway, I wasn't prepared for the profusion of art decorating the next room we entered. Pieces by artists I knew from my father's work as an architect and my mother's as a painter crowded the parlor.

Fabulous Art Nouveau chairs, couches, and end tables covered in lush velvets in wine colors. Grape, ruby, and rose stained art glass lamps twisting and turning on their wrought iron stem-like bases. Garnet and crimson rugs scattered all over a gleaming parquet floor. A pink-cheeked Renoir of a child at a piano hung above a fireplace carved out of marble the same shade of pink. Other colorful impressionistic paintings by Monet, Manet, Matisse, and Cassatt graced the claret-colored walls. Sensual white marble statues of lovers in various poses stood on pedestals in the corners and in front of the windows, and bronze busts occupied tabletops.

"Is this your work?" I asked Madame Alouette, indicating the sculpture.

"Yes, and this," she said, pointing to a white marble bust on the mantelpiece, "this is my son."

I wasn't expecting to come face-to-face with Jean Luc. He was staring out at me, almost as surprised to see me as I him. His almond-shaped eyes gazed intelligently, all seeing. Were they the same midnight blue as his mother's? From the lock of hair Madame Alouette provided, I knew that Jean Luc's hair was dark brown, but now I could see it had once fallen in waves over his forehead.

The shock of seeing him in three dimensions, of learning what he looked like after hearing him inside my head, literally made me unsteady on my feet, and I put out a hand, grabbing hold of the back of the chair closest to me.

"Are you all right?" Madame Alouette asked. "You've lost all the color in your cheeks."

"Yes, yes, I'm fine. I just . . . I'm fine."

She looked at me with her eyes both kind and wary at the same time. And I didn't blame her. Who was this off-balance woman, practically a stranger, in her living room, becoming weak while looking at a bust of her son? I should have turned to her and reassured her I felt fine, lied and said I'd forgotten to eat that day, but I couldn't turn to her, not yet. I couldn't glance away from the sculpture.

Were Madame Alouette any less talented, my reaction might have been less intense, but she had been a student of the brilliant Auguste Rodin and it showed. The technique she used to carve the stone had produced results as close to real life as I'd ever seen. I was almost certain if I reached out and touched it, the stone would be warm, not cold, and I would be able to feel Jean Luc's pulse beating in his neck.

I took in more of his features: a broad forehead, an aristocratic nose with a slight bump high on the bridge, a small mouth with full lips. A sensitive, seductive face, one that seemed to be inviting me in with a secret smile playing behind the stoic pose.

"I suppose I should introduce you to my son. This is Jean Luc Forêt," Madame Alouette said. As tears filled her eyes, I felt tears fill my own.

He was dead, I reminded myself. He was dead, and even my being there was absurd. The voice I heard, that I believed belonged to the man this used to be, was my imagination. We are not meant to speak to people after they pass over. It cannot logically be done. Picking up a message from the departed, from the ether, was one thing; conversations with a ghost, quite another.

But what if that was happening? What if it was an aberration, a mistake of time? And if it was, I blamed my mother. For the hundredth time, or the thousandth, I cursed my mother for having children. A witch who has abilities and powers like hers? Didn't she understand what she would be passing on?

"He was very handsome, don't you think?" Madame Alouette asked, with a twist in her voice. As if she were like any mother matchmaking, trying to interest a young woman in her son.

I looked away from the marble and turned to her. "Yes, he is."

She frowned. "Do you speak of the soldiers like that because you are in touch with them? Because you hear them speaking to you?"

I had been unaware of my use of the present tense until her comment. Another mistake. I'd need to be more careful of how I spoke. In truth, no, I never referred to them in the present, but to me Jean Luc wasn't gone.

"Yes, I suppose I do," I lied.

"Can you ever talk to them without one of these?" she pointed to the crystal orb I'd made which hung around her neck.

"No," I said, not filling in the rest . . . not saying what I wanted to . . . that I never could until she came to Monsieur's atelier.

Madame Alouette seemed to take stock of where we were. "Forgive my manners. Would you like to sit down? Have an aperitif?" I had almost declined when it occurred to me that if I stayed, perhaps she would show me Jean Luc's room. Maybe I could peek at his things.

"That is such an imposition," I said, in that polite way one did before one accepted.

"Not at all. You would be giving me a great

gift. Allowing me to indulge in talking about Jean Luc for a bit longer."

She rose and went to the sideboard, where she reached for a bottle of Lillet. As she poured the golden-orange wine, I noticed a round table across the room covered with at least a dozen silver-framed photographs. I was too far away to make out many of the details, but I recognized Jean Luc in some of them. Madame Alouette and a man I assumed was her husband in others. I longed to go and inspect them, drink in Jean Luc's features, study his expressions, but before I worked up the courage, Madame Alouette returned, handing me a crystal glass.

While we sipped the aperitifs, she recounted stories about her son. A mischievous child, always curious, he loved going off and exploring places on his own. One of Madame's favorite memories was of the first time she took him to the Louvre. He was only four, but he loved touching her sculpture at home so much and seemed so interested she thought he'd enjoy the excursion. As soon as he saw the *Winged Victory*, he ran up to it and threw his arms around its base and set to howling when she tried, along with the guard, to pull him off. After that, she said, his favorite outings were visiting museums. They'd walk through the Tuileries and go to the Louvre and afterward walk over to Angelina's for hot chocolate.

I nodded; it was a favorite haunt of my great-grandmother's as well, and I went there with her as often as we could. We'd always see mothers and children there, the little boys or girls absorbed in the heady drink, glistening brown with clouds of whipped cream floating on top.

"Until we realized he needed eyeglasses, he wasn't a good student. But outfitted with the correct spectacles, he became an avid reader with at least three books open at once." She smiled, remembering.

Under my dress, I felt the talisman warm against my skin. Was he here with me? Could he hear what his mother was saying?

"Jean Luc went to university in Oxford," Madame Alouette continued, "and then stayed on in England to write a series of articles about castles for a magazine. His stepfather and I were so proud of him. When Jean Luc came home, he got a job with *Le Figaro* and started writing his art column. He loved it. His job gave him an excuse to spend days wandering through Montmartre, searching out artists, studying their work, trying to understand what drove them and our reactions to their work. He was so passionate and cared so much about art. About society rewarding an artist's individuality, not condemning it. And then the war broke out."

Even with all the information she'd fed me, I remained hungry for more. The skeleton of a description wasn't enough for someone starving. She must have read something of my desperation, for suddenly she stood and said, "Would you like to see his room?"

I nodded, rose, and followed her back into the foyer and up a sweeping staircase. Down a hall, she opened a door at the far end on the right.

I smelled the scent as soon as I stepped inside. The same curious concoction accompanying Jean Luc's visits. Exotic and pungent limes mixed with verbena with a hint of myrrh. At once a scent of the past and the present. An odd mixture of times and places.

If I imagined the visits, how would I have known about the scent? Unless Madame Alouette wore it that first time we met. Grieving her son, had she taken to wearing his cologne?

Breathing it in, I responded physically, stirred and excited by memories of the titillating nighttime magic Jean Luc's ghost brought with him. Heat flushed my cheeks, and I hoped Madame Alouette didn't notice.

"It's very distinctive, isn't it? A perfumer we use, just a few blocks from here, created it for him. Jean Luc never wore anything else."

"L'Etoile's?"

She nodded.

"I know that perfumer. He makes my grandmother's scents too."

One of Paris's most prestigious firms, the House of L'Etoile dated back to before the Revolution and their shop on rue des Saints-Pères was just a few doors down from my family home.

If I went there, would they sell me a flacon of Jean Luc's scent? Usually, once they created a bespoke perfume, no one else could purchase it. But what if the owner of the scent has passed on? Was it still protected? Or could I lie and say I'd come to pick up a bottle for him? Would they sell it to me then?

Madame Alouette turned on the light. Bookshelves, filled to overflowing, covered the walls. More books next to the bed, and another pile on the table next to an armchair.

Standing close to his desk, I glimpsed a sheaf of notes and an uncapped pen. An inkwell left open, the purplish ink dried out and flaking on the glass. He must have been in the midst of writing when he'd been called away. To the right, the typewriter still retained a sheet of paper in the carriage. Beside it, a small stack of paper covered with characters. On top of them, a pack of cigarettes and an ashtray, with a few inches of gray ash still inside it.

The covers on the bed were rumpled, and upon them, a book lay open, facedown.

Imagining that last afternoon, I pictured Jean Luc reading in bed, coming across an idea, rising, and going to the desk. He started typing, then stopped to think. Lit a cigarette. He'd smoked as he committed his thoughts to paper and then . . . what happened?

"I know I shouldn't keep it like this in here. I should empty out his closet and give away his things but . . . I can't . . ."

I nodded. Mothers spoke to me like this all the time. "When was Jean Luc last here?" I asked.

"Right before he . . ." She still couldn't use the word. "He'd been home on leave. He and a friend were taking the train back that afternoon. Jean Luc was up here working when I called up to tell him Alain had arrived. Jean Luc came downstairs and I made both of them something to eat and then the time came for them to go. Jean Luc had already packed and left his luggage by the door. He must have forgotten about these unfinished notes and never come back up. The following day was Saturday, and my house-keeper doesn't come on weekends. So no one straightened up the room. Marie fell ill and remained indisposed through Wednesday, when we got the telegram. When she finally returned on Thursday, I told her not to touch anything in here, but just to dust. Since then, that's all she's done. I can't bring myself to straighten it up. If I leave it like this, I can pretend . . ."

"But pretending isn't good," I said. Talking to myself really.

"No. But it's all we have." Was she talking only to herself? Or was I included in the "we"?

Somewhere beyond the door I heard foot-steps.

"Madame Alouette?"

The housekeeper, who I now knew as Marie, came to say she was needed in the kitchen. Excusing herself, Madame Alouette told me she'd be right back. Then she left me in Jean Luc's room.

For the first few seconds, I didn't move. Like a child staring into the window of a toy store, I just eyed the riches before me, overwhelmed with the gift I'd just been given.

"So this is where you lived?" I whispered as I strode over to the bed and stroked the depression his head had left in the pillow so long ago. I half expected it to be warm. But of course the linens were cool to the touch.

I imagined lying on the bed and fitting my body into the space where he'd lain. Would I feel his arms come around me? But I dared not muss Madame Alouette's shrine. I touched the coverlet where his shoulders once had pressed down. Where his hips . . . his calves . . . his shoulders . . . left an imprint.

But like the pillow, all these spots were cold. Nothing of Jean Luc remained here anymore. The apartment had been his home, but he'd left it behind. The most his room could offer was insight into the man, what made him Jean Luc Forêt and not someone else.

I started with his bookshelves, seeking to learn what I could about him through his reading. I passed over the childhood classics we'd all read and concentrated on his adult tastes: experimental literature by the British, Americans, and French, as well as popular fiction. My finger ran along the spines of André Gide's *The Immoralist*, *Dubliners* by James Joyce, *The House of Mirth* by Edith Wharton, Arthur Conan Doyle's *The Hound of the Baskervilles*, and Marcel Proust's *Swann's Way*.

Among the shelves of art, architecture, and art criticism books, I recognized the authors Ruskin, Stendhal, and Clive Bell from conversations we'd had at home. Both my parents were highly critical of these critics.

From the condition of the spines of the books on the middle shelf, I guessed these were Jean Luc's favorites, fiction and nonfiction all mixed together: Victor Hugo's *Hunchback of Notre Dame*, Sigmund Freud's *Interpretation of Dreams*, C. G. Jung's *Psychology of the Unconscious*, D. H. Lawrence's *Sons and Lovers*, and *Phantom of the Opera* by Gaston Leroux. Having recently finished Leroux's gothic love story, I felt a thrill thinking of Jean Luc poring over the words and wondering when he'd read it—and what if we'd been reading it at the same time?

I took the book off the shelf and let it fall open
to a random page.

> Know that it is a corpse who loves you
> and adores you and will never, never
> leave you! . . . Look, I am not laughing
> now, crying, crying for you, Christine,
> who have torn off my mask and who
> therefore can never leave me again! . . .
> Oh, mad Christine, who wanted to see me!

I shivered and put the book back. As I did, a
volume with a curious purple stain on its green
spine caught my attention because of its similarity
to La Lune's signature crescent-moon shape.
Was it wine that colored the leather? Certainly
not blood. I pulled out the book. Oscar Wilde's
The Soul of Man Under Socialism, a dry title
indeed. The book fell open to a familiar passage.

> Art is the most intense mode of
> Individualism the world has known.

Beside it, in ink, Jean Luc had written:

> The soul of the artist fighting the
> mediocrity of the masses. An artist, like a
> lover, cares not for convention. In fact,
> convention is his enemy.

A memory opened in my mind. My father and I
after dinner, reading Jean Luc Forêt's column

on individualism, quoting this passage from Wilde's essay. My father became excited. For exactly that reason, my father explained to me, freedom of expression should be defended at all costs.

As I flipped through the pages, I found several more highlighted phrases.

"Know thyself" was written over the portal of the antique world. Over the portal of the new world, "Be thyself" shall be written.

The notion appealed to me; I wanted to write it down and send it home to my father. He'd appreciate it every bit as much as I had. For a moment I envisioned the spirited conversation Jean Luc, my father, and I might have had around the dinner table. My mother, smiling her little cat smile, agreeing with just an elegant nod of her head while my father had much to say and many questions to ask.

"He loved to read," Madame Alouette said. Her return startled me.

I turned to her. "So do I." What made me say that? To voice aloud what we shared? She looked at me gently. Sensing my emotional reaction to her son, or caught up in her own?

"If there's anything you'd like to borrow, please do. Jean Luc loved lending his books to his friends."

Overwhelmed by the offer, I searched the shelves, reading through the titles. How to know which would give me the deepest view into the man's soul?

"I think I'll just take this one," I finally said, referring to the Wilde already in hand. Surely not the most romantic of his books, but all the annotations in Jean Luc's handwriting were too intriguing to ignore.

"I am sorry to rush you, but we are having a little dinner this evening and I need to dress," she said, gesturing to the door.

"May I just look out of the window first?"

"The window?"

"Just for a second. To see the street from here." As I asked, I realized how eccentric a request it must seem. But how to tell her I wanted to gaze upon what he had gazed upon? How to explain I wanted to fill my eyes with what he had seen?

"Certainly, it's a lovely view," she said, and opened the curtains for me and I looked down onto Parc Monceau. "One of his first *Ma chère* columns from the front referred to this view—you must read it."

I stood at the window for a few moments, trying to see what Jean Luc had seen, but Paris wasn't dressed in lights because of the war and I couldn't see anything but a dismal foggy night settled over a patch of darkness.

Chapter 13

Ma chère,

Here in the dark, as the kerosene burns, I try to summon your perfume and pretend I smell it instead of this stink. All around us, all the time, lives are lost. Every minute of every hour of every day and night. We steel ourselves from what we do as we carry the wounded out of danger, getting their blood on our hands, our boots, our uniforms . . . as we ship them off to the temporary field hospitals or, worse, send them back home for burials. We try not to think of the dead who we have no choice but to bury here on the battlefield.

Breathe, breathe, I tell myself, when the enormity of the loss overwhelms me. When I think of the achievements the world will never know. What great novel will never be written because its author was blown up. What wonderful painting that could have brought such joy will never be painted because its artist has expired after losing too much blood.

We march on roads and through fields that have become cemeteries. Nothing picturesque and peaceful like the ones we have at home. There are no graceful cobblestone paths here. No stained glass windows in artful mausoleums.

There is no romance in the impromptu graveyards at the front. Nothing like Père-Lachaise in Paris. If I were home, I would escort you there today. It is a perfect place to ruminate on love. Shall you go for me?

Take the metro, of course—Père-Lachaise is too far to walk. Before the war, there were always tourists visiting the famous resting place . . . but since then, other than sad funeral parties burying a soldier, the mysterious memorial park is rarely crowded.

After walking through the refined wrought iron gates, turn right. Père-Lachaise is laid out like a small town with street signs clearly visible, so if you ask the caretaker for a map, you should have no trouble getting about. Lofty trees shade the allées. Flowers bloom, bees buzz, birds fly, squirrels and rabbits and cats make the cemetery their home. There is much life there in the land of the dead. Just as there is here at the front.

The first tomb I want you to visit is on avenue Casimir Périer, the same name as the tiny street in the 6th arrondissement, but here it is in the seventh section. You will see it from a distance for it is one of the tallest monuments in the area. Not as high as the leafy trees offering shade, but soaring nonetheless, the way well-designed High Gothic structures do.

When you arrive, pause to take in its melancholy grandeur. Then stroll around its perimeter, peer inside its open arches at the two stone effigies, lovers sleeping side by side on their funeral biers.

Peter Abelard was a twelfth-century philosopher and theologian at the cathedral school of Notre-Dame. Considered the boldest thinker of his time, he was quite famous. Héloïse, the niece of a secular canon named Fulbert, was a young woman renowned for her brilliant prose writing, who spoke Latin, Greek, and Hebrew. Yearning to learn even more, she persuaded her uncle to hire Abelard to teach her.

At thirty-nine, despite his fame and popularity, Abelard remained chaste. Héloïse, in her early twenties, was as well.

The great meeting of their minds led to a meeting of their souls and eventually their flesh, even though the political and religious climates of their time forbid their being together.

Abelard wrote he was "all on fire" for

Héloïse and decided "she is the one to bring to my bed."

Despite knowing sex was a sin, neither could resist and they met in secret, insatiable, they both wrote, exploring each other with a passion that until then they'd devoted solely to their intellect.

"My hands strayed more often to her bosom than to the pages, love drew our eyes to look on each other more than reading kept them on our texts," Abelard wrote.

And then Héloïse became pregnant.

"Oh, how great was the uncle's grief when he learned the truth, and how bitter was the sorrow of the lovers when we were forced to part!" Abelard wrote.

To protect Héloïse, Abelard took her to Brittany. There, they wed in secret and she went to stay with the nuns in a convent in Argenteuil while Abelard returned to Paris to make amends. But Héloïse's uncle, believing Abelard had cast off his niece, greeted him by having him brutally beaten and castrated.

Compared to our time, the Middle Ages were so unforgiving. So patriarchal. Humiliated, Abelard resigned as a teacher and became a monk. Héloïse, believing she was without other options, gave up her child and became a nun. And yet their love didn't wither, didn't die.

For the next twenty years, Héloïse and Abelard continued to meet spiritually and emotionally in letters, pledging their love for each other over and over.

I emerged from the subway and, seeing the green trees ahead, experienced a mild surge of anticipation and dread. Why, of all the columns, had I chosen the one that sent me to visit the place I feared the most?

Reaching the tall wrought iron gates, I stopped. The deafening noise assaulted me. I didn't hear one voice. Not one set of words but a symphony of screaming. A horrific song of pain and sorrow and sadness. Much worse than I'd feared.

Quickly I stepped back, away from the gates. So frustrated, I wanted to cry. Why did I need to hear all this? I wanted to follow Jean Luc's column, that's all. Just take a walk. Would I not be able to?

Anna had reassured me the practices I was doing would help me learn to control my powers. But I needed a solution now. I tried something she had recently suggested.

Reading through some old texts, Anna found a description of a mystic, who, in order to hear long-gone voices, missed messages, and forgotten words hanging in the atmosphere, slipped into an unfocused state akin to daydreaming. Therefore, in order to stop hearing them, she suggested I needed to be totally focused on the present. A tiny pinprick of pain might be enough of a distraction to keep the noise at bay.

I pressed one of my fingernails into the fleshy part of my palm. A bit deeper, and then deeper still until it actually hurt, and then I stepped back inside the gates of Père-Lachaise. Solemn silence greeted me. With some nervousness, I took a few steps farther. The dead were not calling out. At least not yet.

This technique, albeit painful, was preferable to the horror in my ears.

In the distance, three women with a large bouquet of flowers walked toward me. I let them pass, and then, opening the sheet of newsprint, I continued reading Jean Luc's column, wondering how many other women had come here with his words in hand. How many others had taken this same pilgrimage?

Yes, I've told you an unhappy love story. Not to make you cry, but rather to offer hope. Separated, love doesn't tear, doesn't break; bonds can grow stronger.

As you gaze at their tomb, Ma chère, think of their love and how almost eight hundred years later it still inspires. Think of us. Only separated for this short spate of time.

"God knows I never sought anything in you except yourself. I wanted simply you, nothing of yours," Héloïse wrote.

Walk around the tomb, search for the symbols of love, of piety, of faithfulness, not so much to God as to each other.

Without trouble, I found the tomb, and when I reached it, I did as Jean Luc suggested. As I peered in, I released my finger, took away the pain. I wanted to hear Jean Luc's voice explaining its significance.

Instantly a cacophony of voices greeted me. Not all alarming, not all intimidating or ominous, not all forlorn, but all overwhelming. I tried to hear Jean Luc in the din, but couldn't pick him out. In my room under the Palais, there were no other dead to drown him out. But here there were too many.

It wasn't my frustration or the two sleeping lovers on their bier that moved me to tears, but the sweet stone puppy with floppy ears asleep at Abelard's feet.

Jean Luc's column included another quote from Héloïse to read after I'd seen the dog.

Ma chère, don't read the next quote from Héloïse until you've noticed the dog, the sculptor's symbol of constancy.

"Let me have a faithful account of all

that concerns you; I would know everything, be it ever so unfortunate. Perhaps by
mingling my sighs with yours I may make
your sufferings less, for it is said that all
sorrows divided are made lighter."

I pressed one hand to my chest, touched the
talisman under my chemise. I'd learned the charm
remained at my body temperature most of the
time. Like any piece of jewelry, I wore it without
noticing it. But when I thought about Jean Luc,
when I reached for my amulet, it reacted—he
reacted—almost immediately. The temperature
change of the crystal affected me in a number of
ways. I became more alert to the sounds in the
ether, as if I could hear the air. And my body
responded as any lover's would, knowing the
other was near. My breasts tingled and my
womb clenched. As if preparing for lovemaking,
my pulse quickened and my blood seemed to
thicken. And the heat! The lovely heat that
traveled from the skin where the talisman lay,
down to the cleft between my legs.

Yes, even there, in the cemetery, touching the
charm, feeling Jean Luc, I throbbed and closed
my eyes and let myself dream for a moment
that my lover was really near, coming to meet
me. He would arrive and take me in his arms,
and he would touch his lips to mine and I'd feel
that same heat, but now it would be from his

flesh and he would be real and my response would be met by a like response and there in the shadow of the ancient lover's tomb he would press up against me and I would feel him, I would feel Jean Luc, and the pressure of his want all up and down the length of my body, and I would know what I wanted was what he wanted.

My reverie shattered with a lonely sound, a crow's caw. I opened my eyes and looked up to see a large black bird against a background of gray clouds. The warmth was gone and I was conscious only of the dampness that promised yet more rain. The crow called again, circling me. I shivered. He seemed to be watching me as intently as I him. Looking back at the newspaper clipping. I read the next of Jean Luc's instructions.

> I think I will let the next grave find you. A little treasure hunt of sorts. Keep your eyes wide, Ma chère. Look for another symbol of the kind of love that, one day, I hope to prove you and I share.

Maybe because of the soft rain now falling, the solemn atmosphere, and the menacing crow, I was reluctant to venture deeper into Père-Lachaise. The shadowy cobblestone alleys looked sinister and unwelcoming. But I'd taken time off from the shop, and come so far. Certainly, the cemetery possessed its ghosts, but they wouldn't harm me.

I'd heard Adolphe Thiers, prime minister under Louis-Philippe, tugged at visitors' clothes if they got too close to his tomb. And that strange translucent lights were visible to those who paid homage at the grave of Allan Kardec, the famous spiritualist, whereas nonbelievers were subject to the terrible scent of sulfur.

But I wasn't there to disturb the inhabitants of the City of the Dead, and hoped they would all understand that as, accompanied by the crow, I searched out Jean Luc's surprise.

I missed it at first and, when I reached the road marked *Chemin Denon*, went back and retraced my steps. There were tombs with broken bronze doors, fanciful angels atop gravestones, sorrowful statues of robed women weeping at the foot of a sepulcher. Nothing fitting the theme of Jean Luc's column.

And then the crow cawed loudly and flew down to perch atop a solemn and simple casket-shaped stone memorial. From the distance, it appeared to be the least adorned gravesite I'd seen. Almost more interested in the bird than the hunt, I inched closer.

The rectangular coffin nestled between two larger tombs. Nothing about it commanded interest. There were no flowers, no trees, no plaque, only block letters carved into the front lip: *Famille P. Legay.*

The name meant nothing to me. I was just

turning to go when the crow, with one last loud caw, took off, flying over my head and into a nearby tree. And that's when I saw what Jean Luc wanted me to see. What the bird had hidden.

He'd been perched on the sculpture gracing the sepulcher, but with him gone I could see it clearly.

Rising as if out of each side of the stone came two sculptured arms from the elbow down, meeting in the middle, holding hands. A man's arm and a woman's arm made of bronze, once shining, now a sour verdigris color from years of exposure to the elements.

Extremely realistic, from the veins running up his arm to her manicured nails and lovely bracelet, the lovers' hands were united forever above their tomb. Eerie, haunting, eternally clasped, the memorial was poignant and utterly magnificent.

None of the others, of so many who journeyed here because of what I wrote, found it. Only you.

"What a romantic you are, Jean Luc," I whispered. "Sending me on a pilgrimage to an ancient lovers' tomb to reassure me, to reassure every woman who read that column, about everlasting love. I wonder how it helped you deal with what you faced on the battlefield to remember this tomb. Yes, we live, and yes, we die. But our passions can survive beyond us."

Chapter 14

"Reports are the tsar's mother is distraught. No one has any information as to the whereabouts of Tsarina Alexandra and the children," Monsieur Orloff said as I walked into the apartment to find him, Grigori, and two other members of the Two-Headed Eagles discussing the news from Russia.

Monsieur looked up at me and nodded. "Anna will be with you in just a moment."

"Why would the Bolsheviks harm them?" Grigori asked, his voice strained.

It must be so hard, I thought, for them to be here, so far from home, so worried about the family they knew and loved. Even though many criticized the royals and said they were out of touch and the country desperately needed a cleansing, the Romanovs remained beloved by many. And to hear Monsieur tell it, the way the Bolshevik regime had taken over and grabbed power was so brutal, they actually aroused sympathy for the tsar and his family among some nonsupporters. The last thing they'd intended.

"Because they are brutes, Grigori," Monsieur said wearily. "Because they are brutes. The Dowager is in exile, she has no money, she's afraid for the lives of everyone in her family. The time for action might be upon us—"

"Opaline, I'm so sorry to keep you waiting." Anna came bustling in to greet me. She and I were soon out the door.

Outside, dusk settled over the city as we walked to the metro. After my experience at Père-Lachaise I'd told Anna that I was desperate and determined to find some way to control my powers now. I'd shown her the silver sheets I'd found at my great-grandmother's house in hopes they might hold a clue, but she couldn't make sense of them. In order to help, she said, she needed certain tools and potions she didn't keep in the apartment. Even though Monsieur didn't visit her secret chamber, he knew of it and tolerated it. But only because she promised him she'd never keep anything suspect there in case the police ever got wind of her abilities and forced an inspection.

So when necessary, she called on her cousin Galina Trevoda, who was, like Anna, a Russian mystic schooled in the occult, and borrowed her workspace.

The metro left us off at rue de Courcelles, and we walked two blocks before turning onto rue Daru. Halfway down the street, I saw the gold onion domes of the Cathédrale Saint-Alexandre-Nevsky afire in the setting sun.

"But this is a church," I said to Anna. "I came here with my parents a few weeks ago for the wedding of my mother's friend."

"Picasso? The painter who married the Russian dancer?" Anna asked.

"Yes."

"Well, this is where Galina lives and works. She's the cathedral's caretaker."

"Do they know?"

"That she's a mystic?"

I nodded.

"The bishop is her brother, so no one delves too deeply or looks too closely. Yes, she must be careful, but really no more careful than any of us need to be these days."

We entered the stone edifice and went into the narthex and past the holy water font.

"At the wedding, I saw people filling up jars from here. What were they doing?" I asked.

"We don't bless ourselves with the water the way Catholics do; we take it home to drink."

Our footsteps echoed as we crossed the foyer and stepped into the nave.

A whole golden universe opened up before me, glittering and glowing.

"It's stunning," I said, marveling at the opulent interior. "So different when it's not crowded. I couldn't see any of it during the wedding."

"The church was built almost sixty years ago," Anna said, "long before anyone dreamed so many Russians would emigrate to France. Its congregation far exceeds its space now."

A mysterious atmosphere, redolent with

incense, swirled around us. In the still silence, I heard a bird's wings flapping and looked up into the golden mosaic of the high vaulted apse. Almost afraid to see if it was a crow, I watched for it to come swooping down, but it stayed invisible.

Like the ceiling, the walls were decorated with ornate gold and jewel tone mosaics. In every corner, golden shrines glittered in gilded niches. Icons graced every table. Not an inch of the interior was unadorned. I looked at Anna's face, at my hands. The reflection bathed both of us. We too were turned to gold.

"It's like being inside of a jewel box."

"You don't need to whisper," Anna said as she hooked her arm in mine. "The service has been over for hours. Come, it's this way."

She led me behind the sacristy, through an arched gilt door. We entered a hallway. Gone were the mosaics and icons. Here the walls were bare stone. The only adornments, the clergy's robes hanging on hooks and various religious objects sitting on utilitarian shelves.

We came to a narrow iron staircase. I dreaded taking the first step. Were there burial chambers here too? Would the voices reach out to me?

Anna had already started. "Opaline?"

"I'm coming."

I followed her down the steps, which emptied into a crypt. Narrow, darkened passageways led to the right and left. The cooler temperature reminded me of our underground at the Palais, though far more damp.

"There's a world beneath every building and street in Paris, isn't there?" I asked.

Anna nodded. "When the architects found these particular grottoes, they were going to close them up, but the bishop asked for them to be connected to the church, because every soul requires secret places for contemplation as well as open spaces for celebration."

"Are people buried down here?" I'd begun to hear far-off murmurs and feared the messaging had started up again in this dark, dank foreign place.

She shook her head. "No, those are flesh-and-blood voices you hear from up above, traveling via air shafts."

As we continued on, the murmurs lessened and became inaudible and all was silent except for our footsteps. When it seemed we could go no farther, Anna turned right into one of the dark alcoves and stopped in front of a wooden door.

Before she could knock, it creaked open.

I froze. Too unsettling, the ambiance, like being inside of an Edgar Allan Poe poem or Leroux's underground opera house, made me anxious. Letting out a shout, I jumped back just as a pale, luminous face appeared in the doorway.

"My dear, dear Anna. I'm so glad to see you," a lyrical female voice with a heavy Russian accent greeted us.

In the darkness, the woman's head seemed disembodied. Not hidden in the shadows, but part of them. Then she opened the door wider, and I saw how a trick of the light and Galina's black hooded robe combined to create the frightening effect.

The two cousins embraced and kissed each other's cheeks, and then Anna introduced us.

"Come in, come in." Galina opened the door wider.

Following the women, I stepped over the cracked stone doorjamb into a small chamber lit with candles. The walls were covered with dozens of embroidered silk wall hangings. I recognized astrological signs I used on my talismans and the runes and symbols from my mother's books and the silver sheets I'd taken from the bell tower. These were the keys to the portal where she practiced her dark arts, to the spirit world beyond what science has been able to explain.

My mother learned to be who she became in Paris twenty-four years ago, before I was born. In running away from her, I'd come to the same place, thinking I was escaping, but over and over again I kept running headlong into my own version of the same crisis she'd faced.

Coincidence, I thought, was merely the word we gave occurrences we couldn't explain any other way.

"So you are Opaline," Galina Trevoda said. "I've heard much about you."

"And I you," I responded.

While not as striking as her cousin, Galina looked more ethereal. Her parchment skin and pale lips set off black, glittering eyes that made me think of the jet I worked with. Anna told me she was in her seventies, but Galina didn't appear any older than her fifty-five-year-old cousin.

"Welcome to my humble abode." She smiled and gestured to the tiny cell. "So I will leave you to your work and get back to mine. I have chores upstairs. Just come find me when you are ready to leave, Anna." She turned to me. "I hope your time here is productive."

After Galina closed the door behind her, Anna offered me a seat at a small table in the corner of the room, already set with a tea service and more candles and covered with an embroidered silk cloth, a large pentagram in its center.

"Let's get started and see if we can find you some relief. I know how frightening messaging is for you, especially since you think you're under the power's control instead of the other way around."

"Yes, and the cries at the cemetery and down in the catacombs, they've intensified. I need to block them out, Anna."

"The first thing you have to do is let go of being frightened. If the spirits feel unwelcome, they leave behind a residual psychic sludge. The universe has bestowed a marvelous gift upon you . . . the kind that should be treasured, but you don't see it that way, do you?"

"No. You've said that before, but the messages . . . the voices . . . are so invasive. I don't know where they come from or why they come to me at all."

"I believe they derive from the unchallenged universe and the uncharted waters lying between our consciousness and the next realm." Anna made broad expansive gestures as she spoke, her bracelets noisily orchestrating her words.

I was attempting to keep up, but I didn't understand. Anna, sensing my confusion, explained.

"The lockets allow you the opportunity to give all of these souls a voice. The last gift the earth has for them—a way for them to comfort those they've left behind. When people pass on suddenly, especially when taken under unnatural circumstances, like wars, murders, or violent accidents, what's been left undone and unsaid haunts them.

"We talk of ghosts haunting us, our homes, our graveyards, but it is the other way around. The souls of the departed are haunted by *our* grief. We need to give *them* solace and put them at peace so *they* can move on. More so for their sake than for our own. To help these departed souls be able to do that is truly a gift."

My sudden tears surprised me. Reaching up, I

brushed them away. When I replaced my hand on the table, Anna took it in her own.

"It's hard, I know. It takes a toll. But you need to see it for the miracle it is."

"It may be a miracle to you, but I can't tolerate it. I need to be able to stop it."

"I know, and I'm going to work to help you take control as much as possible."

"Only as much as possible?"

"It's not in my power. I'm only human. We believe there are spirits who assign abilities such as yours based on available candidates."

"You mean some otherworldly spirit chose me to do this?"

"Yes."

"God?"

Anna knew about my religious upbringing. Or lack of it. My father, a Christian turned atheist, believed only in the power of art. My mother, although born Jewish, eschewed all formal religion, but believed in both the power of art and of magick and claimed they were connected and that every true artist was part magician. Neither of my parents schooled me or my siblings in any faith other than faith in ourselves. I didn't want to insult her by questioning her belief.

"It's all right if you don't believe," she said as if reading my thoughts. "You're not insulting me, Opaline. I've never judged you. You know that. Faith isn't ever easy to embrace, especially in times like these. With so many millions of men being wounded and dying, of course one questions the validity and the justice of any being who would allow such atrocities to take place. Don't worry. It's not necessary to have faith in order to understand what's happening to you and learn to control it better. Religion, spiritualism, magick, and alchemy are all aligned. I see it like a big kettle hanging over a fire. Everything that's not of our plane, that's not visible or tangible, has been thrown in and cooks. Some people take out a spoonful and taste a formal religion. Others a mystical or pagan tradition."

"And you taste a little of each," I said.

"I do." She smiled. "My mother was a mystic. I learned from her until she died. Orphaned. The nuns took me in and taught me their religion while managing not to destroy mine. I became a composite of my mother's knowledge and the church's teachings. I stand in a unique corner of the room."

I'd never heard her story before but understood her better now that I had.

"So, let us see what we can do for you. Even if you are a little heathen, can you keep an open mind to the idea of the spirit world? To the concept that there are powers beyond our ability to understand?"

I'd seen my mother accomplish strange feats. I'd heard objects speaking to me since childhood. Since coming to Paris and making my first locket, I'd heard voices, pitiful, searching, pained voices. I had no choice but to keep an open mind. I nodded.

"First we need to test the limitations and reach of your abilities. Then our goal will be to try to train you to lower a curtain—or shut a door—on the voices when they come unbidden and hopefully still allow you to focus on them when you need to."

"We can do that right now?" Even though she'd couched her comments with maybes and uncertainty, I only heard her sliver of hope.

Anna laughed. "Always so impatient. We can start, but it might not happen all in one session."

"How long?"

"I can't tell. It might take several weeks, perhaps months. There's no way to know how much training you need. How adept you are. Before we begin, though, we should talk first about the ramifications of this training. Opaline, I'm going to try to teach you to—"

"I opened the door, there *has* to be a way to shut it—" I interrupted her.

"Yes, there will be a way to shut it. The issue is that there's a real possibility that if you shut it even once, it might stay shut."

Picturing a large metal door like the one to the vault under the shop, I imagined shoving it closed.

"Forever? I might not be able to open it again for even one voice?"

She nodded.

If she was right, if I did close it forever and stopped hearing voices . . . if all the voices went away, Jean Luc would go away too. Was the risk worth the loss? I shivered. What did it mean that I could even ask myself that? What was Jean Luc really but an incorporeal dream?

"You still want me to try?"

I nodded. "I think so."

Anna stood, went to the shelves, and began pulling down jars. As she opened one after the other, taking out pinches and handfuls of dried leaves and powders, the cavern became redolent with a strange, mysterious scent. Adding a few drops of oil to the mixture, she ground it in a mortar with a pestle and then poured it into a glass. In the candlelight it glittered gold, almost as if she'd ground down some of the mosaics from the walls of the cathedral above us.

Next, Anna uncorked a dark green bottle and poured some of its liquid into the glass. Suddenly I smelled apples—the scent that always accompanied my messaging. Usually it made me queasy, but there, in the cavern, it caused no ill effect.

Finally, Anna unscrewed a jar, dug in a spoon, scooped out honey, and stirred it into the concoction. An aura appeared around the mixture, as if it were lit from within. Or was it just the candlelight's reflection?

"You've always said that when you make the lockets you smell apples."

"Yes."

"Do you know why apples are connected to the talismans?"

I shook my head.

"Try to remember that very first time. Tell me about it."

I closed my eyes and thought back. "I was in the studio . . ."

"Picture it in your mind. Do you see yourself there?"

I nodded.

"Look around . . ."

In my mind I glanced around the workshop.

"Do you see anything unusual? Pavel loves apples, was there one on his table?"

I shook my head.

"Look down at your workspace," Anna said.

"Yes, yes. I can't believe I forgot. You'd brought tea right before the customer arrived. Apples and little cakes.

"I put the plate of food away when I went to help Madame Maboussine. Her son had been killed at the front, she said. And she'd remembered how her grandmother had worn mourning jewelry and wanted to memorialize her son in that old-fashioned way. As soon as she handed me the lock of his hair, my head filled with noise initiating an avalanche of pain. Suddenly the scent of the apple—still on my fingers, I suppose—became overwhelming."

I told Anna how the next day, while working on the design for the amulet, I incorporated the apple quarters into the design. I was basing the locket's design on an ancient Etruscan rock crystal amulet I'd seen in the Louvre. An orb nestled in two bands of gold. One wrapping it horizontally, the other vertically, with a hook at the top for a cord. A lock of hair sandwiched between two halves of the crystal. I was drawing it when Anna came into the workshop with that afternoon's tea. Once again bringing little cakes and apples cut into quarters. I'd stared at the fruit, the sections, the slices, suddenly getting the idea to cut the rock crystal into slices like the apple, then etch in the symbols for the soldier's astrological sign along with his birth date and death date and decorate them with his birth-stone. A commemoration of his being born and mourning of his being gone.

"So the apple was connected to the talisman twice."

"Yes, the first time when Madame Maboussine came in and I'd been eating the apple . . . its odor still on my fingers. The second, while designing the piece. I hadn't realized it."

Anna nodded. "Let me see your palm." Reaching

out for my hand, she turned it over and studied the underside. She'd first done this a long time ago, when I was thirteen and we'd just met.

She pointed to the crescent-moon-shaped scar on the fleshy part of my thumb. "I don't remember this from before."

"While I was working on the talisman later that day. I cut myself with a carving tool. It slipped."

"And bled?"

"Quite a bit. It made me sick to my stomach."

"Was that the first time you became nauseated in relation to the talismans?"

"I hadn't thought about that connection before, but yes . . ."

"So you'd been aware of the smell of the apples before, but the scent hadn't made you sick. That only happened when you cut yourself?"

"I think so, yes."

"And now, still, you conjure the smell of apples when you work on a piece and feel ill."

"Yes."

"Did you hear Madame Maboussine's son's voice while you made the locket?" Anna asked.

"No, that didn't happen until I gave it to her and she put it on. At first it was just a faraway whisper. A young man's voice: *Tell her even though I'm gone, she's my mother forever. Tell her, please, for me.*"

"What did you do?"

"I excused myself, got up, and went into the

showroom, thinking someone was there. But there wasn't. I opened the door to the staircase, thinking I'd heard someone below, but the stairwell was empty."

"You didn't realize yet?"

"No."

"Or you didn't want to."

"I was convinced I'd heard someone whispering. His voice was that clear and distinct. I just didn't know where it was coming from."

"How did you feel?" she asked.

"Confused and afraid."

Anna nodded. Then, in the quiet, I suddenly heard chanting. Panic rose in me like bile.

Anna noticed my expression. Instantly, she tried to calm me. "I hear it as well," she said reassuringly. "It's the monks chanting."

I relaxed.

"I believe that in the moment you cut yourself and bled over the soldier's hair, you lowered the curtain between our plane and the one beyond."

I shivered.

"What is it?" she asked.

"A saying in my family having to do with blood."

She nodded. " 'Make of the blood, a stone. Make of a stone, a powder. Make of a powder, life everlasting.' Is that the one?"

"How do you know it? Did my mother tell you?"

"No. I knew about it before I met her. Most of us who are involved in the occult here in Paris know of it. It's referred to as 'the curse and the blessing of La Lune.'"

"But it wasn't complete. I remember my mother sitting with me in the bell tower the year I turned thirteen . . . an ancient worn leather-bound book opened before us. La Lune's grimoire—my mother explained how the spells were encrypted in the text. My mother said there is a quarto of missing pages that were believed to contain a poem, each canto holding a secret of the universe. Each, an enigma revealing a power. To ensure the poem never went missing, La Lune wrote out each canto separately and hid them somewhere else. My mother discovered the blood stanza when she was just about my age, in her grand-mother's house. The others, she told me, were still lost. But I think I might have found them."

I fingered the ring I wore on my right hand. The ruby floret given to me by my mother when I first got my menses. Part of the La Lune legacy, she'd said, and told me it would protect me and never to take it off.

Anna nodded at my hand. "The crescent on your thumb . . . is it the only one on your body?"

"No, I have a birthmark on my back in a similar shape."

"The sign of every Daughter of La Lune."

"My mother only uses that name to sign her paintings. The real La Lune died in the sixteen hundreds."

"And all her female descendants are called Daughters of La Lune. If you'd let your mother school you in their rituals, you'd be able to use them to quiet the voices."

"But I didn't want to learn. I'd grown to hate what made her different. What kept me and my sisters separate from everyone else. I just wanted to be normal."

What did I even know about a normal life? Did I have a taste of it with Timur? Maybe for a moment, but my powers hadn't even allowed me to enjoy a normal relationship with him.

"All right. Let's see what we can do about it now. The German philosopher Nietzsche said if you gaze too long into the abyss, the abyss will also gaze into you. This is a dangerous journey we are undertaking. You must be prepared. First, I'd like you to drink this . . ." Anna handed me the glass of golden liquid she'd concocted while we'd talked.

"What is it?"

"A combination of herbs, honey, and juice to make you less nervous and more receptive."

"It's safe?"

"Of course." She took the glass from me, tipped it to her lips, and sipped. Then she handed it back to me and I drank it down, surprised at its deliciousness, relieved the fermented apples didn't nauseate me.

The chanting I'd heard before started up again,

more loudly this time. The sonorous ensemble of men using their voices as instruments seemed to be coming through the walls and the ceilings to surround me like a cloak, cosseting me, seeping through my skin, entering me. I closed my eyes and the gold and jewel-toned mosaics from the cathedral swam in the darkness, a kaleidoscope of rubelites, peridots, wine-colored rubies, midnight sapphires, royal amethysts, citrines, sea green emeralds—fractured facets of gems— brilliant and blinding.

"Open your eyes," Anna whispered.

She looked like a portrait in stained glass. Her face and clothes turned into prismatic designs pulsing in time to the chants. I floated on the sounds, lifted up in invisible arms.

"Opaline, can you hear me?"

I responded but too softly, and she asked a second time. I made a greater effort. "Yes." The word sounded loud and harsh in my ears. As if the entire world coalesced in my voice.

"All right. You can close your eyes again. Just listen and relax."

I sensed a light pressure on my forehead in between my eyebrows. Then heat. Her finger pressing warmth into me.

"Can you feel this? This is the spot we need to focus on . . ." She took my hand and replaced her finger with mine. The heat dissipated. "This is your third eye . . . In Hinduism it's called the eye of clairvoyance; in Buddhism it's called Urna . . . in Egypt, the Eye of Osiris . . . in Hebrew they say it is the eye of the soul." She took my hand away and replaced my finger with hers. The heat returned. "Once I've taught you to open your third eye, you will be able to use this portal and reach inside yourself and access all your abilities. You will be able to speak to the voices through your third eye."

Her pronouncements merged with the chanting until they were one and the same. Her words, their rhythm. Their cadence, her phrases. Her finger burned my skin. Setting me on fire. All calm left. Anxiety took over. Raged. Nightmare images filled my mind. A black smoking field . . . smoldering trees . . . the bitter stench of hair on fire . . . my hair?

Reaching up, I tried to push her hand away, but she held fast. I wanted to rise . . . run . . . get away from her . . . from the chant . . . from the fire. Around my neck the talisman felt hot . . . heat increasing every second . . . heat devouring me . . . Suddenly faces swam into my mind. Unfamiliar. Each in uniform . . . tattered . . . dirty . . . torn . . . Each face—younger, older, fair, swarthy—each in agony . . . suffering, in pain . . .

One by one, I saw them, suffered with them, then watched as their misery seemed to melt through and each face lost all its color and settled into a peaceful black mask.

Who were these men? I didn't understand my own vision. Until I saw one I did recognize. Madame Maboussine's son. She'd shown me his picture. Twenty-one years old. His face contorted. Screaming mouth hole. The shout no less frightening for its silence. His expression exploded, distorting, finally settling into a pale, sad smile.

And then I knew I was seeing the men I'd messaged. In the process, they became part of me and I them. And while their final peaceful visages should have comforted me, they didn't. Their terror was imprinted on me. I was reliving it.

I started to scream—at least I thought I was screaming—but it was their collective voices I heard, their horrible, terrified shrieks and openmouthed bleeding cries.

Anna's pressure on the spot between my eyebrows increased. Their voices and my screaming softened, lowered, turned into bells, large bronze bells, clanging over and over, and even though they were no longer hideous, they were still clamoring, still disturbing.

I couldn't listen anymore, couldn't watch. I needed to quiet them, to silence them, to stop the pictures and the sounds, and I pushed myself away from the table and stood up and then there was nothing but blackness and blessed calm.

Chapter 15

Once I'd recovered from my fainting spell, Anna made me tea laced with cognac and lavender honey and served me little Russian tea cakes her cousin had left for us and insisted I try to eat. But I couldn't. She sat with me and encouraged me, but all I could do was cry. My tears of frustration flowed freely, and she tried her best to comfort me, but I was inconsolable. I'd put so much faith into our session. I'd expected to walk away with the ability to be in control. Instead, nothing had changed. I'd only learned that if I tried to close the portal, I might never be able to open it again.

"It's a gift," Anna said, smoothing down my hair. "And you need to embrace it and trust we will find a way to help you live with it."

"It's not a gift," I insisted. "It's a nightmare."

"Part of the secret to being able to control it is not being so frightened of it . . . not hating this ability quite so much."

"Anna, the war is right inside my mind. I hear these men who have died. Some are still caught up in their pain, haven't forgotten it yet, are traumatized by it. Others are so worried about those they are leaving behind, they can't sever the connection. Lost, missing their families, they are in some terrible limbo."

"But they don't stay there, do they?"

"What do you mean?"

"Let's agree you are receiving messages the soldiers leave in the passage vortex between life and death. That these final thoughts linger in some kind of psychic tunnel waiting for you to retrieve them so the soldiers can take their last step out of this realm."

"Yes, fine."

"And once you listen to the messages and pass them on, the soldiers move on?"

I nodded.

"So if you focused on that, maybe you would be more accepting. After all, none of them stay with you, do they? Once you give a mother or sister or wife her talisman, that soldier's voice is gone, isn't it?"

"Yes . . ." I wanted to tell her about Jean Luc, but something stopped me.

She didn't notice my hesitation.

"So your actions relieve them of all their pain and suffering. You unhaunt them, if you will. Do you see?"

I nodded.

"That's why it's a gift. You give them the permission they need to move past the pain and step into the light."

"And if I were to keep hearing a voice, what would that mean?"

"I'm not sure. Has that happened?"

If I told her about Jean Luc, would she think there was in fact something wrong with my mind? That I was making him up? What if she called my mother in Cannes and my parents came to get me? Would Jean Luc come with me? What of my work at the shop? The help I was giving the women who came to see me? Could I abandon them?

"No, it hasn't," I lied.

"So if you look at the process this way, wouldn't the burden feel less onerous?"

"I suppose. I just wish . . ." I shrugged. "I still wish I didn't need to bear witness to their agony."

Once again, she smoothed down my unruly hair, and then bent down and kissed me.

"Let's go home. We won't give up, Opaline. We'll work it out."

I lay in bed after Anna left, my hand creeping up to my chest, cupping the talisman. I kept thinking about the ramifications of what I'd undertaken. If I closed the door and couldn't open it again, I would be letting go of Jean Luc.

The gold began to heat against my skin. I turned on the light, and I pulled out the book of Jean Luc's columns I'd borrowed from Madame

Alouette and opened it to where I'd left off. The next column after the one about Héloïse and Abelard.

Don't read that one.

Jean Luc's voice.

"Why?"

It's too sad and you're already so very sad.

"How do you know?"

I was with you today.

"How does this work?" Suddenly shy, I put my hand up to my chest. I hadn't yet gotten used to the idea of him being able to see me without me realizing.

I'm not totally sure myself. I'm not always cognizant of you. But when I am, I have a feeling I'm warm. Which isn't how I feel the rest of the time.

"Do you try to see me or does it happen without you making an effort?"

I have to make an effort.

"Can you hear me too? What I'm thinking?"

If you direct a question to me in your thoughts, but it's far easier for me if you do speak out loud.

"How do you do it?"

I don't know.

"How does my voice sound to you when I'm just thinking?"

The same. As if we are connected by hollow threads that allow sound to travel back and forth. But I'll always let you know I'm there. I won't spy on you.

"How?"

The warmth.

"Where are you the rest of the time?" I asked.

I don't know. My awareness isn't constant. But when I am with you, I'm in the least amount of discomfort. Not that I'm ever in acute pain. Oh damn, I've spent my life using words precisely and now I can barely figure out my state of being.

I laughed. Then thought how odd—either I was laughing at an invention of my own mind or at a ghost. And if he was an invention of my mind, then I was ill, wasn't I?

You aren't.

He'd read my thoughts.

I may not be quite real the way people in your life are, but I'm myself and not someone you invented. Just think, Opaline, if you were to invent a fantasy lover, wouldn't you make him much more exotic than me? I'm just a bourgeois journalist who can't even dance well.

And then he laughed. I'd never heard him laugh before. A joyful sound, it reminded me of the time before the war when young men drank champagne with women in cafés and bought them violet posies and the sound of cabaret music lingered in the air, mixing with the perfume women wore, all making the very streets of Paris, like the lives lived there, seductive and delightful.

I loved the sound of Jean Luc's laughter and tried to memorize it, for I feared this strange experience would not last. The dead do not linger for long. Jean Luc would do what he must and move on.

I'd been sitting up in bed, my back against the pillows. It seemed one of them had slipped down and I reached to prop it back up. But the pillow sat in place. What was I feeling?

"Jean Luc?"

Yes.

"Is that you?"

Yes, I'm trying to get the hang of this. So you can feel that, can you?

"I can."

I heard a soft chuckle.

And this?

He'd moved his hand to my shoulder and stroked it. Though I wasn't quite feeling a hand. The warm breeze seemed to have coalesced into a form.

"Yes. Do you feel anything?"

No. I don't seem to be whole. I don't get hungry or thirsty either. But I have emotions.

"You're upset about your men."

More than upset. If I'd been smarter, I would have realized we were walking into a trap. I would have—

"Stop. Please. It's pointless. Regret isn't like

grief; it never lessens, just stays the same. A little hard ball in the pit of your stomach."

What do you have to regret?

So he hadn't listened to the whole story I'd told Anna.

"A boy went off to war, and all he wanted was my promise to wait for him."

You didn't give it?

"No."

Why?

"I should have, even if I didn't love him. Realized he needed me and it wouldn't hurt me to just tell him. But I didn't love him. Not the way you wrote about love in your column. A grand love, you wrote. Did you have a love that grand?" I asked him.

No. I never did. Did you?

"No, and I wouldn't want to. It would be too painful if it failed."

But to experience it once—even if it is painful—don't you think it would be worth it? Wouldn't you want to know what that kind of intensity is like? Wouldn't you want to feel that deeply?

"I don't think most people can. Not the way I imagine it."

Tell me what you imagine.

Leaning over, I shut off the light. If we were going to have a complete conversation, it wouldn't be as peculiar in the darkness. I'd be less conscious of the empty room.

"I wouldn't think it happens easily or often. Never for some people. I imagine a love like that is like a fire . . . starting with a spark and growing into a blaze . . . becoming an engulfing passion too hot for most people to withstand."

But don't you think a passion that strong would last? Even as glowing embers. Always illuminating the blackness. Always giving some warmth in the cold.

"It seems so tragic to me, but you make it sound wonderful."

And it would be . . . to always possess the memory of what was possible. Of what could be. Tell me, what do you think it takes to make that first spark?

"What does it take to make a grain of sand become a pearl? They say the sand is an irritant. Maybe love starts that way too. You're alone in yourself and then meet someone who upsets your balance, who you can't quite explain away or put in a comfortable place. Someone who shakes your very soul. Who has ideas that jar you and make you think. Who does more than understand you, who understands what you need."

Who shakes your soul. That's lovely.

The warmth around my shoulders slipped down my back. Encircled my waist. I'd been kissed before, often enough by Timur, by Grigori, but Jean Luc's kiss wasn't like theirs. It began dancing on my lips, pressing on my mouth, and at the same time on my breasts and then at the same time between my legs. Creating sensations all over my body in the one instant. I became the spark about to combust. I smelled his scent of pungent limes, verbena, and myrrh. So intoxicating, at once forbidden and teasing. Like the ghost who now lay on top of me, beckoning me to slide into his dark embrace and get lost within sensation.

How was he stroking me? How could he be moving me to distraction? How was this ephemeral being making my heart race and my breath come in shorter and shorter spurts? A force building deep inside of me beat to a rhythm I couldn't hear but my blood responded to. A spark burst into tiny tickling flames, the flames licking the cleft between my legs, my legs pressing together as the gathering tightened and tightened more and then exploded into fragments of fire . . . a hundred tiny pinpricks of sensation reaching up and up and then finally slowing, easing, so nothing existed but the feeling of my heart pounding with excitement and the sound of the blood rushing faster and faster.

And then it ended. As I caught my breath, I waited to hear what he would say. How he would describe what had occurred.

"Jean Luc?"

No response.

"Jean Luc?"

I waited, but still no response. If he'd been there, he wasn't any longer. The tears came then and surprised me with their intensity. I wanted him to be real. He made me feel as if I belonged to someone and someone belonged to me. As if I'd found my place in the world. Except he wasn't in this world with me. His body had burned in a terrible explosion that destroyed dozens of lives. Ash on a field at the front. He wasn't supposed to have died there like that. I was sure of it. He was supposed to come home. So we could meet. So a true spark might have ignited. So when he kissed me, he'd be able to feel my lips on his. I fell asleep with tears still flowing, clutching the talisman, wondering into what darkness my phantom lover had disappeared.

Chapter 16

In the morning, I went down to the shop and suffered through the work waiting for me, looking at the clock every quarter hour until I could finally take off my apron, put down my tools, and tell Monsieur Orloff I would be going out for a few hours on an errand during my lunch break.

With Jean Luc's talisman against my breast, with his words in my ears, I walked to the Louvre. Because I hadn't grown up in Paris, only visiting my great-grandmother for short periods, there were many attractions I either hadn't seen or hadn't seen enough of—like the great museum. And since I'd moved to Paris, the Louvre had been closed for more days than it had been open to the public. As I approached, I hoped that afternoon would be an exception.

Ahead of me, the ancient palace that had seen so many kings and queens, tragedies and intrigues, stood solid against the ravages of time. Stepping onto the plaza in front of the museum, I felt a surge of anticipation at visiting another of Jean Luc's haunts. I had one of his unpublished columns with me. I'd copied it out so I could bring it and not miss a step of its instructions.

The Louvre was in fact open. Inside, the sheer size and grandeur of the palace overwhelmed me. To reach the first stop on Jean Luc's tour, I climbed an ornate marble staircase. He'd written about how often he thought of the royalty who'd taken the same steps so long ago, so long dead. The concept intrigued me.

We walk in the footsteps of so many who are forgotten. What of them lingers? Do we leave some aspect of ourselves in the places we live and others we visit? If my eyes could see a plane other than this one, would the atmosphere be crowded with people who'd passed through the same halls?

I reached the first landing. Had Jean Luc stood here? Gazing up at the tall ceilings, every corner and crevice decorated in the most elaborate designs of the era, I wondered if he'd noticed the same details.

I stopped at a high arched window overlooking the courtyard. Where war-weary Parisians walked now, in search of an hour's respite, kings and queens and nobility had once trod the same ground, weary of their own wars.

Ma chère,
The inconstancy of love is easy to speak of. We bemoan a lover's treacheries and make light of an ex-lover's faults. What I think of out here is the love immortalized in art. For those who hear of it in song, or on the stage, or who read of it in poetry

or novels, or who see it in a painting or sculpture—it is everlasting. And offers solace to those of us who witness endless examples of instantaneous disaster here, in the muck and mud, amidst the sounds of cannons and gunfire.

Once you enter the museum, turn right and go into the Richelieu wing. Take the staircase to the first floor, and opposite the café, walk to room 4, where you can find objects from the Middle Ages. Here is our first stop on our lovers' journey: the tapestry of a lady and her love. In the 1400s, when this lovely piece was made, the most popular story told was *The Romance of the Rose*. It tells the tale of a suitor's progress through a garden of love. Here in this tapestry, he is offering her a declaration of his devotion. Look, even the animals and the flowers encircle and bind the lovers together. Step closer and look at the gift he is giving her—a heart—a symbol of his love.

Next, you will need to go to room 37 in the French collection. Stand in front of the small painting called *Le Faux Pas*, painted by Watteau in 1717. Of the time, Voltaire wrote that it was the age of licentiousness, and freedom was expressed not only in how people indulged in pleasures, but how they were celebrated in the arts, music, and poetry.

Stand closer and enter into the intimacy of the two lovers. A staged game of love and chance. Be the voyeur.

Have you ever watched two people make love? If you aren't observed, it can be exhilarating. I did once and was mesmerized by the passion with which the man kissed the woman and held her. The delicate way she responded. For several minutes, I couldn't even take a breath.

Before I could follow Jean Luc's instructions to the next room, his voice stopped me from moving forward.

What I didn't write was . . . If I were there with you now in the gallery, I would touch your neck behind your ear, with my lips, and whisper to you to just look at the painting. Not to turn to me. And while you studied the Watteau, my lips would travel down your neck until you'd need to put your hand out to steady yourself.

Jean Luc's lips pressed on my skin. Indeed my neck was warm, growing warmer still as I studied the small painting. My cheeks flushed. A mother and teenage daughter entered the room, their presence an intrusion.

I moved on and followed Jean Luc's instructions to the next room, where my next assignment was to study a painting entitled *The Bolt*, by the French master Fragonard sometime around 1777.

Positioning myself in front of the canvas, I studied the violent and sensual embrace between a man and a woman in her bedroom. Although it was a fairly small painting, Jean Luc wrote that it burst with love and desire. He said I should examine first how the strong shaft of light, almost the focal point of the work, illuminated the three major clues as to the painting's meaning: the man pushing the bolt on the door as he grabs his lover, the rumpled messy bed, and the ripe apple on his lover's nightstand, which symbolized the fruit of Eve, the fruit of sin.

Had I ever stood so long in front of a painting before? The longer I remained, the more fully I entered its dark sensuous world. I sensed the tension in the male lover's legs as he pushed against his mistress. And her teasing halfhearted retreat away from him. But why was he bolting the door when, from the appearance of the room, they'd already enjoyed their amorous respite? Was he unbolting the door and she stopping him from leaving?

Suddenly, I started to see erotic symbolism in every aspect of the painting. Every inch seethed with unspent passion. The upturned chair looked now like legs up in the air. The vase and the roses suggested the woman's genitals. And the bed itself. I sighed. It echoed the woman's sensuality, suggesting folds of flesh. Oh, to be with Jean Luc in that bed with its deep downy pillows that looked like breasts, enclosed by the blood-red velvet curtains keeping out the world.

Alone in the room, I shocked myself by pressing my hand to my breast and holding it there. Feeling the pressure. Wanting it to be Jean Luc's hand. Wanting him to be there in flesh and blood and pressed up against me the way the man in the painting pressed up to his lover. The sensations between my legs were so strong I leaned against the wall. How could I be aroused like this, alone, with no one near? Just from looking at a painting, from reading a dead man's words?

There were more paintings to stop and stare at and wonder about, but I ignored them as I thought about a man who knew the Louvre so well that from a trench in Vichy he could put together a lover's art tour and recall the room numbers of these works and their nuances.

It wasn't just his romantic nature I thought about as I headed to the next piece; it wasn't just his knowledge. Jean Luc's delight delighted me, his interests interested me, his fascinations fascinated me.

And now we come to the most erotic and strange piece of all, one which might make you uncomfortable. I ask you to begin your journey from afar. Do you see the full-size marble sculpture of the sleeping figure? Slightly to the left? Wait. Don't look at its name yet. Don't circle it. Position yourself so you are looking at the figure's back. Take in the curves and the languid pose. You want to touch it, don't you? Run your fingers down the sinuous spine. Feel the satiny skin. If there are no guards in the room, do it. Dare it. Risk it. You won't be disappointed. Finger the curve of the waist, thrill to the velvet. Almost impossible this is stone, isn't it? You want to slip your fingers between the figure's thighs, don't you . . . to feel the warmth . . . so inviting, isn't it?

Now, slowly walk to the sculpture's feet and then around so you can view the piece's other side. Let your eyes travel up from the ankles to the calves, the knees, the thighs. Surprised? Ah yes, so was I.

There in all their crude beauty are his genitals. Now, Ma chère, look at his chest. How is it possible? Beautiful female breasts as well as a fully formed penis.

Gaze on the face of *The Sleeping Hermaphrodite*. What a marvel, isn't it? From some angles a lovely naked woman and from others a lusty young man. Curves and cravings.

According to scholars, this work was typical of Hellenistic art, designed to tease and provide surprise. The statue is a Roman antiquity found in 1608. Eleven years later Cardinal Borghese commissioned the great Italian sculptor Bernini to carve the sumptuous mattress as a base.

Do you know the story of Hermaphroditus, son of Hermes and Aphrodite? The water nymph Salmacis fell in love with the handsome boy and tried to seduce him, but he rejected her. Unable to resign herself to the loss, she begged Zeus to unite them and he did, merging them into one bisexed figure.

Scholars at the Louvre say this "utopian combination of two sexes is sometimes interpreted as a half-playful, half-erotic creation, designed to illustrate Platonic and more general philosophical reflections on love."

The eroticism of the god lying in abandon, half asleep on the sensual bed, repels some who gaze upon him, but not I. I find this hermaphrodite the ultimate embodiment of the coming together of man and woman. A metaphor for sexual desire, a visualizing of the dichotomy in each of us, for don't we all, whether man or woman, want to be taken and take, want to be aroused and arouse, don't we all want to desire and be desired and find that one soul who completes us as we complete them?

Aristotle said it best: "The aim of art is to represent not the outward appearance of things, but their inner significance."

The column came to its close. I stood, staring at the hermaphrodite. Imagining Jean Luc beside me. And then I heard his voice.

For me, and hopefully for you, Ma chère, the sculpture is titillating, yes? This is the miracle of art to me, why we must preserve and protect it. The artist alone can take the grotesque and make it beautiful, can take the confusing and explain it. The individuality of each one of us who creates must be protected and encouraged. For only in art do we learn who we are and of what we are made.

Chapter 17

When the last post of the day was delivered, Monsieur finished sorting through it, crossed the room to my workstation, and ceremoniously handed me a small package with my mother's handwriting on the label and an assortment of stamps in the corner.

Usually my father wrote, adding an addendum from my mother. So something from her alone aroused my curiosity.

Inside, well wrapped to protect it from the journey, I found one of her miniature triptychs: three paintings hinged together and folded up into a compact objet d'art no larger than a book. The delicate wood framing had obviously been done in my father's atelier, in Art Nouveau lines as sensuous as my mother's own painting style.

During the Middle Ages, triptychs were a standard format for altar paintings and adorned many churches and cathedrals. Smaller versions served as movable chapels for their owners to pray to while traveling.

Borrowing the form, my mother created these folded works of art to hide and reveal secret messages. Since she'd first started painting, the year before my birth, her style never strayed far from highly detailed and often erotic symbolism.

One could never just glance at a painting by "La Lune," as she signed her canvases. You needed to study it for quite some time, over days or weeks, to understand all it concealed.

I placed the "painting with doors," as I'd called these when I was a little girl, on my worktable and moved the lamp so it shone down on it.

The triptych's wings were shut, and pictured on the front were large wrought iron gates leading to a garden. The scene looked familiar, but at first I didn't realize why. Then, looking more closely, I recognized the gates at Père-Lachaise. Not opening to a garden, in fact, but to the parklike cemetery I'd visited just days before.

Twilight settled on the cemetery in my mother's rendition, just as I remembered. Birds hid in the branches of leafy trees shadowing cobblestone walks. I picked up my magnifying glasses. Could they be? Yes, they were crows. A chill crept down my arms.

I opened the wings, revealing the interior three panels. The one in the center, the largest, arched at the top, was flanked by two slightly smaller panels. Just like its religious counterparts, the piece was meant to be read from left to right.

In the first frame, I sat where I was sitting at that very minute, bent over my worktable. A man stood behind me, his body long and achingly sensual. Leaning over, he watched my efforts, his hand on my shoulder.

Something about him looked familiar. I peered more closely at his face. Impossibly, I made out Jean Luc!

Almost as if summer had instantly turned to winter, I shivered. How did my mother paint him? And how cruel to depict him as if he were alive, teasing me into imagining how it would look if we were together. Jean Luc was my insanity. My delusion. Proof of how slight a hold I held over reason and rational thinking. Nothing more than a phantom lover I'd created out of my guilt and frustration.

Why had my mother sent me this taunt?

With trepidation, I read the next frame. Jean Luc and I sat on the settee in my sitting room below the shop, entwined in a languorous embrace. His strong arms wrapped around me, his lips pressed against mine. The muscles in his neck tight and tense with ardor. I blushed that my own mother had painted me in the throes of such a passionate hold.

In the last frame, Jean Luc and I stood side by side, in front of the fountain in the gardens of the Palais. Around us, the rosebushes blossomed with flowers so lush and ripe I could smell their heady, spicy scent just by gazing at them.

She'd painted us from the back. Not touching. Or so it seemed at first, and then I noticed the tips of the fingers of his right hand met the tips of the fingers of my left. A fire-like glow emanated from where they connected.

I'd stumbled on a clue.

Returning to the first frame, I reexamined the scene, looking for and . . . yes . . . finding another glow where Jean Luc's hand met my shoulder. Exploring the embrace in the middle painting, I found the same glow where his arm touched my back and even found a tiny blaze where our lips joined.

Turning the object around, I studied the scene at Père-Lachaise more closely. The crows' eyes smoldered with that same warm orange-yellow light. Tiny flowers at the base of some of the trees, tombstones, and mausoleums burned with it as well.

There was a message here, but I couldn't decipher it—not yet. The very fact of this object overwhelmed me and distracted me from working out the puzzle. Why and how had my mother created this? How could she know about Jean Luc, much less what he looked like? She possessed talents, both as an artist and a witch, but even this seemed beyond her abilities. Maman could read the future, but only in a general sense. She could create spells and potions to heal, to harm, and to help. She could slow the ravages of time upon the human body and enchant and influence other people.

Unlike the witches of old wives' tales, she could not raise the dead. Or fly. She could not change the past or travel there.

She might have sensed my distress, but could not have been privy to my very actions. She was able to sense my moods, but not read my mind. Or so she always swore.

I certainly hadn't told her anything about Jean Luc in the weekly letters my parents and I exchanged. We visited several times a year when they came to Paris, either to see my mother's dealer or when my father obtained a commission. Most recently, we'd all gone to Picasso's wedding to his new wife, Olga, just a few weeks before. But then I hadn't yet met Madame Alouette. Or heard from Jean Luc. And I'd never told my great-grandmother about him—so she couldn't have written to my mother about my sad obsession.

And yet, in my hand, I held a series of paintings that not only depicted Jean Luc but also illustrated our trysts . . . portraying him as if he were flesh and blood in instances that had occurred—I'd felt him behind me at my worktable, and certainly making love to me in my bedroom, and I'd gone to Père-Lachaise because of his column.

Only the fountain scene hadn't occurred.

Being well acquainted with my mother's style, I knew it would take me days to decipher everything she'd included in the triptych, suss out the clues and their meaning. But I didn't need time to interpret the overarching message. The triptych celebrated our love as if it were real.

I continued studying the cemetery and noticed inscriptions on the mausoleums and tombstones. Names and dates. My mother never did anything accidentally. The engravings must be part of the message. Picking up a pencil, I proceeded to copy each of the names and the numbers onto a sheet of paper. After finding them all, I applied the simple cipher she used in all her paintings—each number standing for the letter in that position in the alphabet.

Finally, I understood the message and realized the same message appeared on the silver leaves I'd found in La Lune's bell tower.

Make of the blood, heat.
Make of the heat, a fire.
Make of the fire, life everlasting.

No less cryptic than the numbers, really. What was she trying to tell me?

I worked at the puzzle on and off that night and for the next two days. I didn't like to give up when it came to my mother's artful challenges. And she didn't make it easy for me to give up. Maman believed we all needed practice in dealing with mysteries and, by working out the riddles, we were honing our abilities for times of crisis.

But after three days, I gave up and telephoned Cannes. Our housekeeper said my mother was on a sketching trip. I left word for her to call me.

The mystery of the triptych's meaning would need to wait.

By Friday, my mother hadn't been in touch. That night, after the shop closed, I decided to try once more.

In my bedroom and while sipping wine, I resumed studying it. Before I'd tried with magnifying glasses; that night I used my jeweler's loupe, searching for other clues. And I found them. In the shadows inside cracks and crevices on the tombstones and mausoleum lintels, I found yet more runes and symbols. Their meaning eluded me. In the morning I would ask Anna if she knew what they meant.

Why hadn't my mother sent a letter with the painting, explaining what it was she wanted me to know? My father always said she needed to create drama, but I'd never found this habit endearing the way he did. Happier in the dark than the light, she preferred the moon to the sun.

The more I studied the minuscule signs, the more they looked familiar. And then I realized why. I opened my armoire. From under a pile of handkerchiefs, I pulled out the dozen silver sheets I'd found in the bell tower at Maison de La Lune. There, etched in metal, were the same symbols in the same order on the last page. But I hadn't understood them when I'd seen them the first time. Neither had Anna.

Frustrated, just after midnight, I finally gave

up. As I did, the depression that had been hovering on the edge of my consciousness all day descended. What was I doing in Paris? Why was I fighting the facts about what my life had become? Surrounded by war, by loss, by death . . . so steeped in it, I'd manufactured an alternate reality populated by imaginary men. I was a fraud and my talismans were toys.

Pacing my small room offered no relief. At home in Cannes, we'd wander the beaches at night. When our minds wouldn't allow our bodies to rest, we would prowl around the jetties while the phosphorescent surf played around our ankles. While in Paris, I couldn't even venture out alone after dark. There were government curfews, some-times enforced, sometimes relaxed. But Anna had asked me to observe the nine PM cutoff, regardless. With so many lonely, wounded soldiers in the city, streetwalkers strolled the avenues and boulevards at night, hoping to make some money. Anna didn't want me to become entangled with any drunken soldiers.

Well, I was tired of the rules. If a soldier approached me, I would just keep walking and ignore him.

Outside I found quiet. No sirens, few cars. The streets of Paris were eerily unwelcoming, but at least everything existed in three dimensions. Walking on cobblestones, looking above me at the stars, I focused on the facts of the world around me, not the fantasies I kept crafting in my little room. The buildings loomed large in the moon-light; footsteps of one other late-night pedestrian echoed in the still night. Glancing over I saw a lasciviously dressed woman hurrying in the opposite direction. Crossing rue Royale, I walked under the archway and into the Louvre's courtyard and kept going until I reached the quai du Louvre. I descended the wide stone steps down to the path running along the river, the quai des Tuileries, and made my way as close as I could get to the water.

But this was nothing like walking by the sea in Cannes. I missed the scent of salt, the sound of the waves crashing, the give of the sand under-foot. Instead, the swiftly flowing river smelled cold and slightly metallic; the stones underfoot were uneven and unforgiving. Only the moon was the same. At that very moment, the same moon was shining down on the beach at home. And the soldiers in the field. And the tombstones in the cemetery.

The path appeared empty. I was alone. With no destination in mind, I just kept moving forward, hoping I might walk into proof that my mind wasn't infected. Or even proof that it was. I just wanted an answer.

If I could just know I wasn't insane, I could live with the discomfort. I could withstand the bittersweet romance with a lover whom I knew I would lose one day. I could tolerate the noise. But this lack of proof? This uncertainty? That's what I couldn't endure anymore. Were the voices in my head or in some other place? Was I making up Jean Luc, or was he a trapped soul communicating with me?

And if Jean Luc was real—if any ghost could be real—then this love affair was doomed, wasn't it?

I'd reached the oldest bridge in Paris, the Pont Neuf, and stood underneath it. Water swirled in eddies around the bridge's piles. So many had walked across its span since it had been built in the sixteenth century. How many times had my ancestor, the original La Lune, traversed it? Had she stood here and stared down at the water, missing her lover, wondering how she could live with the mistakes she'd made in trying to recapture what she'd lost, what she'd destroyed? Had she ever stood here and wondered if the river would welcome her and offer her the release she so badly wanted . . . freedom from longing, from loneliness?

Despondent, I climbed the stairs to the street level. I meant to turn away, not to walk out onto the bridge. But I did. I walked halfway out, stood at the railing, and stared down.

Paris's bridges cross from the Left to the Right Bank. For many, they also span this life to the next. Every week, broken soldiers jumped off this bridge and the others, unable to cope with how the war left them.

The thought alarmed me—not because I found the idea abhorrent, but because I found it so tempting.

What would it be like to disappear into that blackness? To feel the shock of cold water swiftly surround me? To sink into the river's murky, colorless depths?

Would I find Jean Luc then? Finally? On the other side? And what a nasty joke if he looked at me like a stranger, proving I'd imagined him. Why continue living with this question of sanity? So what if all those women did need my help. If I was a fraud, I wasn't helping them anyway.

I leaned over the railing. The river looked even more sinister. A snake waiting for her next feeding.

The sound of far-off footsteps advanced. To the right, far in the distance, a figure approached. A few more steps and I made out a woman. A few more and her gait became familiar. Clouds shifted in the night sky, and her namesake, *la lune*, shone down, illuminating the color of her hair and then her very features.

"Maman?"

She reached me and pulled me close to her. "I came to take you home."

"To the Palais?"

"No, to Cannes. It's too dangerous in Paris for you."

"I'm careful. The sirens warn us and the shelter at the Palais is very safe."

"Yes, the war is hazardous, but I meant what you are doing with the talismans and how it is affecting you. That's the true and real danger."

"No, I can't leave my job."

"But I can see it in your eyes, *mon ange*." It was what her grandmother called her, "my angel."

"How did you find me? I didn't tell anyone I went out."

My mother gave me her most beguiling smile. The one that said everything: *I love you. You know who I am. You know what I can do. We are mother and daughter—how can you even wonder?*

"But why now?"

"You haven't finished working out the message in the painting?"

"No."

"And you're questioning everything you should be embracing. It's all a gift, Opaline, but you're being tortured."

"A gift? You mean the voices?"

She nodded.

"Some gift. I think I'm becoming as crazy as the owl lady who used to live next door to us in Cannes." I hadn't thought of Madame Sorette in so long. Our delightful but crazy neighbor who kept an aviary of almost a hundred owls she believed were all Greek gods.

My mother laughed at the memory. Deep

throated and velvety. My father always said my mother seemed sensual even when she buttered bread. He was right. If there were any men around, they would have come running at the sound of that laugh, like dogs sniffing out a bitch in heat.

"You need to come home so I can teach you how to use your talents. Every Daughter of La Lune is born with them, but only through training can you control them."

"How do you know what's happening to me?"

"I studied. I trained. And lest you think I'm so prescient, Anna wrote me, Opaline. Mystics like her can help, of course, but not teach. You need to come home. This Jean Luc is torturing you, isn't he?"

"I didn't tell Anna about Jean Luc."

"No, you didn't." She smiled again.

"You think he's real?"

"I don't know. I can't travel your threads."

"Threads?"

"I wish I'd convinced you to study with me when we had the chance instead of rushing through the lessons now. La Lune taught me that each of us has silver or gold threads that tie us to other realms. On them, we can travel past this plane and go back and forth to other planes. I believe you are walking out into time and encountering all these lost souls who need help in cutting their threads and moving on. None of us can walk on one another's threads, though. You can't on mine; I can't on your sisters'. But I can see them—" She took my hands and pressed her fingertips to mine. "I can feel them here, Opaline."

As she spoke, I became conscious of a slight warmth where our fingertips touched.

"I can't come home, not yet. I have to stay here and help the widows and mothers as long as the war rages. I would be selfish to leave. I feel as if what I'm supposed to do here isn't finished."

My mother's silence lasted for a full minute.

"But so far sweet Anna hasn't helped. Are you sure you won't come home with me?"

I nodded.

"Always so stubborn. *So* stubborn. You know I can't stay here and train you. I have the twins and Jadine to take care of. Please, reconsider."

At that moment, the sirens screamed. I looked around in a panic. There was nowhere to go. We were too far from either bank. Maybe it was all for the best. If the bombs fell on us, if they took us, then I'd go to Jean Luc in whatever place he was and we could be together. My mother was a fully evolved witch; she'd most likely be able to keep herself safe no matter where she was.

The first bomb hit deep in the city to the right. Close enough that we could feel the vibration through our feet. A huge explosion of orange-red flames and smoke filled the sky.

Grabbing my hand, my mother pulled me. I

resisted. I wanted to stay. To watch the fireworks, to tempt fate.

"Opaline," she yelled just as the second bomb hit not as far away. The bridge shook as the sound echoed through the canyon of the city streets. The lights were brighter, this one much closer.

My mother screamed my name, tightened her grip, and dragged me, using an inhuman force I couldn't withstand. She ran, towing me with her to the end of the bridge just as the third bomb hit the far end of Pont Neuf. The explosion rocked the ground. We went flying. Thrown by the power of the blast. Incredibly, my mother never let go of my hand, and we landed more softly than seemed possible on a patch of grass quite close to a large plane tree.

Gasping for breath, I sat on the ground, the trunk of the tree at my back, looking at my mother. At her disheveled hair, dirt-streaked face, ripped duster. Smiling at me, she shook her head.

"You were born stubborn, Opaline. The next time I tell you to come with me, you come. Do you understand? We're going home."

Even there, sitting under the sky smoky from the bombs, hearing the cries of people who were scared and hurt, not knowing what would happen next, I remained sure. I shook my head.

"I can't."

"Then you are going to go on suffering."

I stood. Stumbled. I'd twisted my ankle in my

fall. "I'm going back to the Palais," I said. "Do you want to come with me? I'm sure Anna would be happy to put you up."

"No, I'm going to your great-grandmother's. I want to see how she is. Why don't you come with me? I brought something I need to give you. It's there with my bags."

The maison remained undamaged. Grand-mère and all the soldiers were awake and drinking champagne—celebrating, they said, that they'd survived this most recent encounter with Bertha.

I retired to my room, my mother to another. I undressed, turned off the light, and climbed into my bed. On the bridge I hadn't been frightened. But now, with all quiet once again, with the smooth cool sheets pulled up and the down pillows under my head, I began to shake.

And then I heard a knock on the door.

"*Entrez*," I called out, expecting my great-grandmother had sent her maid to make sure I didn't need anything.

The door opened, and in the pale yellow light from the hallway I saw my mother. Her long wavy auburn hair tumbled down around her shoulders. She wore a peach-colored dressing gown cut low. The lamplight in the hallway illuminated the ruby necklace encircling her pale peach skin and set the stones on fire. I'd never seen them glowing like they were then—like embers, I thought, about to burst into flames.

Stepping into the room, my mother switched on the bedside lamp and then sat on the edge of the bed. Reaching out, she smoothed my hair.

"I'm sorry we argued. Sorrier still you won't come home with me. I guessed as much. I understand you feel like you have a mission to fulfill here. I brought this for you. It won't solve all your problems, but it will help some . . ."

She handed me a book. It fit in the palm of my hand. Made of cordovan leather with gold tooling on the front, elaborate letters spelling out five words.

THE DAUGHTERS OF LA LUNE

"It's our history, and our rules. La Lune guided me to find it in the bell tower when I was just about your age. She taught me its lessons. I always dreamed I'd be the one to teach them to you. Promise me you'll study it?"

I took the book from her, held it, and heard far-off music. Soft and lilting. Bells and harps. If the stars sang, certainly this would be their song.

The music grew louder when I opened the book. I touched the smooth parchment paper and breathed in its antique scent. I read my name printed on the frontispiece.

OPALINE DUPLESSI,
THE 44TH DAUGHTER OF LA LUNE

Turning the pages, I discovered a highly illustrated account of our family, going back to the sixteenth century, followed by a list of rules of witchcraft and then . . .

"What are these?" I asked my mother, pointing to what appeared to be the first of many complex recipes.

"Spells. Those we've collected over the years, and some new ones I've created."

"This is a grimoire?"

She nodded. "Yes, your grimoire. And it's protected so no one else can steal it or alter it."

"But why is the last third empty?"

"Each of us is charged with creating our own magick, Opaline. There's room there for you to make notes and preserve your discoveries for future generations. You found the silver sheets, didn't you? Those fit into the book, with space on them for you to engrave your own spells."

"How can there be so much I don't know about you, about us?" I asked.

"You didn't want to know." She smiled her mystical smile again, leaned forward, and kissed me on the forehead. "I know you won't come home now, but you will come home when the war is over; promise me you'll come then?"

"Yes, as soon as the war is over, Maman."

Getting up, she turned off the light and walked to the door. She stopped, her hand on the jamb, and looked back at me.

"*Mon ange*, your Jean Luc is real. How else could I have seen him to paint if he wasn't?"

Chapter 18

The following afternoon, I went down to the vault again, this time to choose tsavorites and emeralds and amethysts of various shades for a brooch of my own design. The large cluster of grapes could be pinned to a lapel or taken apart to make a set of earrings and a smaller cluster brooch.

Monsieur Orloff offered me a rare compliment, saying "Your piece is very well conceived," and then he added several more grapes to the top, making the triangle a more interesting shape after the two grapes were separated out for the earrings.

I'd found eight amethysts so far, large ovals with a lovely deepness. The facets flashed a tiny bit of pink when I held them to the light. My book of gems said that the royal purple stones becalmed their wearer but also increased awareness and psychic ability. Considering my state, I was almost afraid to handle the gems.

I'd just picked out another stone when I heard a noise. Was Monsieur coming down to the vault? I'd been there a long time. Perhaps he needed me.

When he didn't appear, I continued my quest. I found a ninth grape, and then, while I searched through the drawer for the tenth, the noise came again but from a more clear direction: from the chamber backing up to the vault.

Working quickly, I emptied the bottom three shelves of objects, removed the shelves themselves, extinguished my light, and then extracted the loose mortar from the wall as I'd done before.

Immediately, I heard a cacophony of sounds. Just like last time. How much of the din was happening in the present? How much of it, the past?

I tried to press my fingernail into my palm to create the distraction I needed, but it didn't help.

Through the peephole, I watched the men settle. There were no clues about their affiliation from their shoes, but I did see the butt end of one rifle. And then another.

Straining to hear anything to help me identify the language they were speaking, I pressed my fingernail deeper into my flesh, but the symphony of noises continued to roar in my ears.

Did these men have so much blood on their hands that they carried the screams of the dead with them? If that was true, then they must be German soldiers.

I needed to tell Monsieur Orloff, but dreaded how it would feed his paranoia. What if instead I went to the police and—

Some object flashed close, too close, to the peephole. One of the men had dropped something. As he bent to pick it up, his face was only the thickness of the wall away from mine. Had he seen the crack? Seen me?

As quietly as I could, I quickly pushed the piece of mortar back. What could he see from his side? I'd taken precautions, again shrouded the vault in darkness. But could the light from their torches illuminate my face?

And if he had seen me? Were they pointing to the wall now, discussing whether or not there'd really been a girl there? If they looked again, they'd see nothing. Would they try to break through the wall? And the person who'd seen me—had he gotten a good enough look to recognize me?

Shaking, I gathered up the amethysts, tsavorites, and emeralds I'd come for and left the vault.

What if they were building a bomb and were planning to blow up the Palais? Should I go to the police straightaway? No, I needed to tell Monsieur first.

I climbed upstairs and prepared to tell him, but found Monsieur occupied with a client, showing her a variety of his signature linked bracelets—the top of each link pavéd with gems. Women usually bought more than one, collecting the colorful bracelets until a few inches of studded chain covered each wrist.

I couldn't interrupt him when he was with a client. No one could break that rule, not even Anna.

I went back to work, trying to distract myself by arranging the stones on my drawing of the brooch. Only a few minutes had passed when the sirens started.

"What an interruption these are," I heard Monsieur say to his client. "You must come with us to our shelter."

I walked out of the workshop as I heard her arguing that her driver was outside and she intended to go home, and with two of the bracelets.

As dangerous as the bombs were, as many people who'd died or been wounded by flying glass and falling stone, others had become angry at the war, at the interruptions, and found satisfaction defying the danger.

"I'll walk you to your car then, Madame Blanche."

Anna stuck her head in the workshop to tell me she'd wait for Monsieur, but that I should go down to the shelter.

When I arrived, Grigori had already made himself as comfortable as possible. Five minutes later, after locking up the jewels on display in the shop, Monsieur and Anna joined us.

Grigori and his father didn't greet each other but merely nodded. So they'd been arguing again. Anna broke the silence.

"What did Madame Blanche buy, Pavel?"

Intently examining his son, who'd picked up a book and was leafing through the pages, Monsieur needed to ask Anna to repeat her question.

"I asked what Madame Blanche purchased."

"An emerald and a sapphire chain bracelet."

"There's no question, the war has certainly been profitable for those who own textile mills," Anna mused.

Monsieur directed a question to his son, his voice even gruffer than usual: "You are coming to the meeting tonight regarding the Dowager, correct?"

Grigori looked up. "Yes, I said I would."

Monsieur nodded. "And when we're there, please don't ask me again. I've told you. There is a place for you in the operation. You must trust me to explain it at the right time."

Grigori shrugged and returned to the book. Anna frowned at his bowed head and turned to Monsieur. "Has there been news?"

Monsieur sighed with exaggerated futility. "No one has any more information about the fate of the family, no. Additional wild rumors are circulating suggesting where the empress and the children might be in hiding. One day it's the Ukraine. Another it's a dungeon in the Winter Palace itself. No one knows. It's taking a terrible toll on the Dowager."

"I can imagine how painful this must be for her. Her son dead and not knowing the fate of his wife and her grandchildren. She herself in hiding."

"And she herself without funds," Monsieur said.

I saw Grigori's mouth twitch, as if he wanted to say something but was holding back.

"These brutes who took over our country are criminals," Anna said. "But all over the world, they are praised for their bravery. When will everyone realize what they did? When will they be ousted from power? Will we ever go home, Pavel?"

"No," Grigori said, looking up from his book. In his voice, a determination that disturbed me. "We won't ever go *home*. Our *home* isn't there anymore. The revolutionaries broke the system, changed the rules."

Anna looked at him with sympathy, seeing his anger as an expression of pain. "You miss it too, don't you?"

"The past is over," he said. "We can't keep looking back."

Anna winced at Grigori's harsh tone. Monsieur frowned.

"You are upsetting your stepmother, Grigori. The past is over, but there is a future that is waiting, yes? There is always a future and—"

Monsieur broke off. I'd heard it too. The damn sirens starting up again. He went to the door, opened it, and listened.

"This is bad, isn't it?" Anna asked.

"Yes," Monsieur said.

Grigori paced, then stopped beside the north wall, the same orientation where downstairs, in the vault, I'd found the peephole looking into the tunnels that Monsieur Orloff didn't own, that must belong to one of the other nearby shops. Bending down, he picked something up off the floor. A piece of the mortar like the one I'd dislodged.

"What is this?" he asked.

Monsieur Orloff examined it. "Some mortar from the wall, I expect."

Grigori stared at the wall as if trying to see through it to the other side.

I should tell them about the vault now, I thought. But before I said a word, Grigori caught me by surprise by mentioning the very subject I wanted to bring up.

"How safe is your vault, Papa?"

"As safe as the vault in Van Cleef and Arpels and Cartier and any of the banks on rue Royale. The same concern built it."

"That's still where the tsar's treasure is?" Grigori turned and asked his father. "You haven't moved it?"

The tsar's treasure? What was Grigori talking about? I'd never heard it referenced before.

"There is no tsar's treasure."

"But if it did exist—that's where it would be, yes?"

Monsieur glared at him.

I turned to Anna. "What are they talking about?"

"A few years ago, a rumor circulated that to

safeguard his future, and the future of his family, at the first sign of the uprisings and dissent among his people, the tsar sent gold and treasure out of Russia."

"Before the revolution?"

"That's the rumor, yes," Monsieur interrupted. "But it's not true."

Grigori picked up the story. "So my father says. To protect us all probably. But I believe the story. The tsar was no fool. Supposedly, he gave each of a dozen trusted emissaries a portion of his holdings and sent each one out of Russia to live in another country and safeguard his wealth."

"Why are we discussing this foolishness?" Monsieur asked his son. "Why are we talking about this now?"

Grigori's gaze went from the wall back to his father. "Because you said the Dowager is almost destitute. Because we're living in dangerous times. Because I've heard rumors the Bolsheviks are on the hunt for that treasure to fund the revolution. And would stop at nothing to get it."

"What is it you are getting at, Grigori?"

"Just wondering how safe we are. What if the Bolsheviks suspected us and started to follow us, spy on us?"

"Stop. You're upsetting your stepmother." Monsieur went to Anna's side, sat beside her, and put his arm protectively around her shoulder.

"Anna, we are not suspect. Fabergé made sure of that. Everyone believed his story that one of his assistants had stolen the firm's enameling secrets and he'd fired the thief. Why would anyone guess it was a lie? Our friends saw us leave in disgrace, don't you remember? There were no slip-ups." Monsieur was saying it, though, as if he were schooling her more than reassuring her. He then looked from his wife back to his son. "You are not to speak of this again. Do you understand me?"

Grigori rolled the mortar between his fingers, and it disintegrated into powder. He rubbed his hands together to dislodge the dust and then wiped them on the back of his pants.

"Opaline, after our meeting tonight, will you have some supper with me?"

What an unfair trap. Asking me in front of his father and stepmother during a moment of such tension put me on the spot. Especially since I knew Monsieur hoped our relationship would progress and my agreeing would ease the strain between them.

"Yes?" He hesitated when I hadn't answered.

I agreed.

When the sirens stopped fifteen minutes later, we ventured upstairs to the Orloff apartment. Sitting around the wireless, we listened to the news that a German bomb had exploded not far from the Palais. Then, that the reporter awaited more information. We waited with him, worrying, weary of the war and its incessant intrusions. Living in a state of low-level anxiety that at any moment escalated at the sound of the wailing distress signals took its toll. An impact none of us could measure.

After a few more tense minutes, the reporter announced the bomb had hit between two apartment buildings, damaging both. One collapsed. At least five people were dead and many more were feared dead and wounded.

Grigori left, returning to his shop for two more prescheduled appointments. He wanted to be there if indeed his clients arrived. Monsieur said he would keep the jewelry store closed, but wanted to lock everything up. Anna asked me to stay for tea.

Once we were alone in the apartment, she said: "Actually, the tea can wait if you can. I wanted to talk to you."

"Is something wrong?"

"Something I saw a few days ago in the crystals. I wasn't sure about showing it to you, but now I think I should."

We walked into her bedroom, where she lit a candelabra, and then together went through her closet and into her *monde enchanté*.

From one of the very top shelves, she retrieved a crystal ball almost hidden by the ones in front of it. She placed it on the velvet cloth in the center of the card table and sat down. The candlelight illuminated the orb.

Larger than the others, slightly gray, with internal occlusions that suggested a mountain ridge.

Closing her eyes, Anna took several deep breaths, held still for a few moments, and then she slowly opened her eyes and looked into the crystal.

"Yes, here it is again. Can you see anything?" She pushed it toward me.

I stared into the sphere, like looking into the crystals I worked with. I saw a stunning and complex rocky internal landscape but nothing supernatural. I tried moving my head, but saw only the reflection of the candle flames and my own face staring back at me.

I shook my head.

Anna pointed to a spot off center to the right. Straining, I saw a fissure inside one of the rocks, like a break in a cliff.

"I see you here on the edge. And Grigori on the other side. He has his hand out to you. I believe it means you can be the bridge—helping him find his fate. He needs you to give him that chance. I know you are afraid. I'm afraid too. There are storms brewing in these occlusions. Here"—she pointed to a gray mass—"and here. I'm not certain. It could be the war. Or it could be the conflict inside of you. You can't stay afraid of forming attachments because of Timur."

I nodded.

"When I see you in the orb, there are threads wrapped around you, enclosing you. I think they're the voices you hear, creating a kind of barrier between you and your potential both as an artist and as a woman. You are surrounded by the dead. You are allowing them to prevent you from living a full life."

Her words chilled me. Her second sight showed her Jean Luc even though she hadn't named him. And she'd referred to threads. That's what my mother had described to me too.

"You think you can avoid pain by not needing anyone. That if you never love anyone who you can lose, then you'll never feel loss. But it's not true. We're made to love. Even if you think you can stop yourself from feeling, stop yourself from living, your emotions will find a way. They'll trick you when you least expect it."

They already had, I thought. My reluctance to form an attachment to a living man had resulted in my forming an attachment to a dead one.

"You are close to the time when you are going to be forced to make a choice between those \ who are dead and those who are living. Don't choose wrong, Opaline. I promise, the pain you are suffering is worse than the pain you are afraid of."

Chapter 19

I returned to my room to find a note Grigori had left me, saying he had an errand to attend to and asking if I would meet him at Café de la Paix. The restaurant was only a short walk from the Palais, but it had started raining once more.

I didn't really want to go out, but there was no way to reach Grigori and cancel. Not showing up would be too rude. So, feeling trapped but resigned, I changed out of my gored black skirt, white middy blouse, and low-slung belt. Such was my self-imposed work uniform. I owned two identical blouses and skirts, and when one needed laundering, I wore the other. No visible jewels. The gems in the shop were supposed to shine, not those of us who worked there.

From my closet, I pulled out a bottle green silk chemise and held it up against my body. No, too flirty for my mood. Instead, I chose a higher-necked maroon silk dress that set off my hair color without being suggestive.

Checking my reflection in the mirror, I thought the more circumspect outfit a better choice. Plus, the dress would match my ruby silk umbrella with its silver repoussé handle, my great-grandmother's birthday present to me.

Once opened, it revealed celadon-colored silk printed with a profusion of roses in luscious shades of pink. Like having a garden protecting you from the rain.

As I turned away from the mirror, I saw the gold chain around my throat glitter. I removed Jean Luc's talisman. Grigori might ask about it, and I didn't have any answers.

Next, I hesitated over the tray of perfume on my vanity. My instinct led me to forgo the House of L'Etoile's more wanton *L'Eau de L'Amour* for their gentler *Joie de Vivre*. I dabbed some of the floral scent behind my ears, ran my hands through my hair, and then, umbrella on my arm, I left my room, locking the door behind me.

Outside, sheltered from the rain by the arcade, I hugged the wall as I headed toward the Palais's exit. Most of the shop windows I passed were crisscrossed with tape to protect the glass from shattering when bombs shook the city. At La Fantaisie Russe, Monsieur had installed a second plate of glass abutting the window so he could fully show the display cases he was so proud of. But several store owners used the adhesive inventively, making decorative shapes showcasing their wares between the openings. Creative protection from Bertha, I thought.

I walked halfway to the exit, coming up to a shoe store abandoned months before that had remained empty since. Its owner, another victim of war. There were a dozen such shops around the Palais that had been thriving businesses when I had first arrived in 1915.

Of all of the closed shops, the shoe boutique made me saddest because I'd gotten to know Monsieur Maillot a bit and liked his off-color jokes and lovely shoe designs. The way he mixed fabrics and colors, while within the bounds of taste, still shocked a bit. And when he helped you, his fingers caressed the boots or dancing shoes you'd asked to see like a lover. He delighted in his own creations, and it charmed me.

As I passed by, I thought I saw a shadow shift and peered into the darkened interior. Suddenly, too fast for me to react, a hand reached out and grabbed my arm, roughly pulling me inside. I felt my shoulder wrench. Saw nothing but darkness. Then a stench. Wine. Vetiver. Sweat. Garlic.

It wasn't Monsieur Maillot pulling me into his store. Of course not. He'd died at the front. This was some stinking stranger dragging me deeper into the shadows. Suddenly his cold fingers pressed a paper into my hand. Then, grunting, he shoved me in the opposite direction. Sprawling, I tripped on a warped floorboard and landed in a pile of dirty, dusty rags and discarded boxes.

For a moment, I sat there on the floor, stunned.

Not comprehending what had happened. My breath came in ragged gasps. My pulse pounded. I felt a damp breeze and realized the door to the shop hung wide open.

I watched a shadow cross under the arcade. My assailant fleeing. And I was too dazed to get up and go after him.

Standing, I tested my ankles. Nothing broken for sure, not even sprained. My left shoulder throbbed. My right elbow ached. Probably I'd banged it on the wall as I fell. Brushing off my skirt, I took a few deep breaths and walked outside.

I stopped for a moment and leaned against one of the columns, looking out into the garden. I considered going back to my apartment. I certainly had an excuse. But the thought of being alone disturbed me more than the idea of meeting Grigori. I badly wanted a glass of wine and knew he'd probably ordered a bottle already.

Then I remembered the paper and looked down. My left hand still clutched the crumpled sheet my attacker had shoved into my fingers.

Written in black ink were the words:

Arretez-vous, Mademoiselle.

A warning to stop. But stop what?

As I continued on under the arcade, I tried to grasp the meaning of the words and the attack. What *had* happened? Certainly not a thwarted sexual assault? I'd read about soldiers, sick with war fever, desperate for companionship, who came home and raped Parisians. But the man in the shop hadn't touched me except to pull me inside the shop, uncurl my fingers, and push me out of his way.

I exited the Palais out onto the street, with each step more confused but less panicky. Above me, the velvet twilight sky was unaffected by my recent attack and the afternoon's bombing. But around us, the people on the street were very much reacting to the latest tragic assault on the city. After an air raid—whether bogus or real—people poured out of their homes, crowded the cafés, the streets. The relief at the end of the raid needed to be expressed. No one wanted to be alone, cowering. We believed it was our civic duty to celebrate that we'd survived yet another German threat. That they could scare us but not defeat us. We would not allow them to bomb the joie de vivre out of us for more than an hour or two at a time.

I found Grigori waiting for me inside the café, and we were seated by the window. I thought I'd tell him right away about the man in the alcove but, still upset, I wasn't yet ready.

"I've been looking forward to this all afternoon. You always light up a room, do you know that? With your shining copper hair and glowing skin. You're not like anyone else,

Opaline. I think that's what I like about you the most."

He looked at me intently, so intently I needed to glance away.

"Have I embarrassed you?" He laughed.

"A little."

"I should have held back saying that until we'd started drinking. Embarrassment is always easier to take with a sip of wine."

He gestured for the waiter and asked him to fill my glass from the waiting bottle of champagne—one of the few items not rationed.

Grigori held his flute up to me, and we clinked our glasses.

"To an end of these blasted sirens. May we only hear music from now on."

We both drank, but while I sipped, he downed the first glass quickly and motioned for the waiter again.

Through the glass windows, I watched the faces of people who passed by.

"You can see the war in their eyes, can't you?" he asked. I nodded. "Yes," he continued, "Parisians trying to cope with the war, deal with the death and the sadness, and yet, at the same time, not forget this *is* Paris and there are still dancers and painters, sculptors and poets, designers and philosophers living and working and creating while the war rages on."

Grigori took my hand. "Is it the war that makes

you work so hard? Play so little?" His brown-diamond eyes glittered with mischievousness and the wine he'd drunk so fast.

"It doesn't seem the right time to be frivolous."

"No, but it's not healthy for you to spend as much time as you do in the workshop. It's one thing to hold down a job, but all the extra hours you spend meeting with the never-ending line of women who seek you out and making those talismans for them. It's summer, yet your skin is as pale as it was this winter."

"It hardly seems like I'm making a sacrifice considering what their husbands and brothers and sons have given up."

Something hardened in Grigori's handsome face. I'd said the wrong thing. His bitterness at having been sent home from the war with a lame leg was never far from the surface. What bothered him more: the infirmity that kept him from returning to the front, or his jealousy that his younger brother, Anna and Monsieur's heroic son, still fought?

"No, I suppose not. You aren't there and you should be thankful for that."

"Are you thankful?"

He leaned in. "That's a difficult question to answer. Of course, I am relieved. You can't imagine how terrible it is. The living conditions are appalling. Sleeping in those wet, rotten, mud-filled trenches . . . and the cold . . . and the sights . . . I see them in my dreams . . . the mutilations, the blood . . . the gore . . ."

Giving up on the waiter, he poured himself more champagne and gulped it down.

"And yet, for all the relief, there is an equal amount of guilt. But the only way to avoid that, I fear, is to die." He laughed sarcastically. "And I don't plan to do that."

Which was just as well, I wanted to tell him. Even ghosts spoke of guilt.

The waiter appeared again and asked if we were ready to order. I requested the Dover sole and Grigori the beef.

"Rations," the waiter said, with a sorry shake of his head. "Can I suggest the gentleman also order the fish?"

After the waiter departed, Grigori took up my hand again.

"Let's not talk of the war." He smiled. "There is so much beauty still left in the world." He turned to the window. "Look at the moon. At the elegant, wide avenue with such luxurious chestnut trees. And the beautiful Beaux Arts buildings. At the lovely mosaic mural on that shop. The design is delightful, and the colors glow, don't they?"

I took in each of the sights Grigori mentioned, enjoying his ability to notice and describe beauty. As I looked at the mosaics, commenting that they did glow, a man outside the restaurant slowed down as he passed by the window and looked in, right at us. That might not have been unusual except for his expression. Under his hat, his face pinched. His mouth pursed in a narrow line. He glanced away but then turned back again, something sly in his action. As if sneaking another look.

I shivered and crossed my arms, my fingers feeling the gooseflesh on my bare skin.

"What is it?" Grigori asked.

My eyes followed the stranger as he disappeared around the corner.

"Opaline?"

"Did you see that man?"

"No, why, do you know him?"

I shivered again. Was it possible?

"I think I've seen him before."

"Where? Did he do something to you?"

I was surprised by the protective tone I heard in his voice.

"Yes. No. He might be a German spy."

"Opaline! How on earth would you know that? What are you talking about?"

I told him about the vault and the mortar missing from the wall and how I hadn't been sure if I'd been seen, but now thought perhaps I had been.

Grigori's face paled. "This is terrible. And why do you now think you've been seen?"

I explained about the attack on my way to the

restaurant. "He pulled me inside and shoved a piece of paper into my hand and then pushed me toward the wall. I fell. He fled. And when I looked at the note he'd passed me, all it said was *Arretez-vous, Mademoiselle*."

"'Stop'? That's all it said?"

"Yes."

"And you think it was the same man?"

"Yes, the one I saw through the mortar. The one who just passed. He's following me."

"And you waited until now to tell me you'd been assaulted? Not when we first sat down?"

"I was in shock. Shaken. I didn't want to think about it."

"We must think about it, though. If there are spies meeting somewhere beneath the Palais and one of them is following you, we must do something. Have you told the authorities?"

"No, I planned on telling your father, but first he was with a client and then . . . I know how much he hates the idea of having to go to the police and bringing any extra attention to the store and what I'm doing. It's Russia, isn't it? That makes your father so wary of the police?"

Grigori nodded. "But I'm not. Let me take care of it for you. Tomorrow draw me a schematic of where in the vault you were and I'll take it to the police. No need for you to relive it again."

"Would you? That's really kind of you, Grigori."

He waved off my thanks. "And this way we

can leave my father out of it." He sighed. "He's such a difficult man. So stuck in his ways. So sure those are the right ways."

"Why is there so much discord between you?" A brazen question, but their conflicts were disturbing.

"He wishes I was like my brothers."

"You mean, because you aren't a jeweler?"

Grigori shook his head. "He's disappointed in me that way, yes. But it's deeper. Leo and Timur are both his sons with Anna. Yes, they inherited my father's talent, but also Anna's warmth and gentleness."

I nodded. I remembered.

"I, on the other hand, am *my* mother's son. And Papa . . . well . . . quite simply . . . he hated my mother."

"But Anna speaks of you as if she is your mother. She loves you, Grigori."

"She tries to love me for my father's sake. But to both of them I will always be Natalya's son."

"How did your mother die?"

"She didn't die."

"I thought your father had been widowed."

"No, my mother is in Russia. They were divorced when I was three years old. I lived with my mother until I turned twelve and then moved in with my father, Anna, Timur, and Leo. Papa married Anna, who also worked in

Fabergé's studio, very soon after the divorce."

"Your mother must miss you."

"And I miss her. She's wild and exotic. A very well-respected poet."

"Has the revolution been hard on her?"

A mixture of emotions passed across Grigori's face. I wasn't sure why, but he seemed to be weighing my question.

"No, she's a revolutionary. That's a large part of why their marriage ended. They became political enemies. Both were young when they married and didn't know their own minds yet. As they grew, they grew apart. I think Mother ignited Papa's soul, but seared it too. She hated cages and was unable to accept the mores society placed on her. My father was old school, part of the staid middle class. He couldn't accept her radicalism."

"But Anna is exotic and wild too," I said.

"Yes. That's my father's type. But not politically. Not sexually. Anna has been a better wife than my mother ever could have been. I know that. And Anna gave Papa Timur and Leo. Apprentices. With nimble fingers and natural affinities for being a jeweler. Not like me with my clumsy hands." He glanced down at the offenders. "My brothers were already making some of the best pieces in the shop when the war started."

"Did you all go to the front right away?"

"Yes. The French desperately needed bilingual soldiers who could help train Russian troops. The rest you know. Timur died, I was injured, and Leo's gone on to be promoted three times. I think, as much as my father is proud of Leo's heroics, he wishes Leo had been the injured son so he'd have come home. Or that I'd been in Timur's place."

"That's a terrible thought. I've seen him with you. You might rub each other like sandpaper sometimes, but I know he loves you."

Grigori shrugged. "Love? My father saw himself in Leo and Timur. All his talent. All his potential. Passed on to both of them. As for my talent . . . all I am to Papa is a salesman of antiques."

"Your father is a salesman of jewels, that's very similar."

"You are kind to try and mitigate this, but it is all the difference in the world. Even if my father sells his own jewels, it doesn't matter. What is relevant is that he creates them. He is an artist and my brothers were artists and I am a journeyman."

The waiter brought our food, and as we ate, I changed the subject, encouraging Grigori to talk about some of the characters whom he bought the antiques from. A good mimic, he made me laugh with his impressions. Even though his mood lightened, I sensed the murky river running beneath everything he said. The conversation about his father couldn't be all that was on his mind, for he'd lived with that for years. Not for the first time, I wished I possessed the ability to hear the thoughts of the living instead of the dead. It would be far more convenient.

The rain ended, and Grigori and I headed back to the Palais Royal on dark streets lit only with intermittent moonlight when the clouds shifted. He didn't live with his father and stepmother but in his own apartment on the other side of the complex.

"It's kind of you to see me home," I said when we stopped at the entrance.

"I'd like to come in," he said, and put his arm up against the building, enclosing me.

I wasn't immune to his dark eyes and charming manner. And he'd not only entertained but also moved me that evening. But I was thinking about the locket I'd taken off from around my neck before going out. Illogical though it might have been, I couldn't be unfaithful to my ghost lover.

"I don't think so tonight, Grigori. That scare on my way to meet you, it's shaken me. And I've been so caught up with the talismans this week . . . in the stories of the lost men . . . my own lost soldier is very much on my mind."

I'd used Timur Orloff, "my own lost soldier," as an excuse many times in the last three years to keep away other soldiers home on leave. My guilt over what I'd done to him made me fear unintentionally hurting any other man returning to the front. I couldn't be responsible for breaking any hearts just before they might stop beating forever.

I'd never used any excuse with Grigori. He wasn't going back to the front. I'd accepted his attentions, trying them on for size, not encouraging but never discouraging him either. I wondered if his being Timur's brother made it easier for me to be attracted to him. Did my loyalty to the Orloffs encourage me to be with one son because I'd failed the other? The lack of passion I felt was calming. I never worried that being with Grigori would intensify my powers the way my experiences with his brother had.

I'd noticed that, though I liked Grigori, my feelings for him never grew. But my feelings for someone else had grown. And that night, when I gave Grigori my excuse, it wasn't his half brother I was thinking of but another lost soldier. That night, a deeper truth haunted me.

"I thought you'd forgiven yourself for what happened with Timur. You can't dwell on it, Opaline. It's been almost four years. My dead brother is not coming back. And I'm here."

Yes, it was ludicrous. Forsaking a flesh-and-blood man—albeit a troubled one—for Jean Luc, for a ghost.

"He's just in my head tonight."

"Why?"

I shrugged. "Every woman who comes to the shop and wants a memory locket makes me remember all over again."

He dropped his arm, leaned in, and kissed me on the lips. I was at first too shocked to move back. He wasn't rough, and the kiss wasn't an assault, and yet that was how it seemed compared to Jean Luc's ethereal embrace. I knew it was unhealthy for me to be in love with a ghost. Because that's what had happened. I hadn't admitted it to myself yet, but everything about this kiss was proof.

Grigori pulled away first and looked at me askance. He'd felt what I hadn't said in my luke-warm response.

"It doesn't seem possible that as more time has passed your sadness has increased. Why are you allowing yourself to be so preoccupied? My father and Anna have moved on. It's unhealthy that you can't."

It was so easy to let him think it was Timur coming between us.

"I know," I said. "Believe me, I do."

Chapter 20

When I got inside, I locked the door to my room, undressed, and slipped a nightgown over my bare skin. From my jewelry case in the armoire, I withdrew the locket I'd first made for Madame Alouette and stared into its depths at the green river of peridot and the lock of Jean Luc's hair.

I hadn't wanted to wear it to dinner with Grigori. I'd hoped that without it on, I'd feel more connected to the living than the dead. But it hadn't worked.

When I slipped it over my head, the orb came to rest between my breasts. Almost instantly, the gold warmed against my skin. I clasped it.

What was wrong with me? Grigori, a living breathing man near my age and not at the front. That alone made him a catch that anyone would envy. And yet when he'd kissed me, I hadn't responded. His warm lips hadn't moved me the way the ghost's spectral touch had.

The hopelessness of the situation settled upon me like a shroud. How had I allowed myself to fall in love with a phantom? Certainly, there was no future in it—I almost laughed out loud. The man I was fantasizing about, who I was communicating with, was a lingering echo of the past.

My mother had left me with a grimoire and a

list of spells. She'd guaranteed I could control the portal if I studied. And yet I hadn't opened the book. She'd warned me the longer I dwelled in this netherworld, the harder it would be to break the ties.

She'd spoken the spell I needed to use. *Make of the blood . . .*

No, I didn't even want to think the words for fear they'd do their job. I'd rather be lonely with my ghost. Crying for the stolen dream I could imagine as mine if the war had not intervened.

I fell asleep holding the golden orb.

I woke to a dark room and a warm breeze. The rise in temperature confused me. My nightgown suddenly constricted me. I pulled it over my head, dropping it on the floor. Now naked between the sheets, I felt wanton. I fingered the orb resting between my breasts, even warmer than the air.

I'd been dreaming of Jean Luc. I was sure of it. He'd been kissing me. Not the way Grigori had, not tentatively, not asking permission, but rather with a desperation as if he needed my kisses to keep him alive.

A cruel dream since he wasn't alive and I couldn't do anything to bring him back.

But you weren't dreaming the kisses, the wind whispered.

"How long have you been here?"

I don't know. Time isn't real for me. But I loved watching you sleep.

I worried he'd seen Grigori kiss me.

"Were you here when I got home?"

I arrived when you put on the memento mori. I haven't figured out how to get here without that pathway.

So he hadn't seen the scene at the door.

"As long as you are here now." I smiled.

I am.

His ethereal warmth stroked me, from my feet, up my legs, between my legs, around my hips, around my waist, up my back and then my neck and then, when I turned, around each breast.

"I want you to kiss me." How brazen I was, asking for the embrace.

His lips lowered onto mine again as he kissed me, and I kissed him back, certain I was with a man, not a specter. Jean Luc brushed the hair off my face and kissed my forehead and then my eyelids.

Don't open your eyes. If you keep them closed, you'll be able to see me better.

"How are you doing this?"

You must stop asking. I don't know. I only know that I want to be with you and that everything that's happened seems less terrible when I am. All the guilt I feel is still there, but it's as if your very presence is a forgiveness.

The war. There it was again. "You weren't at fault."

I might have prevented it.

"Other than by seeing the future? How?"

If I'd been smarter, I would have realized we'd been exposed for too long. That we should have sought shelter sooner.

I stayed quiet. What could I say about the actions he'd taken in battle? I didn't understand how warfare worked; I could offer nothing but platitudes.

No, you offer me so much more. Solace, for one.

"Wait, I wasn't talking out loud. You just read my mind."

So I did. I'm sorry.

"That's all right. But you said you wouldn't."

I won't. But what's bothering you? I can tell something is.

"So many things. For one, my great-grandmother thinks I'd be better off not listening to my mother and not developing my talents."

What does she mean?

"My mother is a witch who developed her abilities here in Paris against my great-grandmother's wishes. And I've inherited some of those same powers but haven't developed them. They're the reason I can communicate with you."

I don't want you to stop communicating with me.

"Neither do I."

And I don't want to stop kissing you.

I smiled.

You're even lovelier when you smile.

"I don't want you to stop kissing me either."

His hands cupped my face as he kissed me. Not the gentle kiss of someone waking me up but a hungry and urgent pressure. The warmth against my lips.

I wanted more of it, more of Jean Luc. A man not of flesh and blood but of incandescence that suffused me.

He continued arousing me, and as he did, I became the gold that I worked with in the workshop and he the fire that heated me. His mouth was the blue-hot flame that moved up and down my arms and legs and torso and breasts and warmed my flesh, making it hotter and hotter. Melting me. Turning me into another form. I became a circlet of gold, reshaped, with a space for a gem. He would be my ruby, my jewel, in my center.

I writhed.

His warmth flooded the space between my legs; I squeezed them closed, tight, held him there. Released my grip for a fraction of a second and then held him there again. The most exquisite heat tickled me behind my ears, then down my neck, in the crook of my shoulder. Unable to remain still, I twisted and turned in delight. Feeling more. And more. And then felt tickling between my legs, and inside of me, and I couldn't move fast enough or spread my legs far enough apart or press them tight enough together. I heard my name then, a whisper that moved inside of me as if his mouth were up against my cleft, and somehow the sound traveled up into my womb.

Opaline, Opaline, Opaline.

At once a plea and a promise. Too wrapped up in the sensations that his warmth created, I could only moan in response, not even sure I managed to repeat his name.

Reaching out, grasping for shoulders, for arms, I tried to enclose him, but my hands found no hold. For all its pleasure, this one-sided love-making frustrated me. I could not embrace, only be embraced.

"I need to touch you," I whispered.

You are touching me, Opaline. You don't feel me, but I feel you. Lie back, let me give this to you. It's so much more than I could hope for.

He became the jeweler then, his kisses little flames licking my body, heating every inch of skin, twisting and turning me to his will, sending shocks coursing down my arms and legs. Bending me into his design.

On fire, my skin must have turned from pale to rose by now. Inside, the temperature of my blood must have risen to the melting point. He was kissing me and entering me and filling me up with rare, deep purple-red rubies, blood-red, pulsing with their own life, and my thighs spread wide for him and my back arched for him and I opened for him in a way I never could have imagined.

Jean Luc rocked me and caressed me and teased me with his heat, and for long, long minutes I just allowed him to give me all of this blue-hot orange pleasure as I pooled beneath him. Melting gold. Molten metal. Dripping with pleasure, stretching with delight and desire.

It certainly was never like this when I was with my young lover, stealing our time away from his shop at the Carlton, hiding on the beach at night, pretending at love. Never like this with Grigori in his halfhearted efforts to pleasure me.

This desperate lovemaking between two people who could not be together, who should be able to be together, who were defying science and logic to lock together in an embrace, exploded inside.

Opaline, Opaline, Opaline.

Jean Luc moaned my name as he left kisses on my lips, my breasts, inside my thighs, that surely were branding my skin the way we imprinted our jewelry with our maker's mark. The backs of my knees and my ankles. And surely inside my body because waves of fire throbbed inside me. I had no choice but to give myself up to the heat. It was worth it to feel this burning passion, even if it meant I would be scarred for life.

Chapter 21

"I don't want to speak of it here," Monsieur said to me the next day, shortly after lunch. "But you will come upstairs for dinner tonight, yes? I have a favor to ask you."

I couldn't very well refuse.

We worked in companionable silence through the next hour. I was halfway to completing a complex necklace that would be displayed in the window when it was finished. The amount of pavéd surface made it difficult and painstaking work, but I was really only at peace with myself when living inside the process. Even though the magnifying glasses were heavy on my face, they centered me. Bending over strained my back, but at the same time the physical exertion distracted me from thoughts of my late-night visitor and my curiosity over the favor Monsieur was yet to ask of me.

"I need to visit the vault—may I have your key?" I asked Monsieur midafternoon.

"What is it you need?" He came over to my table and inspected the piece.

The necklace consisted of twenty large round sapphires, each cut so as to expose a wide flat table. They were the canvas, the dark blue night-time skies. I'd carved a crescent moon around one side of each stone, pavéd with light blue sapphires, and planned for tiny diamonds in the curve that would sparkle like tiny stars.

"I don't have the stars . . ."

Monsieur looked at me quizzically. "I thought you'd already brought those diamonds up."

"Yes, I did. But when I interrupted this to finish the grape brooch, I replaced them. I didn't want that many stones in my desk."

Nodding, he handed me his key. I threw my shawl around my shoulders and went down the hall to the doorway to the steps.

Despite how much I despised going underground, how much I hated the chalky smell of the dungeons, how the damp got into my bones, how the cries and whines and whispers made me shiver, I had to learn more about what was going on.

Inside the vault, I started removing the objects from the shelves on the back wall. I needed to work quickly. Monsieur would be concerned if I took too long, and I didn't want to alert him to what I was doing. He'd forbid me from getting involved. Anna too would have me stop. They wouldn't want me inviting danger by investigating further, but after the confrontation with the stranger and the note he'd shoved in my hand, I was scared.

At least I didn't waste time picking out stones. The diamonds I required for the necklace were in my smock pocket. I'd chosen them the week before and, as Monsieur had thought, taken them upstairs. I hated lying to him, but I'd needed an excuse for visiting the vault again.

Only halfway through my efforts, I heard voices. Hurrying, I removed six jeweled goblets and three frames, and then two large silver candelabras, almost dropping one. I had to be careful: if I could hear them, then they could hear me.

I dug the mortar out of the crevice, fragment by fragment, hoping once I'd exposed the peep-hole I'd see a more complete clue.

Who were these men? Why were they meeting? And why had one of them warned me away?

Rising up on tiptoes, I put my eye to the crevice and . . . nothing but blackness. Gently I reached in with my forefinger and hit an obstacle. Either plaster or mortar—I couldn't be certain which one because my view was obstructed. I could hear them, but mixed in with other voices, other sounds, I couldn't glean any information at all.

That night at the Orloffs' apartment, there were two other Russian men whom I'd seen at dinner before, Serge Kokashka and Alexi Vanya. Along with Monsieur and Grigori, they were drinking vodka and arguing loudly in their mother tongue when I arrived upstairs.

Anna greeted me warmly, kissing me on both

cheeks and taking me by the arm to sit with her on the couch.

"Would you like some tea or wine?"

I asked for wine and she winked. "For me too."

She filled two glasses and handed me one. The same gold double-eagle insignia on all of her china and silverware glinted in the candlelight as if the bird were preening.

Grigori broke away from the caucus to come over to me. He gave me a formal bow and smile, then pulled me up and kissed me as his mother had, on both cheeks. At the same time, he whispered he'd gone to the police.

I looked into his eyes, and he nodded. Anna, sensing we wanted to be alone, though for very different reasons than she probably thought, busied herself with the dinner. Once she left, Grigori and I sat on the couch and I told him what I'd seen in the vault and that mortar had been put in the crack.

"I must have been discovered, which had to be why I was attacked."

"I'll go back to the police tomorrow. I don't want you to worry. I'm here, Opaline. I can watch out for you. I can protect you."

"Thank you . . ." I wanted to say more but was confused about how to show my appreciation without him thinking I was encouraging him romantically.

Anna announced dinner, and we all sat at the

table. The men continued their conversation in Russian, while Anna and I chatted in French. But once the maid served the soup, everyone switched to French and Monsieur directed his comments to me.

"We hear the Dowager, the tsar's mother, is distraught. The lack of news about Tsarina Alexandra and the children weighs on her more and more every day," Monsieur Orloff said. "No one has any idea if her grandchildren are alive or dead. It's a terrible situation, as you can imagine, and she is not coping with it well."

"Why would they have been killed? What political purpose would that serve?" I asked.

"The Bolsheviks are monsters. They easily could have murdered the children simply to destroy any chance that royalty would ever rule over Russia again."

"But it will happen despite them," Serge said. "If there are no children, there are cousins. Dozens of them. The Romanov line cannot be wiped out so easily."

The soup, a fine consommé with delicate dumplings floating on top, tasted of beef, sherry, and dill. The cuisine served at the Orloffs' combined French food with a Russian sensibility.

"The Dowager," Monsieur Orloff continued, "will do anything to get an answer about the fate of her beloved grandchildren. Are they alive? Where are they?"

"Yes, I know, it's indeed terrible," I said.

Serge and Alexi nodded at me, murmuring their agreement. I noticed Anna had stopped eating her soup to watch me. So had Grigori.

"You know the Dowager Empress's sister Alexandra is mother of the king of England?" Monsieur asked me.

"Yes."

Outside, I could hear the wind beating on the windows, as if it wanted to come in and hear what it was my mentor was asking.

Serge inched closer to the edge of his seat. Alexi kept flexing his fingers nervously. This was an important conversation, but I didn't know why.

"The Dowager is planning a clandestine trip from the Ukraine to England. As you can imagine, it will be dangerous, but she's going to travel in disguise. The trip is a long one and there is a war on, but she is determined to find out what has happened to her family. King George has been using all his power to investigate, but still has no answers. She needs to know more than what the king can tell her."

Monsieur Orloff paused. Anna reached out and put her hand on mine. "You don't need to do this. It's as dangerous for you as it is for her."

"But I will go with you," Grigori said. "I'll make sure you are as safe as possible."

"Do what?" I looked from Anna to her husband.

I'd missed something. I'd lost the thread of what they were asking.

"We want you to go to England. The Dowager Empress is in need of your services," Monsieur said.

"I don't understand."

"We want you to meet with the tsar's mother. To help her," he said.

"How can I help her?" I still didn't understand.

"If she gave you locks of the children's hair, you could make talismans for her and see if they speak to you. If they don't, then she can hope, she can believe they are still alive," Monsieur said.

"But you don't even believe what I do is real," I said to him.

"Yes, he does," Anna said. "It's just Pavel's way to always express his cynicism first."

"Will you do this, Opaline?" Monsieur asked.

I shook my head before I even finished processing the request. "No, I can't. What I do isn't a discovery process. If I was wrong either way, I could cause her so much pain."

"We need you, there's nothing else we can think of," Alexi said.

"The empress is distraught. Grieving," Serge said.

"And I'd be going with you. To protect you. You'll be safe." Grigori gave me a proud, almost smug smile.

"I'm sorry to disappoint you all, but I can't. I'm not a soothsayer."

Anna looked from Grigori to Monsieur. "I agree with Opaline. It is too dangerous to leave Paris, to cross the channel, to go to England with a war raging around us."

Not one of them responded to her.

"Yes, it is dangerous, but the Dowager is a grieving mother who doesn't know if she is also a grieving grandmother. She has five missing grandchildren and can't find out what's happened to a single one of them," Monsieur repeated.

"Do you actually expect me to travel across the channel during the war to meet with the mother of the tsar and the grandmother of his children and tell her the fate of her family? How could I bear the responsibility? What if I was wrong? I don't predict death. I don't read the future. These women come to me, and I tap into some tunnel of last thoughts for them."

"She is desperate, she's lost her only remaining son," Monsieur said. Then he turned to Anna. "Tell Opaline how it feels to lose a son."

Furious for Anna's sake, I interrupted. "I know how she feels. I've looked into the faces of so many mothers in mourning. Don't exploit your wife's grief to pressure me."

I'd never talked back to Monsieur before, and he looked stunned. But I wouldn't let him do this to her. I didn't need a reminder of Anna's anguish. I dreamed of her and other mothers like her. They haunted me even more than the voices of the men who'd died . . . for the men moved on to a place of peace after passing on their messages. All except for Jean Luc. Not moving on, he couldn't let go. There was something he needed to do or to tell someone and hadn't yet figured it out. But this was not the time to think about him. Not with Monsieur and his companions and his son trying to coerce me into taking this trip.

"There must be some other way to find out. Aren't there spies in Russia? Bolsheviks who would take a bribe for the information?"

A shadow passed over Grigori's face. I couldn't tell if it was because I'd referenced the Bolsheviks—this family hated them with an all-consuming passion—or if, despite the risk, he'd envisioned the trip as a way for us to spend more time together. A way for him to prove he could stand up to danger and protect me.

"Every other avenue has been exhausted. We tried bribes, but there is no news we can rely on. They say anything for money. One day that they are alive and hidden somewhere. The next that they were executed," Alexi said.

"Opaline," Monsieur said as he put down his spoon and leaned toward me, "will you at least consider it?"

I shook my head. "I'm sorry, no."

"There is nothing we can offer you truly worth the effort and danger," Monsieur continued. "But—"

I started to protest.

"Hear me out. You are a fine jeweler with a keen eye and a wonderful imagination. To be young and so talented. I envy your future. Once the war is over you will be able to soar, and the pieces you will make will take Paris by storm. I know this. I can see it in your work. I taught you like I taught my own sons. You are almost ready to go out on your own. If you take on this journey, if you help us, then when you are ready, in a year or two, whenever it is, I will set you up in a shop of your own and stock it with all the gold and silver and gemstones you need to open your doors."

The offer took me by surprise. I could hardly imagine how much money it would take to accomplish what he'd suggested. I knew the Orloffs were well-off, as was my family, but this offer required a small fortune. Was Tatania Tichtelew helping finance the effort? I'd seen her in the shop earlier that day.

"No, I just can't."

"But Opaline—" Monsieur began, but Grigori interrupted.

"This is too much. You asked her, she said no. And why shouldn't she? It's not her country, it's not her empress, it's not her problem. You are exploiting her. Opaline"—he turned to me—"there's no reason for you to do this. Or even to sit and listen to any more of it."

Grigori's compassion touched me. The room was swimming. Too many eyes watched me. The rain had become a storm, and outside the howling wind distracted me. My mind was crowded with what everyone had said. It was ridiculous to even entertain the idea in exchange for a shop. If I wanted one, my parents might become my patrons. Or maybe one of the other wealthy women who came to La Fantaisie Russe would want to be able to brag to her friends that she'd financed a jewelry store. My great-grandmother was another avenue. She knew immensely wealthy men whom she sent to our store to buy baubles for their wives and mistresses. Perhaps one of them would want to finance a shop. Besides, I was years away from going out on my own. Or was I ready? Had I in less than four years learned what Monsieur Orloff could teach? Was working with him actually stifling me? Didn't I have ideas for pieces, journals filled with drawings, that he'd dismissed? But how mercenary—to be bribed into taking this trip!

I turned to Anna. "You agree with my decision, don't you?"

"You have a great gift to listen to those who have passed and bring solace to those who are still here, but you should never feel obligated to use it in any way uncomfortable to you."

"But you think I should go?"

"It's not what I think. It's what I've beheld. No matter what I say to you, you will go. This journey is meant to be. It is something you do because of who you are."

"Who I am? A Frenchwoman with no ties to Russia?"

"Because you are a Daughter of La Lune."

Listening to her echo my mother's words angered me. I didn't want Anna to tell me what lay ahead.

"Will you do this for us?" Monsieur asked.

"I'm not ready to . . . I need time to think about it."

I hadn't said no this time, and Monsieur Orloff beamed. The widest smile he'd ever bestowed on me. Anna's eyes filled with tears. Serge and Alexi appeared relieved. Only Grigori was upset, and I couldn't help but wonder why he looked as if his worst nightmare had come true.

Chapter 22

In the end, it was my memory of Timur that influenced my decision. I owed the Orloffs for not giving their son what he had deserved, what he'd wanted, before he died.

There was not a lot of time to prepare for the trip. We would be leaving in three days to travel by car to Le Havre, where Grigori and I would ferry across the channel to Portsmouth and then be driven to the rendezvous in a town whose name I'd not yet been told.

Anna suggested she help me practice trying to read the locks of hair without turning them into talismans in case I cracked the crystals or broke the solder machine. I wouldn't have backups, only what I brought with me.

"I've tried, I can't. I need the crystal and the engravings and elements to work together to open the portal."

"Maybe simply because you don't know how," she said.

"That's certainly possible," I answered.

"Have you been studying the grimoire Sandrine gave you? Has it shed any light on the notes you took about the triptych painting?"

Since agreeing to this mission, I'd been actively studying, trying to find something in the book about soothsaying—about telling the present or future without the use of stones—but hadn't been able to discover anything.

"Why don't I try to help," she said and suggested I retrieve my book of spells and bring it to her secret reading room.

She was waiting for me in her *monde enchanté*. Thick votives, perfuming the air with their sweet scented wax, burned softly, illuminating the crystal orbs and jeweled Russian icons. A beatific Madonna seemed to be looking down at me with a knowing glance.

Today Anna's worktable was decorated with a bright red-and-navy silk cloth, in its center a pentagram embroidered with silver thread.

I handed her the grimoire, somewhat reluctantly. My reaction surprised me. It was only a book—what harm could come to it by letting Anna read it?

As she took it from me, I wondered if she might find more there than I had. Would she discover the secret of the voices? And if she did, would she finally be able to teach me to control them?

What I'd read so far had at least explained a bit about my preoccupation with Jean Luc. Daughters of La Lune, it seemed, were cursed when it came to matters of the heart. Each only was allowed one absolute love per lifetime. And that love, once given, never waned. Even if the man was untrue or died, she was destined to pine for him and never find another mate.

Many generations tried without luck to find an antidote to love. And I didn't wonder at their effort. If there was a potion I could swallow to rid my heart of Jean Luc, I would have gulped it down. If the curse was true, I was in love with an ephemeral spirit not just for now but for always.

I'd read how my ancestor, the first La Lune, lost her lover, Cherubino, and did everything in her power, including selling her soul, to try to regain his love. She'd failed, but even after his death, she never stopped loving him.

And now, over three hundred years later, there I was, also in love with someone who was dead. Who was trapped in that netherworld. Had a cosmic mistake been made? Had what was meant to be been thwarted? Had the war interfered in our meeting? There was nothing in the book about the strange process that made it possible for him to hear me. To speak to me. To touch me with his warm wind.

In searching for an answer, I'd read a warning about necromancy in the pages of my book. The darkest art, it was fraught with dangers. Mistakes created monsters. Preventing an imminent death didn't test the laws that governed us. That was allowed. But raising the dead did. Still, if I could bring Jean Luc back . . .

Anna closed the book and handed it back to

me. "I'm sorry," she said, with a sad, defeated expression in her eyes.

"There's nothing?" I asked.

"There could be everything, but I can't see it. There's nothing written in the book, Opaline, it's all blank pages."

"That's impossible. What do you mean? I've been reading the stories about—"

Anna interrupted. "So you can read it?"

I nodded.

"Then it must be guarded so no one but you and the person who wrote it can read it."

"That's possible?"

"Yes. Rare, but possible."

And then I remembered. "My mother said it was protected when she gave it to me, but I didn't understand what she meant."

"Well, no matter," Anna said, and stood. "I can still try to help. Here, look at this—" She pulled a book off her shelf and opened it to a yellowed vellum page. I stared at the illustration of a compass and notations that appeared to be written by hand, in Latin.

"This is the *Ars Notoria*, believed written in the thirteenth century. This drawing is of a 'megnetick experiment' which allows people to communicate through telepathy using a lodestone and two compass needles. The theory was that when the two needles were rubbed against the same lodestone, they would become entangled with each other. Linked. And whenever one needle moved, the other needle would move the same way. So if someone placed a needle in a circle made of letters and spelled out a word, wherever the other needle was, it would move accordingly."

"And you think that's similar to what happens to me? I've become entangled with a cosmic needle?"

"It's possible the talisman functions as the needle. So if the goal is for you to access the voices without creating the amulet, you need to become the needle yourself."

"Yes. Do you think that's possible?"

"I'm not sure, but we can try."

Anna opened her armoire and began pulling out bottles and jars.

Finished with her apothecary, she placed two beakers in front of me, one on either side of the bowl. The left looked like oil, golden with a hint of green. The other appeared to be rich ruby wine. Into a crystal glass that reflected the votives in all its facets, she poured first some of the oil, and then the other liquid.

I'd read dozens of my great-grandmother's books on witchcraft and the occult. I knew what some ceremonies and spells required. And the grimoire my mother gave me provided me with more proof.

"That's wine, isn't it?" I asked.

She laughed. "Yes. What else could it be?"

"Blood?" I asked.

"Heavens no, Opaline." She picked up a small

paring knife I hadn't noticed. "Now, for your personals. Can I take a nail clipping?"

I offered her my hand, and she sliced off a tiny sliver of the nail from my ring finger.

"And a lock of your hair." She clipped a curl. "Now the most difficult part. I need to collect one of your tears."

"How can I—"

"Close your eyes and try to remember something that made you sad." She handed me a glass spoon. "Use this to capture the tears."

"Couldn't you let me cut up an onion?"

She laughed. "They have to be tears of emotion. I'll leave you alone for a few minutes." Anna rose, leaned down, and kissed me on the top of my head. "You're a brave one, Opaline. I'm proud of you."

I'd worried how I'd manage to cry on purpose, but her words got me started and then I pushed myself to think, with a sinking heart, about my futile, impossible feelings for Jean Luc.

When Anna returned, she put the nail clipping and lock of hair in the depression of a large amethyst crystal geode. Then she lit a tall buttery-colored candle and intoned what sounded like a prayer.

"The powers present are strong, but we ask for them to be stronger still. We ask that they intensify for all of the right reasons and none of the wrong."

Then, using the tip of the candle, she set fire to my hair and nail shaving. A noxious odor filled the room, and I leaned back, away from it. Picking up the spoon, she dripped my tears over the tip of the candle to put out its flame.

Once the concoction in the geode stopped smoking, she anointed it with six drops from the oil-and-wine mixture. Then she wrapped the mess up in a piece of parchment and placed it in a crimson-colored silk pouch with black draw-strings. She held the small bag close to her heart for a moment and then held it out to me.

"Wear this for three days, and then see if you can pull a message from a lock of a soldier's hair without encasing it in crystals and gold. Without the man's wife or mother or sister there. Hopefully, you'll be able to do it."

"I'll try." I took the pouch from her and held it in my right hand.

Anna put her hand over mine. "You've been gifted with a rare power, and despite how it's pained you, you've used it graciously and self-lessly. But never more so than now. No matter the outcome, I want you to know we are grateful for your willingness to help. All of us, myself, Pavel, Grigori, Serge, Madame Tichtelew, the rest of the émigrés, and even those who are no longer here to say it themselves. From all of us, Opaline, thank you."

It was almost a shame Anna didn't need any more of my tears, because of how freely they flowed then.

Chapter 23

That night Monsieur Orloff and Grigori fought. I didn't know why they were in the store after it closed. Or what they argued about. But their heated words carried from the shop down to my apartment, so lying in my bed, I could hear them. If only I could have understood them. Russian is a complicated-sounding language to the French. Our words flow like water, smooth like sips of wine, like the texture of our cheese, silky like my mother's paints on her palette. Russian sounds like throwing rocks into a stream, like chopping wood, breaking branches.

Placing the silken pouch around my neck as Anna had suggested, I tried to go to sleep, but the fight continued long into the night, and so I finally got out of bed, picked up the binder of columns written by Jean Luc, and continued to read.

There were over one hundred. He'd written a column every other week for four years. Plus several that had never been published. A soldier's letters home to his lover. Except there was no lover. He'd only imagined her in his mind. She was as ephemeral to him as he to me. And yet, as I read, I could picture him with his careless smile and hair falling into his eyes. It wasn't the photographs of Jean Luc I'd glimpsed in his parents' apartment that I saw in my mind, but my mother's paintings of him. I'd been too far from the photos to see any of Jean Luc's expressions. But the man my mother had depicted was animated and vital. Yes, wracked with guilt, but also with a yearning for life, sensual and smart, determined and creative. A poetic soul who sent me on lonely treasure hunts around Paris.

The more I read, the more I was able to fill in about him. He was an avid reader who'd traveled as far as China and Australia and Egypt. Sorry he was an only child, he'd had an imaginary friend when he was a boy. Sometimes, in the trenches, he thought about that friend, almost wishing he could conjure him again. A dog lover, he missed his terrier—the dog I'd met at his mother's house. An inveterate museum visitor, he found solace there. Art made him think, wonder, engage in philosophical questioning. Among the list of artists he mentioned whose work he'd studied and appreciated, I was stunned to find my own mother's name. Reading about her work in one of his columns did more than surprise me; because of its context, it stunned me.

Jean Luc wrote he'd been home on leave and gone to the gallery on rue la Boétie, where her work was shown. He'd fallen in love with one of the paintings, wanted to buy it, and was distraught to learn it had already been sold.

Stupefied, I read on, realizing the painting he'd wanted to buy was of me.

Portraits of her sitters illustrated via the items that exemplified them was one of my mother's specialties. She painted my father in the reflections of all the windows of a building he'd designed. My younger sister Delphine, following in my mother's artistic footsteps, could be seen in puddles of watercolors in her paint tin. My brother, her twin, who had all attributes of a businessman even as a teenager, was pictured on a ten-franc note. My mother had painted me over and over in the flashes of fire in a string of opal beads.

Putting the book of columns down, I took off Anna's pouch and replaced it with Jean Luc's talisman. Between my breasts, under my night-gown, it warmed my flesh instantly.

"You knew my mother's work? You'd seen my portrait? Did you recognize me when you first saw me here?"

No. I felt drawn to you, but I didn't realize till just now, as you read it. So that's who you are, the famous painter's daughter. La Lune's daughter.

"Her real name is Sandrine Duplessi, but she signs her paintings that way. Do you know about the original La Lune?"

No, but I'd love you to tell me the story.

And so I told him about my ancestor, a sixteenth-century courtesan, a witch, a painter.

And a spirit who kept herself alive for almost three hundred years, waiting for a descendant strong enough to host her—who turned out to be my mother.

Her tale frightens you.

"It does."

Because of what you might have inherited?

"Of course. Witches' blood flows in my veins. Witches! Who were burned at the stake and were pilloried. Who are shown as old crones to be feared."

Is that why you came to Paris? To escape her and your ties to her?

"No, I came to help with the war effort."

Are you sure?

"Of course."

I'm not as certain, Opaline.

A breeze blew against the back of my neck.

"How do you do that?"

I pull at the energy in the atmosphere. Do you like it?

"It both frightens me and reassures me at the same time. If I physically feel the heat and the gusts of wind, then I know you're not a manifestation of my imagination. Not a symptom of some kind of mental illness. If I feel you, then you are real. Or at least as real as any spirit might be."

You know the reason you can hear me, feel me, is because of the powers you inherited. Your mother is right . . .

I couldn't help but laugh sarcastically.

But she is. If you embraced them, it might help. You could learn to use them. You'd be happier.

"Even you are pushing me?" I shook my head, disappointed for the moment.

The breeze embraced me now. As if he'd put his arm around me to soothe me.

Why are you so afraid of the dark?

I shivered. I didn't want to talk about my fear of the dark. I'd never told anyone what I'd seen there.

What happened? What did you see in the dark?

"You promised not to read my mind."

I wasn't. Your memories aren't the same as thoughts.

"I don't want you to read my memories either."

It's not quite reading them, more like reaching out for them. They have some physicality thoughts don't.

I started to hum a song, trying to block him out. A song I'd loved since childhood.

Jean Luc laughed.

That song you are humming now. You are on a great white horse, wearing a little green dress, and your hair is all curled. Were you six? Seven? A happy moment, wasn't it?

"Yes, my father took me to the carousel down on the Croisette in Cannes, by the beach. How did you know that?"

Your memories are like a mosaic, thousands of colored tiles. But not just on a flat plane.

They're multidimensional and go backward and forward in time. That's where I see the darkness too. Black shadows of fear.

"Well, the world has been a scary place for quite some time."

Jean Luc sighed.

I didn't want us to be mired in my fear. "Can I touch you?" I asked.

I'm not sure.

I reached out. My hand met no impediment.

"And yet you can touch me. It's unfair."

Like this?

A heated breeze flowed around me and caressed me. Molding the wind into hands, he removed my robe and unbuttoned my nightgown with fingers I could not see but felt.

If it weren't for you . . .

"Yes?"

You're keeping me from moving on.

"But that's a bad thing, isn't it? Isn't peace on the other side?"

I don't think so. Not for me. But do you want me to move on?

"No," I cried out. "But I suppose that's selfish of me. You're unhappy and unmoored. You can't stay here for me, you must go."

Not yet. It's impossibly unfair I didn't find you until now. You're who I would have settled down to be with. Who I would have stopped traveling to stay at home with. Given up all the wild nights

and excess of wine just to be with you like this.
Just like this, but you'd be able to see me.

Tears fell from my eyes, dripped down my cheek. The wind brushed them off.

I want to try to make you see me.

"Yes, please." I sat up, leaned forward, searched the shadows in the corners of the room.

Lie down, be still. Keep your eyes open.

I did as he asked. Naked but warm, in my strange little bedroom without any windows, decorated with all the drawings of pieces of jewelry I dreamed of making.

Now, look, Opaline, right above you.

As I watched, a puff of cloud formed. A bit of condensation. A mass of opalescent fog. And in its mother-of-pearl shine, I saw a glimmer of Jean Luc smiling at me, an expression of lust and desire on his face.

It lasted a moment and then, as quickly as it had appeared, dissipated.

I sensed how much effort it had taken him to manifest the image because the wind immediately grew cold and I began shivering. Had he disappeared? Had he crossed a line that would prevent him from coming back? The panic began to build inside me. I started to freeze. And just when I thought all really was lost, the warmth returned, blew over my breasts, between my legs. My shivers had nothing to do with temperature but sensations. My phantom lover had not left me after all.

Chapter 24

Planning for a channel crossing during a time of war proved complicated. Grigori found us passage on a barge taking medical supplies and personnel across to Portsmouth. It was usually a journey of less than half a day, but he warned me that, depending on war games, traffic, and the weather, it might take as long as eight hours. But first we needed to motor from Paris to Le Havre.

The morning we were to leave, we ate breakfast with Anna and Monsieur Orloff. When we were done, Anna handed me a basket.

"Here are apples and ham-and-cheese sandwiches, a bottle of wine, and two canteens of water." I took it from her. "And here is a blanket, since it might get cold on the water." She draped it around my shoulders.

Grigori took our suitcases down to the car he'd hired. Each was as small as we could manage, though mine contained more equipment to make jewelry than clothes. Anna's silk pouch hadn't worked. I remained unable to message without encasing personal effects in the stones and engraving the runes. I was a lithomancer, after all, not a psychic.

Grigori came back. "We're all packed."

Monsieur held his hand up. "There's still a bit of time before you need to take off, Grigori. Come with me, Opaline. I have a gift I want you to give the empress."

I followed Monsieur Orloff out of the kitchen.

"Why do you want *me* to give it to the empress and not Grigori?" I asked, knowing this would sting his son anew.

Monsieur, as was his habit, didn't answer when he wasn't so inclined. In silence, he led me down the hall of their apartment and into the library.

Unlike the vault below the shop, which shone with so much gold and silver that I never knew where to focus my eyes, the library glowed more deeply with a green shimmer that made me suck in my breath. This was not the shine of stones, but the magick I remembered seeing in my own home. The books were glowing. I walked over to a shelf and scanned a row of leather-bound volumes. The letters were all Cyrillic. I couldn't read any of them.

"What is it?" Monsieur Orloff asked. "You seem surprised."

"The books . . ."

"Yes?"

"They are . . ." I struggled, looking for the word. "Are these your books?"

"Yes. Why?"

"What kind of books are they?"

He came over to the shelf where I stood. "Those are all about the history of emeralds."

"And the rest?" I gestured.

"All about jewelry and jewelry making."

That explained the glow. They were speaking to me. Calling out. These books held secrets about gems and metals.

"I wish they weren't all in Russian. I'd like to study them."

"Enough about my books, Opaline." He stood beside his desk. "Come here."

As I strode toward him, I saw him pull out a drawer and extract one of the shop's embossed-leather boxes. When I reached his side, he opened the box. Inside were two gold necklaces. At least twenty-five emerald enamel miniature Easter eggs hung from one. Ruby enamel eggs hung from the other necklace.

First he took the green one and lowered it around my neck.

"It is not about the value of this piece, you understand?" His eyes were boring into mine, his voice a low, harsh whisper.

I nodded.

"It is precious because I've been waiting to give it to a member of the Romanov family for a long, long time."

"Were these eggs on *The Tree of Life* in the cabinet downstairs?" I was sure of it. I'd studied those eggs for years.

He didn't answer, instead continued giving me directions. "Put it inside your dress, hide it under your chemise. Please, do it now."

He turned away so I could partially unbutton my chemise and hide the necklace.

"It's done."

He turned back. Still sotto voce, he whispered: "Give it only to the Dowager Empress and only when you're alone, yes?"

I nodded.

"When you bathe, hide it. When you sleep, leave it on under your nightgown. Yes?"

I nodded again.

He lifted out the red enamel necklace.

"This is for her also. Look here."

Carefully, he showed me a little key hanging at the back of the chain. He detached it and used it to open the center egg, the one with the insignia of the double eagle on it.

Inside was a small scroll of paper. He unfurled it to show me how it was covered with Cyrillic letters. And in its center lay another tiny gold key.

"The note explains who I am and what this gift means to me. That it's just a sentimental gift, you understand? I only mention the red one in the note. The green one is a secret."

He rerolled the paper around the key and replaced it inside the egg.

"And the key?"

He ignored yet another of my questions. "Everything I am telling you is just between us, yes?"

Did he mean for me to keep it from his son? And why hadn't he answered me about the second key?

He lowered the necklace of red over my neck. "This is the one I want people to see. The one I want them to think you are giving to the Dowager. The one I even want Grigori to believe you are giving to the Dowager. Do you understand?"

"No. Why are you keeping this from Grigori?"

"I don't want to frighten you, little one, but there are spies everywhere. Bolshevik spies who watch us, waiting for us to do anything out of the ordinary. We've taken extreme measures so this trip will remain secret. There are only four people in Paris who know you are going to visit the Dowager. But we can never be too careful. If the wrong people discover who you are going to see, they will be looking for a treasure. There have always been rumors I am one of those who was sent out of Russia with some of the tsar's fortune. That, anticipating the revolution, he stashed away riches in other countries. The Bolsheviks are poor. They foolishly believe those stories and are searching for those caches of riches."

"But these are just our eggs, they aren't expensive."

"You know that, and I know that, but the Bolsheviks are suspicious. They might not believe it. If, by some terrible chance, they find out about this journey, if they find you and Grigori, I want you to give them this red necklace. It's not as special as the green one I need you to protect."

"But I still don't know why you don't want Grigori to know." It pained me that Monsieur was hiding this from his son.

"Grigori is a terrible liar under pressure. I've tested him. His eyes give him away. His glance always goes to the right. I want him to believe these red eggs are the ones for the empress so if you are accosted, neither of you puts your life in danger. Just give the thugs the red eggs. Continue on your way. The real gift—the gift of my heart, the gift that will make the Dowager remember Mother Russia and for a little while remember the glory of her homeland—will remain safe under your clothes."

Were there tears in his eyes?

"You understand?" he asked.

I did. Not just his feelings for the country he loved and had needed to leave, but Grigori's sadness too. Monsieur didn't trust his own son the way a father should.

"This necklace you are wearing underneath also has an egg that opens up near the clasp. You will show that to the Dowager."

"That's what the key is in the red egg?"

He nodded.

"But what if the red necklace is taken?"

"That's why I'm explaining it all to you. If the red necklace is taken, the Dowager will be able to find a way to open the green eggs on her own once you've explained how it works. Now, let us go outside and show Anna and Grigori the lovely red enamel gift I've prepared for the mother of the tsar and the grandmother of his heirs."

Seeing the necklace, Grigori's rage turned his cheeks as red as the enamel. The private conversation had angered him. Anna did her best to make small talk and calm him, but it didn't help.

"We have a long drive ahead of us," Grigori said to me. And then, with the most meager of good-byes to Anna and his father, he walked out the door. Before I could follow, Anna grabbed me to her and whispered a last bit of advice. When she let me go, Monsieur said, "Bon voyage." But the words were incongruous with his grave expression of concern.

Every stage of the voyage was difficult. The car Grigori hired was old and the roof leaked in the rain. The roads were rutted and we bumped our way to Le Havre, both of us worried we'd lose a wheel or two.

By the time we arrived, the rain had become a relentless storm that kept the boat in the dock, with all of us on it, for more than four hours before the captain decided it was safe to set sail.

Once we were on the channel, the wind picked up again and Grigori and I huddled in our seats, both of us violently ill. Peppermints or ginger would have helped, but Anna hadn't packed those. The food she'd prepared went uneaten.

Twice I noticed a businessman, an attaché case in his lap, watching us. The third time, my heart accelerated, and without thinking, I put my hand up to the red egg necklace, fingering one of Monsieur Orloff's trinkets.

"What's wrong?" Grigori asked.

I turned to him, faced him completely, so if the man was indeed watching us, he wouldn't be able to read my lips.

"Don't look over there. I don't want him to think I'm talking about him. But there is a man five rows in front of us with his case in his lap. He keeps turning around to watch us."

"My father has scared you. There's no one on the boat and no one in Paris who has any idea of what we are doing."

I knew he was as nervous as I was and just trying to calm me, for all his actions belied his words. He had been inspecting the other passengers when he thought I wasn't watching. And when he wasn't scrutinizing people, he was staring out at the channel, worrying the gold signet ring on his left hand. As he continued, I wondered if he was trying to assuage my fears or his own.

"And if anyone did know what we were doing, they wouldn't care. I know Papa might not think so, but the Bolsheviks have more importan things to do than follow a witch and an antiques dealer to a castle on the English coast. They don't need the Dowager. She's useless to their cause. If she wasn't, she would be dead like the rest of them."

Grigori's words surprised me. I'd never heard Monsieur or Anna talk with such assuredness about the fate of the tsar's wife and children.

"So you do believe everyone in the family is dead?"

He looked away from my face, his eyes traveling to the red eggs around my neck. Reaching out, he fingered one and then dropped it, almost reluctantly.

"No, no, I'm not sure," he said, and looked off to the right, out into the distance.

Grigori's tell, just as Monsieur had described it. Before, I'd considered this a sign that Grigori was easily distracted. Now I wondered if he'd often been lying.

"But you must have some reason for what you said. What is it?" I asked.

"It makes sense to me, that's all. Why would the Bolsheviks keep them alive? What better to do with symbols of a corrupt system, as they say." Grigori spat out the words. Hatred hardening the syllables.

338

No, his loathing for the revolutionaries ran as deep as his father's did.

"Enough of this talk now," he said. "No one is following us. No one is watching us."

The boat rocked as it hit a swell. We swayed one way and the next. I tried not to but moaned out loud.

Grigori put his arm around me. Cold and scared, I welcomed the comfort. His fingers found the necklace, and he toyed with one of the ruby eggs for a few moments, then let go.

"I'm going to try to sleep." He closed his arms over his chest. "You should too. You'll feel less ill with your eyes shut."

Following his advice, I closed my eyes, but the boat rocked too intensely. That, plus my fears about the man five rows in front of us, kept me awake. Through almost closed lids, I continued to watch him turn to look at us several times more.

Ravaging waves kept tossing the boat as if it were a plaything. My stomach couldn't take it anymore. I needed to get up; I was going to be sick. I just managed to get to the railing in time. Leaned over. Beneath me the murky green water churned. I gagged. Once. Twice.

And then the boat pitched so far to one side water sprayed on my face. Righting itself, it held steady for a moment and then went down again, sharply, quickly, and I lost my balance. I didn't care—so sick, the idea of the icy water seemed almost a relief. Falling forward, I watched the waves come closer until arms pulled me back. Away from the inviting sea. I fell backward onto Grigori. When I turned and saw his face, it was etched with worry.

"Thank God," he said. "I thought . . ." He broke off, wrapped his arms around me, and held me tight to his chest. "Thank God."

He'd flirted with me. Befriended me. Shared confidences with me, but until that moment, I hadn't guessed at the depth of his feelings for me. And it surprised me.

When the boat finally docked, ten long hours after we'd set sail in Le Havre, we disembarked in yet more rain. Even on solid ground I continued swaying, feeling as if I remained on board, still sick, still yearning for the shore beneath my feet even though I had it. Or thought I did.

Chapter 25

I don't think we saw the sun once while in England. From the moment we stepped off the ship, during that first night at a dark, dismal inn, in a room too dirty to take off my clothes, and then all during the long drive to Cornwall, the winds and rain never abated.

Winding through a thick forest dripping with rain and smelling of pine, we rounded a bend and got our first foggy glimpse of Fordingbrook Castle. I sucked in my breath as an overwhelming sense of doom settled upon me. Overhead, seagulls flew, their cries sounding like women weeping.

"Do you hear that?" I asked Grigori.

He listened, frowned. "The birds?"

"Don't they sound forlorn?"

"As would you be, living in isolation out here on the edge of the earth."

For that's where we were. The cliffs jutted out over the sea, and the sea went on forever. The horizon line was nonexistent because of the inclement weather—the gray morass of sky and water continuing on and on with no delineation. This was not a lovely view but rather a bleak impasse, a dire warning not to venture forth, not to pass the boundaries of this place, not to try to soar—not with ideas, not with words—but to stay tethered to the earth.

We climbed out of the car and trudged up to the great gray stone castle, Grigori stumbling on the uneven cobblestones. I wanted to reach out and take his arm, offer him ballast, but would he perceive it as pity? Too proud, he could take umbrage so quickly.

The front door opened, and the majordomo came out to greet us. He looked to be in his seventies but appeared fit. He introduced himself as Briggs and ushered us inside as a fresh-faced young man—too young to go to war and still awkward—picked up our cases and disappeared with them.

The castle, Monsieur had told us, belonged to a widowed cousin of the king who worked in the war office and was rarely in residence anymore. The location had been chosen for this assignation because of its isolation as well as its proximity to the port. The Dowager had supposedly arrived directly by boat, under a cloak of secrecy, her identity hidden. We were to address her as Madame Silvestrov. Even King George's cousin didn't know who would be using his house, only that he'd granted the Crown a favor by providing staff and allowing a three-day meeting to take place there.

An attaché waited for us in the foyer. He introduced himself as Yasin Poda, Madame

Silvestrov's aide. Short and round with a balding pate, he sported an elaborate walrus mustache, which made him look melancholy. He smelled of strong tobacco, nutmeg, and cinnamon, which might have been pleasant if it hadn't been so overwhelming.

"I'm Grigori Orloff and this is Opaline Duplessi, the mystic," Grigori said.

As we shook hands, I wondered at the way Grigori introduced me. "The mystic"? I'd never been called anything but a jeweler before and was made uncomfortable by the designation.

Then I heard my mother's voice in my head, offering advice before she went back to Cannes: *You need to open yourself up to who you are, Opaline. Denying your powers is dangerous.*

Introductions complete, Yasin informed us Madame remained indisposed after her trip but looked forward to meeting with us at ten o'clock in her suite on the following morning. He spoke French with the same Russian accent as the Orloffs.

Briggs told us dinner would be served at seven unless we preferred a light meal en suite, which I said I'd prefer. He nodded efficiently and proceeded to show us to our rooms.

The bleak scenery around us filled me with foreboding. As did the small palace. Though lushly decorated as befitted a property owned by royalty, a pall of abandonment hung over it. In the hallway on the way to my room, we passed prints showing the castle's development as it had grown over the years.

While spacious, my lavender-and-powder-blue bedroom contained shabby furnishings. Frayed drapery framed large casement windows looking out over a topiary garden and beyond to a raging sea.

A maid arrived to help me unpack. She offered and I accepted a glass of sherry, and she asked me if I'd like to freshen up or perhaps take a bath.

"A bath sounds lovely," I told her.

I began to undress, taking off my raincoat and hat. I reached for the necklace of ruby eggs and realized I couldn't get undressed in front of the maid. No one was to know I possessed the other necklace.

In the bathroom, I finished undressing, removing both the ruby and the emerald egg necklaces as well as Jean Luc's talisman. I put them inside my burgundy suede jewel case and slipped them under a stack of towels and then stepped into the tub. At least the verbena-scented water was hot. A luxury I didn't take for granted.

As I soaked, I tried to sense if Jean Luc was near. Had he traveled with me out of Paris? Was he even able to do such a thing? How ridiculous—he was a ghost—of course he could travel anywhere he wished. Mentally, I listed the rules I'd noted about his existence.

Can generate heat.

Can speak to me, but without sound. I hear him inside my head, out loud. No one else hears him.

Can move objects but not lift them.

Cannot visit with me if I'm not wearing the talisman—but I don't know if that is his failing or mine.

Unlike in stories I'd read, animals didn't sense his presence. Anna's cat that lived in the shop hadn't noticed him.

I placed my hands across my breasts, suddenly modest, wondering if he was hovering above me, watching. And what if he was? He'd seen me naked before, in my bedroom. But never during the day. He'd always come to me in the dark. I continued listing Jean Luc's rules.

Can see what I see. Almost as if he sees through my eyes. More than once, he'd mentioned sights I'd seen even when I was unaware of his presence.

Is not all knowing. He can't ferret out other people's secrets. He seemed just as confused by the meetings in the tunnels under the Palais as I. Just as worried, but unable to shed light on who the men were or what they discussed.

Can't leave me and go into another part of the store or the Palais or Grand-mère's house when I stay there. He explained he was either in a kind of colorless, odorless limbo or tethered to me.

Never hungry or thirsty; however, he does feel pleasure and pain. The pain, he said, appeared to be a memory of his injuries, but the pleasure seemed new, unique to being with me.

Makes love with heat. He said his body thrummed with delight when he joined me in my bed, and he experienced feelings similar to when he was alive, but more intensely.

Can smell me and prefers my rose perfume to my violet—saying the House of L'Etoile failed with the latter, and it reeked of powder, while the rose smelled redolent and lush, as if he were walking through Rodin's garden, crushing petals under his feet.

I must have dozed off because I came awake with a start, shivering in a tub of cool water, hearing voices drifting up through the open window.

After wrapping myself in an oversize towel, I stood hidden by the heavy damask curtains and looked down. Two men stood in the garden, each under an umbrella, speaking in Russian. At first I couldn't see either of them clearly enough to identify them. Then one of them moved and I saw Grigori. The other remained concealed.

Why would they be walking in the rain? What did they need to discuss that they couldn't talk about in the house? Or were they on their way into town?

After a few frustrating minutes of listening to

them but not understanding anything they said, I gave up. I stayed wrapped in the bath sheet, watching from a distance until the men resumed walking. Still wondering what they'd needed to talk about in the rain, I dug my burgundy suede jewel case out from under the stack of towels. Monsieur had been so adamant I keep the necklace a secret, I'd been afraid to leave it out on the countertop while I'd bathed in case a maid came in.

In the bedroom, I took out a dressing gown from the closet and slipped it on since I planned on staying in for the evening, reading, eating a light supper, and recuperating from the crossing and the miserable night in the dirty inn.

As I lowered Monsieur's enamel treasure over my head, I thought about how secretive he'd been about it and wondered why it was so important. He'd acted as if my life might actually depend on no one knowing it was in my possession. In giving it to me, had he involved me in a mission far more dangerous than he'd suggested?

Later that evening as I fell asleep, my fingers clutching the emerald eggs, I remembered Anna's anxious eyes when she had said good-bye to me the day before. At the time, her words had not struck me as odd or out of place. But now that I'd arrived here and had seen the palace and the grounds, I wasn't sure.

"You will be fine. Just rely on your instincts. Trust what they tell you. Even if black looks white. Inside of you . . ." She reached out and pressed her forefinger to the spot between my eyebrows. The skin immediately leapt alive and warmed. "Inside, you possess ways to find the answers to all of your questions. You are brave and you are strong—don't forget that. Much stronger than you believe."

Had she known from gazing into her glass orbs that something was to occur in the English countryside that could be dangerous? And if so, why had she allowed her husband to send me? Was my mission that important? Why did the Dowager really need a seer to tell her if her grandchildren were alive or not? Why did the royal family not have enough spies or friends in governments around the world to suss out that information? Why send a French jeweler across the channel to see if she could raise the voices of the dead?

Chapter 26

The next morning, I found Grigori and Yasin Poda having breakfast in the dining room. I couldn't be certain, but hearing the tone and timber of Yasin's voice, I assumed he was the man I'd heard talking with Grigori in the garden the night before.

Both greeted me and I sat down. Briggs appeared to see if I wanted tea or coffee. I requested coffee.

"There are strange but delicious things on the buffet," Grigori said, gesturing to the sideboard, where silver domes covered half a dozen dishes. "We're to help ourselves."

Inspecting the chafing dishes, I recognized eggs, tomatoes, and sausages, but needed to ask what the other two contained. One held kippers and another kidneys, I was told.

Nervous about the day ahead of me, I sat back down without taking any of the prepared food. When Briggs came in with my coffee, I asked for some toast but only managed half of one slice.

"Madame Silvestrov," Grigori said, "is in her suite, dining on her own. We're on to see her in an hour, at ten, as planned."

• • •

Precisely at ten, Grigori and I stood in front of the Dowager's door. Grigori knocked; Yasin opened it promptly. Beyond him, I saw a pale yellow sitting room decorated with violet accents. Although it too was a bit shabby, the profusion of flowers cheered it up. Crystal vases of roses and freesia rested on the fireplace, the desk, and the coffee table. I smelled their scent and something darker.

Seated by the window, I saw a young man and a middle-aged woman, both in simple garb. Yasin didn't introduce either of them, and I assumed they were part of the Dowager's retinue.

"Have a seat, please, both of you," he said. "I'll tell Madame you are here."

Yasin walked to the door at the far end of the room and knocked.

The Dowager must have answered him even though I couldn't hear her, because he opened the door. Through the doorway, I glimpsed a small figure in shadow, her back to us, looking out of the windows at the rough sea. Her posture was straight and tall and proud. But the set of her shoulders was defeated. Slowly, she turned to Yasin. Backlit, her face was too dark for me to see. They spoke in hushed tones for a moment. He turned and came back out, forgetting to close the door behind him blocking my view into the other room.

"I'm sorry, Madame Silvestrov isn't well. The trip proved more arduous than she expected. She prepared this, though." He looked at the envelope he now held in his hands. I noticed a gold signet ring on his pinkie of the same two-headed eagle Monsieur revered. It drew my attention because of its tarnish. Gold doesn't tarnish, yet from its color and hue, there was no question it was eighteen-karat gold. Had it been treated? And then, over Yasin's voice as he continued speaking, I heard an off-key whine coming from the jewelry as if it were crying out.

"Excuse me?" I'd missed part of Yasin's explanation.

"I said, inside the envelope are the locks from all of the children's hair, as you requested. How long will it take you to make the charms?"

"I think I'll be making one talisman incorporating all of the locks. Hopefully I can be done by this evening."

He stepped forward to hand me the envelope, and as he moved, I saw behind him, into the Dowager's bedroom. A suite of sapphire-colored enamel objets d'art decorated the desktop. A jewel box, no bigger than the palm of my hand, decorated with the familiar gold double-eagle insignia; beside it, one of the Easter eggs Fabergé was famous for (a larger version of those hanging over and under my chemise). Monsieur had worked on many of the royal eggs, and framed drawings of their designs hung on the walls of our workshop in the Palais. But to see one in person! I stared at the sapphire enamel egg, decorated with the same gold double-eagle insignia, and wondered what treasure it held inside. The last of the trio of objects, a small oval frame, hosted the same insignia at its top. Inside the frame, Tsar Nicholas and his wife and children gazed out, frozen in time by a photographer's efforts.

I became aware of a low-pitched humming. Not the grating sound of Yasin's ring, but a sorrowful thrum. And it was coming from the frame.

Returning to my room, I placed the envelope on my desk, arranged my tools, and set to work at the card table.

When the maid arrived at one o'clock to tell me luncheon was served, I asked her to just bring me something light in my room. I wanted to keep working.

A few minutes later, I heard another knock.

"Come in," I called.

I didn't glance up as she entered. I was engraving the symbols and didn't want to interrupt my effort. "You can just leave it on the desk, thank you so much."

"I'm sorry, perhaps you were expecting the maid? I am not she."

I looked up then and discovered the Dowager, Maria Feodorovna, at my doorstep. Despite her seventy years, she was quite beautiful, with dark, intelligent eyes, very black hair, delicate features, and iron-straight posture.

"May I come in?" she asked in perfectly accented French.

I lowered my tools and stood. "Of course."

She smiled and swished into the room, her old-fashioned long black silk skirts harkening back to an era before the war. Reaching my side, she took my hands in hers.

"I wanted to see you alone," she said. "Without the entourage. I don't know them well. Yasin arrived to be my escort only a few days before the journey. I'm not comfortable around strangers."

"Of course."

"So you are Opaline?" Each word, every movement and glance, bespoke her royalty.

Anna had schooled me in what to do when I met the Dowager, and so I said yes, and then bent into a deep curtsy.

"That's all right, child. Let's forgo the formalities for now. I don't want them to find me afoot. We don't have a lot of time."

I rose from my bow, looked into her face, and saw her humanity etched in deep lines around her mouth and swimming in the sadness in her eyes. The woman's pain, so intense on her lovely face—I felt as if I might drown in it if I wasn't careful.

"Thank you for risking so much to come to me," she said.

"I'm terribly sorry for your loss, Your Highness. It's the least I could do."

"But it is my loss, and yet you put yourself in danger to help me." She patted my hand, and I relaxed a bit. As imperious as she first appeared, she showed kindness and empathy. "Let us sit so you can tell me about what you do and how you do it. There are many mystics in our country, some quite famous, others quite infamous."

She must have been referring to Rasputin, I thought. "I'm humbled, but I'm not a mystic, Madame. My talent is minor."

"Humility isn't necessary with me. I don't find it all that attractive when people make light of their abilities. And from what I hear, you are quite gifted as both a mystic and a jeweler. Monsieur Orloff made some of my favorite pieces. Anyone he's chosen to mentor must be very talented indeed. And I've heard his wife is equally talented in another art form . . . If she is training you as well, I'm sure you will be of great help to me."

The Dowager sat in one of the tapestry-covered chairs at the card table in front of the window I was using as a workstation, and gestured for me to take one of the other chairs.

"Show me how you work," she said.

Even though she sat up straighter than anyone I'd ever seen, her every movement precise and careful, she seemed less a royal and more like a curious grandmother as she pored over my tools and supplies.

I described how I crafted the talismans and then answered her questions about how I came to make the first one. When I explained about hearing the first dead soldier talk to me, she leaned forward a little.

"And how many of these charms have you made? How many soldiers have you spoken with?"

"More than fifty by now."

She put her hand on mine. "Isn't that too difficult a toll on you? Aren't you being emotionally bruised?"

Tears welled up in my eyes. Oddly, no one had guessed. Not even Anna. And I'd never volunteered it. Not even to my mother. My tremendous sense of guilt prevented me from complaining. And now, of all the people asking, offering empathy, it was a woman who'd been consort to the tsar of one of the largest countries in the world and witness to its entire govern-ment toppling. She'd lost everything and yet offered me sympathy.

"It's the very least I can do. Millions of men have died, leaving behind tens of millions of grieving mothers and fathers, wives, daughters and sons. How it makes me feel—" I shrugged. "That's unimportant."

"That's very noble, my child, but you must take care of yourself as well. Listening to the dead has to be very painful. Do they tell you how they died?"

"Sometimes."

"Do they speak of the suffering they endured?"

"Except for one"—I thought of Jean Luc—"no, no, they don't. They aren't suffering when they find me, or I find them. They're haunted by the grief of those left behind and need their loved ones to let them go, so they, the soldiers, can move on. That's why they give me messages to deliver."

The Dowager nodded.

"So they don't tell you about the pain?"

I understood then what she was asking. She needed to prepare herself for what she might hear if indeed I found any of her grandchildren.

"No, they don't."

"I don't think you could bear it if they did."

Or you, I thought, but didn't express it.

"But this one who did tell you, do you know why? What was different about him?"

Ah, how to explain about Jean Luc? What did I even know for certain?

"I don't know, but rest assured, it's not something likely to happen again." My voice broke, and I was embarrassed. No, it wouldn't happen again. There would never be anyone else like my ghost lover.

"It was so terrible . . . ," she said. "So terrible you haven't recovered still?"

How to tell her how difficult it was to hear Jean Luc describe the last attack on him and his men. How for hours afterward I was unable to do anything.

The words of the dead are much heavier than those of the living because each requires so much effort and energy. We take our words for granted. While we live, our minds and our bodies are connected, but once we die and the connection is severed, the soul is awkward on this plane without having a corporeal presence.

Jean Luc said it was like being one with the air, and the feeling, while freeing, was too limitless, too uncontrolled. Ghosts are unhappy creatures, not pleased to be stuck in our realm, uncom-fortable and disassociated. Remaining with us is a hardship.

"Do these talismans you make always work?"

"No. A few times I've created one and not heard a spirit."

"Do you know why?"

I shook my head.

She rose and walked to the window, where she stood looking out at the sea.

"I think I'm afraid of what you do," she said.

"We've always embraced the mystical in our country. The long winters and dark nights lend themselves to tales of the strange and incomprehensible." She turned back to face me.

Behind her, in the sky out the window, the sun peeked through clouds, illuminating her from behind. For a moment she seemed to float there, surrounded by a nimbus of opalescent light, very much an otherworldly creature herself.

"At first I hesitated about meeting with you. And even now I'm not sure I want to proceed."

I didn't know what to think. Grigori and I had risked our lives to come here and meet with the Dowager. Anger bubbled up inside of me, but I couldn't show it. This woman had been the tsarina of Russia. The mother of its last ruler. The grandmother of its now uncertain future. She wasn't like the women who came to me in the shop who knew their sons, fathers, brother, lovers, and husbands were dead. This woman had no idea how many of her loved ones she had lost, had no idea how much deeper her grief would go. Compassion supplanted my anger.

If I were in her place, I might not want to know either.

"We don't need to proceed, Your Highness. If you've changed your mind, we can abort the exercise."

Her fingers worried a string of marvelous pearls looped twice around her neck, their luminosity and shimmer exaggerated by the black silk behind them. Other than two simple gold bands she had on her ring finger, the strand was the only jewelry she wore.

I knew, because the Orloffs had talked of it many times, how the royal family had been stripped of all their possessions. Their vast stores of money, securities, antiques, artwork, and jewels had all been conscripted by the revolutionaries. The remaining Romanovs were broke. Even those who'd managed to escape with some treasures had little left. Most needed to sell their valuables in order to live.

"In addition to the locks of hair, I brought more keepsakes, the few I still have. I wasn't sure if they would aid you."

I watched her withdraw a purple velvet pouch from inside a hidden pocket in her voluminous skirt, open it, and pull out the sapphire enamel box I'd noticed in her bedroom. Twisting the double-eagle insignia, she opened it and stared down into its interior, lost in thought.

I'd never had insights into what people were thinking. Only the dead spoke to me. But I imagined, based on our conversation so far, she was wondering if it would be better to know the worst about her family or be left with hope.

With a sigh, she tilted the box toward me, showing me its contents.

One would have expected emeralds, diamonds,

sapphires, and pearls to be nestled in the casket lined with pale robin's egg blue satin. But none of those would have been worth as much to the Dowager as the items she withdrew.

"This is the first tooth Alexei lost." She placed it in front of me. Next, she took out a faded coral length of grosgrain. "This is a ribbon from Anastasia's confirmation bouquet of flowers."

There were a dozen other small keepsakes, and she described each one to me, lovingly.

"I wanted to make sure you'd have what you needed." Her voice broke. A tear escaped from her eye and rolled down her cheek. She blotted it with a handkerchief embroidered with a royal insignia.

Anna told me they called her the Lady of Tears. In one lifetime, she'd already witnessed the assassination of her brother King George I of Greece, the premature death of her first fiancé, the early death of her husband in 1894, the abdication and then assassination of her son Tsar Nicholas II, the execution of many members of her family during the Bolshevik Revolution, and the dissolution of her entire way of life.

"Excuse me, I just miss them so," she whispered.

"I understand, and I am sorry."

Returning all the items to the box, she composed herself, and once she was again in control, she continued. "So you have what you need, correct? These items will work as a conduit and enable you to make contact with them if they have indeed passed on?"

I nodded, then answered aloud. "Yes, that's correct. I might only need the locks of hair, but thank you for bringing all these other bits and pieces. I might be able to use them as well."

"You won't destroy anything in the process?"

"No, certainly not. What I do is encase a few strands of each child's hair or a sliver of the tooth or a thread of the ribbon in between sections of a rock crystal, then bind that with gold and lock it together. I give you the talisman to wear on a cord, as well as the key."

"How long will it take you to make this amulet?"

"I brought everything I needed with me and should be finished by this evening. We can do the reading tonight if it's all right with you." *As long as it works,* I thought. *As long as the crystals don't crack. As long as the stone's energy intensifies the mementos. As long as the magick has traveled with me across the channel.*

The Dowager picked up her exquisite enamel box and caressed it. "I've already lost my darling son. My entire beloved country. All I have left is the hope of these children." She put the box in my hand and curled my fingers around its cold rectangular shape. Then, with surprising strength, she squeezed her hand around mine with such force the edges of the box dug into my flesh, hurting me. "Opaline Duplessi, I hope to God you fail," she said, and gave me a heartbreaking smile.

I'd seen women weep in my shop, held them sobbing in my arms. I'd heard them speak with grief and anger, passion and pain, pleasure and melancholy about their lost loved ones. But I'd never seen anyone whose smile was as sad, or whose burden as heavy as the tsar's mother's in that moment.

She stood.

"Wait, before you go. I have something to give you," I said.

"I expected you might. My son liked to plan ahead and told me Monsieur Orloff owned a necklace that—"

A knock on the door interrupted her.

"Who is it?"

"Yasin, Madame, there's a visitor here to see you."

Leaning forward, the Dowager whispered: "Only my sister and my nephew the king know I am in England. She's come to visit for the day. I'll come back later, you can give it to me then. I don't trust everyone in this house, and we need to be very careful, you and I, yes?"

Chapter 27

I wept as I placed part of each of the five locks of hair into the recess. I'd brought the finest crystal egg I'd ever found with me. I unfolded and smoothed out the list I'd drawn up of the Dowager's grandchildren and checked the eldest's information.

Olga, November 15, 1895, Scorpio
Tatiana, June 10, 1897, Gemini
Maria, June 26, 1899, Cancer
Anastasia, June 18, 1901, Gemini
Alexei, August 12, 1904, Leo

Once I'd carved the names, birthdates, and astrological signs, I added my tokens. The Ouroboros. The crescent moon. The single star. These, the symbols I'd chosen as my mantra when I'd made my first piece. Even without being trained, I'd chosen the symbolic sentence all Daughters of La Lune were taught. The crescent moon that marks our skin and brands us. The star-shine to shed light on the mysteries we encounter. And the Ouroboros to open magical doors for us.

I never received messages while I worked. When I made the talismans, I was a jeweler.

Nothing else. Not the daughter of a witch. Not a mystic who could divine messages from stones. Not someone who could speak to the dead but an artisan practicing her craft. Designing and building a charm to give its wearer pleasure and comfort. Just a jeweler continuing a time-honored tradition of making mourning jewelry to commemorate and immortalize the love that tied one person to another.

As I worked that afternoon, rain pelted the window, and wind rattled the frame. Newspapers reported the summer of 1918 had been the rainiest season England and France had suffered in years. For us it was only gloomy and wet—for the men at the front it brought misery. There was no shelter on the battlefields, and trenches turned to mud. With soaked clothes, soldiers who were worn down and in already compromised states became ill.

At three o'clock, Grigori came to check on my progress and ask me to tea. I said I'd prefer a tray in my room so as to not waste time. He surprised me when, a half hour later, he arrived with it himself and set it on the desk.

I removed my jeweler's glasses and joined him for finger sandwiches, scones, clotted cream with jam, and a large pot of very fragrant black tea. All despite the war rations in England, which were similar to ours in France.

"How is your work progressing?" he asked.

"It's painstaking, but going well."

"And you haven't experienced any . . . you call them messages, correct?"

"No, I haven't. I usually don't at this stage. The only thing that happens sometimes is I get ill while I'm putting the talisman together." I took a bite of a salmon sandwich and chewed. I hadn't realized how hungry I was.

"But you don't feel ill?"

I shook my head.

"Do you think that means anything?"

I took another bite of my sandwich. "No, probably not."

"What's wrong, Opaline?"

"Nothing, why?"

"When you're upset, you purse your lips, like this." He showed me.

"I do?" I said, surprised. Not so much that I made the same expression my mother made when she was upset. Rather, I was astonished Grigori knew my face so well.

"You do. So what's bothering you?"

"There's danger here. I can hear it, Grigori, like a low-level hum coming from the house itself."

"You're probably picking up on the castle's history. Briggs told me about its bloody past as he was arranging the tray. He said he would never have chosen to serve here had the royal family not requested it of him."

"That may be, but not what I'm sensing. Distant tragedies feel a certain way. Like wood worn smooth. But when I touch the crystals in the lamps in this house, or the marble on the fireplace, I hear a tense sound. High-pitched and jarring. As if the house is bracing for a new crisis. Something is going to happen while we are here. The Dowager must be in danger."

"Of course traveling during wartime is always dangerous."

"I don't think that's what I'm sensing. This feels like specific danger. Do you think the Bolsheviks found out she is here?"

Grigori stood up and came to sit beside me on the settee. He put his arm around me and held me close. When he spoke, he measured each word carefully. "I don't think they could know she is here, no. And I don't want you to be alarmed."

"But isn't she one of the symbols of the politics they've overthrown?"

"Yes. And for the same reason, she is precious to the tsarists and those who want to restore the monarchy." He took my hand in his, reassuring me. "And that's why this trip was arranged in such secrecy. But I don't want you to be concerned. The Dowager is here anonymously as Madame Silvestrov. Only her own staff, the king, and his mother know who their guest is."

"Thank you. I feel better. Now I should get back to work. I have a lot to get done and not a lot of time."

Grigori leaned forward and kissed me. Not a chaste embrace, but not an invitation either.

"Don't let me bother you. But if you don't mind I'd like to stay."

I preferred him to leave, but it wasn't really a hardship to let him stay. So I went back to my makeshift workstation and the talisman while behind me Grigori stood and began to pace. The sound of his footsteps on the carpet, because of his limp, had an unnerving, uneven rhythm. And the longer he kept it up, the more it disturbed me and added to my growing unease.

If all was well, why was I so nervous? Why was he?

"What is this?" he asked.

I turned. He'd picked up the Dowager's jewel box. "Is it Fabergé?"

"I don't know. The empress brought it with her and it has—"

He'd opened it.

"No, don't, it's—"

He stared at me. My tone had been too harsh. What was wrong with me that I was so anxious? Grigori was a fine arts and antiques dealer—he knew how to handle precious objects. Was it just that I always worked alone and found his presence distracting? Or was I sensing something about the tsar's children I didn't want to face yet and felt uneasy because of them?

Grigori inspected the contents, taking them out and putting each on the desk blotter. First the locks of hair, four of them tied with lavender ribbon, one with navy. Next the tooth. Then the grosgrain ribbon.

His face gave away nothing, and he remained silent as he continued searching through the contents.

"Grigori, please don't. If something has happened to the children, what you're doing is like rifling through their coffins."

"What a strange thing to say." His eyes softened. "How hard this must be for you. Spending so much time working the remains of the soldiers. Hearing their voices. I'm sorry I've never really asked you about it before. Does it seep into your dreams?"

Twice in one day now, someone had asked me almost the same question.

I nodded.

"Tell me."

"No, not now."

"Imagine the value you could place on your service if you could ask them questions and they could answer you. Have you ever tried that?"

I couldn't tell if he was teasing or serious.

"No, I haven't. I just accept the messages. It's

not the same as having a conversation," I said. Or at least it hadn't been, I thought, until I'd met Jean Luc.

"You should at least get paid for what you do."

"We charge for the piece of jewelry."

"You should get a fee for the readings as well."

Grigori was a good salesman. I'd been in the shop when he'd charmed clients into paying high sums for a candelabra or an armoire. Several times, I'd heard Monsieur admonish Grigori for being too greedy, but I'd written that off to the friction between them. Was I wrong? Since we'd arrived at the castle, Grigori didn't seem the same to me. Was he more himself on his own, out of his father's orbit, and I was seeing it for the first time?

"Are you uncomfortable being here?" I asked.

"Uncomfortable?" he asked. "No, the accommodations are fine. Aren't yours?"

"No, I meant being away from Paris, here in the country, at this castle, on this mission. You seem anxious and perhaps a little angry."

Grigori frowned, and then, like the sun rising, one of his sparkling smiles transformed his pensive face. "I'm sorry. And yes, I am anxious. I am worried about what you will discover when you finish that charm." He pointed to my work. "I suppose I'm finding it intimidating to be around the Dowager, to be in the same house as her. And I'm concerned she has traveled all this way and you will have to give her bad news. And then we will have to witness her grief. And somehow my father will find a way to make even that my fault."

It all made sense, but as he said it, his eyes kept returning to the ruby enamel egg necklace I wore.

Without meaning to, before I realized what I'd done, I'd put my hand up, protectively covering the piece, and examined yet again the subterfuge of wearing this necklace over the other. Of the request to give them to the Dowager, but only when we were alone.

"Is that a new piece of jewelry?" Grigori asked.

"It is. Your father gave it to me for luck."

And the greatest question: Why hadn't Monsieur wanted his son to know about the real gift? I'd accepted his logical answer, but I wasn't sure I believed it.

Inadvertently, I shook my head.

"What is it, Opaline?"

"Nothing, I should get back to work or I won't finish."

"I will leave you then. When do you think you'll be done?"

"By dinnertime as promised."

I wished I didn't need to read the talisman until the next day. If it was bad news, I preferred giving it to the empress in daylight, when she wouldn't have a long lonely night ahead of her. But time, I knew, was of the essence. No one was aware the empress had left Yalta. For her to be away for more than a few days invited danger.

Monsieur had said it over and over again: the Bolsheviks' hate knew no bounds. The world feared for every member of the tsar's family. And I for this strong, lovely woman most of all.

Once Grigori left, I put down my tools and stood to stretch. His presence had affected me, almost as if the storm clouds from the outside had come in. I rubbed my forehead, feeling the beginnings of a headache coming on. There must be aspirin powder in the house. That would help. Unless of course this was the first harbinger of the fate of the children.

I closed the door, locked it, pocketed the key, and took off for the kitchens. But the castle stretched out too far and the hallways twisted too many times and there were too few lamps lit for me to easily find my way. As I wandered, the shadows danced in macabre patterns, portraits on the walls sang to me, and objets d'art buzzed or murmured.

Maybe Grigori was right and I'd spent too much time invested in the dead. But hadn't everyone in France? In England? In every country in Europe? The four-year-long war had claimed an unfathom-able number of men. Not just unimaginable to me, but to all of us. You could picture a room with a dozen people in it. A theater with a thousand people in it. But enough men to fill a thousand theaters?

I'd managed to reach the main floor of the castle but wound up lost, following a darkened, narrow hallway that seemed to go on interminably. Retracing my steps, I tried to get back to the main staircase. From there, I would try again to find the path to the kitchens. After five more minutes of wandering, I found myself in a gallery.

The room was as long as a half dozen normal rooms and twice as wide as one. The walls were hung with portraits. As I made my way down its length, every ten feet or so I passed under another elaborate crystal chandelier. None of them lit, none of them glittering, but all of them emitting a high-pitched crystalline keening. As if the very crystals were weeping with grief.

With only gloomy daylight filtering in through the occasional windows, I peered into the faces of these noblemen and women, some going back to the fourteenth century. All of these people, I thought, were dead. Like all the souls in Père-Lachaise were dead. Like all the soldiers were dead. Like Jean Luc was dead.

Darling, you are becoming morose.

Jean Luc! I smiled despite myself.

I can go wherever you go, but I'm not happy about being here.

"Why is that?"

Because you aren't happy here. Something is bothering you.

"How can you know?"

I think sometimes I can hear things you are thinking before you acknowledge them.

"Is that possible?"

Is any of this possible?

I smiled again. "It shouldn't be, but it is. I still wonder sometimes if I invented you. The way children invent imaginary friends."

Haven't I proven myself to you?

"I would have thought so. But you're hard to believe in—even with everything you've shown me and all that my mother and Anna have explained, a part of me still believes reading the stones, getting the messages, could be some manifestation of madness. The mind is more powerful than scientists and doctors know and—"

Please stop.

His voice sounded terribly sad, with much angst in just those two words.

"What is it?"

My presence is making life more difficult for you, and I can't bear that. I don't want you to miss me and long for me. I didn't come this far to find you in order to hurt you. All my men dead and my mother suffering and now you are questioning your own sanity.

"No, no. Jean Luc, even if I spend the rest of my life missing you, I'm not sorry. Do you know why pearls are so rare? Each one begins as an accident when a microscopic grain of sand becomes trapped within an oyster's mantle folds. Perceiving the sand an irritant, the oyster then manufactures layers of nacre to soften the irritation. Hundreds of very thin layers covering one another, building up a metallic, mirrorlike luster. Of the millions of oysters, how many contain pearls? Very few. We know to find just one luminous pearl, thousands of oysters must be killed, opened, and searched. And when one is discovered, what a treasure. What value it has. The incandescent glow of a pearl is like nothing else. The colors that play on its silky surface are one of nature's most unique and striking rainbows. I don't have any pearls, Jean Luc. But I have you. And forever I will be able to take out the memory of you and look at it, like the glorious rainbow on a pearl, and remember what it was like to be with you. Would I regret being able to wear a queen's pearls for a day? No. Not even for an hour."

In answer, his warm wind blew against my cheeks. *I wish I believed that. I don't. I've seen grief. You've seen it.*

"You are fixated on the raw, early grief. But think about what happens later. What happens when we build up our own protective layers of

374

nacre and our very misery turns to something beautiful, a memory of love."

He didn't respond.

"Jean Luc?" My voice sounded panicked even to me.

Yes.

"What happened? Suddenly you weren't there, were you?"

No, I wasn't.

"Why?"

I'm not sure.

"Has it happened before?"

Only the last few days. I try to reach you, and it seems you're just too far away. Or I'll be listening to you and then suddenly I feel as if I'm being pulled back.

"Are you telling me it may be time for you| to go?"

It might be. I don't think I'll be allowed to remain in this limbo for much longer.

I nodded, feeling tears springing to my eyes.

The warm wind wiped them away.

But not yet. And not here. Not until you are safely back in Paris. I promise.

What could I say? Was I meant to go to him? I stood beside the window and, hiding my tears, looked out at the sea. What if I just walked out onto the cliff and stepped over the edge? Then we could be together. There would be no separation between us. I could go be with him wherever he went. Life wouldn't separate us.

No!

The word was so loud in my head I put my hands up to my ears. He'd shouted his admonition inside of my very soul.

There is a pattern to all of this, a method, a weaving. You cannot pull the threads out and control it yourself.

"Are you sure? How do you know? Do you believe in fate?"

Don't you? You are a daughter of a witch, a Daughter of La Lune. Isn't that fate? Isn't there a pattern to whom you are born to and whom you become?

"I don't know, I am not sure."

And for what seemed the hundredth time, I cursed my mother and my history. This had been foisted on me. All of this. I leaned forward and pressed my forehead against the cool glass. My headache had worsened. I needed coffee and some headache powder. Resolving to find the kitchens, I walked to the end of the long corridor, alone now, without his voice in my head, and continued on.

Through a door, down a hallway. A stone staircase I hadn't seen before. I smelled the scent of age, of undusted newel posts, of mice behind the walls and spiders that feasted on the neglect. Much older than the rest of the castle I'd seen— from the construction of the rough-hewn beams and cracked stone steps, I guessed this section dated from the Middle Ages.

As I followed the spiral down, the temperature continued to drop. The never-ending circle of steps went deeper than one flight, deeper than two or three. I thought about stopping, going back up. I really was lost. And then I heard a voice—indistinct and far off.

"Jean Luc?"

No response. In silence, I descended deeper, taking another step and then another. Suddenly I heard the voice again. More distinct. Two voices. Good, I could ask for help, get directions to the kitchens.

I hurried. The voices getting louder. I came around another spiral. Only a dozen steps now to the bottom.

Before me lay a darkened cavern. I peered into its depths to find the men, to call out, to tell them I was lost, to ask for help. I saw them. Opened my mouth to yell out—and then instead put my hand up to stop myself from screaming.

Two men stood with their backs to me: Grigori and Yasin. But they were not alone. The Dowager was with them. She was seated in a tall-backed wooden chair. Fury in her eyes as they bent over her, tying her arms to the chair with thick, rough rope.

In Russian, Grigori asked her a question.

And she answered him back, shaking her head no.

He asked the same question again, even more loudly.

She repeated her answer, this time without shaking her head.

Yasin yelled at her.

She only shook her head, no.

With a burst of anger, Yasin pulled a white handkerchief out of his pocket and stuffed it into the Dowager's mouth.

Grigori went to work tying her ankles together with another length of rope. Her expression remained stoic.

And then she noticed me. She shook her head slightly—the regal movement, an order telling me not to try to help but to leave, to escape. Then her eyes met mine. I wasn't looking anymore at the Imperial Dowager who'd ruled Russia alongside her husband. In her eyes she was nothing but a frightened elderly woman begging me to save her.

Chapter 28

My instinct was to run the rest of the way down the stairs, but something held me back. My horror? My understanding that I couldn't fight two men? My shock that Grigori, my sometime lover and certainly my friend, was in the process of committing a violent act against the tsar's mother?

As stealthily as I could, I crept backward up the stairs. Worried my panic could be smelled. That my pounding heart could be heard. Why were they tying her up? I wanted to help her, but first needed to figure out *how* to help her. Rushing ahead wouldn't do her any good if they restrained me as well.

The stairs turned, and I could no longer see into the dungeon. I climbed and climbed up those endless steps. There were servants in the main part of the castle. If I could just get back there, I would find Briggs. Explain. Get him to call the police. Gather the rest of the staff. Take on the two Russians.

Panting, I reached the top of the stairs. Looked around. Of course, nothing had changed. Still lost, I had no idea how to find my way out of the ancient wing of the castle. And I knew if I wandered around for too long, Grigori and Yasin might find me there and suspect I'd seen something.

I forced myself to take deep breaths and assess my options.

I stood in a circular stone room, with ancient tapestries covering most of the walls. Like the rest of this wing, the room appeared abandoned. I turned in a full circle. Trying to see something I could use to help. I focused on the narrow casement windows illuminating the stairs.

Finally, I thought of an idea. Maybe the view would help me figure out where I was.

Peering through the rectangular opening, I looked into fog and incessant rain. Straining through the atmospheric morass, I thought I saw the sea. But that was no help. The whole of the back of the castle faced the sea. I sank to the floor. If I was going to help the Dowager, I needed to understand what I'd witnessed, but first, I needed a hiding place in case Grigori and Yasin came this way leaving the dungeon—they mustn't find me.

A narrow hallway off the main room led to a series of smaller rooms. I chose the last, empty with only a closed, locked door at its other end. From the dust on the warped parquet, no one had ventured this way in weeks, maybe longer. I sat down on the floor, leaned up against the door, and tried to think through everything I'd seen and what I needed to do.

I pulled the long chain from around my neck and

wrapped my fingers around Jean Luc's amulet. He was no seer, no witch, and no wizard. His voice in my head couldn't solve this for me. But he'd become, in a way, my strength. My trajectory to the abilities I'd denied for all this time. Only when I spoke to him, when he was by my side, when he made love to me, did I allow there was really more to this plane, to this dimension, to my senses and my talents, than I'd accepted.

But what good would any of that do me now? I hadn't learned how to harness any of my other abilities. I didn't even know what skills were available to me. I'd read most of the history my mother had given me. I'd studied some of the spells. But I hadn't yet begun to practice, and without practice, I remained a neophyte, incapable of effecting any magick.

The only way out of this was through logic and determination. As my fingers fussed with the talisman's gold chain, I realized I'd twisted it up with the ruby enamel egg necklace. Still trying to think through my dilemma, I disentangled the two.

What did Grigori want? I tried to remember anything unusual I'd overlooked during the planning of this trip. Or on that last morning when we said good-bye. Yes, there had been some tension over Monsieur giving me the necklace. I'd never quite accepted Monsieur's reason for not letting his son take on this task. Or why he wanted me to hide the emerald eggs from him. And when I'd asked, Monsieur had seemed disturbed by his own admission that he was afraid Grigori wouldn't be able to hide its existence.

Buy why was its existence so important?

I pressed the spot between my eyes where Anna had shown me my third eye slept. I needed all the insight and intuition it offered now. The answer to this puzzle lay in small moments and odd comments. What had I seen but missed? Not knowing there was a secret, what had I overlooked?

Monsieur's hatred of the Bolsheviks. Anna's fear of them. And Grigori . . . I pictured his face when he'd told me how the Bolsheviks had destroyed the Russia of his father's generation. I pictured Grigori as he described his mother and her revolutionary poetry. Not ashamed at all, as Monsieur's son should have been, but proud of her? Yes, Grigori was proud of his mother's revolutionary roots. When he'd talked about what the Bolsheviks wanted, about who they hated and how determined they were, he'd been angry. So had Monsieur Orloff. But now, thinking about Grigori's comments differently . . . he'd never decried the Bolsheviks. He said they'd destroyed old Russia . . . it would never be the same again . . . the land his father and Anna wanted to return to had vanished.

But he'd never expressed regret. He'd only spoken facts.

Was it possible? Was Grigori a secret member of the very political party his father and Anna despised? The very opposite of a tsarist sympathizer? A spy in his own father's house? Had Monsieur Orloff sensed his son's betrayal on some deep visceral level? Anna too had said things that seemed harmless, but now, if I read them with this new knowledge, they took on an entirely different meaning.

When she said she thought Grigori might find his destiny with me, I'd assumed she meant it in a positive way. What if she hadn't? What if she'd seen it but didn't understand it?

If Grigori was in fact a Bolshevik, then coming here to meet with the Dowager suggested what?

What were they planning to do with the empress?

He'd told me the revolutionaries were obsessed with destroying the symbols of the monarchy. But if they'd wanted to, they would have killed her already. So then what did they want?

Monsieur often talked about how the Bolsheviks were in desperate need of money. Suddenly the antiques store took on a changed appearance. Was Grigori helping fund the movement from the heart of Paris? Were the cracks I'd found in the vault's wall an effort to break through into that treasure trove so he could steal from his father and give the party money?

My imagination spun wildly. This was all a

story I was inventing. Like Jean Luc . . . making it up in my mind.

Except hadn't my mother proved he wasn't my invention? And seeing the Dowager tied up was no invention either.

The enamel eggs around my neck—the ruby ones on top of my blouse and the emerald ones next to my skin—began to hum and vibrate. What was the real meaning of the two necklaces? What hadn't Monsieur Orloff told me? Why had he taken all of the emerald eggs off of *The Tree of Life* to give to the Dowager? *Why those eggs?*

I reached inside, pulled out the hidden necklace, and held the eggs up to the window. I'd seen them almost every day for nearly four years, locked in the display case, hanging off the sinewy sculpted silver branches. Now, inspecting them, I looked for anything atypical compared to the other eggs we made. The fine workmanship, a hallmark of Monsieur Orloff's artistry, was evident. Perfect enameling, refined designs, tiny exquisite stones set in the bands, crossing the eggs horizontally or vertically. My jeweler's glasses were still in my smock pocket and I put them on. But even when I looked at the work magnified, nothing shouted out.

Then, turning one egg, I examined its back and noticed a miniature lock in the center of the horizontal band. Examining another, I discovered it was locked as well. I looked at a third. All of them were locked. I studied the ruby eggs. Only one was locked. The single egg Monsieur had pointed out up by the clasp. The one with the note folded up inside of it.

Removing the small key from the end of the chain, I opened the ruby egg. As I unfolded the paper, a second, even smaller key fell out. I picked it up, examined it and then the note. All in Cyrillic. But I didn't need to be able to read it to guess the purpose of the second key.

Refolding the paper, I enclosed it once more inside the egg. The second miniature key was difficult to hold. My fingers covered the ridges and notches, preventing me from fitting it into one of the emerald egg's locks. Trying to position my fingers farther back, I fumbled and the key fell.

The chamber wasn't well lit. The casement windows didn't allow in much light. I couldn't see the key on the stone floor. Had it fallen in between a crack? Getting on my hands and knees, I searched and finally, after a frantic five minutes, found it a few feet away, where it had bounced.

Picking up the key once again, I held it more cautiously, careful to keep a grip on it. I'd almost maneuvered it into the lock when I fumbled again. This time, I was prepared and tried to catch it. Instead, I watched in despair as it fell into one of the dreaded cracks and disappeared from sight.

Chapter 29

For a few minutes, I sat on the floor staring down into the crevice. Had I actually dropped the key? The enormity of my clumsiness weighed on me. Fishing around in my smock pockets, I found my jeweler's tweezers. Gingerly, I pushed them down into the crack, hoping to reach the key, but the hole was far too deep.

Frustrated, I began to question what I was doing, wasting time trying to open the necklace. How could the enamel eggs matter now? Why was I focusing on them instead of how to get out of this maze and help the Dowager?

Because Grigori and Yasin wanted something from her. What if it was the necklace?

Rooting around in my pocket again, I searched for anything I could use as a key. I needed to know what hung around my neck. Why were the eggs locked? Why was the necklace so precious that Monsieur had lied to his son about it? Was it the clue to the scene I'd witnessed down below?

My fingers found a two-inch-long gold rod. A remnant of what I'd heated and stretched upstairs, planning to use as a binding around the Dowager's talisman. It would work fine if I could heat it. I thought about the soldering torch in my bedroom. Just above me somewhere upstairs—

near and yet impossibly far at the same time.

I tried to remember what I'd read in the grimoire my mother gave me. There'd been a spell for putting fires out. Another for drawing water to you. One for sending it rushing away. Had there been one for creating fire out of thin air? I thought so, but I couldn't be sure. There must have been. The book contained dozens and dozens of spells, but I had been lax in learning the lessons of my heritage and how to harness my power.

Heat? How could I summon heat?

And then I thought of Jean Luc. He was a source of heat. I grasped his talisman and closed my eyes. Tried to connect and summon him.

I felt nothing.

I grasped the talisman tighter.

"I need you," I whispered.

Still no answer.

Had he in fact left? Was our time over? He'd just warned me it was becoming more difficult for him to come to me and one day he'd be gone. But so suddenly?

"Jean Luc?" I heard the panic in my voice. "Jean Luc?"

And then, ah yes, I sensed him. That delicious warm breeze. Weaker than ever before, but there.

Not quite time yet, but soon.

"I need you to help me. I need your heat."

You possess your own, Opaline. Just claim it.

"But how?"

You know. I think you've always known.

"I don't. Tell me."

Nothing. Silence. What did he mean?

In my desperation to understand what Jean Luc meant, to help the Dowager, I finally stopped trying to make sense. I had to save her. That's all I knew.

Holding the small rod between my fingers, I focused on it and willed it to heat. I *told* it to, insisting it warm so I could use tweezers to bend it into a shape I could fit inside the lock.

My whole body went rigid. My eyes saw blood-red blackness. For a moment, it seemed as if I'd in fact stopped breathing. I put all of my weight and my energy and my life force into the two inches of gold pressed between my fingers.

The gold began to heat . . . In seconds it became so hot I could barely hold it. The only pain I'd ever welcomed. If anyone had told me I'd be able to do this, I would have sworn it was impossible. How had I— No, there was no time to think through this wonder. The Dowager was in danger and I needed to find out if the reason was contained in the chain of eggs I wore around my neck.

Working as fast as I could, using the two random tools I happened to be carrying in my pocket— the tweezers and a file—I fashioned the soft gold into a makeshift key with three notches mimicking Monsieur Orloff's key for the ruby eggs—just a bit smaller. Calling on my memory of the original.

Done, I put the new key on the stone floor to let it cool and harden before trying it out. If I used it while it was still soft, I might break it. Only then did I realize how badly I'd burned my fingertips. Closing my eyes, I tried to cast the pain off in the same way I'd brought on the heat and felt the intensity lessen. Not a lot, but enough for me to pick up the key and fit it into the egg. Feeling the lock catch, I turned it.

The lock sprung open. I pried apart the egg's shell and peered inside.

I stared down at a brilliant blue diamond that must have weighed at least ten carats. Teardrop-shaped, and as flawless as any I'd ever seen. A sliver of ice, shimmering, frozen, dazzling.

Opening the next egg, I found a heart-shaped pink diamond. Sparkling like a rainbow on fire.

Inside the next egg sat an oval canary diamond. In the next, a pale green diamond. In each of the thirty green enamel eggs, I found an extraordinary colored diamond. A king's ransom—a tsar's ransom's worth of jewels. Each glittered and shone and twinkled in my lap like a droplet of colored water in sunshine. These were worth enough to bribe an army, to rescue a royal family, to rebuild an empire. It wasn't a rumor. The stories were true. I was staring at part of the treasure the tsar, worried about rumors of a revolution, had entrusted to Monsieur Orloff to take out of the country and secrete away for a time when his family needed them.

And now, the tsar's mother did need them and Monsieur had entrusted them to me to give to her and I was going to fail. Unless . . .

Was this what Grigori and Yasin wanted? The Bolsheviks required money. Could I trade the diamonds for the Dowager's life? For mine? Could I trust Grigori to take the stones and leave us alive? What if their plan had been to steal the jewels and destroy the great Romanov matriarch as well?

Carefully, I replaced every stone into its hiding place, locked each egg, and then slipped the treasure-laden necklace back over my head and under my chemise.

Then I opened the ruby egg that had held the original key. Once more, I unfolded the note, this time wrapping it around the new key. I now guessed the note explained about the hidden stones in the emerald egg necklace. Or perhaps it was a message meant to be found to throw some-one off the track of the other necklace. Knowing Monsieur as well as I did, I guessed the latter.

After putting my tools and my glasses back in my pocket, I stood. I needed to find help from someone I could trust.

As quietly as I could, I crept out of the stone

archway, nervous to be leaving the safety of my shadowed hiding place. But I wasn't going to waste any time trying to find my way through the maze of rooms. I was just looking for a way out. And I found it. A window large enough for me to crawl out of. Opening it was relatively easy, and in moments, I was outside in the dripping rain, standing on the soggy grass.

I took several deep breaths. Dampness filled my lungs. The fog hung heavy over the cliff, so misty I could only see a few feet in front of me. My urge to run almost overwhelmed me. What did I care about the woman bound and gagged, deep inside the castle? She wasn't my sovereign; I wasn't her liege, but only a jeweler who made watches . . . who heard voices. Incapable of being a heroine in an adventure story.

Except how could I leave her? A terrified woman who'd lost her son, her country, perhaps even her grandchildren.

But this wasn't my battle, wasn't my family. I took my first steps away from the castle wall. Started to run. I would find the road. Someone would stop. I could go to the police, send help for the Dowager, then go back to Paris. No, to Cannes. I never needed to go back to Paris.

But I could still see the Dowager's eyes boring into mine. I couldn't just leave her. Especially when around my neck I wore what might be all it would take to save her.

Turning, I stared at the impossible building, trying to figure out where exactly the ancient wing was, but the fog and the last renovation hid the clues. I was just as lost looking at it from the outside as on the inside.

I circled around it, knowing I'd come to the front or back entrance soon. My plan was to find Briggs. While I could have been wrong, I believed what he'd intimated to Grigori—that he worked for the British royal family and had been lent to the castle for the occasion. I'd tell him what I'd seen and he'd be able to get help.

I'd reached the east end of the castle and turned. Around the corner, I saw Grigori and Yasin walking toward me. Consternation on their faces.

"We've been looking for you," Grigori said. "Where did you get to?"

I hadn't realized how much time had passed. I searched his face. Did he know something, or was I projecting my fear?

"I was working when one of my headaches started . . ." I'd decided to tell him as much of the truth as I could. Not at all sure I was calm enough to lie well. "Sometimes fresh air helps. I've been walking."

He eyed my smock.

I shrugged. "I didn't think to take it off. When I feel a headache coming on, the sooner I can get outside, the faster it goes away." Surely he remembered me talking about my headaches and would believe me. "Why were you looking for me? Do you need something?"

He smiled. I was confused. His eyes were as gentle as his touch when he took my arm. "The empress is indisposed, and I went to your room to see if you'd like to join us for a light supper."

Yet again, I questioned what I'd seen. Had it been my imagination? Perhaps my mother had been wrong. What if I was ill? What if I saw and heard things like the crazy owl lady after all? And she simply sensed what I saw and believed it to be real. This man holding my arm, whom I'd kissed and made love to, wasn't capable of anything sinister. He was an antiques salesman. Yes, he was bitter he'd gone to war for France and been handicapped for life. But Grigori wasn't evil.

"I'm sorry the Dowager's ill again," I said to Yasin.

"It's often difficult for Her Highness to deal with the upheaval and sadness she's had to endure," he said. "She said to tell you she'd very much be looking forward to meeting with you in the morning instead of tonight. If, in fact, you will be finished."

"I will."

"Good. Now let us enjoy our supper," Grigori said as he led me to the entrance to the castle and away from help.

Chapter 30

As I took a seat and waited for the staff to serve us, we made small talk. The effort of pretending all was well proved almost as painful as the burns on my fingertips, which I tried to keep hidden in my lap. Briggs came in with the food and offered us a choice of cold chicken or meat pie. There was also wine, but I was afraid to take more than a few sips lest it affect my alertness. I sensed I needed to keep my wits.

"How is the talisman coming?" Grigori asked me.

"Almost finished," I said. "There's some burnishing and polishing to do."

"Did you get any information on the fate of the family?" Yasin asked.

"I can't tell anything until I'm with the person connected to it. Do you think they are alive?"

Yasin shook his head. "I don't think they are."

"Why is that?" I was looking for a clue, wanting him to say something to give me some insight into their plans. And at the same time, I tried to appear naïve. My only chance of saving the Dowager was to keep these men from thinking I knew anything. I had to be able to walk away from them when tea was over and summon help. If I seemed nervous or asked the wrong questions, if I made them suspicious, they might trap me too.

"Why would they kill the tsar and keep his family alive?" Yasin asked, rhetorically.

"The children and the empress were, after the tsar, the manifestation of the corrupt royal system," Grigori added. "The Bolsheviks would have no use for them, other than the pleasure of destroying them."

Was he saying it with relish? Whenever we'd spoken of this before, I'd always thought he repeated the Bolshevik propaganda in order to explain the atrocities that were occurring in his homeland. But I'd been wrong. It was clear to me now that Grigori Orloff believed in the Bolshevik cause.

The conversation drifted to other topics. The men demolished the pie and the chicken. When we were done, Briggs came in to ask if we needed anything else.

I eyed him. Was he as safe as I thought? Or had he been lying too? Was he in on the plan to kidnap or murder the Dowager? And what of me?

Back in my room, I walked back and forth in front of the windows. And then, reminded of Grigori's incessant pacing, I stopped. I sat down and worked. And worked. The basket weave I'd chosen was taking much longer than expected. The complicated pattern of gold threads lacing over and under one another occupied my mind and at the same time allowed it to wander, to try to come up with a plan I could execute on my own.

By ten o'clock, I was desperate to take action, but still not sure what I should do. If I could get to a telephone and not be overheard, I could call the local police. But I hadn't seen a phone and I didn't know how to go looking for one without arousing suspicion when, for all I knew, everyone in the household was part of the plot.

Still weaving, I must have fallen asleep at the table. When I woke, long past midnight, the moon shone through the windows, illuminating the finished talisman. The crystal looked alive; the gold glimmered. I picked it up. I couldn't hear any voices but sensed they were indeed there, waiting until a connection could be made via a loved one before imparting their terribly sad information.

It was the first time I'd ever made a piece of jewelry in search of proof of death, and I hated having done it. If I ever saw the Dowager again, if in the morning I figured out a way to help her, to free her, she was sure to ask. How could I be the one to deliver this horrible news?

I barely slept and went down to breakfast early, hoping I might find Briggs alone and talk to him, try to get a sense if he was indeed innocent or part of Grigori and Yasin's band of thugs.

But both men were already at the dining table,

half done with their breakfasts, and I couldn't figure out how to get the butler alone.

"Did you sleep well?" Grigori asked.

"No, I didn't. Too anxious about today. About giving the empress the talisman. About what it will tell us."

"I'm afraid it won't be possible for you to spend a long time with her," Yasin said. "We've received a message from London and they want her to leave as soon as possible."

I nodded as if everything made complete sense, but I was confused. Was I really going to meet with her?

"I'll come and get you as soon as Madame is ready."

What game was this? How were they going to bring me to the Dowager? How were they going to get her to pretend she was all right when \ she'd spent the night in a dungeon tied to a chair? Or had she? Was the scene I'd witnessed some kind of torture to get information from her? Had they decided to let her go? But they couldn't— she'd seen their faces.

At ten o'clock, Grigori knocked on my door and told me the Dowager was ready for me. Together we walked to her rooms. Yasin opened the door and led me inside, through her sitting room into her bedroom. The heavy forest green damask drapes were drawn. Only a small lamp was lit. The room and the woman sitting by the

window were shrouded in shadows. Dressed for travel,
the Dowager was all in black, with a hat and veil covering her face, black gloves on her hands.

I walked toward her, but Yasin stopped me before I came too close.

"Can I have the talisman?" he asked. "I will give it to Her Highness."

I handed it to him. He crossed the room and handed it to the Dowager.

She held it in her palm and looked down at it.

"What should she do?" he asked.

"I need to show her," I explained. "I need to hold it as well."

He seemed concerned but then nodded and gestured.

I approached and stood close to her. I tried to peer through the veil and into her eyes, but her glance was cast down, looking, it seemed, at my handiwork.

"If Your Highness would hold on to the talisman, I need to put my hands around yours."

She nodded and did as I asked.

I put my hands around her gloved ones.

I'd expected children's voices to come all at once. Was sure of it. But I heard only the distant ticking of a clock and waves hitting the rocks. Maybe I'd been wrong. Perhaps I hadn't sensed the children's souls waiting for their chance to speak to their grandmother.

"They . . . your family . . . your grandchildren . . . they aren't talking to me, Your Highness. They are still alive."

I expected her to say something. Just a few words of thanks. Someone of her breeding would have acknowledged my efforts. But she remained silent.

I released her hands. She dropped the talisman on the table.

How odd, I thought. Wasn't she going to take it with her? Her grandchildren's memorabilia was contained within the crystal. How could she leave it behind?

Yasin appeared at her side, helping her up.

"The car is waiting," he said to her, and then turned to me.

"I believe you have something for Her Highness?"

Pavel had told me only to give her the second necklace, the necklace with the emerald eggs, if she was alone. But we weren't alone. And moment by moment I was becoming less and less certain she was the Dowager at all, but an imposter. Could the real Dowager have left the talisman behind? Wouldn't she have clutched it to her chest, cherishing it and the hope it had offered?

"Yes, I do," I said, and took off the chain with the ruby eggs dangling from it. As I gave the decoy necklace to her, I prayed my hand wouldn't shake. "Monsieur Orloff wanted me to give these to you and tell you they are from your son. A gift he planned on giving you himself one day."

I watched the woman pretending to be the Dowager take the piece of jewelry and barely glance at it as she slipped it into a black satin reticule.

Together they left the room. I watched their backs as they walked through the sitting room and stepped over the threshold and into the hallway. I watched as the stranger dressed in the Dowager's clothes turned the corner. As she walked out of sight, the panic inside of me bubbled up and soured my stomach and then I did start to shake. From head to toe. My fingers worst of all.

Chapter 31

Somewhere in this godforsaken castle, the mother of the recently executed tsar of Russia sat tied to a chair, her feet and her hands bound. A gag stuffed in her mouth. I had no doubt, if she wasn't already dead, she would be soon. I surmised they wouldn't kill her until they safely held the necklace.

And now they did.

Even though it wasn't the real one, even though there was nothing inside those pretty red eggs. They believed they possessed what Monsieur had sent me to deliver.

"Well done, Opaline. You made an old woman very happy," Grigori said. We were in the foyer, watching the Dowager and her party leave. "Did you tell her the truth? Did you really not hear any messaging?"

"I really didn't," I said as I put my hand up to my forehead and rubbed it. I knew why I hadn't heard anything. The talisman that was now in my pocket would only have worked if held by the children's true grandmother, not a fraud dressed in her clothes.

"Another headache?" he asked, with what seemed like real concern.

"Yes, a terrible one. I think I need to take a

powder and lie down for a little while. Is that all right?"

"Of course. We're not departing for at least two hours."

"I'll go to the kitchen. I'm sure they can find something."

"I'll get it for you," Grigori offered, "and bring it to your room."

I had no choice but to let him.

A few minutes later, he knocked on my door and came in carrying a small tray. I took the powder in water. "Thank you. Now I should lie down."

He left. I waited a few minutes and then got up. I wanted to find Briggs and find out if there was a phone. Even if they were in on the charade, I could come up with an innocent enough reason to need the phone. And then I'd find a way to call the police. If I bumped into Grigori, I'd just say the headache hadn't gone away and I wanted some tea.

But when I arrived at the kitchen, there was no one in sight. Had all the staff been sent off already? Was anyone left in the castle but Grigori and me? And the Dowager?

I searched but found no phone in the kitchen. Taking a glass of water, as an alibi in case anyone remained behind, I left and made my way to the library. No phone in sight. Was it possible there wasn't one? No. This castle belonged to royalty. Modernized, electrified, there must be a phone. Even if no one currently lived here, people had been living here as recently as four years ago, Briggs had said.

The clock on the mantel chimed. I'd used up a half hour. And I hadn't found a phone and I didn't know how to get to the Dowager. And then I remembered the prints of the castle in the upstairs hall. A series showing how it had evolved over the centuries.

I made it back to the hallway without being seen and examined each print. The dungeon must have been part of the original building. I started there and then, by studying each subsequent print, finally understood the layout of the east, west, and center wings. I knew my location. And hers. And now how to get there.

I found the older wing of the castle, then the stone room, the staircase, and finally the dungeon. With shaking hands, I tried the door, afraid I was not going to find the empress alive. When I opened it, I found myself staring at a lifeless woman sitting in a chair, her head falling on her chest, her chest not moving.

I was too late. "I'm sorry," I whispered.

Then I heard rustling. Was it Grigori? Had he found me? I turned around. No one was at the door. The noise continued. I turned again.

The sound wasn't emanating from the door but from the Dowager. She'd raised her head. Was twisting in her seat.

First, I removed her gag.

"I thought it might be those men again and wanted them to think I'd expired."

"Well, it worked. I thought . . . Thank God you didn't, Your Highness."

I untied her hands and went to work on her feet. Then I helped her up. Wobbling, she had to take two turns around the room before her circulation returned to her limbs and she could stand on her own.

Amazingly, she wasn't scared, but angry and full of fury. "These are the monsters who destroyed everything that ever mattered to me. Hurry, child, they will be back and I need you to help me."

"But how?"

"I own a gun. You have to get it for me."

"But they packed all your things. Yasin and your maid, who was dressed as you, left."

"I should have been more suspicious when my own maid came down with a stomach bug on the boat. But the gun is still in the room, I'm sure."

I turned to go, took five steps, and came face-to-face with Grigori.

Chapter 32

"I thought your head ached," Grigori said as he took my arm and pushed me down into one of the other chairs and then, before I could respond, began to tie my arms behind my back.

The Dowager rushed over and tried to intervene, but he shoved her and she went sprawling onto the floor.

He hadn't yet gagged either of us. I started to scream: "Help, help!" The Dowager joined me. Grigori looked at both of us and laughed.

"Scream as loud as you want. Everyone is gone but Fodor and I. Oh, you don't know who Fodor is. I think you know him as Briggs. He's one of us."

"What do you want with me?" the Dowager asked.

"I? Very little. We've taken the jewels my father hid all these years and they are on their way to Russia. I've done my job. There are some people arriving later this evening who want to talk to you, Your *Highness*." He spat out the word. "And I promised to give them that opportunity.

"As for you—" Grigori turned to me. Sadness in his brown-diamond eyes. He gave me one of his smiles—not dazzling but tinged with despair. "I wish you'd stayed in your room. Minded your own business. We were leaving, you and I. We were going home to Paris." He shook his head. "We were going home, Opaline. I was going to make sure you returned safely before I left for Russia."

I didn't doubt the sincerity in his voice. In fact, I decided to take advantage of it.

"Grigori, please don't leave us here. I understand you're a Bolshevik and your principles are against the monarchy, but there's a difference between ideology and murder. And murder is a terrible burden to bear for the rest of your life."

He cocked his head, as if listening and weighing my words.

"You saved my life on that ship," I said. "I know you weren't doing it just because of this rendezvous. I saw your face. I know what's inside of you. You saved my life—are you really going to be the one who also ends it?"

His face twisted into a mask of grief as he wrestled with his personal emotions versus his politics. "I didn't plan on having feelings for you."

"But you do."

He shrugged. "This is a time of war in more ways and in more places than one. In a time of war sacrifices must be made."

A few moments passed.

"How can you leave your father? Your family? Your country?"

"My family? My country? My father never loved me. Not really. Not with his soul. And France has never been my country. I used France. Used her naïveté. Used her willingness to believe everyone wants to be in Paris instead of Petrograd. Used your city's tunnels to hold secret meetings under the shop in order to plan all this. And now that I've done my job and secured the diamonds, I'm going back to Russia as a hero to work for the party. I've done what I came to France to do." He spat out the name of my homeland.

"The Rainbow Diamonds?" The empress looked at me.

I nodded.

"I'd thought so. Nicky told me about them so long ago. He said he had given them to your Monsieur Orloff to safeguard. Did you bring them with you? Is that what you were going to give me?"

"I was," I told her. "But they took them."

"My father-in-law handpicked each of those stones," she said. "Collected them. Treasured them. The finest colored diamond collection in the world . . . He gave them to my husband . . . and from my husband they went to Nicky . . ." Her voice trailed off.

"And now that fortune will help to fund the new party, the new Russia. Stones!" he said. "Glittering, gaudy stones. Blood money."

All his emotion shone in his eyes. What I'd

thought of as resentment had been hatred. I'd misread so much about this man. So had his father. We see what we want to see when we look at someone. Like a diamond before it has been cut. We can guess at its brilliance but can't see the faults until the stone has been cut and polished. Only then can we glimpse inside and see the occlusions and the clarity.

"You should have stayed in your room with your ghosts, Opaline." Grigori's voice cracked. He turned. And left. The door clanged shut. A key turned. The metallic sound echoing like the final punctuation to Grigori's words.

"They have taken all of my treasures, haven't they?" the empress said. "My son, my grand-children, my country."

What did she believe? What was she asking? What did she really want to know? I decided I would wait. If we survived this and if she asked again, then I would offer her the talisman and together we would learn the fate of those five precious children. But was there any reason to conjecture about what I'd sensed and tell her nothing but a hunch? Did she need to know that here and now, while we were alone in this ancient underground cell? So deep belowground that, despite it being August, we were freezing cold. As I started to shiver, I worried about the empress, who'd been left here overnight.

She needed heat. So did I. What were we going

to do to survive? I shut my eyes and tried to reach Jean Luc. He'd been so distant since I'd gotten on the boat. Barely here. He'd warned me. He was already leaving. Drifting away. But I couldn't bear to let him go.

Or maybe I wouldn't have to. Maybe this was all meant to be. Maybe the Dowager and I would be left to die here. Maybe this was the end of my time on this plane. Perhaps that's what Jean Luc meant. Had he known? And when the end came and I was released from this body, would my soul find his?

My shivering increased. The Dowager's teeth chattered. I struggled against the ropes but they remained taut. Frustrated, I jerked my arms downward. Had I heard a faint squeak? I repeated the action. The rope wasn't giving but the wooden slats of the old chair were. For another minute or two I yanked and tugged, each exertion producing more creaking until I heard the first splinter. Keeping at it, I continued moving my arms up and down until the wood finally gave out and the chair rail clattered to the stone floor. With the echo still ringing, I disentangled my hands from the rope.

Jumping up, I rushed to the Dowager and untied her. Her skin was cold to my touch. Once I'd helped her stand, she leaned on me, unsteady on her feet.

"Are you all right?" I asked.

"I will be. It's just so cold down here. We need to keep moving," she said as we began to pace. From one end of the cell to the next. Back and forth. After ten minutes of this, she stopped.

"This won't do. We must find a way out," she said. "A way to open the door."

We searched the room together, inspecting it, both of us hoping we'd find something, but we failed. It was hard to give up, but after an hour, we realized there simply was nothing down here but the chairs and the rope and bottles of wine. I cracked one open on a rock, one for me and one for her.

"What are we going to do?" I asked.

"We're going to think of something. I haven't survived so much to die at the hands of those filthy Bolsheviks who've stolen everything from me."

"Not everything," I said.

"What do you mean?"

I reached inside of my shirt and pulled out the necklace and gave it to her. "Your son's gift to you," I said.

She took the necklace from me and inspected it. "There is a key?"

"He told you that much?"

"Yes, he said there would be a key to open it."

"They took the key. They think they've got the real necklace. I don't know how long it will be before they realize their eggs are hollow. But we need to get out of here and find safety before they do. I will make you another key when we get out."

"Did Monsieur Orloff tell you about the necklace?"

"No, only that it was a secret gift. And he gave me an identical necklace to wear on the outside of my clothes in case anyone followed us."

"He is a smart man. My son chose well when he chose him." She fingered the eggs. "If Monsieur didn't tell you about the Rainbow Diamonds, how did you know?"

I told her about making the key myself and opening them.

"What did you make a key with?"

"I'm a jeweler. Miniature locks and keys are part of my designs. I found a bit of gold in my pocket and heated it."

"With what?"

"My fingers."

"Your fingers? I don't understand."

I told her a little about myself and my heritage.

"A mystic. One got us into this trouble. How ironic if one were to get me out."

"I'm not a mystic."

"Would you prefer 'witch'?"

I nodded. Even if I didn't live to use it, the time had come to own it.

"Can you make a key to get us out of here? To unlock the door?"

"I don't have any gold or tools."

"If it's gold you need . . ." She held out her hand, showing me her two rings.

"Even if there's enough there to fashion a key big enough, I would need more heat than I can generate. More heat than my own fingers could withstand."

Behind me warmth caressed the back of my neck, as if someone were blowing on my skin. I turned around. No one stood behind me. But I knew. Jean Luc was there. He'd come back.

I closed my eyes and saw words in the triptych I'd deciphered. The same words I'd read in the grimoire.

Make of the blood, heat.
Make of the heat, a fire.
Make of the fire, life everlasting.

The talisman around my neck began to generate heat. It traveled down my chest, down my arms, out my fingers, into the room. Like swimming in the sea at home when I was a child, I floated on the feeling and let the waves of warmth lull me. The Dowager's teeth stopped chattering. The room grew warmer. I thought about the amazing nights I'd spent alone in my bed, with Jean Luc setting me on fire.

And then I knew what to do. I wasn't sure if it would work. But I needed to try.

I worked the gold into a key. The metal became hotter than I could bear, but I couldn't stop. This pain was Jean Luc's last great gift to me. All of his energy, all of his effort, his good-bye. Tears dripped down my cheeks as I fashioned notches and ridges. Then I put the warm, soft gold into the lock and let it remain there. The lock would imprint on the gold and form the key. Once it cooled, we could use it to escape.

I won't be there on the other side of the door, Opaline.

I heard what Jean Luc said and nodded, but was afraid to speak.

I'm trying to stay with you, but I don't have any more time. It's pulling me. It's not dark anymore, my darling. There's light. Brilliant light.

I pictured that light, the white light of a flawless diamond, welcoming Jean Luc to the next stage of his journey.

I put my hand on the key in the door. I wasn't seeing what was in front of me. I pictured an unblemished diamond shattering and sending out incandescent splinters of rainbows until there was no light but only that dazzling white light.

The key had cooled. I turned it. Heard the tumblers move.

I opened the door.

I let the Dowager go first and then followed. I sensed that when I stepped across the threshold I would be leaving Jean Luc behind. I hesitated a moment. Then felt her bony fingers grip my wrist and pull me across from what was to what would be.

We both knew it as soon as we reached the first floor and looked out the window. All the cars were gone. We were alone in the castle. Grigori had left us in the dungeon to die. But we were not going to die. We both knew that too.

And I knew something else. Something I didn't want to know.

The talisman around my neck had grown cold against my skin. For the first time in more than two months, no warmth emanated from it. No heat. Jean Luc had gone. My phantom lover had left me for good.

Chapter 33

The Dowager knew where the phone was, in a small room off the library. It was really no bigger than a closet, save that it had a window. She called her sister, and Alexandra said she would arrange to have a local constable come to pick us up and cautioned us to be careful until help arrived. Even though I was certain everyone else had departed and we were the only ones still there, we locked the room from the inside and remained, both of us cowering behind the curtains that pooled on the floor.

The next hour passed slowly. We had been in shock, but the longer we waited, the more the reality of what had almost happened to us sunk in. Both of us jumped at the castle's every creak. Were trees brushing against the window, or had Grigori come back to check on us? Was that a gull crying, or was someone calling out in Russian? What if the people Grigori had mentioned came before nightfall? What if they arrived before the police?

Finally we heard a car's tires grating gravel. The Dowager took my hands, closed her eyes, and bowed her head, whispering a litany of words under her breath. Even though I couldn't understand her, I knew she was praying that help had arrived. Friends, not foes.

And it had. We were taken to a safe house where we were well taken care of for the next twenty-four hours while the royal household prepared the ship to take her back to Yalta and arranged my passage to France.

And then it was time to go.

The Dowager touched my cheek and gave me a wise and sad smile. Around her neck, under her dress, the Dowager wore the emerald egg necklace. But on top of the black satin bodice, the talisman I'd made for her hung on a silken cord. She reached for it and held it tightly in her fist.

"You know, it was your magic that saved me and gave me hope when all hope had been lost. I will keep your magic orb with me always, but not to use as a gateway to whatever doom my family may or may not be experiencing." She shook her head. "No, I will hold on to this for the promise it offers of a future, one in which they, like me, have been rescued. And that someday, in this life or the next, I will be reunited with them."

Then she took off one of her gold rings we hadn't needed to melt, and handed it to me.

"Will you take this as a token of my thanks?" she asked.

"I would be honored."

She kissed me on each cheek and then let me go.

I was immensely relieved to see her off without

our trying to learn the fate of her grandchildren from the talisman. The entire enterprise went against the very purpose of my ability. My job was to bring solace, not stir up turmoil. My hearing the children's voices would have caused her nothing but pain and sorrow. She wouldn't have been a mourner asking for closure but rather a woman who still had hope having it dashed. And in not asking me to discover her grandchildren's fate, she had in turn given me a great gift. I never had to see her face dissolve in agonizing grief, a sight I never would have been able to unsee, never have been able to forgive myself for causing.

If I'd been traveling alone, I would have been nervous on the crossing back to France, worried that Grigori had found out I'd survived, but the Dowager had arranged with King George to have one of his guards escort me safely home. The return trip proved as smooth a journey as the voyage over had been rough. Little had I known then that Grigori had been the Bolshevik spy I was searching for on the way over.

Now I dreaded what faced me back in Paris. I was going to need to tell Monsieur Orloff and Anna about Grigori. I'd witnessed their sorrow and watched them mourn when Timur died. But he'd died with honor. I feared this in its way would be worse.

They listened to my story without emotion, but when I finished, Monsieur broke down. He sat at their dining room table and put his head in his hands and wept like a child. Anna put her arms around her husband and began to whisper in his ear. I stood to leave them, he to his grief and disappointment and she to the job of comforting.

I'd reached the door when Monsieur called out.

"Opaline, don't go."

I turned.

"You should stay with us. Mourn with us. You are part of our family. You've suffered too. This has been tragic for you as well."

"But I've let you down. Because of me, Grigori is gone. You may never see him again."

"Because of you?"

"If I hadn't discovered what was going on in the castle, hadn't realized what their plan was, he and I would have returned home. I'd have done what you asked—made the Dowager's talisman and given her your gift—and Grigori's trespass would have gone undetected. And I let Timur down. Because of me he died without hope."

Monsieur rose and came to me. He put a hand on each of my shoulders and looked into my eyes. I'd never stood so close to him. Never noticed his eyes were the exact same brown diamonds as Grigori's.

"Because of you, one of my sons died believing he was well loved. Even if you think you should have given him more hope than you gave him, he didn't. He loved you, little one, and he believed you were going to be here when he came home."

"How do you know—"

"He wrote to me," Monsieur interrupted.

I looked at Anna, wondering why she'd let all this time pass without telling me. But she looked as surprised as I was.

"Pavel, why have you said nothing before now?" she asked.

"I didn't know before now how Opaline felt. That she thought she could have done more." He turned back to me. "He wrote to me and said how happy he was and how much he loved you and he believed you loved him back. And having read his words," Monsieur said, "how could I ever be anything but thankful to you? My child was not alone in his last thoughts because of you, darling girl. For that, I will always be grateful. So grateful I must make sure you understand you are in no way responsible for Grigori's escape. He was his mother's son. I never really faced that fact, never wanted to see it or admit it. But he was. I've always feared one day he would return to her and to the new Russia." He shook his head slowly, with regret. "No, you aren't responsible for me losing my son. But you are responsible for saving my sovereign, for protecting the Dowager."

He kissed my forehead, and I felt one of his tears moisten my skin. "You are a gem, Opaline. And I am forever in your debt."

I went down to my bedroom. Depleted. Exhausted. It was going to take days for me to process what had happened in England. Perhaps years to understand it. But it would have to wait. Now that I had delivered my news, there was only one thing left on my mind. And I did not know how I was going to face it or cope with it. Jean Luc was gone. He'd left when we were in the castle and he hadn't returned. The talisman around my neck was nothing but a cold crystal bauble, as empty of magick as my soul was of hope.

I needed to return the books Madame Alouette had lent me. But first I had to finish reading the rest of his columns. I spent the next few days going over and over his words, his phrases, his insights. Grieving for him in a way I'd never grieved for anyone.

Finally, on Thursday evening, I took the walk he wrote about in his final column, the one he'd written just before meeting his death.

He'd invited his *Ma chère* to take a boat ride on the Seine. There were no tourist boats anymore. Not during war. But I found a tugboat and paid the captain handsomely to let me stand on the bow as he took his final trip of the day. So while twilight settled over the city, as the magical *l'heure bleu* descended, as the boat journeyed on the gently flowing river, I read Jean Luc's last words and shed the last tears for him I would allow myself.

Ma chère,

As the boat takes you down the Seine, look at the people going about their lives on the banks of the river. Life goes on whether we want it to or not. Sometimes here, I think of Paris and am amazed people are still baking bread—even if it's brown bread—and going to the museum, and walking in the beautiful gardens and washing their clothes and punishing their children. Amazed anything but this hell exists.

Does something truly exist if we are not there to witness it?

Just because I cannot see those people going about their business doesn't mean they aren't doing it. Just because they don't know of my existence in this rat-infested watery trench doesn't mean I'm not here.

I love the Seine. The river is the heart of the city. And you are the heart of my heart. The water is our lifeblood, mixing, mingling. The bridges are our hands meeting. One side connected to the other. We can't be together in the flesh, but you can look through my eyes and see what I saw and feel what I felt. You can know that even here, so far from you, I hold your heart in me. Like the precious gift it is. And I will hold it within me always.

FEBRUARY 5, 1919

A brilliant sun warms the winter afternoon as best it can. Through an open window a bird's song drifts in from the garden. None of the roses are blooming, but the hard tight buds will be appearing soon. Spring is only weeks away. I can hear it.

The war ended in November, and our world is slowly returning to normal. There are baguettes made of white flour in the bakeries, meat in the butcher shops, men of all ages in the street, and women are dressing up again in shimmering silks with fringes and sequins.

My great-grandmother is once more entertaining in the grand style she enjoyed before 1914. She plans to enjoy her celebrity as one of the last great courtesans as long as there are gentlemen who still arrive bearing gifts of perfume or jewels in exchange for a delightful evening's entertainment.

I haven't seen Madame Alouette since visiting her home to return Jean Luc's columns, but every so often, in the pages of *Le Figaro*, I read about the work she and Madame Ladd are carrying on with the wounded soldiers.

The stream of grieving mothers and sisters, daughters, wives, and lovers visiting number 130 has stemmed. Our door is now open for customers shopping for jewelry to celebrate life, not grieve death. My wartime services are no longer required, and I have been relieved of my duty of freeing lost souls from their families' mourning.

Monsieur and Anna's youngest son, Leo, returned home a true hero. His presence has done much to relieve the sadness in the Orloff home caused by Grigori's transgression and defection—old friends have reported seeing him in Petrograd—and the finality of Timur's death.

My job is mine for as long as I want it, the Orloffs told me, and when and if I am ready, Monsieur is prepared to fulfill his promise. I keep the idea of a shop of my own, shining like a beacon, in my sights. I want it. I'm almost ready for it. But I feel my work at La Fantaisie Russe remains unfinished. I sense there is an important lesson still to be learned.

I returned home to Cannes, as promised, a month after the war ended, to study with my mother. This time, I wanted to. I was both anxious and eager to claim my heritage and understand it. Over dinner one night, I gave her back the ruby necklace I'd stolen from her that day at the dock and was surprised when she smiled and told me she'd been happy when I took it. It was a rite of passage for women like us, for Daughters of La Lune, to strike out on their own, she'd said.

Now back at La Fantaisie Russe, in the glorious Palais Royal, I am alone in the workshop. Monsieur has taken an assortment of bracelets and rings to a client's home for a private showing. Anna works in the front of the shop. Leo, who's taken up his old spot at the other workstation in the studio, is down in the vault, overseeing the repairs. The crevice through which I'd seen the Bolsheviks meeting—as it turned out the men I'd seen weren't German spies after all, but Russians working with Grigori—has been cemented over, but the walls need fortification.

As I sit at my station, setting pearls into a diadem for a wealthy New York socialite visiting Paris and staying at the nearby Ritz Hotel, the bell rings, signaling a customer, and I hear Anna open the door and welcome someone in.

"I'm hoping you might be able to help me?" A man's voice. A honeyed voice, deep and rich like caramel.

"Of course, Monsieur," Anna says.

"My mother purchased this here last year. And these gold threads broke. Might you be able to repair it? It's quite dear to her. It has my hair in it."

"But of course," Anna says, then hesitates. "This is one of our lockets, but how can it be?" She sounds incredulous.

I put down my tools and take a step closer to the door.

"How can that be, Madame?"

"You said your hair is inside?"

"Yes. My mother brought it here."

I take a step closer and peer out. I can see Anna's back, but not the soldier's. Only his shadow. I lean against the doorjamb.

"This was the kind of talisman we made for women who lost loved ones in the war. But you are here, very much alive," Anna says.

"Ah yes. Well, there's an explanation. You see, during the war I was badly wounded. I almost died. In fact, I spent six weeks unconscious. During that time, no one knew who I was. When I'd arrived at the hospital, my identification papers were so drenched and muddied they dissolved when the nurse tried to read them."

"And so they told your parents you were—"

"The rest of my unit had been found dead, so yes, they told my family I'd been killed."

"Oh, how lucky for your mama." Anna's voice cracks. She is unable to hold back her tears, thinking of Timur, I know, of her lost son who would never be coming back.

I can't hold back my tears either. I wipe at them as I step out into the storefront and look at the man standing in front of Anna, holding one of my talismans in his long, lovely fingers.

The soldier sees me. My eyes meet his. They

are midnight navy—the color of a sky full of stars with a full moon shining. The same color as his mother's.

Even through the blur of so many tears, I know his face.

Does he know mine? Does he remember the weeks we'd spent in some kind of miraculous communion with each other? Does he remember that somehow, while his body rested in deep slumber, his soul had left and met mine?

Jean Luc's brow furrows. He cocks his head and looks at me as if he is trying to place me.

I take one more step forward.

"I made the talisman for your mother, and I'd be happy to repair it." My voice quivers.

"Have we met?" he asks me. "Everything about you is familiar. But I don't know your name."

"Opaline Duplessi," I say, extending my hand.

"I'm Jean Luc Forêt," he replies as he grasps my trembling fingers.

The flow of warmth is immediate. I can see from his expression he feels it too. No, he doesn't remember, but he hasn't quite forgotten either.

We remain there, hands clasped together, like those beautifully weathered bronze hands on the Famille P. Legay tomb in Père-Lachaise. But we are both alive and generating a heat I'd believed I would never feel again.

It will take some time to figure out what exactly

happened and then more time to explain it to him. Or perhaps that isn't necessary, because all that matters is that we will have the time now. We will have all the time he thought had been stolen from him, all the time we will need to visit all the places he'd dreamed about while at the front. All the time it will take for me to show him I am his *Ma chère*.

Author's Note

As with most of my work, there is a lot of fact mixed in with this fictional tale.

Paris during the Great War is described as close to the truth as possible. The bombings, strife, rations, numbers of dead and wounded are all based on fact. You can visit all the streets, bridges, buildings and churches, museums, and cafes I wrote about except for the shop where Opaline works, La Fantaisie Russe in the Palais Royal. However, I did base it on the jeweler Georges Fouquet's very beautiful boutique, which you can visit in the Musée Carnavalet. The tunnels under the Palais do exist and were used for all kinds of clandestine operations during the war.

There were indeed laws in France forbidding fortune telling and necromancy so as to prevent charlatans from taking advantage of the grieving, and while there were many types of spiritualism practiced, I am not aware of anyone who worked with talismans the way Opaline did.

Anna Coleman Ladd's "Studio of Miracles" did exist and restored dignity to countless men, but there wasn't a sculptor there named Denise Alouette. Jean Luc's mother, like him, is a character of my invention.

Le Figaro was and still is one of the great

French newspapers, but there never was a *Ma chère* column.

Thousands of Russian émigrés flooded the city in those early years of the twentieth century, but there wasn't a jeweler named Pavel Orloff that I am aware of. For generations there were rumors—still unproven—that the tsar sent emissaries from Russia to other countries, well before the revolution, with treasures to safeguard, but the Rainbow Diamond collection I described in this novel does not exist.

As far as I know, the Dowager Empress never undertook a secret journey to England during that last year of the war. It is true, however, that in her lifetime, she claimed to never believe her grand-children had all perished along with her son. She always held out hope.

Acknowledgments

To Sarah Branham, my amazing editor, for her patience and creativity and insight—if this novel shines—it is because of her.

To my wonderful publisher and friend Judith Curr for her steadfast faith in my work.

To the legendary Carolyn Reidy, CEO of Simon & Schuster, whose respect for authors makes all the difference.

To Lisa Sciambra, Hillary Tisman, Andrea Smith, Suzanne Donahue, Haley Weaver, and everyone whose hands this book passed through—your hard work and creative thinking is greatly appreciated.

To Alan Dingman for covers that somehow get more and more beautiful every year.

To Dan Conaway, no writer could have a better agent, and I could have no better friend.

To Taylor Templeton for her patience and cheer, and everyone at Writers House whose help is invaluable.

To Inezita Gay-Eckel without whom I would never have found La Fantaisie Russe, and that's just the beginning. You opened up the magical world of gems to me and became such a dear friend in the process, thank you. And to all the other wonderful professors at L'ÉCOLE Van

Cleef & Arpels in Paris. The week I spent with you learning about the art of jewelry-making influenced every page of this novel.

To Temple St. Clair whose inspiring talisman I wore each day when I sat down to write—there *is* magic in jewels.

To Simon Teakle Fine Jewelry and the staff at Betteridge Jewelers, both in Greenwich, Connecticut, who never chased me out and answered endless questions as I researched this novel.

To each and every one of my fabulous friends, but especially Liz and Steve Berry, Douglas Clegg, and Randy Susan Meyers.

A special thank-you to Natalie White, director of Client Services at AuthorBuzz.com without whom I wouldn't even have time to write.

I also want to thank readers everywhere who make all the work worthwhile (please visit MJEmail.me for a signed bookplate). And to the booksellers and librarians without whom the world would be a sadder place.

And as always, I'm very grateful to my family, especially my father and Ellie, the Kulicks, Mara Gleckel. And most of all, Doug.

Center Point Large Print
600 Brooks Road / PO Box 1
Thorndike, ME 04986-0001 USA

(207) 568-3717

US & Canada:
1 800 929-9108
www.centerpointlargeprint.com